DUPLICITY

Toni Lee

Powerhousepress.com, Inc.
Atlanta

Published by
Powerhousepress.com, Inc.
P.O. Box 50473
Atlanta, Georgia 30302
www.powerhousepress.com
sales@powerhousepress.com
(888) 524-6873 fax: (404) 753-8257

BOOK DESIGN BY TONI SCOTT-DANIEL

LIBRARY OF CONGRESS CATALOGING-IN-PUBLICATION DATA

ELECTRONIC BOOK VERSION
ISBN 0-9678469-1-9
Copyright 2000 by Toni Elizabeth Lee
All Rights Reserved
developed and printed in the United States of America
January 2000
First Edition

This book is dedicated to
my Mother
Valmarie Colley Lee,
whose iron will is my driving force, and
whose voice I hear in the words I write,
in ever-present spirit with visible
representation and without.

ACKNOWLEDGEMENT
AND THANKS

First to the Spirit Most High, the High Counsel, the Orisha, my Ancestors, Charlotte, Guides and Protectors in addition to Priestess' Ayoka Lanloke, Omi, Oyabi, and Chief Ojamu.

Also to:

My dear, kind, diligent son Alvis Lee Baynes for being the wonder of my life, and remaining as the best thing I have ever done.

My Father Alvis A. Lee, just for being my Father when so many are and were not. Enough said. My family for their love, encouragement and belief in my abilities, and all manner of support during the writing of this book.

My editors at different stages - Malaika Adero for her outstanding insight into the written word and the fragility of new authors, and Dr. Marcia Riley Elliott for her impeccable knowledge of the English language.

Tina McElroy Ansa for her continuous love and support, and Jonee' Ansa for all he is and all he is to her.

Beverly Guy Sheftall for her wisdom.

Zakiyyah Muhammed El Shabazz for being my constant cheerleader, and to Aisha, Sharif and Amenia Irons for being hers.

Atty. Sharon Marquetta Chavis for 34 years of friendship, support, patience, love and a wonderful legal mind - in this life and now in spirit.

Atty. Lourdes Neely Coleman for an array of stuff and a wonderful infectious laugh that can lift a mood in no time flat.

Aziz Faz for being a perceptive, knowledgeable guide in Morocco, and Larabie and Ali for their participation.

Jackie Green and Hi-Tech Travel in Dallas for being the best travel agent possible, and taking me to Morocco, so that I could take my readers with me.

Bill Ziegler of the Miami Metro Zoo for giant reptile lessons.

Conne Ward Cameron for teaching me to be a better researcher.

Patrice and Elise Coleman, Tony and Millicent Small, Gail Bibb, Annsonita Robinson, Carl Nunn, Carl Roberts, Amoyewa Skaggs, Ju Ju Ferrell, Jamilah Shakir, and Norma Chappelle for hoards of reinforcement.

Toni Scott-Daniel, for the artistic interpretation of my words.

Denzel Washington for sparking the light that became "Duplicity" during the shooting of Glory, and to Salli Richardson for appearing on the scene and continuing the inspiration.

All of the nurses, support staff and friends, Doris, Carolyn, Ali, Darryl and the guys, Johnnie, Nancy, Chinito, Ms. Blue, Ms. Georgia, Linda, Veronica, Jean, Julia, Donna, Sunyic Lee, Dr. Brooks, Dr. Stephens, Glenda and Mike Callendar, Sister Marilyn and others who cared and supported my mother during her long illness. Without them, I would not have been able to think clearly, long enough to write. Many thanks to Myrna, Morgan and Edena for their love of her.

All of the test readers who were honest and free with their opinions, and whose critique has kept me honest. They are too numerous to name and I am certain I will forget many, but will try. Please forgive me for the names missed, but they are in my heart. They are in no particular order other than that provided by bad memory and inadequate notes.Alvis A. Lee, Jim Trotter, Audree' Irons, Amoyewa' Skaggs, Shomari Lateef, Gail Mayo, Whitman Mayo, Ann Robinson, Angela Mills, Charles Mills, Myrna Colley Lee, Morgan Freeman, Rasheeda Ali, Sam Pollard, Ethan Ealy, James Quarles, William Hudson, Rosita Castillo-Lewis, Grace Ellis, Shomari Lateef, Dr. Bernard Harris, Cynthia Cole, Makha Konate', Joyce Williamson, Dot Greason, Bousara Whitaker, Sharon Johnson, Tab, Gail Bibb, Dr. Clark White, Victor Chavis, Tony Harris, Harriett Harris, Seyume, Joe Jowers, Bill Ransom, Soraya' Merkerta', Jeannette Guillermo, Henri Dana, Shirley Taylor, Vernon Preston, Dr. Cornelius Stephens, Tony Small, Millicent Small, Richard White, Pat White, Carl Roberts, Alan Ricca, Dr. Bill Cleveland, Sara Reed, Fran Burst, Carl Nunn, Bolaji Bailey, Marilyn Broyhill, Cheryl Marshall,Carl Anthony, Monica Freeman, Adrian Anderson, William Clark, Michael Carmichael, Denise Stinson, Blanche Richardson, Conne Ward Cameron, Frederick Johnson, Barry Burls, Lori Beard Daily and all the people I am certain I've forgotten to name, who are nonetheless greatly appreciated.

To Mannie Baron whose efforts are appreciated and have not gone unnoticed. To the Powerhouse team, Kevin Hicks, Jeannette Guillermo, Robert Ryan, and my publicist Carletta Hurt, for all of her hard work and diligence. Finally, for my Mother, for all she was and is, and the many incredible gifts she left me.

DUPLICITY
A NOVEL BY TONI LEE

PUBLISHED BY POWERHOUSEPRESS.COM, INC.

CONTENTS

1 DETERMINATION

He moved with exceptional speed and agility for a quardragenarian, darting in and out of the crowd, hot on the heels of the only contact he had to Archie Dayton, the slippery, slick thief he had been pursuing for three months. The young man he was following past the vendors at the Labor Day Weekend Arts Festival leapt over the persons and goods of jewelry makers, ran by painters and weavers, under canopies, into tents and out again preventing Clinton Creech from getting close enough to stop him. The crowd was too thick to draw a gun, so he was forced into foot pursuit. Once again, Dayton had reduced an operative of his caliber to absurdity. He wondered, as he leapt over a seeing eye dog, whether he would have time to make Dayton pay for the continuous indignities he caused him. The possibility of not catching Archie was his greatest regret about giving up the job.

Clinton's partner Gerald started out right behind him, but went back for the car hoping to meet them on the other side of the field. Clinton and his brother ran six miles every morning for exercise, so he was the logical choice to continue. He could feel the effects of chasing a twenty year old though, despite his ability to keep up. The kid came out from between two food vendors into the open field that made up the Mall, Washington Monument Park - once used for the March on Washington in the sixties and the Cherry Blossom Festival since. With minimal obstructions, only youth and speed came into play.

The kid was younger, but Clinton was very fast having placed second in the 400 on his college track team. The kid ran steady and hard, but Clinton gained on him and lessened the gap to about twelve feet between them. The kid turned around and saw the distance closing, made a wild yelling sound and propelled himself forward with longer, faster strides, pulling away an extra three, four then five feet.

Clinton knew that the time it would take to pull his gun would be too much lost to recover. He also suspected the kid would not stop running even if he fired a warning shot, and he would actually have to shoot him.

1

He really did not want to snuff out the life of another young black man, even if he was a thief, when it was his boss that they wanted anyway.

On the cross street, at the other end of the field, Clinton saw a black BMW pull up, smoke puffing from the tailpipe in the brisk Spring air. Even with tinted windows, Clinton knew it was Archie.

As the kid fast approached the car, ever increasing the gap between himself and his pursuer, Clinton stopped and pulled his gun. The young man ran, jumped into the passenger's side just as Clinton shot into the front, driver's seat window. Because of the trajectory, the bullet entered at a slant, went in through the side window and out of the front window. The tires screeched, rubber burned and smoke rose from the back wheels as the car fishtailed and sped down the street. There were no tags on the back. Clinton sucked his teeth in disgust as he realized that he had not touched the driver he assumed to be Archie behind the dark tinted windows. He walked to the curb to wait for Gerald.

He sat down, holstered his gun beneath his dark rust Perry Ellis sports jacket and watched the crowd at the festival for a while, then the clouds moving lazily across the sky and a flock of birds fly in V formation and land in a group of trees that lined the street. He wiped off his shoes, hummed a couple of songs, talked to a child who walked by with her parents and petted a cocker spaniel who stopped to sniff his shoes. He waited for what felt like an eternity before Gerald appeared in a gray Ford. Clinton rose, dusted off his dark brown wool gabardine slacks, smoothed his dark brown, tailored silk shirt and got in the car.

"Clint, I'm sorry. I couldn't get here any faster. The car got stuck behind another one with a flat tire. I had to help the guy change it in order to get here this quickly."

"It's alright Gerald. Today just wasn't the day to catch Archie. Who would have thought that he would use a kid to transport the booty from the Vandeleer's estate? I never imagined he was that bright. I think I have underestimated him."

"I know what you mean. We have to figure out his weaknesses. Once we do, maybe we can move him into the right situation for him to give himself away."

"I hope you're right, but it is becoming evident that it won't happen before I leave. That's a bit disappointing, you know?"

" It might still be possible. We've got the Black Caucus Fundraiser. He'll be there. Months of research for him all wrapped up into one night. He wouldn't pass it up for all the tea in China."

"Yeah, you're right. Maybe then." The two men drove off as the sounds of the city traffic silenced their banter about the upcoming event.

2 HOME FIRES

Twenty seven hundred people filled the International Ballroom of the Washington Hotel, and another thousand overflowed into the Crystal Ballroom. Black elected officials, cabinet members, leaders of the House of Representatives, representatives from major corporations, prominent black businesswomen and businessmen, top civil rights leaders, actors, singers, entertainers, athletes and religious leaders came with their missions, agendas and most prized possessions. Furs, jewelry, gold, silver, diamonds, emeralds, rubies, sapphires and Rolex watches lay atop gorgeous designer dresses, Armani suits and beautiful well cared for bodies - a haven for Archie Dayton.

Clinton and Gerald began their work early that cool, late September day and continued through the Secret Service's three o'clock sweep of the exhibit hall and Main International Ballroom in preparation for the President's evening arrival. The sweep, unfortunately corresponded with the Caucus Wives' annual fashion Show. The eleven agents they brought with them, didn't seem enough in all the confusion caused by the two simultaneous events and the forty five hundred guests milling around.

Once, Clinton spotted two extremely well dressed young men checking out the goods imported into the Hotel by a host of wealthy women, anxious to participate in and observe the display of latest fashions from top designers. As if they had a sixth sense, just as Clinton was about to focus in on them, they quietly left the ballroom through the main door and separated quickly. Clinton followed the taller of the two out of the Connecticut Avenue entrance of the hotel and watched him get into the passenger side of a black van with no license tag attached. As the van pulled off, Clinton returned inside, checking with the agent guarding the coat or rather fur room via walkie-talkie. Assured that no intruder had surfaced, Clinton went about his rounds.

The presence of the young men let Clinton know that Archie had scouts casing the guests for him. He had become too visible to do so himself - at least that was the logical assumption. Archie was not always logical.

4

Clinton felt anger crossed with admiration when he thought about Archie. Clinton had to admit that despite the fact that he was an annoying, cunning, pain in the neck, Archie did have his own style. Clinton left to change for the evening's festivities - with no sign of
Archie before his departure.

◊

Grace Creech, a small ebony colored woman with sparkling eyes and smooth skin, sat on the edge of the bed and watched her husband Clinton get dressed for the Congressional Black Caucus Annual Legislative Weekend Dinner. He was, after all their years together, the most irresistible man she had ever known. She liked everything about him. The way he looked, the tone of his voice, his bow legs, his smile, the way he smelled and felt, his relationship with their son, his mother, sister and brother and his father Big Clinton, before he passed away. Her whole world was wrapped up in the tall, fine black man with the hairy chest and broad shoulders, naked to the waist wearing only tuxedo pants who was cutting a path in their bedroom carpet as he looked for all the pieces of clothing she had already laid out on the bed for him.

She handed him the Kente cloth cummerbund as he started across the floor toward the closet. "Clinton, here you are."

He took it, kissed her on the forehead and said, "Thanks baby."

In his early forties, Clinton was six feet two and had the pecan coloring of his mother. His weight stayed at about one hundred and ninety pounds without an extra inch of fat on him. He was broad shouldered and deep chested like his father Big C, and had a thin low waist and slightly bowed legs like his mother. His face was peaceful yet sharp, with a straight nose - a mixture of his African and Native American ancestors. His voice was a medium tone, but had a silkiness to it that made you think of riding down a fairly calm river on the back of a raft, but without the rapids and falls - only an occasional dip and sway. He was very muscular and women noticed him far more than he realized.

As she watched him preparing for the night's work, she wondered if he thought that coming home while in the middle of a job would make her change her mind about wanting him to quit the FBI. Usually, when he worked on a case as intensely as he had been on the present one, he would not come home for days, or weeks. As he tied the bowtie, he could feel his wife staring at the back of his head and knew that his lame scheme was fairly worthless.

◊

Grace stood up from the bed and went to help her husband with his tie. She was about a head and a half shorter than her husband so he bent down to her. He loved her immensely, as she did him. He hoped that they could make it through the evening without further discussion about his leaving the job. He regretted having come home to prepare for the evening. He knew it was a bad idea when he saw the concern in her eyes.

"Clinton, are you going to regret my pushing you into quitting for the rest of our lives?"

"No Grace. I'm a grown man. Your nightmares and the apprehension are not worth it."

He picked her up , hugging and kissing as her braids fell in their faces. She held onto his neck as he walked her over to the bed and lay her down gently as he lay on top of her, still mid-kiss. Then he broke the kiss and looked at the beautiful remnants of West Africa laden in her features.

"You're going to wrinkle your tux."

"I know, and I don't care."

"I see."

"Grace, I am alright with this decision. It's done. I can teach at the Academy, and if I get bored I can become a consultant. Not a problem." He knew it was not quite the truth, but he would deal with it. Of that he was certain.

He kissed the top of her forehead, the side of her face and down to her neck. He straddled her and began unbuttoning her blouse and kissing her chest. She moaned a little then said "Honey, you're late."

"Uh huh" he replied as he ran his tongue down to the fullest part of her breast. All of a sudden a small person's voice could be heard from the stairs.

"Mommy? Where are you. I need you to come start my game again for me, and we don't have anymore fruit roll ups. We need to get some."

Clinton rolled off of his wife and straightened up her blouse, just as their five year old son Eddie came in the room. Grace sat up. Clinton stood and finished dressing.

"Alright Eddie. Let's get your game straight and later we'll go to the grocery store, O.K.?

Eddie ran over to his mother and kissed her on the cheek. "O.K. Mommy." He looked at his father and asked "Where you going Daddy, all dressed up?"

"I have a big party to go to for some very important political people. You have to dress up to attend. You understand?" Clinton looked at his small son who moved to sit on his mother's lap.

"Yeah . . . like on Halloween?"

Clinton laughed and replied "Well sort of, but not in costumes."

Eddie looked at him and said "But then why do you have on yours?"

Clinton was a little taken aback but smiled, picked up his son and held him while talking. Grace watched with amusement. "Well this is just another form of a suit. A special suit. You understand?"

"Yes Daddy, like the minister's suit at church, but not like my Icon, Superhero costume for Halloween."

"Right Eddie. That's exactly right. You are so smart! You are truly your mother's child and your daddy's heart." Clinton kissed his son and lowered him to the floor.

"Eddie, go back to the playroom and wait for me. I'll be right down. I just want to talk to Daddy for a minute, O.K.?"

"O.K. Mommy, but hurry."

The child left the room just as Clinton finished putting on his jacket. Grace went over to her husband and hugged him as if she would never see him again. He felt the tension in her back and shoulders and tried to rub it out of her, but he knew only his change in occupation would help the situation. He loved being an agent, and knew he would miss it terribly, but there was nothing in the world he loved more than her. He held her close, until she almost dissolved.

"Baby, it will be alright. Relax. This is the last time."

"I know . . . but the dream last night was so strange. I was running down a beach, chasing and playing with Eddie. Neither of us had on shoes. I could see you up on the pier fishing, and threw you a kiss. You threw one back. All of a sudden a huge wave came in from the ocean and washed Eddie away first, and I could see you drop your fishing pole and begin to run toward us, but then the wave forced me underwater very quickly, before I could even finish screaming for Eddie. I know this must mean that you left us and I really am not comfortable about tonight. You be careful Baby. Extra careful. You have my whole life tied up in this tuxedo."

He kissed his wife passionately and wiped the tears that were welling up in her eyes. She was generally calm and collected so he was concerned. At that moment, there was no doubt in his mind that he had made the right decision about leaving the job. He would not cause her this much pain so unnecessarily again.

"Baby, I will be fine. I'll come home as early as I can, but it might be late, so don't worry. I love you completely."

"Me too."

They kissed and he left the room. When he saw Eddie while passing the playroom, he went in and kissed his son on the forehead. "Bye big boy. Be good and listen to your mother."

"O.K. Daddy. I will."

Clinton left the house, went out to his blue, Buick sedan, reached into the glove compartment, removed the holster and his automatic gun and put them on before getting in the car. He never performed this ritual in the house. He looked up at their bedroom window and saw his wife looking down at him, and regretted not waiting until he reached work to arm himself. He waved at her and she smiled and blew him a kiss. He got in the car and drove off, away from the most important people in his life.

He drove in silence for a minute till a chill came over him. So great was the feeling he pulled over on the side of the road. He sat, wondering a moment then drove back to the Washington Hotel for the most prestigious event of the year for black politicians and half of the rest of Washington D.C., and his last night as an agent.

3 SWIFT AND IMMEDIATE TRANSFORMATION

As he walked into the hotel, he was glad they called in an additional seven agents. From the front door, through the lobbies and bars, to the mezzanine, the place was lit up with chandeliers and glittering dresses of sequins, lame' and sparkles. Clinton could feel Archie's presence, moving in and out of Washington's black elite without detection. He began to see Archie in the unescorted young women who wore too little dress, too much perfume and an air of capture that emanated from their pores and poured into the evening with every breath they exhaled. He suspected that Archie used not only young men, but young women as well as scouts and possibly junior thieves for this kind of event. Clinton glided through the hotel feeling the spirit and vibrations from every guest he passed. He was on top of his game the early part of that late September night.

It was as if he could read the intent of everyone he saw. With the additional man and woman power from the Bureau, he was able to allow his intuition to run free and pick out every petty thief and con artist who had come. Instinctively, he knew who to single out for questioning and Gerald and the other agents reeled them in and determined their motives. Sophisticated devices, fake identification and makeshift entry equipment was collected during surveillance as the night progressed, but no one caught could be directly linked to Archie. Though the path seemed clear of Archie's presence and influence, there was something more ominous seeping into Clinton's skin via the collection of attendees.

In the main Ballroom, a rush of exhilaration filled the air when the singing group Boyz II Men took the stage. Clinton moved around the room honing in on any and all irregularities. FBI Agents along with city police were stationed on every guest floor to guard against room theft while the guests were out because many used safety deposit boxes, but more did not. Clinton and Gerald never really believed that Archie would attempt any real theft during the event, they suspected he would pass himself off as a respectable member of the community, and befriend a couple of people in attendance who had the power and influence to hook him into

9

a chain of potential victims. They intended to prevent that.

Once the singers finished, Mayor Byron Metcalf welcomed the attendees, as did members of the Black Caucus, the Black Caucus Foundation, and Congressional Black Caucus Chairperson Congresswoman Charlotte Nelson Hampton the civil rights activist turned politician. She was revered by many and hated by more, especially anti-abortionist and radical thinking white supremacists. Clinton liked and had great respect for her.

As the politicians, seated in order of seniority, introduced each other and made grand, eloquent speeches about the state of things at hand, the condition of human existence to come and the hope of life in the future, Clinton could feel Archie near. He slowly scanned the area and spotted him.

Gerald was on the opposite side of the gigantic room. He spoke to him on headset. "Gerald, look at this fool sitting at the table with former Heavy Weight Champ Oscar Davis. You see him? That boy has more nerve than a little bit!"

Gerald craned his neck and found the table where Archie, dressed to the nines, was carrying on polite conversation with the boxer and his wife as if sipping Sunday tea .

"Uhm, you're right. He's at back and center though. He might be arrogant, but he's not totally stupid. By the time either of us get to him, he could slip out of the room and out of sight. The only time we could do it is when the President enters to speak and nobody is allowed to leave the room. Then on the other hand, he knows that we can't take him out of the room either and that too much commotion would cause the Secret Service to get nervous and we would catch flack. Slick dog."

"We have time. You call Secret Service and tell them what we are doing and I will get to Archie. I'll take Louis with me, and you send Robert from your direction."

Clinton moved toward Archie, wondering how to execute the task tactfully, without confusion. Just as Congresswoman Hampton took the podium to introduce the Vice President of the United States, Alton Bouregard, a flash caught the corner of his eye and made him stop. He saw a Caucasian man assembling something under the table where he was seated. A second look proved it to be a crude, homemade handgun, whose parts were being taken from under the tablecloth, with flat parts taped to the bottom of the plate in from of him. Clinton stopped and spoke softly to Louis.

"You go ahead slowly, but don't move in on Dayton yet. Keep your distance and wait for my instructions."

Louis nodded and proceeded. Clinton called Gerald on the headset as he moved closer to the man who was near completion of the gun assembly. "Gerald, alert Secret Service. Caucasian man assembling a handgun here. I think there is a problem . A major one and I don't know if the target is Hampton, the Vice President or the President himself, but it isn't good ."

"Done."

As Congresswoman Hampton began speaking, the man became agitated and fidgeted in his seat as he completed assembly. Clinton moved in closer and two secret service agents began closing in from the side-rear to avoid detection. Just as Ms. Hampton finished her best white house joke, the man stood up and pulled the gun out from under the table but terrified of the task he had undertaken, he was a bit wobbly and took a minute to steady his stance. Clinton ran toward him and as the tall slender man aimed the gun at Hampton Clinton tackled him and the gun misfired causing the bullet to hit the wall behind and about ten feet above her. Ms. Hampton ducked behind the podium, Clinton, the man and the gun crashed down on the beautiful china, goblets and silverware, breaking the round table as its inhabitants screamed and scattered. Clinton held onto the crazed man and wrestled the gun away from him as he shouted "Baby killer, baby killer!" toward the podium.

Pandemonium broke out. Archie took the opportunity to slide out of the back entrance as many of the dignitaries screamed and ran for the exits, alarmed by the gunshot. Clinton snatched the flailing, screaming man to his feet and the secret service agents came to assist. Shaken, Hampton was quickly escorted off the stage with the other politicians. A calm but great commotion went on to get the Vice President and President out of the area quickly. Within a few seconds a chorus of police sirens could be heard at the loading docks, and more law enforcement people in and out of uniform appeared from everywhere. The banquet was for all intents and purposes, over.

After the assailant was in custody, Clinton stood with Gerald amidst the mass of dishes, broken glasses, heap of tablecloths and an army of hotel personnel trying to restore order to total disarray.

"Well, not quite what we planned, huh?"

Gerald laughed as he replied, "No, but all in all, still a good job. We just thought we could confine our nut cases to one a night."

"Maybe it is a fitting way for me to go out, you think? The whole pursuit of Archie has been too ludicrous anyway. Might be right. I just keep feeling that something else is going on though. I just can't put my hands on it right now, but it doesn't feel good."

"Well it will all be a memory in the morning Clinton. Just think, when you wake up, you don't have to be anywhere, or do anything in particular for a while. Ain't life grand."

Clinton laughed and said, "Yeah man, if you say so. Would have been better if we had caught Archie at something we could hold him on though."

He rose, patted Gerald on the back and started out of the door. "I'll see you tomorrow evening for racquetball, right?"

"Sure Clinton. Enjoy your first day of retirement."

◊

When Clinton pulled into his driveway, he didn't see Grace's car however a police car with its parking lights illuminated was parked in front of the house. Clinton's heart dropped down into his stomach, and he felt more fear than twenty assassins and forty Archie Dayton's could have ever mustered in him. He put his gun in the glove compartment and got out of the car as the policemen walked toward him. He recognized the cop as someone he attended the academy with years before, but could not remember his name. Clinton walked to meet him, greeting him cautiously.

"Hi Man, how have you been? I haven't seen you since the early days." "Hi Creech, it has been a long time." The policeman, Anthony Bishop seemed subdued and cautious.

"Well what brings you here, is it Anthony?" he said as he remembered his name.

"Yeah, that's right. Uh . . . I have some bad news for you and when

I recognized your name on your wife's insurance card I felt I should be the one to come talk to you."

Clinton's heart began pounding like a Conga drum. He had done this before when he was a cop. He had delivered unthinkable news to some unsuspecting family member who did not want to hear. He often thought he could feel their pain and bewilderment, but he was wrong.

"Clinton, let's sit down in the house for just a second, alright? Let's go inside."

Clinton nodded and started toward the door, but when he reached it, he could not get the key in because his hand would not stop shaking. He had terrible visions running through his head and contemplated which version was reality. He thought about Grace's dream and wondered if she and Eddie had run off of a bridge into the Potomac or some other malady. Anthony took the key from him and unlocked the door. Clinton braced himself against the doorjamb as it opened, and mustered up all the adulthood and strength he could find in the recesses of his being.

"Anthony, just tell me. Are they alive?"

"Clinton, let's go inside."

"I don't think I can make another step without knowing."

Anthony took a deep breath, stood up straight and prepared for whatever came next, hoping to execute his task with grace and empathy.

"No Clinton, they are not" he said softly.

Clinton felt as if he was falling from a very high cliff into an abyss of blackness with no sides, bottom or end. He forced himself to go inside and sit in the closest chair he could find. Anthony closed the door behind them and placed the keys on the foyer sidebar. He poured Clinton some spring water, and sat it beside Clinton on an end table.

"How did it happen Anthony?"

"It appears they were coming from a grocery store because there were groceries in the back seat of the car, when a drunk jumped the median and hit them head on. We believe that your son died on impact. Your wife lived long enough for the ambulance to reach her, but it was too late. She died as soon as they got her on board. Her internal injuries were just too massive Clinton."

"Oh my God." Clinton became visibly shaken, his leg jerking slightly as he tried to respond. "Was she conscious enough to know that Eddie had been killed?"

Anthony hung his head.

"Anthony, please tell me. Did she know that Eddie had been killed?"

Anthony raised his head and wiped the tears from his eyes. He had great respect for Clinton, and also came from a family of cops and a mere hour before felt compelled to deliver this news instead of leaving it to a total stranger. He wondered why at that moment.

"Clinton, yes. Man I am so, so sorry."

Clinton felt as if he were a leaf at the height of autumn, breaking away from its lifeline and falling to depths unknown, lifeless - never to blow in the gentle breezes or weather the torrential storm again. He could only lay in the crush of similar broken, battered, brown, crackling debris that once made a vibrant collection called a tree. He leaned over with his head in his hands as tears quietly fell from his eyes. There was no sobbing, just water. "Oh my poor baby."

Anthony quietly sat in a chair opposite Clinton and thought of his own family. After nearly fifteen minutes of silence, he stood up. Anthony stood as well, following his lead.

"Thank you Anthony, for being the one to tell me"

"I only did what I knew you would do for me."

"I'll be alright, go ahead and go home to your family and guard them with your life."

Anthony nodded and patted Clinton on the shoulder and gave him his business card.

"Thanks Man." As the door closed, the sound echoed in Clinton's head like the bars of a prison cell. He walked from room to room and gazed at every item on a shelf, wall or table. Then he went to Eddie's room, looked around until he found his son's cap and put it in his pocket,. He went to his and Grace's bedroom, and took a picture of the three of them from a frame on the dresser and put it in his pocket. He entered the walk-in closet and stood in front of Grace's clothes, glaring into their very fibers as he remembered countless occasions in which she wore nearly every item in the closet. He finally chose a long pale turquoise, silk scarf, pulled it down from a hanger and buried his face in it, breathing the faint scent of her favorite perfume, Joy.

He remembered buying it for her years before, despite her complaints about the exorbitant price, though she loved every whiff. He wanted only the best for her.

He put the scarf in his coat pocket, and found one of Grace's small, gold hoop earrings, went downstairs for ice, a large needle, cork, cotton, matches and alcohol. He put the ice on the front and back of his earlobe and held it there for a few moments, and tried to think of some meaningful thought but his mind was still a blank. He heated and cleaned the needle, pierced his earlobe, cleaned the wound, and pushed the earring through his ear with an emotionless, tearless, glazed over gaze into the mirror.

He went to the office down the hallway, and wrote a check to himself which he put in his pocket, and another to Will along with a deposit slip. Out of his and Grace's joint savings account, he wrote a withdrawal slip and sealed all of it in an envelope .

He picked up the phone and dialed.

"Hi, its Clinton. Meet me at Mother's house. I have something very important to tell all of you. Call Justine and Clarissa and ask them to come please and call Mom and let her know we are coming." He hung up, went downstairs and out of the front door, got in his Buick and went first to the morgue to identify them, and then to his Mother's.

He stumbled out of the car, walked up the walkway and through the open door and into the room where his mother, brother, sister, sister-in-law and young nephew Jarrett were. He barely heard the crying, Justine's horrified screams and the rapid-fire questions that Will was asking. Bernice didn't cry, but watched her son intensely as she held Clarissa with one arm and Justine with the other. Once his initial questions were answered, Will held Jarrett close and sat in Big C's favorite Lazy Boy, rocking the small boy. He watched Clinton's detached behavior and felt almost ashamed that he could not think of an appropriate, wise phrase that would supply balance and stability to his younger brother. Clinton stood in the corner and watched the women with slight disinterest. He could feel his mother and Will focused on him, but hadn't the energy to consider what they thought or their obvious concern.

After a few moments, Clinton pulled Will out onto the front porch to talk to him. Will sat the dozing child in the seat and joined his brother outside. They sat in the two rockers, with Clinton falling hard into the seat . The solid thud of his rear end hitting matched the feeling his heart had each time he attempted to think of Grace and Eddie, so he quickly sent his mind back to the blankness that was fast becoming his companion.

"Will . . . I cannot put my whole life into a hole in the ground. The morgue was enough. I can't watch my baby and my woman have dirt thrown on top of them and cremation is inconceivable. You understand?"

"Yes Clinton, I do." Even though Will and his recently-separated-from wife Barbara fought constantly, he couldn't imagine her death, unless he had the opportunity to kill her himself. That he imagined on a daily basis.

"I need you to bury them for me. Sell the house and give all the stuff away if you want to. I don't care. I know this is a lot to ask."

Clinton did not even glance in his direction while making the request. He gazed at the stars, one of his favorite pastimes all their lives. Will was frightened for his brother. He had been so responsible and solid his entire life, breezing through the most difficult tasks. When Big C died, it was Will who initially fell apart while Clinton made all the funeral arrangements and shored up their mother. Will had never seen such a blank expression on Clinton's face.

Clinton's emptiness seemed to reach new heights when coupled with the guilt he felt by placing such a huge responsibility in his brother's hands. He knew that Justine, and her parents would work with Will to do his family justice. He could no longer be concerned with the vacant shells that made up their bodies when the essence and vapors of his life were floating out in the universe. He couldn't add insult to injury by placing them in the cold ground as well.

Will could not refuse his brother anything, but worried about Clinton detaching himself from the grief process. He studied his brother from head to toe. He was dressed in a tuxedo, bowtie still perfectly tied, a silk turquoise scarf tied around his neck, a small baseball cap sticking out of his inside jacket pocket, and there was evidence that blood had trickled from the earring in his ear, down to the collar of his shirt. An earring in Clinton's conservative ear was inconceivable in itself, and the whole picture alarmed Will further.

"Clinton, you know I will do anything you ask, however they are so importa . . ."

"Were Will, that's just it. Were. They are no longer here and at the moment, nothing is important to me."

Will patted his brother on the back. "Sure Clinton. I'll do whatever you ask."

Clinton reached in his pocket and gave the envelope to Will. "This should take care of everything you need. The house information and your Power of Attorney is in the top center desk drawer, and here are the keys. Justine needs a new car. Give it to her. The title is in the bottom drawer."

"I'll handle it." The sounds of crying and whimpering could be heard through the screen door to Bernice Creech's house. Justine kept trying to talk but her sobbing drowned out coherent communication. Clinton seemed not to notice.

"Thanks." Clinton rose and started down the steps toward the street. Will stood and watched him.

"Where are you going Clinton?"

Hands in his pockets, and without looking back, Clinton answered "I think I need to walk. He stared at his shoes for a second. "Yeah, I need to walk Will."

"Alright. I'm going inside and check on the women." Will Creech watched his brother move down the same street they grew up on, away from the same house both he and Clinton were married in. He watched his silhouette for a moment until Clinton disappeared from sight and into the night. He stood for a moment, wondering, then turned and went back into the house - the sound of the screen door accentuating the women's cries and the night's silence .

4 FAUX PAS

The walk from Hotel Hasna on Mohammed the Fifth was about as calm as Marrakech could become at any time of the year, other than Ramadan. Generally the city was one massive hustle of colors, sounds and glorious smells of spices and food. He liked the small hotel with its peach colored marble bathrooms, and mixture of French and Moroccan furniture. He even liked the shops at the base of the stairs that led up to the street and the highly polished wooden artifacts that glistened in the windows. The outer walls were more a yellow shade of rose than most of the buildings in the city, considering all of the buildings were some shade of rose or the other, and it had bright blue trim - another oddity. These qualities alone endeared the small, quiet hotel to him.

It also appeared to be family owned, but maybe it seemed that way because generally Marrakechiis were so polite and gentle with one another and touched each other easily, like family members. During his stay in the country, it had been commonplace to see two men walking down the street holding hands. Most of them appeared to be father and son. That touched him somehow, and made him think of Big C.

Whenever he walked, he was pleased to be staying in a hotel with a named cross street, Rue El' Imam Ali - a rarity in this city. A blessing if ever he could recognize one. He had spent countless hours during the first two days of his stay looking for street names, to no avail. It helped to stay in a place that was surrounded by money also. The Societe' Pour Le Development Des Achats Par Le Credit was next door and the Credit Agricole was directly across the street. He didn't know what they meant, but where there was "credit," there was usually money so his natural instincts and nose for money could guide him when his knowledge of French failed him.

He turned at Place de la Liberté and his old standby Restaurant Le Jet D'eau, down Echchouhada. He had made this practice walk twice in the last two days, and knew that it took exactly twenty-five minutes. This night should not be different.

He watched a lone woman in a bright green djellabah and high heeled shoes that were run over toward the outside of her foot as she walked in front of him. She seemed neither afraid nor apprehensive, despite the fact that it was two o'clock in the morning and that this street was not nearly as busy as Mohammed the Fifth. She had no reason to be afraid in Marrakech. Women appeared to be quite safe, and actually far more powerful than he had imagined for an Islamic country. They seemed to be quite equal actually, when he thought about it, and abuse of a woman was out of the question. The King, the Honorable Hassan II had seen to it that laws protected women - really protected them, not just lip service.

As he looked down at his own black tennis shoes, and the few feet not hidden by robes and djellabahs that passed him by, he could not remember if any metropolitan area he had worked in before had as many varied sidewalks as this city of Marrakech. Even in the semi-dark of the moon-lit night, he could see the small blocks in the wide walkways, creating a grated system of lines and squares only two or three inches apart. But there were no slabs with periodic cracks two feet apart - the stride of a grown man or a stretching child - in the cement to send his mind back to child's play and the concerns of his luck, should he step on the line. Such diversions were useful when preparing for his work. Somehow the mind wanderings actually helped him focus on the task at hand. What had his mother always said? "An idle mind is the Devil's workshop?" He laughed at the thought. He started out as a shop apprentice, but by now, he and the Devil had formed a corporation.

As he neared his destination, he allowed the sounds of the busy night to creep into his range of thought. At six feet four inches, he was taller than most of the people he passed this cool Autumn night, but fit in easily dressed in a long black djellabah over black slacks and t-shirt, a black kufi and a small black leather bag over his shoulder. The feet of the passerbys seldom shuffled in this city and the beat of the long garments worn by still so many, even in these current times, made an interesting sound. . . akin to water softly lapping against the side of a boat as it rocks gently, drifting without purpose. He had been thinking about moving to a beach house lately or maybe buying a boat. The money from this job could easily pay for it . . . that is if he ever got to do the job.

People never seemed to sleep in this city. It was hard to comprehend, given their religious convictions and devotion to Islam. Possibly he was looking through Washington, D.C. Baptist Church eyes. Being a Moslem seemed odd in and of itself with all the repeated praying, bowing and kneeling. He couldn't claim to have a handle on Christianity either though since he had not stepped foot inside a church in twenty-two years.

Occasionally, he looked into the faces of the people he came in contact with and basked in the familiarity of the features he saw. He saw John Harrison, a neighbor in DC in the face of an elderly man that he passed. A young woman dressed in a long green dress looked like Essie Phelps, his first crush in junior high school. Another woman looked like his automobile insurance agent.

He reached Quadissia, then turned right, moving into the New City, the Hivernage district. Some had well lit courtyards while others were dark and secluded. Red and ochre were splashed throughout the neighborhood in the form of shutters, tile awnings and tile roofs, but of course, all atop rose and creamy rose colored homes. Giant woven textiles made of yarn and fabric in colors of rust, cream, red, black and an occasional hint of purple, hung from the sides of houses whose courtyard walls had breaks in them and allowed him to gaze at their beauty through the soft moonlight as he walked. The further he traveled, the wider the streets became, the larger and more grand the houses - and fortunately, the fewer the people.

He turned the corner at the beginning of a stone wall which was higher than any other he had seen, with a breathtaking mosaic band at the top that dipped down into Moorish arches of purple, rust, pale blue and cream colored mosaics that gave the appearance that you could walk straight through them. This would have been useless however, since the solid stone wall of what appeared to be rose quartz or amethyst in the subdued light, would quickly stop any entry . He could not imagine what a quartz wall would cost, or if it had to be imported. Brilliant, giant red gardenias lined the sidewalk and a hedge of rosemary bushes three feet high stood oozing its pungent fragrance between the flowers and the wall.

The entry door to the gate and the car door for the garage were both cedar, highly polished with solid silver studs arranged in beautiful designs which repeated the mosaic design at the top of the wall. He recognized it as some sort of Berber markings of the indigenous inhabitants of Morocco, but he had not seen them before and could not identify the people from which it came. The wall and entrance alone spoke to the unique taste of the occupant of the home, and somehow gave him an odd chill down the back of his neck as he thought of what she might be like, or more accurately, look like. He knew from his research that she was unmarried and he hoped that she was not a night person but would be asleep when he arrived, considering the lateness of the hour.

He got a whiff of some wonderful smell, as he walked the length of the property, in an effort to be certain he was in the right place since street names and numbers were nearly nonexistent in this King's city. The house appeared to have been two massive homes at one time, and even at that, it took up the same space as the four large homes directly across the street and went from one corner to the next. He estimated it at eighteen to twenty thousand square feet. He counted on what he knew about Moroccan order and the reliability of tradition, and guessed that the office would be on the main level, off of the courtyard. Casually he walked all around the house, checking all sides. There were no lights on inside, at least not on the second floor though the wall prevented him from seeing the first floor.

It was still and quiet, with only the distant sound of a lone truck somewhere down the main street. The night was cool and a slight breeze brushed across his bushy eyebrows like the soft touch of a woman's finger as she played with the curly hairs of his beard and eyebrows during the fondling, afterglow that followed lovemaking. He took a deep breath of the fresh night air laden with the smell of olive and cedar trees, and the sweet smell of what he thought were roses, although that seemed illogical to him in this region.

Foot traffic had nearly disappeared with the last change in direction and he was alone when he stopped and fondled the intricacies of the mosaic and quartz wall for a moment, on the side away from the street light, as he checked in all directions for watchful eyes. Confident all was clear, he pulled up the long robe, before jumping up two feet to grab the top of the wall. The caution he used to quietly come down into the mansion garden was in complement with the natural disguise of his dark brown skin and black clothing.

Once he lowered himself to the courtyard grounds, he could scarcely believe the glorious smells and sights evident, though palely lit by the moonlight beaming between the trees. The garden was filled with palm, lemon and olive trees and one glorious cedar pushing its pungent smell into the air from its center position. Immense cacti fifteen to twenty feet tall filled some of the rock gardens, bordered by brilliant bursts of red color emanating from potted geraniums, miniature orange trees; red, white, pink and violet impatiens, and pots filled with tropical plants. Severely angular birds of paradise jutted up from metallic pots that bordered stone filled pathways between the black and white checked tile pathways, and were surrounded by philodendrons and hundreds of rose bushes bearing roses of every color imaginable.

Carefully, he quickly shone his flashlight around the outer courtyard checking the shadows and found that there were salmon colored Mojave roses in the corners of the yard with huge flowers whose petals were actually mixed apricot and carmine; and beautiful white roses at the center of several of the rock gardens as brilliant red ones resided in others. Far off on the opposite side of the lavish yard was a beautiful fountain with a small pond that meandered out into four tributaries that came back together to a small pool. He heard no trickling water, and realized that the water was turned off. He wished for the cover of the sound of moving water, but Cest' la vie'. He turned off the flashlight.

The most appealing flower was closest to him, the pale lavender Blue Girl tea rose with its silvery glimmer. He recognized this one in particular because it was one of the few pleasant memories he had of marriage to his former wife Barbara. The Blue Girl was her favorite, so he filled one corner of their backyard with the roses and built a gazebo for her in the middle of the flowers. Later, when the kids were born, she would take the babies out and nurse them in the peaceful, fragrant sanctuary. Whenever she became too difficult to deal with and talking to her became nearly impossible - which was often - he could usually lure her to the gazebo which would calm her down enough for them to discuss the issue at hand. The Blue Girl worked quite well for a few years with its lavender glow, but ultimately, even it could not help the turbulent marriage.

Gigantic covered L-shaped cages on both sides of the garden appeared to be for housing birds, although he heard no birds. The faint smell of mint was everywhere. He could not visually identify the mint in the lush garden because of the low light, but there was no mistaking the scent. Although he tried to stay on the checkered, mosaic tiles as he moved toward the back door, he accidentally stepped off of the path once, crushing the low ground cover plants and immediately smelled the strong, distinct smell of spearmint.

He was well hidden by the foliage in the massive, surreal garden as he slithered toward the rear doors of the elegant urban estate. Using tools he retrieved from his black bag, and with the skill of the master he had become, he opened the glass doors with ease and entered the cool, breezy inner courtyard, careful to keep out of the light. Too easy he thought as he stealthily moved along the wall toward a doorway. The height of the two story room was easily thirty-five feet, topped by skylights from the second floor which shone silver moonlight down on the fountain that softly trickled water from level to level in the center of the lavish, tropical garden of the inner courtyard. Although there were not nearly as many flowers as in the outer garden, the smell of roses, hibiscus and jasmine was strong as they spew forth their glorious scents from pots which adorned the walls of the great room. On each side of the room were two massive zelliges, glittering mosaic tiles of many colors, with blue and rust being most predominant . Two massive, curved staircases at opposite ends of the open room led up to the second floor balcony and the rooms overlooking the waterfall.

He thought, as he moved closer toward the first door, that this was the house of a terribly sensuous woman. Most of his jobs were in Europe the past few years but European women didn't have the fire of African women who could warm a man down to the hair on his little toe while just walking down the street to the market. A strange chill flashed in weird patterns across his back and down his arms as he checked the courtyard again before entering the room.

◊

Slowly, in the dark shadows of the second floor, the figure of a woman moved slightly from behind the pillar on the balcony to watch the thief entering the room below. A giant hulk of a man joined her side, looming greatly in the darkness. They were both dressed in soft, silk, flowing robes that swayed in the gentle breeze that rose from the air circling in the courtyard. Naseer Aajiz moved closer to the woman and began to speak softly when she, Saa'iqa Mastoora, coldly and abruptly waved her hand in front of his face, silencing him immediately. From the doorway below, Will Creech was alerted to some movement in the house and stopped to listen. Saa'iqa and Naseer moved fully into the shadows. Will scanned the courtyard quickly but discovering no one, entered cautiously.

◊

Once inside, he used the small flashlight and began searching for a safe, safety deposit box or other device containing the vast jewels that a woman with this sort of wealth must have. The room was filled with expensive tapestries. There was an exquisitely plush Persian rug of muted colors of lavender and blue on the floor, and wooden and silver artifacts placed on modern Moroccan furniture with angular backs and bright colored woven fabric between highly polished wood, which Will inspected and examined with the speed and accuracy of one who had searched for riches often. He checked under lamps, behind long, heavy drapes and modern paintings by Morocco's new movement of young, upscale painters to no avail. After a quick look, he left the parlor and slithered along the courtyard wall to the next open door, still under the watchful eyes of Saa'iqa and Naseer.

It was dangerous taking so long to find the stuff. There was something else about being in her house that made his wrists cold, as if freezing rain was beating against the point where his hand and arm joined on the underside. Maybe it was his age.

He got down to the business of finding loot, starting with the large cedar bookshelf against the wall behind the beautiful wood, marble and leather desk. The room was huge with fourteen foot ceilings and tall, deep, elegant Moorish windows made of gueps from top to bottom, the carved plaster work with hand-cut surfaces as fine as lace. The floor was adorned with intricately patterned burgundy, cream and green Arabic rugs and large throw pillows of matching colors. Tapestries combined with

French modern art decorated the cream colored walls and hopefully, hid a safe. After a thorough search through the bookcase, Will checked behind the wall hangings and under the rug. He ran his fingers along the walls looking for hidden doors and buttons.

Frustrated by the futile hunt, he shone the flashlight beam in a sweep around the room attempting to discover missed hiding places. Next he moved to the desk, whose drawers were all unlocked and contained only papers written in French and Arabic. Baffled by the lack of clues, he thought for a moment then shone the flashlight beam on the ceiling and carefully searched every inch, starting at one corner and working his way toward the center. Because of the strength and busyness of the patterns, it was quite difficult to discern the normal shapes from any additional or unusual ones, but Will was patient and searched diligently. Midway, the light revealed the small square outline of a door quietly hidden in the intricate, hand painted cedar ceiling with patterns and shapes of rust, indigo, white, black and green.

He smiled to himself as he searched through his bag until he found four large suction cup devices. With familiarity of the task, he placed two of the cups very high on one wall and activated the suction function by flipping the levers on the sides. Once secure, he pulled a six inch wide banded rope from each mechanism and attached them to the second set of cups. After carrying the new set of devices to the opposite wall, he repeated the method of attachment and activation. With all of them in place, a double clothes line was formed about seven or eight feet from the floor. With a two foot square webbed cloth which he attached with Velcro tabs and laced to the clotheslines, he formed a platform directly under the ceiling door.

Looking up past the apparatus to the ceiling door, Will smiled slyly and whispered to himself, "Oh I do appreciate creative victims" as he checked the stability of the contraption.

Once certain, he swung himself up like a trapeze artist, and boarded the platform - which placed him directly beneath the concealed door. With a screwdriver he probed the perimeter of the safe for alarms and triggers, and found none, but he found no opening apparatus either so he tried pushing the door. A good choice. It opened slowly, as if by hydraulics, and lowered a safe with a combination knob on front, about ten inches down from the ceiling.

He whispered, "Really nice."

Using a stethoscope like the eccentric he was, he opened the safe and removed the jewelry, leaving the hidden papers. Will seldom used modern devices to execute a robbery. It seemed undignified to him somehow, and an insult to Jack's teachings. Once the safe was open, he found five flawless diamond necklaces, three strings of pearls, five pairs of diamond earrings, eight diamond rings the smallest of which was a five Carat - and three sets of incredibly exquisite antique Berber jewelry, including one nose/ear ring, two older rings and one antique Berber Khatem, a tall silver ceremonial ring, over a hundred years old, still worn by some of the women . When finished, he closed the safe door which rose up into the ceiling, disappearing into the pattern once again. Quietly he lowered himself to the floor, and disassembled the suction devices.

◊

The tension on the balcony almost rivaled Will's nervousness as he slowly exited the office. No attempt was made to stop him. Saa'iqa fumed quietly as she watched the thief who possessed such unbelievable audacity, sneak his way along the walls and out of her back door. Naseer, towering over her, watched both her and Will as he carefully left the house. As soon as the door closed, he stepped into the subdued light on the balcony but she stayed in the shadows. The increased light made the irritation on Naseer's chestnut colored face somewhat visible as he spoke.

"He does have great talent, but is a foolish individual."

"Yes." she replied, "It was quite interesting to see him in action. We could not have been in a better position for a demonstration." She sucked her teeth at the end of the sentence, and topped it off with a small "humph."

Naseer watched her carefully, as he always did, trying to read her body language though the darkness made it quite difficult. He hoped she was disgusted, the only appropriate reaction to the situation in his opinion. He decided to test the waters. "I warned you of the danger of hiring a foreigner. There are enough Marrakechiis here who could perform the tasks we nee . . ."

Saa'iqa turned suddenly and stared at him, the cold intolerance in her glare was felt, if not well seen - even in the dark. He silenced. She wondered what could have possibly come over her long time friend to cause such behavior. Since this mission began Naseer had been jittery and extremely opinionated. She tried to think back to a time when he had spoken to her in the same manner but could only remember once, when she was twelve and he was fifteen. He was at least six feet three even at that age and towered over her small frame then, as he still did. A visiting student from the U.S. had been the cause of his outburst then. Maybe he had some deep dislike for Americans which only manifested itself under stress. It was unpleasant for her to treat him like the hired help he was, but he was. She spoke to him in a calm, smooth voice he had heard before, but not directed at him - one that meant danger was imminent.

"As you well know, I have no patience for disobedience and insubordination. I will take care of this idiot myself. Your opinion has been heard."

She moved back toward the edge of the balcony and looked down at the peaceful fountain. She had watched it in amazement for as long as she could remember. She then continued to speak with her back to Naseer and her hands tightly clinching the railing. Her voice dropped half an octave and became almost a soft, syrupy hiss as she responded.

"However, your tone is unappreciated. Tomorrow, I will see to Will Creech."

Naseer raised an eyebrow slightly, noting the tone of her response and then bowed and backed away, leaving her alone in the dark. As he walked back to his room, a slight smirk came over his face as he considered the annoyance she was obviously feeling. He allowed the gray silk robe to fall from his muscular body glistening with moisture from the warmth of the night. Left wearing light silk pajama pants, he lay in on the foot of the bed, rubbed the dense hair on his chest, walked to the window and watched the soft shadows of the Atlas Mountain range in the distance. He had the urge to scream the fears he felt about the task they were embarking upon. He longed to hold her, and take away the need, but he doubted that he could. Instead, he sighed, closed the balcony doors and lay on the bed until sleep took him over.

5 WILL

Working always made things brighter and clearer the next day. Nothing like it. Despite the dangers and uncertainty, or perhaps because of it, Will loved being a thief. Must have been what he was born to do. The walk to the Restaurant Le Jet D'eau was a very short one and the morning was crisp and beautiful. Le Jet had croissants, and he was even able to get eggs there, much to his delight.

Before going to the restaurant, he went west on Mohammed the Fifth to the news stand to get a copy of "The Messenger of Morocco" the only English written newspaper he could find and a copy of "Le Matin," a French paper that he could muddle through some sections of with his minuscule knowledge of the language. After securing his morning dose of news, he walked back past the hotel to the restaurant.

Jet D'eau was in a new, modern six story building on circle Place de la Liberte. It was pink with gray trim and huge gray marble facade columns. Six major streets met at the intersection, and a massive stone, circular structure sat in the middle of it that looked like a fountain, but there was no evidence of water or water spouts. The shape of it resembled a sundial of sorts, with disjointed and parallel marble sections comprising the whole. It was a curious structure to him.

Seated in Saa'iqa's navy blue Mercedes, she and Naseer watched every move that Will made from down the street. In the daylight, it was evident that Naseer was a gargantuan man who seemed ill fitted for the large, luxury sedan. He wore a black fez which only highlighted his gold flecked, chestnut colored skin. His thick black beard was striped with thin gray slithers at random places from his ears to his chin. His eyes were as black as coal, with long lashes that curled up toward his perfectly arched eyebrows on the top, and down toward his chin on the bottom. His nose bore the ageless beauty of Arab ancestry, and was straight, yet broad, and his eyes the depths of Berber heritage. The hair that could be seen from under the Fez, as with that of his beard and his chest, was course and thick, with a density that caused it to have a spongy feel to the touch. His lips were full and straight, his neatly manicured mustache covering most of his top lip. He watched Will Creech walk down the street with great intensity, as if reading Will's thoughts with every step.

Saa'iqa's face and head were covered by a brilliant purple veil and scarf, revealing only her equally brilliant, blue-green eyes. Her skin was a light reddish, yellow hue like the color of finished bamboo, and smooth looking around the outside of her large, wide, almond shaped eyes. Striking would be the first word to come to any person's mind who got even just a glimpse of her. They watched Will enter the same restaurant.

Naseer spoke first. "It is odd that a man in his line of work would eat in the same place every day."

"Not odd . . . arrogant!" replied Saa'iqa just before getting out of the car, wearing a black djellabah which covered her from neck to toe. She walked across and down the street and into the restaurant, passing the farmers in mule driven carts with giant wagon wheels, numerous mothers on scooters taking their children to school, and men and boys on bicycles carrying cases of drinks they were delivering, or books or nothing at all as they moved mechanically down the street. Although the street was four lane, two on each side going in opposite directions, at any given time during her crossing, there were eight to ten different vehicles along side one another, pushing and nudging gently in an effort to get ahead of each other and vie for space. And then there were the street vendors on their bicycles carrying heavy laden baskets of mint for NAA-NAA, Moroccan mint tea - the national drink, making their way toward the Place of the Dead and the souks - the market - for their day of trading and selling. She made her way to the restaurant, fairly unnoticed, blending well into the crowd in her traditional, if not a bit conservative dress.

Will was sitting at a table sipping the hot, sweet mint tea while reading The Messenger, when that feeling of cold rain on his wrists crept up on him, not abruptly, but slowly with a strange intensity. He lowered his newspaper and looked up to find the most brilliant blue-green eyes he had ever imagined in any of those erotic fantasies he was prone to have, staring at him, lashing and piercing through the newspaper. The suspense of wondering who was under all of that clothing and behind those eyes was better than an orgasm for a man who thrived on the unknown. "Was she saying something?" he thought. Stunned by those provocative eyes, he struggled to reply to the words he could barely hear her speaking.

"Mr. Creech? You are Will Creech, are you not?"

She was talking to him in a wonderful, light Moroccan accent with a touch of French! He tried to imagine how she knew his name. It was very hard for him to concentrate. He explained that he had not expected anyone to know him in this city.

Confusion in her eyes, she replied "Oh . . . well I was hoping you were the person who called . . . but it wasn't your voice at all. My name is Aisha Moustapha and I well, I guess I made a mistake."

This was just too good. Who would have thought that he could come here and meet a confused African woman with sexy laser eyes, who needed his aid? "Please, sit down and explain. Maybe I can help."

She had always liked this part of the game and wondered why arrogance and gullibility seemed to go hand in hand. She sat down and explained how she had a "highly specialized occupation", which she could not go into at this time, and that she received an anonymous phone call at her home in Casablanca hiring her for a job here in Marrakech.

"No, thank you," she answered when he asked. She wasn't hungry but thought tea would be nice.

She said that a messenger brought money and instructions to her, stating that she should come to Marrakech and wait at a small hotel on the opposite side of town for further instructions. Well she did, and was still waiting, but nothing had happened for a whole week until she received a call that morning telling her to meet with Will Creech at the Hasna Hotel. She went there and the clerk told her that she could find him here. She hoped that he was her employer, but now she was more confused than before.

Will watched her movements, trying to gather as much information as possible about the woman who was speaking. There was little he could tell other than the obvious things about her eyes and the confines of her clothing, except for the exquisite jewelry she was wearing. Although he questioned their authenticity, she appeared to be wearing a ceremonial Berber necklace and a ceremonial ring, a Khatem, both of which were either genuine antiques or very good replications. Although he did not know if the wearing of this jewelry was considered to be for everyday wear, he doubted it seriously. Of course, he had no idea what else she had planned for her day.

"Ms. Mohammed, I believe you and I are in the same boat. I'm still waiting for further instructions myself. I tell the clerk how to reach me nearly every time I leave the hotel."

She thought, "Of course you do you fool! Where and how did he learn discretion?" Being the professional she was however, all she said was "Well what do you make of it Mr. Creech? Why would we be given such instructions? Do you sup . . ."

Before she could continue, a waiter approached and asked if Will was American - then informed him of a phone call at the counter. Will excused himself, asked the waiter to see to Aisha and then went to the telephone. Aisha was careful not to make eye contact with the waiter as she politely declined in Arabic, his offer of food.

Having completed his brief conversation, Will returned to the table saying "Well it does get curiouser and curiouser."

"I beg your pardon . . .curiouser?"

"From Alice and . . . never mind."

He admitted to the line's utter unimportance in the larger scheme of things and told her about the message left for them by the caller. They were to meet a blue Mercedes on the corner by the hotel in exactly three hours in order to attend a meeting with their employer.

"Did you order something to eat?" he asked, but she explained her lack of hunger.

In the natural order, according to the ethics of Will Creech, he suggested that they go back to his hotel room and wait until it was time to meet the blue car, if that was all right with her. It was so automatic for him. A split second later, he could only contemplate how stupid his invitation actually was. Aisha was covered from head to toe and there were probably many more rules of etiquette you could break here than he ever even thought about in the States. He thought, "So what now? Was she going to jump up and scream to the entire restaurant about his impropriety? Would he be flogged or have his hand cut off or some such?"

He couldn't help but wonder why he knew so little about Morocco. He knew about other Africans. He knew Nigeria extensively and loved the ways of the Yoruba, at least most of them. He was very familiar with Egyptians and even spoke some Egyptian Arabic. It did him little good in Marrakech. He felt quite connected to the people of Cairo, white folks constantly tried to make the world believe that they were not black people, but he could feel the kinship. Go figure. Even when Anwar Sadat was alive and on the news daily, looking just like Norman Lear's sitcom character George Jefferson.

"Why wouldn't this woman say something . . . or at least scream? Who spoke last anyway?" He held his breath and contemplated. He looked around the restaurant and wished he had opted to sit out on the terrace under the crisp morning sun. That way, if she did choose to scream, there would be less embarrassment. He could step back into the shadows and stare at her as everyone else surely would at that point, and act as if he had not a clue what her problem might be. He remembered that the traffic noise could grow deafening, and decided to remain inside for breakfast.

The waiter appeared just as Will was about to say something. He waited before speaking, noticing that she lowered her head while they were being served, and assumed the gesture had something to do with their culture, although he had not noticed any other women being quite so demure.

As was the tradition when serving mint tea, the leaves were stuffed into small glasses, like the ones Americans use for their morning orange juice, then placed on the table in this case in front of the patron, thought sometimes held on a silver tray. The server, and they all seemed to be men in this country, then began pouring the tea from about two inches from the opening of the glass, then progressively raised it higher and higher; sometimes as high as two or more feet from the glass as they poured. In this way, they could aerate the tea and check to see if it creates foam in the top of the glass. If there is no foam, the drink is considered to be inferior, would not be served and new tea would be made. Will was pleased to see the foam.

"Please forgive me Ms. Mohammed. By no means did I mean to suggest anything improper. You tell me what you would like to do."

Saa'iqa finally raised her head and looked directly at him, then chuckled at his nervousness, causing her eyes to sparkle and dance - captivating him even further. "Please Mr. Creech, think nothing of it. I spent several years in Parisian schools and have adopted many Western ways. I only dress traditionally in Marrakech in order not to draw unnecessary attention to myseli. It is best, considering the type of work I do."

"And exactly what is it that you do Aisha?"

"Oh I think that will become pretty obvious to you in a very short time . . . you know, when we meet our employer Mr. Creech. Your thinking makes the most sense however, I would prefer to come to your hotel room, but our customs are still very strong. I will meet you in about thirty minutes rather than enter with you if that suits you?"

He gave her the room number and wondered what else he could do to make this visit easy.

She told him she would go browse at the newspaper shop on the corner until he left the restaurant and she was certain he was back in his hotel room.

◊

This was sort of new for him. Usually, his parameters were defined and the rules were clear. As he brushed his teeth, he thought about all the women in his life and how many times he had been through this ritual. He was a grown man in his mid-forties and he still anticipated every new relationship with a woman as a possibility for permanence. "Why was that?" he wondered as he rinsed the suds from the brush and the sink. The only constant woman in his life had been his wife Barbara - a serious bitch on wheels. He had fought nicer bar room brawlers in his younger, fighting days. She was steady though and reliable, and he could not think of a better mother for his children - he certainly couldn't take that away from her. He thought he needed all that at the time. On rough days, he wasn't sure that he didn't need it still. But today he felt, would be a good day.

After checking the hallway to be certain she had not been noticed, Saa'iqa removed the brown contact lenses she had worn while walking through the hotel lobby. A Moroccan woman in traditional garb, with blue-green eyes is a little more conspicuous than she could afford to be today.

Just as he was drying his hands he heard a knock on the door. He tried to remember if he had heard her coming down the hall at all. He had not . "This woman," he thought, "must be a thief too." And she must be a good one for him not to have been aware that she was that close. Interesting women really turned him on. Dangerous women were ecstasy.

She knocked, he answered, she entered and they exchanged small talk. "Come on in and make yourself comfortable. Can I get you something?"

She walked into the room, thinking of how much Americans seemed to always sound like John Wayne. Men, women, it didn't really seem to matter. The use of the word "on" in his sentence was actually quite interesting, as if it potentiated the action of entering. She could hear good old John in some long lost scene from the cinema adding that extra, and generally unnecessary word in order to make the "little lady" feel more welcome. She wondered if this was also Will's intent, or just mindless habit embedded in his psyche from massive doses of television he must have watched, as all Americans seemed to, as a child.

"Yes, may I have a mineral water please? Do you mind if I remove the djellabah because it is so heavy, and the room is quite warm."

This was certain confirmation to Will of his prior suspicions of having been blessed by somebody's God this day, be it Baptist or Moslem. "Honey, you can take off whatever, and as much of it as possible," he thought.

"Sure, whatever makes you comfortable Aisha." he said.

Once she removed the scarf and veil, he was stunned by the sheer beauty of this woman. Her face reflected the best of powerful, strong features of the original people of this continent mixed with the colorful eyes and intensely pointed aura of a European heritage; complemented by her golden bronze complexion. He couldn't quite find the right group of people to match her features with. Something about her looked particularly Egyptian and pointed, and yet there was the distinct look of rounded Moroccan features, with full lips and a strange mixture of French characteristics. He had never seen another person like her in his life. The combination of features slightly reminded him of a Blackfoot Native American woman he knew once. Saa'iqa's skin was absolutely flawless with only a small, flat black mole on the bottom of her left cheek. Her coal black hair was twisted up into a thick bun and secured to the back of her head by a large silver comb. She was somewhat hairy, with a soft down on her face, and smooth eyebrows that he suspected might run together if she allowed them to get out of hand. She was small, probably no more than five feet three inches tall, and probably no more than one hundred and ten pounds.

Will poured the mineral water into a champagne glass and sat it on the table near the sofa. As he returned to the bar, Saa'iqa began pulling the large garment up past long legs, a short brilliant green skirt and double breasted, tailored jacket, to remove it over her head when the djellabah got caught in the comb in her hair. While struggling, she asked Will for help.

Happy to oblige, Will pulled the surprisingly heavy, woolen clothing up with a little more zeal than was necessary, throwing her off balance and plummeting toward the floor. In a fast agile action commensurate with the moves of a top rate second story man, he caught the small woman easily in his arms, the fabric completely covering her face. She broke into a glorious laugh that gurgled and bubbled like Eartha Kitt's voice, only a half octave higher.

He was embarrassed and hurried to free her of the confines. Once he got the garment over her head, he pulled it down behind her back, placing their bodies very close together, his arms encircling her body. He apologized profusely for nearly injuring her. She assured him that he responded before she was hurt.

"That's good," he replied, "I wouldn't want any part of your body hurt. Do you have any suggestions as to how we might engage ourselves for the next couple of hours?"

Seductively, with the purr and gravel of the best Kitt performance she answered, "I suspect you already have a little something in mind."

"Huhm . . . huh . . . huh . . . you are not at all what I expected Aisha."

She smiled coyly and answered, "I suspect you're quite right about that too Mr. Creech." She moved closer to him, lightly pressing her body against his. He pulled her even closer, kissing her passionately for a few moments, but keeping his hands still, then pulled back and watched her intensely before speaking.

"Yeah, lots of contrasts and surprises. What else do you have up your sleeve?" he asked.

"Why don't you look up there and see."

Delighted by the invitation, he kissed her again as he began unbuttoning her jacket, revealing no blouse nor undergarments. He removed her jacket and allowed it to fall to the floor without ever interrupting the kiss. Once her skirt was unzipped and on the peach colored, tile floor, he was in awe of the magnificent woman clad only in black panties and heels before him.

He picked her up and carried her to the bed, gently laying her down. Standing beside the bed, he unbutton his shirt and removed it. As he began unbuckling his belt, she reached up and caressed his rock solid stomach softly.

He took her hand in his and began kissing the inside of her wrist first, then worked his way down her arm, past her inner elbow to her shoulder. Positioning himself on top of her, they kissed passionately as he removed the comb from her hair, allowing its full length to fall upon the pillows and off the edge of the bed. He noted that it was not completely straight, but somewhat coarse and wild. It made for an even greater turn-on as he kissed his way down her neck and across both shoulders. She caressed his neck and upper back with her fingernails and fingertips. He ran his tongue under her chin, down to what would be her Adam's Apple were she a man, causing her to moan ever so slightly.

Never breaking her gentle writhing movements under this wonderfully erotic man, with her right hand, Saa'iqa opened a compartment on the top of the massive ring on her left hand. Will nuzzled and kissed her collarbone, his warm breath causing small shivers under the surface of her skin. The jingling and tinkling of the Berber necklace and earrings, which he could see now were solid silver with ruby studs and intricate filigree, was almost sensory overload for a jewel thief who loved women.

She pressed a small release button on the side of the ring, enabling a two inch needle to ease out.

◊

He loved them all, mind you, but women like this one were especially delectable with their perfect bodies and powder soft skin. It was wonderful to be with a woman who smelled like a woman should instead of those tacky walking perfume displays too often disguised as females back in the States. The kind you smelled from twenty feet away or who suffocated you if you were unfortunate enough to enter the same elevator, or hell, the same room with them. "No class!" he thought. Aisha only smelled as if she had bathed in a tub full of flower petals and softly scented natural oils.

Wouldn't it be great, he thought, to lounge in a huge tub or Jacuzzi and soak in the softly scented oils of Morocco with this breathtaking woman; the water lapping softly against the inside of her thighs and rocking them gently, lulling them into sensual bliss. He smiled to himself when it occurred to him that he was thinking about water again - then using the tip of his tongue he began to make small circular movements down from her collar bone. Increasing the circles slowly, he ran his tongue along the outermost perimeter of her right breast, relishing the softness there, then with decreasing movements, worked his way to the wrinkled aureole. Applying very mild pressure at first, he pressed the tip of his tongue into the hard nipple in tiny rotating movements, then sucked it lightly before repeating the process again with slightly more pressure with time. She groaned softly and arched her back somewhat, pushing more of the perfect mound of flesh into his hot, receptive mouth.

◊

"Oh my, oh my, oh my - merciful Allah be praised for the skills you have allowed this man!" she thought as his sucking, pushing movements became more rapid and prominent. She seriously contemplated her time schedule and whether or not she could rightfully indulge in pleasure with so much to do. Just as he decided to move to the other breast, the small break in sensual charging allowed her the clarity to return to the task at hand. As Will licked across the top of the left nipple, Saa'iqa positioned the needle directly above the nape of his neck. He slowly sucked the hardened nipple, causing her to sigh audibly. She plunged the needle firmly into his neck and kissed his forehead gently. Will jumped slightly, startled by the sharpness. Soothingly, she rubbed his back as he spoke.

"Aisha, baby, your nails are . . ."

She closed the roof like, ring compartment and gently stroked an increasingly distressed Will on the shoulder. He began to experience some involuntary muscular jerks and twitches while she lay quietly beneath him.

With extreme difficulty, he spoke again. "Aisha . . . there's some . . . something wrong. "Why couldn't he move? What was happening to him? Why didn't this woman do something?" he wondered.

Will's spastic jerks became more pronounced as he lay atop the beautiful African woman with the dark, long flowing, wild hair who remained calm and still as could be - considering a man who was a hundred pounds heavier than she, was shaking and flailing around on top of her.

"Do not bother to fight Will Creech. It's useless. Accept the fact that you can no longer command your arms and legs. Ahh . . . see . . .the involuntary movements are calming now."

She stared up at the ornate ceiling with plaster relief in symmetric patterns of gold, peach and blue above the room as she kissed his forehead and rubbed his back gently and lovingly, and spoke to him in a voice that was smooth as silk and drippy as Michelle's Favored Creme Syrups.

"I am Saa'iqa Mastoora, your former employer. You were instructed to come to Marrakech and remain anonymous until you were contacted. A simple thing to do for most people. You could have acted like a tourist; visited the Dar Si Said Museum or Djemaa El Fna and watched the snake charmers, seen the sights and soaked up the vast African culture. Not you however. Instead, you robbed three houses in a four day period, the last of which was mine! How has one so impatient become so adept in this field? I cannot understand this. You must be an idiot savant. I simply cannot afford to allow such greed and stupidity to expose even the slightest bit of information about me or the job for which you were hired."

◊

Finally!! He wasn't shaking so much , but he still couldn't move his hands toward her throat the way he had been willing himself to do for the last couple of minutes. What a cruel revelation he thought, as he tried to at least enjoy the feel of the smooth skin on her chest ; his face laying against it. More than one person who knew him had said that his attitude about women would be the death of him. What irony. He smiled, or at least meant to, at the thought that he wished she had waited another hour or so. Well he supposed he should count his blessings that she was not

38

some deranged psycho who would mutilate him beyond recognition, causing his mother distress when she saw his dead body.

◊

Maybe, she thought, she should have waited an hour or so before killing him. It had been a long time since she'd been with a man who was not intimidated by her or that she did not find disgusting and loathsome. This one was just stupid, but clearly physically wonderful. Other than Naseer, who worked out like a fiend, most Moroccan men she came in contact with seemed to have very little interest in staying in shape. She relished the dark brown skin that was perfectly tight, the feel of muscles everywhere she had touched and the strong, sinewy arms of a climber. She envisioned him as a rock climber as she gently rubbed his hair, now that he was calm.

"I regret wasting such talent, but I do detest insolence. I suspect from this beginning that you would be an exceptional lover as you are a thief, and I wish I had time to indulge, but I have too much work to do now finding your replacement. Good-bye Will Creech."

Will stared blankly while struggling to speak. Without attempting to move him off of her, she called out to Naseer in only a slightly louder than normal voice. There was a very brief fumbling with the door lock heard before Naseer and two other men entered the room, all wearing gloves, closing the door quickly behind them. The two men lifted Will off of Saa'iqa and placed him on the opposite side of the bed, face down. One of them noticed the unusual gold and malachite watch on Will's left wrist.

Will watched as some mountain of a man gathered Saa'iqa's clothing and gave it to her. She got up from the bed and all three men turned away while she dressed.

Very odd behavior, thought Will. Killing a man is acceptable, but looking at a naked woman is not. If he could only get up, he could catch them all by surprise. He put up a tremendous struggle on the inside . . . but no body parts seemed to respond as far as he could tell.

Once her skirt was on, she told Yakub and Aamil, the assistants, to retrieve her jewelry along with the rest of the jewelry he had taken all week and wipe every item in the room clean of fingerprints to assure there was no trace of him or them. They were also to remove the surveillance equipment they used to watch Will's movements all week. When they were finished, they were to take this body to the coast, weight him down and drop him into the ocean at least fifteen miles off shore. She made it clear that they would have to answer to her if they made any mistakes.

◊

As Will watched he realized his concerns about his mother's reaction to seeing his body were in vain. He always thought that "sleeping with the fish" was something out of a gangster movie, but suddenly realized that there would be no policeman to hunt down his remains, wished he was imputrescible like plastic, able to survive the sharks and fish until someone could find him and free his mother from the agony he feared she would suffer with his death. Or maybe uncertainty was better for her. He no longer knew. Now he wws goonieg hv otnbbdsio . . . jwo vcmxz; . . . "What had happened to him?" He had at least been thinking straight before that point. Everything had become a jumbled mess in his head.

◊

Saa'iqa buttoned the top button of her jacket. When she bent down to get her shoes, she moved very close to Will's face and spoke to him.

"Poor Will Creech. I wonder what you are thinking now. Earlier today you asked me what my profession was. Do you think you know now? Huhm? I'm very good at what I do, so feel honored that you have died at the hands of one of the best."

She stood slowly, watching the occasional blinking of Will's eyes, and asked Naseer to bring her purse and djellabah to her.

The six foot seven, two hundred and sixty pound man complied. Yakub and Aamil began cleaning away fingerprints as Will struggled to say something. Saa'iqa was inserting the brown contact lenses when she heard some faint sounds coming from him. She leaned closer to hear, amazed that he could even attempt speaking at this point in his poisoning. She knew her weapons well and this one should have killed him five minutes ago. She had great admiration for his fortitude.

Will knew he was slipping away. He wondered how this could have happened to him? He was supposed to be smarter, more streetwise than this!! He must have one clear, unjumbled thought in his head. He must have some clarity, something distinct and unafraid.

Shhhhh . . . listen.

He could hear the water softly lapping against the side of . . . of . . . of what? No matter. He could see her up ahead in the mist . . . her wonderful, long brown arms stretched out to reach him. She was swaying and humming like she always did when she was waiting for one of them. He could hear the water gently hitting the side of . . . of . . . well anyway, he had to call out to her . . . to let her know he was there; to know that she was with him.

Saa'iqa moved even closer so that she could hear Will's weak voice whisper the word"BERNICE."

"Bernice you say?" said Saa'iqa as she stood again and took the djellabah from the patiently waiting Naseer and pulled it over her head. "I wonder if this Bernice knows there is a man who calls her name with his last breath on earth. What an amazing woman she must be to deserve such love and devotion."

Will's eyes slowly closed. Saa'iqa watched him briefly before securing the veil over the lower portion of her face. She told Naseer to finish the work there and meet her at Djemaa el Fna in two hours. She then walked to the door, which Naseer opened for her exit. He bowed slightly as she left the room.

"BERNICE?"

Will couldn't see her anymore but he could hear her wonderful voice humming in the mist . . . keeping in synch with the gentle, steady lapping sound and the rocking motion he felt. He hoped the laser eyed woman wouldn't speak again. Lord knows she felt good, but under the circumstances, the last woman's voice he wanted to hear was certainly not hers. He wanted that low, deep Baptist church hum from the woman who still had arms strong enough to carry Ms. Berry from the garden where they were weeding, to her car when she had a stroke three years before, and still had the strength to drive her to the hospital. He wanted to reach those arms and be wrapped up in their gentle embrace, held and nurtured by her unconditional love and wondrous devotion.

Shh . . .

There she was again singing low . . . sounding like Marion Anderson, Mahalia Jackson and Tina Turner all rolled into one. Lord he loved that voice . . .gently . . . softly . . . humming "Were you there?" his favorite spiritual . . . singing just for him the way she always had, no matter who else was listening, no matter what else they thought he knew that her voice with its smooth roughness was raised only for him. He was unafraid for her then. He was calm and his thoughts were clear, with no pain. He had protected her even at that moment, as he had always wanted and intended to do, even when he was unsuccessful.

Quietly, he lay still and listened. He listened, no longer concerned with his physical surroundings. He listened with every fiber of his being as he entered a cool long tunnel bathed in a glorious warm light that became brighter directly in front of him. He could hear her singing now, soft and low, deep and gruff and the sound of water lapping against the side of his pathway became more rhythmic as the gentle breeze of the corridor played with the hair on his face and the light seemed to warm his bones, yet bathed him in coolness all at the same time.

He could hear her singing as it became fainter and stronger - singing just for him.

"Were you there when they nailed him to the tree?

Whoaoaaooo, sometimes it causes me to

tremble, tremble, tremble.

Were you there when they nailed him to the tree?"

The light was whiter, lighter, bluer, and brighter as she began to hum again and the coolness was oh so soothing, and the water lapping. . . lapping . . .lapping . . . lapping . . . gently lapping . . .

6 CONNECTIONS

She could not figure out why she had been rocking so fast for the past ten minutes. The evening started out so calm and peaceful. Ethel Waters -whose father thought naming her after his favorite singer and actress was a cute thing to do - her neighbor from down the street, brought over the most unguinous fried chicken she had ever seen or tasted in her life. They combined it with the fresh vegetables she fixed that afternoon - cabbage, squash, turnip greens and cornbread - and had dinner together. Of course she had to soak up some of the grease with a paper towel before she could eat it, but ultimately it turned out well. "Two old widows having dinner together so that they wouldn't notice how alone they were," she thought aloud as she rocked more vigorously by the minute.

Ethel and she made a pact that whenever they had the "widow's dinner," they would not discuss anything about their dead husbands, only the future and events to come. They held pretty true to that and had done so for the previous eight years of Wednesday nights. She remembered for a moment how much she missed her husband, an activity she seldom indulged in of recent. It was simply too much to bear. Too many years of joy, pain, trials and tribulation to reduce to a widow's blithering, idiotic efforts to subdue feeling the obliteration of loneliness.

She couldn't sit still any longer and nearly leapt out of the rocking chair and walked to the edge of the porch. She looked around the neighborhood wildly for a moment, down the street to the left toward Rhode Island Avenue, where all the houses on her street had neat little yards, spotted lights on porches and in windows and an assortment of cars parked all along the street. She walked out to the middle of the street and began speaking to the ether. "Something is just not right! I can feel it being all wrong now just make it clear. Make it clear."

From across the street, she heard a familiar voice that she would have preferred not to at that moment. Her neighbor Buck Echols, who gained great pleasure from harassing Bernice had been sitting on his porch watching her. Some days it seemed that his greatest joy in life was waiting for her to do something that signaled old age, despite the fact that he was older than her, so that he could laugh at her behavior and pending senility.

"Only thing that ain't right woman is your head! Out here talking to the street lights in the middle of the night. Only thing clear is that you need to go find you a man, and get you a little bit so you can take the edge off all them years of gittin' none!" He left his house and joined her in the middle of the street.

"Look Buck, I don't have the time right now for your . . ." she tried to say before he cut her off.

"Now my friend Joe down at the lodge, still thinks you are a 'comely woman.' His words, not mine . . . I wouldn't use any words like that . . . comely . . . what does that really mean? Anyway, I guess you still a good looking woman, I know you was fine when you was young. Jessie Jane hasn't let me look at no women in so long, I can't really tell anymore."

"You got no more sense than you did when we were young either. Thank you but no, you old fool." she laughed.

"Well now you let me know if you change your mind though. Joe is ready! I mean r-e-a-d-y." He executed a kind of Fred Astaire dance move, while hooking the other arm around an imaginary woman's back.

She smiled at him and started back to her porch. "Don't hold your breath Buck."

Conscious of city safety, he checked up and down the street for any sign of movement before he went back to his house, leaving her with "Alright then."

She sat down in her rocking chair and was quickly reminded of the uneasy feeling she had that made her look up and down the street restlessly. She had come out on this warm, summer evening after Ethel left, to read Toni Morrison's book SONG OF SOLOMON because she never got a chance to savor it when it came out years before. After reading JAZZ and BELOVED, she wanted to soak up every word this woman had to say. She pushed her glasses up to her eyes again, and opened the book to find the page where she had stopped reading, yet couldn't really focus on the search. There was no place quite like Washington, D.C. she thought as she watched the tip of the Washington Monument bobbing up and down as she rocked. She had been born there, and would probably die there - loving it to the end.

She tried to shake her feeling of uneasiness, but it was still alive and well. After a few minutes of reading, she sat quietly, contemplating the name Hagar and her role in the book. Must be something with these progressive black women and that name, she thought. She went to see that beautiful film a few years ago, by that young woman in Atlanta - somebody Dash - about the Geechies. She had a character named Hagar in there too who was a woman after her own heart. When that girl said "She might not have been born in that family but she was here now and that she was a fully growed 'Oman,' and if she couldn't say what was on her mind, then damn it all to hell!" Bernice nearly jumped out of her seat and shouted Amen!! At least that was what she heard, and frankly didn't want to know if it was any different.

Having had some in-law trouble in the early years of her marriage, she could relate completely to that Hagar, but just sitting here on the porch rocking in her chair, she could not in all her sixty-nine years remember one real woman named Hagar. Didn't mean anything necessarily, just one more thing she did not know firsthand. Her father-in-law never did like the fact that his son married a woman with a child. He had a serious case of that "fruit of my loins alone" syndrome that a few black men, maybe men in general seemed to ascribe to. Never did seem to fix it for him when she and Clinton Sr. had two more children together.

"What? Who called me? Which one was it? It doesn't feel like the twins" she said out loud before realizing it.

Then she looked around to see if anyone saw her, like Buck, lest he or another neighbor send someone from the mental hospital to collect the crazy old lady in the brick house with the dark green and yellow trim and giant sunflowers growing in the yard. It had happened to old people before. She knew it because she saw it on Sally Jessie Raphael or that other woman's show where one guest killed the other one, or maybe it was Oprah; she couldn't remember. Just more evidence for cause to exile her to the funny farm when they show up and ask her questions to test her sanity that she wouldn't know, she thought. She realized that she was probably watching too much television, and made a mental note to read more.

If there were an Olympic event for rocking chair rocking . . . she could have been a contender! She stopped the chair abruptly and took off her glasses, placing them on top of the book which was laying in her lap, and looked closely at the signs of the night.

The sky seemed especially clear that evening and more endless than usual. Sometimes it had edges and definitive points of beginning and ending, but now, those perimeters only curved at the limit of her vision, hiding its vastness from her inferior human eyes. She never fooled herself into thinking that people were any more than minute particles floating around as if in a huge hot air balloon - equally as insignificant to the operation of the larger entity, but nonetheless there.

There had been times in her life when she had been arrogant enough to believe that she had been elevated from her "particle" status. That happened occasionally when she was still teaching and some small child from a poor family that had been so messed up by the system that he or she believed they couldn't learn and she had been able to help them turn around their hopelessness and absorb the information. At those times, she deluded herself into thinking she had been promoted to dust mote status or some such. Reality would usually find some way to kick her butt back in gear however, because after all, a dust mote is merely a collection of dust particles. No elevation can occur alone. Maybe, if she added up the many children whose lives she touched, and they allowed her to stand with them, they might all equal a half a mote.

Sometimes these mind wanderings helped one get to the bottom of what was happening. Rocking . . . doodling . . . trying to miss the cracks in a sidewalk; they were all busy work designed to help a person think or not think - whichever was appropriate at the time.

She was clearer now. It was her eldest. Something was happening and it was not good. She could feel the cold now. Just thinking of him normally made her warm and at peace. Whenever he took trips overseas though, she seemed to have more of these anxiety twinges, but nothing like this one had ever happened before. He could always touch her soul.

She had an overwhelming urge to cry, and couldn't understand why in the least. She rocked very slowly and deeply, allowing the chair to go to the limit of both ends of its repetitive movement. She began humming the old hymn "Were You There?" soft and slow, deep and clear the way she did when she and Ms. Henderson would do during their soprano and contralto duet at church. Needless to say Bernice was the contralto. A lump was forming in her throat, and she felt some sort of weight or force leaving her and drifting up in pastel colored, air-driven swirls that split and changed from one to many wispy shapes that simply dissipated into the night air. She slowed her rocking even more, and softly called out to her eldest son and watched the sound drift up to the suddenly, strange darkening sky and travel beyond the rounded edges to infinity. Tears streaming down her smooth brown cheeks, Bernice Creech barely whispered . . .calling for her son, to whatever forces would hear her concern.

"Oh baby what is happening to you? What can I do for you ?"

She listened, hoping for some assurance; some ease to her worry. There was only silence. Not even the swirling forces continued, only silence so overwhelming and profound that it seemed to take over all the street lights, and reflections of the line of side mirrors on the parked cars, and the glow from the tall wooden, antique lamp that her Aunt Bessie Lee gave her when she got married and all the darkness in the street, and the sky, and the shadows of the shrubs around the side of Buck's house and the sounds of the cars on the street, and the puppy whimpering from its spot behind the Chavis' house two doors down the street. The deep ominous, overshadowing still rattled around inside itself, inside of the universe. There was only quiet that hurt her ears and intense, devouring cold that smacked of the chill of a massive necropolis where the souls of many long gone lay buried and finished beneath the ground. She sang.

Were you there when they nailed him to the tree? Were you there when they nailed him to the tree?"

She rocked quietly and stared up at the stars in the sky and soaked it in, nearly suffocated by the dead still of the night, whispering his name with soft undertones of the bewilderment she felt.

"Whoooooooaaaa, sometimes it causes me to tremble, tremble, tremble."

Tears flowed down her face as if a faucet had been turned on, and she was wracked with both physical and emotional pain throughout her pores. Her stomach hurt and she was freezing and hot at the same time, but for some reason she felt compelled to sing on, and for one minuscule nanosecond, she thought she heard him call her name.

"Were you there when they nailed him to the tree?"

She stopped singing and stared into the night, wishing for the tranquillity in her soul that was reflected in the abyss of the firmament above.

"Were you there when they nai . . .

She was silent for a moment, trying to listen for any sign of clarity, but there was no answer that she could discern. After a while she lifted her voice, always slightly lyrical, and musical, even when uttering a single word.

"WILL . . . ?"

7 AFRICAN DESCENT

BARUMP - BARUMP - BARUMP - BARUMP - BARUMP - Ah - uhn - ah - uhn - ah - uhn - ahBARUMP - BARUMP - BARUM - BARUMP - Ah - uhn - ah - uhn - ah - uhn

The pounding of her hooves was enough to make a person's heart stop! The roar was thunderous and seemed to be in slow motion, Dolby Sound like a movie soundtrack that nearly drowned out the jet engines of a Boeing 727 that was taking off from Wilson Airport, just a few miles down the road. There was something quite special about working on a nature reserve that was only a few miles outside a busy metropolis and one of the busiest airports in the world.

BARUMP - BARUMP - BARUMP

Trying to run at Olympic speeds without the benefit of the training, skill or natural ability necessary to do so, was far more than a notion! The peradventure of his situation was not only frightening, but equally exhilarating, though he felt that he was fast reaching his excitement quota.

Ah - uhn - ah - uhnSNORT - BARUMP - SNORT - BARUMP

"My goodness!!" he thought.   "What had thinking about? Where was my mind?" He questioned the wisdom of being out on the reserve while he was unfocused, though he could find no real source for his distraction of several weeks. It was rare to see a rhino at all, and he knew that, or at least he should have known that Impala Point was not really a safe place to wander into at six am in the morning, the only time they were likely to be seen.

BARUMP - SNORT - Ah - uhn - ah

After working for a year and a half at the Nairobi National Park, he knew these animals well enough to be much more careful than he had been on that day. He had been able to stay ahead of her because rhinoceros were not as quick on the start, but could wear a person and most animals out in the long run. He knew his time for keeping ahead of her was about up and though there were many trees in the forest to his left, none were accessible for him to climb. Literally, he could see no trees for the forest . A strange twist on the old adage, he thought. He searched the terrain for an answer.

"Well, ask and ye shall receive they say." He wondered who "they" were, and why ordinary people always referred to "them;" but could not sustain such a frivolous line of thought at the moment. He needed an escape when what should appear straight ahead but a small cliff. He would have to remember to be more specific in his future requests. It was too late to turn and go in another direction with no more room for maneuvering than the hair's width between her nose and his ass. There was a pool at the bottom of the upcoming ledge that was filled with . . . well he didn't have time to dwell on the negative.

Upon reaching the edge, with little hesitation, Clinton Creech glanced back briefly at the halting rhino as he leapt off and down the edge of the cliff yelling "Ohhh shit". . . the short journey down to the cold, icy pool below. When he hit the chilly water he sank a few feet and found he could touch the bottom of the shallow pool. Although he could not dwell on it, he found the information comforting. He recovered quickly, surfaced to the top, then swam at breakneck speed toward the shore.

Aroused by the loud splash, African spoonbills, saddle-billed storks, crowned cranes, sacred ibises and Egyptian geese took flight; two Grant's gazelles, one Thompson gazelle, and a hippo sought refuge while a massive crocodile slithered into the water to check out the commotion - all, just what Clinton needed at that moment. He pulled his knife from the belt holder and prepared to fight, knowing the reptile would reach him before he could touch the shore, which it did.

Although he had tangled with a few monkeys, a kangaroo, a wildebeest, a baby lion and a few snakes in his time, he had not been in a crocodile fight before and his only knowledge of such came from the PBS shows he had seen on television. He surmised gratefully, from the length from its eyes to the tip of its tail, that this was a relatively small croc, only seven or eight feet long, but big enough to feel it could handle Clinton obviously. He had read in a book when he first came to Kenya that the Nile crocodile in particular, could grow to be twenty-five to thirty feet in length. The fact that his battle was not with something so overwhelmingly gigantic gave him significant hope and resolve for the ensuing struggle.

He marveled briefly that he was concerned about the prospect of his continued life.   It had been years since he anticipated living through a dangerous situation.   More often than not, sheer survival instinct would kick in and he would struggle his way through the numerous events that had threatened to end his life.   In all those situations however, he could not recall having a thought about anything past the moment of eminent danger.   He had not considered family, or material things, or friends, or creature comforts or anything else in the past.   At the moment the crocodile reached him, he envisioned his nephew Jarrett's graduation from high school, and how he wanted to see that event, despite the fact that he was far from graduation age and that Clinton had not seen him in years.   Maybe it was an odd thing to consider at such a time, but it seemed to fortify him as he saw the humps of the croc's eyes coming toward him.

The fight was on, with Clinton treading water wildly to keep his foot out of the crocodile's mouth.   He had watched the creatures eat before and knew that if it got hold of a limb, it would twirl it around until it was ripped from the socket, while pulling him down and drown him.   He was lucky that the gyrations maneuvered him into an opportune position for delivering the first blow to the reptile's underbelly.   The crocodile thrashed around, his tail crashing into Clinton's ribs, causing excruciating pain.   Clinton stabbed it on the back a couple of times hoping to buy enough time for an escape, but realized that the scales and what felt like bone when he struck a blow, prevented him from penetrating deeply into flesh.   He recalled that he also read in an article that if you could hold the crocodile's jaws together, the opening mechanism was not nearly as strong as the closing mechanism and you could subdue the animal in that manner.   At that moment, he could not imagine what kind of crocodile the person writing the article was discussing, because it most definitely had little to do with the reptile he was fighting who was offering no such opportunity.

The crocodile grabbed for Clinton's arm in an effort to subdue its prey, but Clinton was fast and pulled away just in time for its tooth to merely graze his arm leaving only his shirt sleeve yanked from the armhole and dangling in the massive rows of crocodile teeth.   With every movement, Clinton grew wiser.   He had always been a natural fighter.

They wrestled and tussled, alternating the advantage for nearly ten minutes when finally, and luckily since the combination of treading water and fighting was a most tiring task, the nearly worn out man was able to subdue the creature with a series of fatal knife wounds that landed between the front legs and into the heart of the croc.

Slowly it sank to the bottom of the water as Clinton swam the last fifteen feet toward shore, unaware of a second, slightly smaller crocodile headed his way. When he realized the situation, he barely had time to move, avoiding the certain loss of a leg, but sustaining a tooth tear to his calf. He swiped a gash in the animal's nose with his knife, causing it to halt momentarily, and buying himself enough time to escape from the water.

Just as he pulled his entire body onto the shore, a tour bus with a sign on the side that read KENYA SAFARI TOURS, pulled up and parked about thirty feet from the edge of the pool. It was filled with a diversified group of tourists from several different countries and Clinton's co-worker, a Kenyan native named Martin Lincoln. The bus, designed for photographic expeditions, but not open because of the inherent dangers, held four Japanese adults and three children; two Swedish couples; a South American couple; three East Indian men, two English women and a couple from the United States - all heavily laden with camera equipment. Martin jumped out of the bus and ran toward Clinton who in turn, limped quickly toward the bus - closely followed by the crocodile who seemed undaunted by the change in terrain.

Confused by the arm flailing and incoherent shouting, Martin stopped running and tried to assess Clinton's odd behavior. He seemed to want him to turn around and go back to the bus, but the older man was at a loss as to the reason. About that time, Martin could see the crocodile pursuing Clinton at top speed. With new understanding of the situation, he quickly returned to the bus and started the engine.

The tourists, now also aware of Clinton's dilemma began snapping and filming the event; delighted with the excitement. Some of them were cheering him on some were yelling in fear but most were greatly engrossed in recording the pursuit. Luckily, the strange noises coming from the strange box seemed to discourage the crocodile, causing it to retreat to the water about the same time that Clinton reached the bus. He turned and saw the animal leaving, limped a few more feet and jumped into the bus. Lincoln took off.

Appreciative of the better-than-they-could-have-ever-imagined show, the tourists ceased their snapping and applauded the escape joyously. A thoroughly embarrassed Clinton bowed slightly in an effort to silence the group, just before sinking down into the seat, wishing greatly to disappear.

His khaki pants and shirt were in shambles, torn and ripped as if they had been in a paper shredder. There was blood running down the side of his face, off of his arm and pouring out of his leg. The beige of the clothing, the red of the blood and the brown of his skin all joined together in a sort of mosaic, modern art piece that looked like a Chagall, as painted by Dali. He looked far worse than he felt , which was oddly invigorated and charged.

"What happened to you?" Martin asked. "I could see you while the group was taking pictures of the zebras and the Thompson gazelles, then you just vanished! I drove around looking for you until I heard your scream. I could tell from the way the 'shit' trailed off that you must have ditched in the water."

Clinton was grateful that the tourists had finally lost interest in him and returned to photographing their surroundings like good little visitors. There were far more interesting things than an American tour guide with scrapes, cuts, bruises and gashes to watch. At that time of morning, there were many animals in the park for them to photograph. As they moved across the forty-four square mile range, the beautiful African sun shone brightly upon a herd of Masai giraffes as they debouched from the forest and moved onto the plains. More zebras, warthogs, ostriches, wildebeests, impala and eland provided food for the tourist's biological and mechanical eyes. They were even blessed enough that day to see a few cheetah taking a morning stretch.

Partially out of necessity, but mostly out of a need to stall, Clinton got the first aid kit from a compartment behind his seat and began cleaning and bandaging his wounds. Martin was a very meticulous man who had been doing safari work for thirty-four years. He had trained Clinton, and constantly warned him of taking chances and being careless with the animals. Explaining this from some intelligent angle would be far more palatable than spouting out "stupidity" as the reason for the hole in his leg, thought Clinton. The problem would be finding that intelligent angle.

No knowledge nor wit was forthcoming. The bare truth would have to do. It wasn't worth a lie, so Clinton limned the account of his escapade.

"Mzee, I was looking for a good place for them to see the Thompson gazelles when I happened upon a mother rhino and her baby. She didn't care for that too much and proceeded to let me know it at a good rate of speed. I ran out of ground and ended up in a pond with more critters, then you and my audience showed up."

Martin was a soft spoken thin man, about five feet eight inches tall with bronzed, milk-chocolate colored skin and arrow straight posture. He was also a very perceptive and patient man who recognized the difficulty Clinton had with explaining the situation, and did not press nor admonish. The fact that Clinton used the word "elder" or "Mzee" when addressing him, informed him of the weight of the explanation. Sometimes it seemed to him, that this fearless young man from the States had a death wish. As quick, bright and agile as he was, it would not seem that he could be as distracted as he became in the most dangerous situations. He was an amazement to Martin, and though he decided not to pry into Clinton's world too deeply, devilishness nearly prompted him to see if he could get a full blown, full length Kiswahili conversation out of the American who spoke it well, but was shy about doing so. He suppressed the urge successfully and remained light and superficial in his inquiries.

"How is your leg and which animal did that?"

Clinton was always grateful when Martin allowed his lack of good judgment to slide by. "The second crocodile . . . the one you saw."

"There were two!?" After Clinton nodded affirmatively Martin continued. "Uhmm. We will get you to the infirmary. Malika will love this. By the way, Paul called on the radio and said there is a woman at the office waiting for you."

Clinton seemed very surprised. "Is she African?"

"He didn't say," Martin replied.

Clinton searched his memory bank, attempting to identity the woman. He lived in an apartment building in Nairobi where several women who worked for the United Nations also resided. Although generally, he kept to himself, he had shared a couple of meals with a young British couple - a man and a woman, and had attended a play with a Kenyan woman. He had been fortunate enough to be invited to her home beforehand for dinner and eat the best ugali, corn fried with onions, tomatoes and potatoes - and sukuma wiki, a kale stewed with spices - he had ever had. She could cook western dishes as well, and filled his plate with fried chicken - deep fryer style like home.

They were not serious by any stretch of the imagination and she seemed to understand that he had no plans to be so. As hungry as he was after the running, fighting event he experienced with the rhino and the reptile, despite the fact that it was still very early in the day, he hoped it was a dinner invitation from her, but couldn't imagine why she wouldn't just call. Her showing up could be a dangerous opposition to his commitment to detachment. He hoped not. He would regret losing her friendship as well as her cooking.

He had successfully stayed unattached, despite the fact that he seemed to be a magnet for women. He never understood their attraction to him. He was actually quite conservative in his activities and could count the times he pursued a woman in his entire lifetime, on one hand. He considered himself "O.K." looking, and had actually been called handsome a few times over the years, but he always assumed that people were being polite, and really didn't know what else to say.

He was pleased that the morning tour was scheduled to be a short one, and that he did not have to cut any time off of it for the customers, with his need for medical attention. Although he had tended the wounds, he could not fully stop the bleeding from his leg and knew he needed stitches.

He rode through town thinking about the move to Nairobi from the Liberian village he lived in for the six months before. The small town of Kakata, about sixty miles from Monrovia was pleasant enough. He taught industrial arts at Booker T. Washington Institute for about a year before the ever changing political climate of Liberia became more volatile than he cared to deal with. There were too many people with too many issues in the small country. He left and moved close to Nairobi, living at first in the nearby wilderness with a small group of Australians who were returning to nature. He bored of their neophyte outlook quickly and moved into the city - the first major city he had lived in for more than four years. He could not understand what this recent move toward urban living meant in his continuing evolution. He didn't even understand what he was evolving toward. There were still times when the car sounds bothered him immensely, and made his teeth hurt and temples throb.

When they arrived at the Tour Office which was at the edge of the park, just before town, a limping Clinton, Martin and the tourists entered the waiting area - the latter of whom were chattering happily in their respective languages about the events of the day. Martin directed them to the desk, then told Clinton he would see him after his visit to Malika; which he hoped wouldn't be worse than the crocodile bite.

Hobbling toward a hallway, Clinton searched the room for the face of a familiar woman. There was an assortment of people preparing for their tours of the park as well as the city of Nairobi that were conducted by a sister company in the same building. Most of the tourists were European, a great deal of whom were British. In the tradition of vacationers, they were dressed in a sea of Khaki clothing and Safari hats with a sprinkling of African cloth here and there. There were several East Indians and a couple of Asians visiting as well and a few children. The roar of excitement, as expressed in all their different languages was continuous, and it was difficult to hear, even if someone was calling his name.

As he made his way toward the hall, while trying to look over the sea of heads, there seemed to be silence falling over the room. Less people were talking and more were turning to look at him, many in shock. He was still preoccupied with his search and the struggle to get to the doctor's office without bleeding profusely, and was slow to recognize their growing silence. Once the change in behavior became apparent, he began to look up into the frightened faces of the uncertain tourists.

Across the room, still not in his view, sat a lovely black woman, dressed in a black European chic, Christian Dior pants suit with antique brass buttons down the front. She also noticed the increasing silence and looked for the source.

As Clinton moved across the room searching for the woman who was there to see him, people began moving out of his way so that he could see. Several gasps rose from the crowd, but they all tried not to obstruct his view, as if granting a dying man his last wish to see. During one such parting of the wave of bodies, he caught a glimpse of and was surprised to see his twin sister ,Clarissa, seated across the room. She had her pen poised as if to write on a legal pad placed on top of the briefcase in her lap, but she was stretching her neck to see what others were looking toward. He wondered why he didn't know she was there. He had always been able to tell when she was nearby. It might have been the injuries or maybe she was pregnant. Before Eddie was born, he had trouble connecting with her the . . . he shut out the thought and called her name out loud.

The crowd turned in her direction, awaiting her response.

Delighted to hear his voice, she put her work in her briefcase and walked briskly toward him until she saw the condition he was in. She stopped and stood for a moment, somewhat in shock before running to his open arms. They embraced warmly, then she held onto him tightly, with tears welling up in her eyes. He said nothing because he wanted any affection he could get from his sister, but nearly passed out from the pain of the pressure against his badly bruised ribs.

"Clinton what happened to you . . . you're all bloody and wet and it looks like something tried to tear you apart?! What happened? And did I say wet?"

She backed away slightly, and offered him support as they moved down the hall. In the background, Clinton could hear one of the Swedish tourists, who was with him and Martin in the park, talking to the crowd of shocked and increasingly worried onlookers, "It was wonderful! He was our guide and we all got pictures." Then there was a roar of questions and comments as he and Clarissa went to Malika's office.

She could always make him smile with her spontaneity; a lot like their father's personality had been. Bright, quick and off the cuff. He explained that he surprised some animals as they hobbled down the hall. She looked a lot like Clinton yet different, but with the same coloring, short curly hair, a tight, thin, shapely body and deep sultry eyes that nearly matched his in intensity.

While he was delighted to see her, he wanted to know what had brought her to Kenya. She explained that she and their mother had been trying to reach him by telephone for the past week or so with no success. Since she had to be in Mombassa and then Nairobi on business for her firm's largest client, Claude Duparc, she promised their mother Bernice, that she would find him because she was worrying herself sick about Will. Clarissa asked Clinton to go home because their mother really needed him.

The pain on his face in response to her request more than rivaled the pain caused by any animal bite. He was briefly numbed by the thought of returning back to the States, an act he had avoided so thoroughly and for so long. Didn't she know what she was asking? Didn't she understand what an unreasonable request that was? He wondered. He was quite thankful that they had reached the infirmary door. He stopped and looked at the worried face that looked more like his mother's than his own, and tried to read the urgency of her plea. She was not one prone to over exaggeration or hysteria, and her concern seemed quite genuine; of course it would have to be for her to make such a request. "Here is the infirmary. Rissa . . . you know I can't go home."

Clarissa sighed heavily as they entered the room.

Inside the clinic was a tall wiry African doctor, putting away supplies. She appeared to be in her early fifties and exuded self confidence and control. She turned in response to the voices coming in the door to find the tattered, wet Clinton with blood all over him and a disproportionate amount of it running down his leg. Shaking her head in disgust, she got down bandages and scissors and placed them on the examining table where Clinton automatically sat, picked up the scissors and began cutting away what was left of his pants leg. Dr. Malika Lateef retrieved cleansing agents and antibiotics from the shelf as she looked at Clinton and sucked her teeth slightly.

"Clinton . . . so what about the soccer game on Madaraka Day this year? It's still a few weeks away. Are you going?"

Clinton smiled slyly at her as he continued to further demolish his clothing in an effort to expose the damaged leg. She was a hard woman, but he liked her a lot and was always pleased when she did the unexpected.

"I might go, but I haven't decided yet. You going?"

Clinton finished removing the pants leg and Malika stared at the open, gaping wound, then around the side of his thigh. "Didn't I put fifteen stitches in this same spot when you fought with the wildebeest?"

"No, it was the other thigh. See . . . here's the scar."

"You are right . . . silly of me to forget." She smirked slightly before putting a cleaning solution on a cloth.

Clarissa watched them both curiously before asking the obvious question. "Clinton, what happened to you this time?"

"I met up with a crocodile."

Clarissa gasped, "Crocodile!" and then moved back a step as if one were in the room with them. Malika began cleaning the wound. Although Clinton seemed totally unaffected by this action, the vigor with which the doctor scrubbed caused Clarissa to turn a little green. Malika took it upon herself to address Clarissa.

"Oh this is not uncommon. I have repaired him on many occasions due to injuries sustained from charging, defending and slithering animals. You should consider a relationship with some other man young woman, because this one's days are purely up to chance."

As if very accustomed to such statements, Clinton replied, "Malika, this is my sister Clarissa."

"Nice to meet you Malika."

Malika stared from one to the other for a moment before speaking. "And you . . . and which one of you is older Clinton?"

"Actually I am by six minutes."

"Which I've never been allowed to forget!" replied Clarissa.

Malika responded "Twins? You never told me you were a twin Clinton. That explains quite a few things." She looked from one to the other, searching for the resemblance which was not readily recognizable. Fraternal twins seemed to carry more family overtones than direct like-ness, and yet if either one gained or lost a considerable amount of weight or if Clinton grew facial hair, it would have been very difficult to connect them as family members she thought. Additionally, they were not quite the same complexion with Clinton being a couple of shades lighter than his sister. The skillful doctor and Clinton continued conversation easily while she applied stitches.

Clarissa was not handling the blood and perceived pain nearly as well as her brother. At his suggestion, she walked over to the window and looked out at the beautiful Kenyan landscape with its vast prairie, distant hills and orange golden setting sun. It was as peaceful as anything she had ever seen. She always loved these meetings in Africa; so different from the bustling streets of Paris, her home. There was no wonder Clinton gravitated toward this area. He needed some peace.

◊

In between stitches, Malika watched Clarissa curiously . Everything about this woman's body language read in opposition to Clinton, she thought. They fascinated her.

"I have heard that twins sometimes complete each other. Could it be that you possess the abandon and aggressiveness and your sister the caution and gentleness, Clinton?"

Clinton contemplated the correct answer, least likely to set Malika on some course unrelated to the matters at hand. Although he usually didn't mind the diverse and often educational "preaches" as Martin called them, at the moment, he wanted to get through the repair job on his leg and down to the matter of his brother Will. Before he could answer, and possibly because she sensed his hesitation, Clarissa responded while continuing to look out of the window.

"Well right now, all I possess is a weak stomach, and personally if it is his, I wish he would take it back!"

Malika noticed the slight smile on Clinton's face and wondered if it was because of what Clarissa said or because she had let him off the hook by answering for him. These people covered for each other so easily that she suspected that they had done so their entire lives - maybe without really realizing it. Multiple births and their distinct idiosyncrasies had always been profoundly interesting to her. She nearly went into obstetrics for that very reason. Being a general practitioner was far more practical for this region however, and the part time position with the tour company enabled her to keep up the clinic outside of town. Clinton and his sister had grown very quiet and pensive. With the suturing complete, Malika announced that she had to get something from the storeroom, allowing them time to talk.

When Malika left the room, with the needle at rest, Clarissa left her window refuge and sat on the examining table next to her brother. He asked her to tell him about Will. She explained that Bernice had called her, very upset about Will missing her birthday. He had not done that for as long as either of them could remember, and had always used every opportunity possible to pamper and spoil Bernice - especially on her birthday, Christmas and Mother's day. Clinton agreed that this was extremely odd and asked if his secretary, Lacy or his kids had heard from Will. Clarissa responded no, and that Bernice kept having dreams about Will being on a boat . . . drifting slowly away from her as she stood on the shore.

Clarissa looked out of the window and became nearly entranced while she told of the misty vision her mother had described to her.

"She said she could see fog for miles and miles, drifting and swirling around in strange round and oblong patterns of thick, billowy mist in shades of gray and yellow that would clear momentarily when she waved her hand, only to obstruct her vision again within a few seconds. During those cleared times, she could see Will standing on the rear deck of a wooden boat with the word "Gossamer" painted in white letters on the back. He was reaching out for her while trying to speak, but no words were heard from his mouth. He was dressed in black, but the boat was white and peach colored with tall masts like a sailboat. It had fishing gear on it too, like a shrimp boat, and two engines in the rear, about ten feet below where he was standing. Mama was on the shore calling out to him, but couldn't hear her own voice either. He just kept drifting further and further away . She couldn't wave her arms fast enough to keep the fog from between them, until she could not see him anymore in the heavy mist and fog, leaving her on the shore, silently yelling out his name. She said she fell to her knees and into the mud, screaming for him not to leave, but could neither see nor hear him although she did not feel he was completely gone either - only unseen."

Clarissa turned and looked at Clinton, returning to the worldly existence around her. "Now Mama says she can't feel him anymore and he does seem to have disappeared. She keeps talking about his "presence" being gone."

Malika entered the room in enough time to hear Clarissa's comments about Will's spirit and their mother's connection to it.

"Please excuse me, but from what nation has your mother descended? A woman who not only bore twins, but is connected to the spiritual world in such concrete terms! I should like to meet her someday Clinton. Her capabilities sound like those of the Dogon or Yoruba. What is her name?"

Clinton looked at her steadily and said, "Bernice, but I don't know . . . not about her . . I mean our African ancestry. I know she has some Cherokee in her . . I think."

Malika was astonished but kept it to herself - at least most of it. She was Kikuyu, and knew the name of every ancestor on both her mother's and father's side for the last three hundred years, and every major event in their family story. She was the daughter of a Mau Mau and a follower of Jomo Kenyatta's teachings. She knew her neighboring people, the Kamba, the Luhya, the Luo, the Kisii as well as other groups of original people and the immigrants who had come to her home. She knew the Samburu, Turkana and Hamitic people in the north, and had at least a basic knowledge of their histories. She relished in tales of the mighty Massai, who developed little interest in the matters of whites until most recent times. It was this comprehension and respect for other people of original Africa that made Kenyans able to survive colonialism without losing themselves.

Maybe slavery on foreign soil made American Africans so disjointed and lackadaisical about their heritage because they felt no real connection to the earth. Though she fought the urge, she pitied them. She always felt that the dirt beneath her contributed to the brown of her skin and that the rain that fell on the ground of Kenya was made of recycled tears from many black mothers and fathers. She was not a visitor in her own country, and though she wished these American Africans could see it, they were not either. Surely enough black tears of joy and sorrow had fallen on the soil of the United States for them to know that they were at "home" and had a history that couldn't be taken or written away. She felt anger and sorrow at the plight of these intelligent, yet strangely unconnected people, who seemed to recreate their history every two generations or so.

A couple of years before, she heard that a man from Burkina Faso reserved several hundred acres of land for American Africans to know that they always had a home, and could return whenever they wanted to. He was an old man now, but required that his family and heirs keep the land for just this purpose for the duration of time, so that this could always be fulfilled. She had considered this unnecessary and a bit eccentric when she first heard it, but as the years went by and she had seen more Americans that seemed confused and unaware, she understood the wisdom of the older, wiser father; yet doubted it would ever come to fruition. There would be so much understanding necessary for them to even know the gift and sacrifice of his deeds, let alone what to do with it. Often, she found American Africans exasperating, yet beautiful - like young children. Attracted to the shallow, baubles of life, avoiding the deeper expansive qualities we share as humans.

Malika responded to Clinton, slightly perturbed with him, for all the thoughts in her head. She aggressively placed bandages over his wound.

"You American Africans! I find very few of you who understand that all you are and do are a result of your bloodline and heritage. Your ancestry!"

With the gentleness of the charging rhino Clinton encountered earlier, Malika took the hypodermic from the table and abruptly administered Clinton's antibiotic shot. The action quickly sent Clarissa back to her window retreat. Clinton barely raised an eyebrow.

"Bernice . . . I cannot remember what that name means." Malika continued. "None of us has been named accidentally you know. Your mother may well be a highly spiritual woman."

With that said the fireball of a doctor walked across the room and replaced the supplies in the storage cabinet. Clinton and Clarissa watched attentively, waiting for her next comments. Malika walked out of the room, never looking back and calling to them over her shoulder, "Nice to meet you Clarissa. Do not run anymore today Clinton."

They watched momentarily, expecting her return. When she did not, Clarissa said "Interesting woman." Then she turned to her brother.

"To say the least!" Clinton replied.

Clarissa resumed their original conversation. "Clinton, mama needs you to find Will. Please go home. I'm worried about her and I can't leave Paris right now. Besides, I wouldn't know how to begin looking for him." She sat on the table next to him and began rubbing his back. He got up, crossed to the window and looked out.

She continued. "Clinton, it has been five, nearly six years now. You can't stay away forever."

"If I could, I'd go back. I've tried. Don't you think I've missed mama and tried to go home for at least a visit in all this time?"

Clarissa walked over to her brother and hugged him from behind, placing her arms around his waist and laying her head on his back. When they were young, she thought she would always be taller than he was, but of course that didn't last. As they got older and he outgrew her so quickly and completely, she found that laying her head against his back was one of the most wonderful experiences she could think of whenever she was upset or worried. Somehow the width and breadth of him made her feel protected and loved. She had always been thinner and he more solid. Now, as adults, he stood a full head taller than she, and his back only got broader and more capable of carrying the heavy burdens he too often took on . . . until he retreated. His back had always worked for her, but what could she do for him when he felt overwhelmed?

She had felt the sum total of her ineffectiveness to make his life easier the night of Grace's death. Despite her countless and seemingly endless tears for him, her deep and undying love for him, and her strongest and most sincere wish to take away his pain and gouge out the eyes of the vile and despicable offender, she was totally powerless and prostrate to make even the slightest difference in the building of the armor that instantly clad him in massive and overbearing sorrow. She willed for time to return before that fateful day so that she could fix everything, but her prayers went unanswered and he slipped further and further away from her , unreachable for a very long time. The pain she knew he was feeling was excruciating, and she felt drained as she struggled not to cry. She had hoped to find him less affected.

She steeled herself and spoke to him again, in a calm and loving voice. "Clinton . . . if I could, I'd take all the hurt from you and carry it myself for a while. You've had it long enough. Maybe I could disperse it differently if it were mine to handle, but I can't and you can't let it guide you this time. There's nobody else as capable as you to find Will. Clinton . . . you have to do this. You know that don't you?"

He looked out at the nearly set brilliant golden orange sun and the few and distant trees on the plains while he examined his aloneness. He had spent so much effort not going home; not thinking about the people and things there. Will had always had a dark side that Clarissa would be inept at uncovering clues about, let alone tracking their brother. She was right.

That realization only caused greater pain.

He took a long deep breath and let out an equally long sigh, pleased with the love he could feel against his back in the form of his closest friend. He never beat up on her or harass her like other boys did their younger sisters while growing up. It always seemed too inappropriate to even consider. She was then, as now, the sweetest human being he had ever known in life, except for Grace. Even thinking her name made his heart ache and a lump rise to the top of his throat and struggle to burst through the skin of his Adam's apple. He didn't know how he could do this thing his sister asked. He simply did not know.

He rubbed Clarissa's arm gently and let her love penetrate the turtle's shell he had been carrying on his back for so long and said "I know."

8 GRIT AND GUMPTION

She had to be very careful not to step in the slimy mud which seemed to go on forever and made her nervous about sliding into the bog to her right. It would have been so much easier to do if she didn't have on those damned flip flops she used for bedroom shoes, which for the life, of her she could not figure out why she had worn them to a swamp. Must be related to the reason she still had on her nightgown though . . . both too ridiculous to think about at the moment. She was on a mission.

She could hear Will's voice faintly calling her name but the mist with its swirling yellow, gray and tonight, pink fog was too thick to see through. As she craned her neck to look for him while still moving toward his voice, she mistakenly stepped into some of the muck on the shore. She never did like the feel of mud between her toes, squishing and oozing like something spoiled and rotten.

When she was a child and visited her grandmother in Florida every summer, she had seen more than her share of mud; enough for two lifetimes. The mud beneath her in this particular swamp was red, and equally unpleasant. Red mud in a swamp, she thought, must be an indication of her being in Georgia, or somewhere close by. She wondered if it was really possible to have such or if it was just a continuation of the aberration she was experiencing. Maybe it had significance because in a manner of speaking, Georgia was the home of some of her ancestors. She, on the other hand, had always been a city girl at heart and in practice.

"Why in the devil do I have on these stupid, little, nearly useless shoes in this misty, murky mess?" she thought to herself, but seemed to say out loud though she didn't remember her mouth opening or moving, despite the fact that she certain that she heard herself say it loudly and clearly. The shoes were quite annoying. The swamp was quite strange with its voices and noises and whispering thoughts from strangers and friends and ancestors some dead and gone, some alive and well. After a moment, she heard him speaking to her in a strange, deeply guttural, raspy voice that floated and drifted toward her through the multicolored haze.

"Oh my goodness, he called me 'mama' this time!" she nearly screamed.

Will had not done that in years, not since he turned nineteen. He always called her Bernice. Said it was to protect her vanity because a woman as young as she was, who looked as good as she did, should not have such an old son, therefore he would not give her away with such a title. Feeling the onset of self doubt that hits some women in their forties, at the time it sounded like a good idea and she gleefully accepted his offer. Clinton Sr. objected mildly that Will would get too grown for his own good, but his protests didn't last long. Nobody in the family could stay upset with Will for long. Of course Will began calling him Big "C" that same year.

As his voice became more and more faint while he continued to call her "mama," she tried to figure out the purpose of him being in a swamp. She called out his name, but when he didn't answer she stood motionless in the mud and concentrated with all her might on seeing his face. He was there, in her mind- her beautiful son. His face was so strong and powerful looking with his straight jaw and sharp eyes. He looked more like his biological father every day. Much too fine for his own good and certainly not for any woman's good. His face began to disappear from her concentration and she could hear her grandmother clearly saying, "Baby child stop standing in that mud! You wanna ruin that nightgown?" She turned quickly, nearly falling into the dreaded mud, and looked for her sweet Nana, but could not see her anywhere. There were strange things going on in this swamp. She was grateful it was daytime there.

She thought for a moment about the stately Indian woman who had always been in her life and the struggle it had been to get her to move from her home in New Smyrna Beach, Florida up to Washington, D.C. when she became too old to care for herself. That of course, was not until she was ninety-six years old. Nana Lizzie was a statuesque, reddish-brown woman who, for all of Bernice's life, wore a long, single braid that hung down to her waist, She was shapely, about five feet nine inches tall, thin at one hundred thirty five pounds, heavy chested and lanky. Her hair had been wavy and pitch black when she was younger, and only turned slightly salt and pepper when she reached her late seventies. It never became completely gray, not even at her death at the age of one hundred and two.

Bernice thought about the small, neighborhood general store her Nana Lizzie owned that was attached to her house by a long wooden walkway that creaked and cracked as she crossed over to get candy that Nana would give Bernice when her mother Velma was not paying attention. Nana Lizzie was a strong-willed woman, who was not prone to taking much of anything off of anybody. Bernice adored her strong hands, and straight back, and everything else about her.

Lizzie, a full blooded Muskogee Indian, had been violently raped one evening, by two white men passing through town, while she was walking home from delivering pies she sold to local restaurants. Velma, Bernice's mother, was the blessed result. Lizzie - born in the year of emancipation - and her husband, Moses Cole, lived in the black part of town.

Moses worked for a Turpentine company and was a distant part of the Washitaw/Turnicus clan, Nat Turner's family, and part of the original people from the Louisiana territory. He was dark red/brown with a wide, straight nose, and tight, curly hair. He was six feet five inches tall, thin, about one hundred and eighty five pounds, muscular, and had a big booming voice that made people move back a step when listening to him, usually because they were startled by the resonance, power and depth he put out. He never found Lizzie's rapists, or the family's history would have been different. He always treated Velma as his own.

They thrived during reconstruction, and were well respected in the community by blacks, Native Americans, and the few whites they came in contact with. Lizzie was fair, outgoing, active in community affairs and education for children. Her eldest daughter Louise, whom everyone called Lou, was well read, well mannered and stuck to her mother like glue. Sometimes, as a child, Bernice would sit with her aunt Lou on the wooden walkway and watch Lizzie's sixteen cats hunt for small animals and lounge in the hot Florida sun. Lou looked a great deal like her father. Dark skinned, short tight hair, long arms and a high waist. Moses, was less outgoing, but was a man of his word at all times with everybody. He never made a promise or a threat that he didn't keep. His mere presence made others in the community feel calm and unafraid as the Ku Klux

Klan ran rampant across the Florida countryside.

Moses lived in New Smyrna as a married adult, but his immediate family was from Loudiwici, Georgia - forced to flee when his younger uncle, Duff Cole, took revenge on some men who killed his sister, Moses' aunt. The story goes that Duff was a slim, fair skinned young man in his early twenties, who was a staunch civil rights activist in the small, eastern Georgia town near the coast. Duff had been making many strides in the community. He was organizing and mobilizing blacks to take stands and to make new demands.

After harassing him in town at the local black church, some whites, bound to halt black progress in their tiny community, decided to ride out to his home and stop him, or at least scare him. Aware that they were pursuing him, after days of harassment and a particularly nasty incident at the church, Duff hurried home, but took evasive action to try and draw them away from the house.

Duff had a younger sister Sheink, who was fifteen years old at the time, and a deaf/mute. Their parents, Douglas and Minnie Cole had borne fourteen children over a twenty-eight year period, so they came in all shapes, colors, sizes and had overlapping ages with uncles younger than nieces and nephews. On that day, Sheink, the final and the youngest, was in the house when the five men arrived at the one hundred and sixty acre farm located at the edge of town, headed toward the city of Jesup. They called out for Duff, who had by-passed his home and run straight into the woods near the eastern corner of his parent's property, nearly two and a half miles away from the house. He assumed that if they could not find him, they would leave. He traveled deep enough through the thick Georgia pines not to be seen, and unfortunately, not to see well either. He waited. And waited. And waited. And waited.

About twenty minutes later, he decided to go to the edge of the woods so that he could see, but was horrified by the sight before him. The wooden framed house, with the white paint and yellow trim, was roaring in flames and five white men, who Duff had grown to know too well, were riding off on their horses. Duff began to run toward the house frantically calling out Sheink's name, though he knew it was useless to do so. Even if she were still alive, she couldn't hear him. As he ran he tried to remember if anyone else would be home at that time of day who could help

Sheink get out; but he knew that his entire family was working out in the back twenty acres. Sheink seldom went with them, but stayed in her room reading, her greatest joy in life. He shuddered to think of what Sheink might have been going through while he was running for her life, and his own sanity.

The house was blazing with flames shooting high up on the second story, out of every window, and he was only halfway there. He ran faster, shouted louder, but the flames roared a deafening dirge of death for his sweet sister, who probably never knew what was happening from her second story room until the flames met her at the steps. He ran, and prayed harder than he had ever done before as vivid pictures of his baby sister during happier times, who had endured so much and had learned to deal with her physical challenges with the grace of a queen over the years, played havoc with his mind and heart. He could barely stand the pain of her apparent death as he reached the house which was in full blaze from chimney to foundation, the walls and roof caving in and crashing down into giant piles of flaming rubble that crackled and hissed like the snake that was injecting the venom of hatred and vengefulness into his heart. He fell to his knees and prayed for her soul, and his family's, and his own because revenge was all he could think of at that moment.

He screamed and charged at the house though it was clearly demolished and incapable of bearing life, especially not that of a young defenseless girl who must have lived her last moments in incredible pain and sheer panic. He took long pieces of wood and tried to poke at the fire in hopes that somehow she had hidden from the flames, that somehow she escaped despite the fact that he was standing on the ground, poking at second story furniture from his parents bedroom. His pain was unbearable and his anger as hot as the flames before him. He didn't even notice the burns on his arms until three days later when he awoke in his Aunt Doreen's house with his mother sitting on the edge of the bed beside him.

He was inconsolable and silent. He didn't explain. He didn't try to tell them what happened to Sheink; he didn't answer any questions. He merely cried. He cried all day and all night until his fair complexion was beet red from his swollen eyes to his chin. His mother, who was mourning the death of her baby girl, was terrified that she would lose him as well to some madness. She could only speculate and had no real way of determining what happened. At first his father yelled at him, demanding an explanation, but the tears had been so continuous that there was no way to enforce his requests. So they all waited patiently, while afraid that he would never recover and be lost forever.

After four days of tears, they stopped - suddenly. He uttered only one sentence.

"John Manson, Stud Shaw, Angus Bright, Ethan Steed and Charles Encoe decided to burn the house down in order to stop me from organizing and making protests in town."

The family was in shock and began discussing what should be done before he cut them off.

"Ain't no need in y'all talking about the sheriff and all, specially since you know it's no use. I'm gonna take care of this myself, by myself. This was my doin' and this will be my fixin.'"

Protests came from his father, aunt, mother and remaining sisters, brothers, nieces and nephews including Moses, but he heard none of it. Only got out of the bed, put on his clothes and started out of the house. His father stopped him.

"Son, I don't know what you got on your mind, but I done lost one child and I don't want to lose another one before I die. Please don't go anywhere and do nothin' stupid. Stay here and let's figure out what we need to do." Douglas said.

"Sir, I'm sorry, I can't do that. You always taught me to be a man, now let me go be one. This was my mess. I guess I was an uppity nigger like they said I was, thinking I could make a difference in the way all us live, but all I did was get my baby sister Sheink killed. I got to take care of this and I am askin' you to let me be the man you always taught me to be."

His father stared into the bright red face with the light green eyes of his white grandfather, let go of his youngest son's arm and hoped it would not be the last time he touched him alive. He nodded at Duff and moved out of the way. Duff walked out on the porch, pulled his hat on his head and walked down his aunt's stairs to the street, and across the railroad tracks. Nobody saw him for a week, not even for Sheink's funeral.

◊

Duff sat on the edge of Sweet Baby's bed and thought about how good that woman was in bed, and how grateful he was that if his last sex in life was the one he had just experienced, he couldn't have had a better one than with her. She could open her legs wider and take more of him in than any other woman he had ever known. Most couldn't handle him and complained that he was too big. He didn't seem to hurt her one bit, and she did wondrous things with her stuff. He had been seeing her for at least two years off and on, not necessarily in the daylight either for all the town to see. Sweet Baby didn't care though as long as he brought her some money, occasional flowers and a new dress every once in a while. He had plenty of money from the mill job, and loved to see her body in dresses that other women wouldn't dare wear. He stared into the closet door and wondered which one he would wear.

He got up from the bed and looked through the closet for a dress that would be big enough and plain enough for him to put on, and be fairly inconspicuous. Sweet Baby didn't have too many inconspicuous clothes. She didn't even understand the concept of "low key,". She was a tall, healthy country girl, and she carried it well.

Way in the back of the closet was a long, gray, flannel dress with pink and green print trim that surely must have belonged to her mother because it was too big, and too plain for Sweet Baby - even for church. It was flowing, not too narrow, with a partial lace bodice, and lace around the wrists with white pearl buttons down the front , sleeves and the bustle. He laid it out on the bed and looked at it for a few moments before picking it up and trying it on over his naked body. It fit. The sleeves were a little short, but not so much that one would notice. It was long enough for his deceptive purposes, and would hide his shoes - the two most important necessities in his opinion.

He was grateful that Sweet Baby, whose real name was Saffronia, had left the house. He didn't really want her involved and the less she knew the better. No one would connect him to her since their relationship was mostly a nocturnal one. He looked around the sparse room and tried to memorize all the furnishings - the sleigh bed with a beautiful patchwork quilt of yellow, orange, brown and blue-green that her mother made for her and an oak chest of drawers; the white lace curtains, the blue and white walls with wainscoting and the assorted width pine floor. There were endless figurines and doilies all over the room and on every surface. They were porcelain, and wooden, and ceramic, and cloth, and clay, and of every culture. There were Choctaw and Creek, and Cherokee and Muskogee dolls and toys and games, and African and Haitian fetishes, baskets and jewelry hanging and laying everywhere. There was even the porcelain cat tea pot that he bought for her when he went to Savannah the year before. Men brought her things, happy to have her sexual favors. He knew he was at least one of her favorites. He never was foolish enough to think he was her only.

He took off the gray dress, searched for and found a pair of scissors in the top dresser drawer and cut the right side pocket off on the inside, creating a big hole. Then he removed his rifle from the closet and slid it inside the long, cut dress pocket to see if it would fit and be concealed. It worked. He went back to the closet and found a long, heavy, lavender, crocheted shawl and wrapped it around his shoulders to see if it fell below the pocket. It was enormous and hung all the way to his calves in the back, dipping well below the pocket. He laid it on the bed and then found a scarf in Sweet Baby's drawer that matched the shawl, wrapped it around his head and looked in the mirror.

He was not very tall, only five nine and his face was somewhat feminine looking, especially with the scarf on. His eyebrows were thin and straight, and he had long eyelashes, a small nose and mouth, and high cheekbones. His mother was half white and he and his brothers and sisters came out a myriad of colors and shades, running from Sheink, who was oak tree brown, to him at almost piglet pink-white. He surveyed his greenish/hazel eyes, and sandy colored mustache then picked up the water pitcher on the stand, poured water into the bowl and shaved off all of his facial hair. When he finished, he used some of Sweet Baby's makeup and did his best to make himself look like a woman. He had watched her apply her own paint enough times. He was glad to have her example because nobody in his house ever wore what his father referred to as the "devil's paint."

He put on a little rouge, eye liner and lipstick then put the scarf on and some earrings. He looked at himself in the mirror and marveled at his resemblance to a woman, fortunately not his own mother. He certainly didn't want people thinking that he was her. He finished dressing, put the gun deep down in his pocket and left the house. He went outside and mounted his sorrel horse named Buckin' Bo Boy and rode toward town, but stopped at the edge of town near Baskin's livery.

He tied Buckin' Bo Boy around the back of the warehouse next door and walked through town, unnoticed by whites, eyed cautiously by blacks at first. Whites generally paid no particular attention to a mulatto woman walking down the street but after a short block, blacks seemed to understand what might be coming, and quickly, but calmly cleared the streets, careful not to bring attention to themselves or Duff lest they be accused of being involved with any devilment he might have in mind. He walked for about a block, crossed the railroad tracks, and the courthouse and went into a local saloon called The Roost. He walked directly up to the table where John Manson, Stud Shaw, Angus Bright, Ethan Steed and Charles Encoe sat playing cards. They didn't even notice the woman they assumed was white, or a cleaning woman until they heard the first shot and Angus Bright hollered, grabbed his chest, fell over and hit the floor. The rest went so fast that they never even had a chance to go for their guns, or even scream and curse obscenities. Everyone else in the room was under the tables or on the floor behind the bar. He was fast, directed, goal oriented, efficient and then absent.

The second he was certain they were all dead, he nearly flew out of the saloon and ran around the back of the building, snatched off his women's clothing and with his own underneath, transformed himself into a man again. He stashed the gun and clothes in a box that he had put in the alley earlier, wiped the rouge and lipstick from his face, put on his hat and calmly walked around the building to the other side of the street back down the back alleys to Buckin' Bo Boy. He mounted the horse and left town immediately, headed west and never returned.

Most of the family moved away within three days because the pressure was too great for them to stay, and they assumed it would only get worse. Although it was not exactly clear who had actually killed the five men, questioning bore out the fact that they had burned down the Cole's home, and white folks began to put two and two together. Young Moses and his new wife Lizzie were some of the first to go, gone by sundown the next day. Others of the Cole clan went south or west, and all but Doreen left because she refused to be displaced by the actions of vengeful whites.

In one act, an entire family consisting of thirty-eight separate families was transformed and their destinies altered, but none of them minded ultimately since they all did so safely, and they all loved Sheink and Duff dearly. White folks didn't seem to make too much noise after some questioning, because even they found something distasteful about killing and burning a deaf and dumb child, even if she was black. There were no more black casualties in Loudiwici of Sheink's nature for many years. Despite all the grumbling of white supremacist groups prior to the incident, there was only one more hanging in the city until 1912, and that was about sex with a white woman - a clear and known taboo for a black man at the time. Duff's actions could have well sparked a Rosewood sort of incident, but then sometimes there is justice and equilibrium in the universe.

Duff became a local legend in the small town of Loudiwici. For many years after, whenever kids were playing and one of them would execute some sort of bravery, or insanity the others would say to him or her, "Well you feeling real Duffy today, aren't you?" They all understood what it meant.

Bernice, of course never met her great, great Uncle Duff, but she had heard the story many times as a child. As she moved cautiously through the swamp, she thought about the grit and gumption her ancestors possessed. She had several examples of self determination from which to draw, on both sides of her family, and could see the traits carried out in her children. She listened briefly for the voice of her Uncle Duff though she hoped not to hear it because he was certainly of the dead and she had refused to think of her swamp as a harbinger of such news up to that point.

She listened carefully for Will's voice, but only heard a banging noise, far in the distance. She tried to maintain her concentration so that she could stay connected to him but ultimately, Bernice watched Will's face slowly drift away, forced out by the banging echoing in her head - an intrusion that seemed forceful, adamant and determined somehow.

9 JUST A SIMPLE COUNTRY HOME

Bernice bolted upright in the bed from her swamp visions and tried to get a grip on the ruckus that seemed real and surreal simultaneously. The man's voice shouting from downstairs forced her out of the sound, dream filled, if not restful sleep, quickly down stairs past numerous pictures of her family hanging on the stairwell.

"Mama! Mama!," shouted the man's voice from downstairs.

Barefoot, she threw on a pink velour robe and whispered hopeful thoughts as she moved fast toward the banging. "Will, oh Will?! Please be Will."

She looked through the peephole, gasped a few small breaths, unlocked the three dead bolts and flung open the door so she could bear hug her youngest son Clinton.

"Child I'm so glad to see you! Give me another hug. I know this is a sign of good things to come."

Clinton and his single suitcase, entered the house and the two of them talked about the cold weather in Washington for the time of year and how warm Kenya was. Bernice confessed that she was not sure he would come from the conversation she and Clarissa had a few days before. He admitted it was a struggle and that he almost did not get on the airplane. They held hands for a while and basked in their love for each other before parting for the night.

Clinton bade his mother a peaceful rest and went to sleep in what had always been his room. It had changed little over the years and most of the sports trophies he and Will earned as kids were still in place. There were a few extra soccer awards - a sport that neither he or Will played. He moved closer to read the name on the silver plated stand and found it belonged to Jarrett, his nephew. He wondered what the child must look like and how tall he was as he drifted off to sleep nestled between the red plaid flannel sheets on the twin bed with Will's old baseball bat still leaning against the wall.

◊

The smell of coffee and the sound of Bernice's deep voice singing Billye Holiday's "Lover Man" opened Clinton's eyes and heart to the warmth of being home. It had been so long since he called anyplace home that even the thought seemed odd, but looking around at the pictures and articles he knew so well made him ache inside at the joy and pain of being there.

◊

She was going to give him ten more minutes before she went upstairs to wake him. He never liked fancy things for breakfast like Will. As a child, he had her cooking Eggs Benedict and trying to follow that complicated recipes for crepes and such. Clinton was plain and steady, just like his father. Eggs, grits or cottage fries and toast. No meat. She could always count on him for anything she ever needed until the accident. She was glad he had come home. She sure needed him, she was thinking when he walked into the kitchen fully dressed in blue jeans, desert boots, a heavy cotton shirt and ready for the day.

"Sure smells good. Think I'll fix some French toast to go with it, if you don't mind."

Bernice turned and looked at him oddly. Never does pay to think you know what's going on in another person's head she thought. "No problem, I'll fix it for you."

Clinton poured a cup of coffee, sat at the table, and watched Bernice cook in the same yellow and gray kitchen he had seen her cook in since the fifties. Although she had redecorated the rest of the house since Big Clinton's death, the kitchen went untouched, except for the gray and yellow flowered wallpaper. The yellow Kenmore refrigerator she had painted to match the tile, was an updated version of the older, original Fridgidaire that was in the house when they bought it in 1956. The speckled, yellow, and gray linoleum tile floors were unchanged as were the yellow counters, and yellow cabinets with gray trim. Over the years, the ruffled curtains did evolve from yellow and white to ruffled gray and yellow flowers and there was a glass topped table with cane backed chairs that she bought during the mid-eighties.

She kept humming "Lover Man" as she took out the skillet and started the French toast. Clinton couldn't help thinking that his mother must have been something else in her day. She was still a good looking woman, and only ten or fifteen pounds heavier than her weight as a young woman he guessed, remembering pictures of her during those days. When he was a kid and attended the same junior high school where she taught, half of the fights he got into were because some hormone crazed adolescent made crass comments about his mother's anatomy or their wishful intentions. That kind of talk usually made Will insane when he was young, and kept him in the principal's office. Will always was her favorite and although she would never have admitted such a thing, both he and Clarissa knew it. It was good to see his mother looking so well with only a few extra gray hairs in her thick head of hair. He fingered the edge of the yellow outlined flowers and leaves of the Correlle plate in front of him as he spoke to her.

"Mama, did Will say anything to make you think there was something wrong the last time you spoke to him?"

"No honey, just that he would be out of town for a couple of weeks and would call when he returned. About a week after he left though, I had the strangest feeling one night, while I was out on the porch reading and then I couldn't feel him anymore. He was just gone."

"Feel him? What do you mean?"

"Well ever since each of you were born, I feel a connection to all of you, but I can almost feel Will's presence physically, as if he is standing right beside me. Although it is definitely there, my bond to you and Clarissa is not as strong, I suppose because you are so connected to one another, being twins and all. I can still feel you and Rissa, but I can't feel Will now. At least not while I'm awake but I keep having these strange dreams about him."

"What kind of dreams?"

"They aren't clear enough for me to explain yet, but I keep hearing water in the background, and sometimes I think there is a boat, but I'm not sure and I keep stepping in mud. What do you think has happened to your brother Clinton?"

"I don't know Mama. . . I just don't know."

They spent the next hour discussing Will's love life and restaurant equipment business while trying to figure out the best place to start looking for him. Ever since Will and his wife Barbara split, he had not spent much time with one particular woman. Even Clinton remembered how unattached and uncommitted to women Will had insisted on staying. It appeared that he had not changed during Clinton's absence.

Clinton finished breakfast and decided to begin his trek with Will's secretary, Lacy, before going to Will's apartment. He thought he had made it through the conversation with his mother without discussion about his own life, but alas, just as he was about to leave the table, she reached her soft hand over, placed it on top of his and looked deeply into his eyes and through to his soul - as only she could.

"Son . . . was it so difficult for you to come home, even now?"

"Please Mother. Let's not discuss it. I'm here. I'm going to find Will and though I miss and love you, I'm going back to Kenya as fast as I can after everything is straight. So please, let's just not talk about it."

She could barely stand the pain in his eyes and wondered whether or not other mothers experienced similar emotional oneness with their children. When the accident first happened, he was in so much pain that she did not think he or she would live through it. He was an instant emotional recluse and she became physically ill - throwing up and carrying on through the funeral - and his absence.

Her connection didn't seem to be related to their physical well being, but to their emotional state however. She thanked God for that! All the dangerous stuff that Clinton and Will did as kids surely would have killed her if that were the case. She seemed to key into confusion, anger, hurt feelings and the physical pain if it was related to those emotions.

Will must have thought he was capable of handling his predicament before he disappeared from her, at least up to the last few minutes. There was no long term telegraphing of pain to come or confusion or doubt. Actually, she felt there was not much conflict in him. He must have resigned himself to something and then he just vanished. She had not thought of that before. Will resigned to something.

Suddenly she shook at the combination of thoughts that Will could be beaten by something and accepting of that fact. Would he have fought back frustration to protect her if things had gone really badly? Maybe so. He probably would have been careful about his emotional state if he thought there was no way out. He would have done anything to protect her . . . or hide his real pain from her. The possibility of a defeated, resigned Will and the present impact of Clinton's renewed pain and possible danger brought tears to her eyes.

◊

All he could think of was the grief he was causing already. He had not been home twenty-four hours and he was causing this woman to cry. Traveling had numbed him to this deeply, close and personal pain. He sincerely wanted at that moment to find Will and get away from people who cared about him and whom he cared about. He longed for the gentle breezes of Kenya, and the sound of wild birds and parting, rustling bushes as they revealed the efforts of Thompson gazelles and their day-long search for food. A reflection of the peaceful simplicity, devoid of emotional anguish he found at home. He gently picked up his dear mother's hand and kissed it before speaking.

"I'm going to Will's apartment first if you still have the key. It will be all right Mama."

"I know son."

◊

The crisp, cold air of Washington seemed to sharpen his senses somewhat. He had grown accustomed to looking out for danger from the obvious, but being back home made him think about relationships and people with hidden agendas while he was walking down the street to Will's apartment. Animals, fires and skydiving had clear, distinct problems. Women, men, jobs, cars, relatives and people in general - that was the stuff nightmares were made of: unpredictable and dangerous.

He walked into the modest building and caught the elevator up to the eighth floor to Will's apartment. Although there was no graffiti in the elevator, he couldn't help thinking that some kid must have thought about scribbling his or her name across the middle of the back wall and looked closely to see if it had been painted over. The place was clean enough, but children were everywhere in the complex. He could hear them in their apartments tuned into Saturday morning television cartoons and in the courtyard playing strange war games he could not recognize. He even saw one running through the hallway dressed up as a turtle, and another as a robot with a mask or something. He was amazed that Will had not moved to a more bachelor like atmosphere after Barbara took the kids and left.

He reached apartment 846, put the key in and opened the door to find a room full of rent-a-room furniture. It was pleasant enough, nothing special. Everything in the room was mauve, gray and sea green. It looked a lot like it did before Clinton left the country but more sparse somehow, though he couldn't put his finger on the reason.

A dead plant sat in the corner, attempting to hold on to the few green leaves it had of life. Clinton touched it to determine if watering it was in order but the last of the leaves fell to the dirt, set free by the movement of his hand. A small mirrored bar was on the left with an assortment of wine and liquor on the counter behind it. Small throw rugs of beige and gray lay unobtrusively under the glass topped coffee table and end tables, all atop an immaculately clean mauve carpet.

Clinton moved into the drab, undecorated kitchen. The counters, cabinets and appliances were all white, and there was not so much as a colored dishtowel, a department store kitchen print of herbs or flowers, nor a brightly colored mug holder, or mug for that matter to brighten up the cold space. He opened the refrigerator door to find a carton of cranberry juice, a bottle of Hunts ketchup and two molded green grapefruits. He quickly shut the door and moved to the sink, where two long stemmed wine glasses were; one with a woman's lipstick lips imprinted on the rim. He used the corner of a paper towel to carefully pick it up by the lower portion of the stem and place it in a plastic bag he pulled out of his pocket.

He laid the bag on the counter and went down the hall into the bathroom. It was fairly neat with only a little hair in the sink and a brush on the counter. Again there was no color and no nick-knacks that people seem to accumulate over the years in rooms in which they spend a great deal of time. The toothbrush holder had been removed or had fallen off the wall and never been replaced, and the toothbrush was in a blue, plastic carrying travel case. There was no toothpaste in the vicinity, nor in the medicine cabinet above the sink.

He moved on to the equally boring office. The prints on the wall were standard national discount chain variety, modern landscapes and doll faced children in pastel colored matting and chrome frames. Imitation wood melamine furniture comprised the furnishings, with a few cheap novels and a stack of invoices strewn across the desk. Something about the room simply did not look as if Will really worked there on a daily basis. The pencils were in place and a clean, unwritten legal pad lay on the corner of the desk. Clinton picked it up to see if any impressions had been left from previously written pages. He didn't see any, but brushed the lead pencil across the page anyway to be sure. No imprint appeared.

Was there no place in this house that reflected the wild side of Will, he thought as he entered the bedroom. Clearly not in there. The bed was made which in itself made him suspicious, and there were no clothes on any chairs or on the floor. He moved to the closet and found Will's clothes hanging neatly in the closet which seemed to host a sea of navy blue and beige slacks and jackets without one red, black or teal shirt amidst the collection of white ones and the neatly lined up row of shoes were all black or brown. He could not believe that Will had become so conservative or organized in his forties.

He continued to search the room, looking under the bed and in Will's private bathroom, only to find no clues to his whereabouts. As he was about to leave, he noticed the Romare Bearden print hanging on the wall, obviously a mass reproduction he thought. Nearly out of the room, something urged him to take a closer look at the signature. He did, and to his astonishment, he realized it was a Bearden original.

Clinton slowly sat down on the bed, contemplating the wonderful colors and shapes which were the artist's trademark. The frenzy of activity of the piece nearly matched the mass of confusion in his head. What would Will be doing with a Bearden original in this apartment full of rental-a-look stuff? He could not imagine how much the artwork cost, at least one to three hundred thousand dollars, but his years of training in the Bureau told him it was not in keeping with the standard pay of a restaurant equipment supplier. Not with two kids. He wondered what Will had gotten himself into as he stared blankly at the silk-screen.

Walking back down the hallway to the elevator seemed quite surreal to him. The children running past him seemed to be going in slow motion, their arms flailing about wildly as they chased each other and laughed at the joy of it all. He contemplated his relationship with his brother, and for the first time, had genuine fear for his well-being. He could remember times when he was a kid and Will, who was five years older, had hunted him down and tickled him until he wet his pants. He never seemed to get too upset though. It was just Will's way. Clinton watched the group of kids as they squealed and chased each other up and down the hallways and through the lobby - happy and carefree. Then he left the building and headed to see Lacy.

When he pulled his mother's 1989 maroon Cutlass in front of the Capitol Restaurant Equipment building in a warehouse district in southeast Washington, he was amazed at how little it had changed. Other things in his hometown had shifted and altered under the weight of time, but this building looked just like it did before he left. There were still large wooden flower pots filled with Blue Girl roses up the stairs on both sides of the long ramp leading to the entrance door. The building itself was cinder block painted turquoise, peach and yellow with a twelve by twenty foot yellow sign with giant black letters with peach shadows that read "Capitol Restaurant Equipment Commercial Suppliers," with the telephone number underneath. No changes seemed evident - even down to the sign missing "au" in the word restaurant. He had always wondered if there was some hidden meaning to the formation of the words Rest and Rant, but Will never seemed to care before, and obviously still did not.

As he walked into the outer office, he was reminded that Lacy was a human oxymoron of the most interesting type. She was a very average looking woman with an incredible looking, far more than average body that many a starlet would kill for and any Mack truck would stop for. She wore conservative clothing that fit her perfectly, a suit that day - snug, but not too tight.

The walls were filled with neatly stacked books and files that had their own cardboard cases with titles, and what looked like two inches of dust on them. Her desk was neat as a pin except in the upper left hand corner, which was filled with haphazardly stacked papers, stuffed into manila folders. She was putting away files in a beautiful, antique oak file cabinet which sat directly beside a spray painted metallic gold one. Her desk was an expensive cherry, perfectly polished, Queen Anne wooden antique with an oxblood colored leather top, and her bright, brassy blue Ergonomics chair pulled up to it. The office reflected her style.

She had her back to Clinton, but he had no trouble identifying the vespine silhouette he often marveled at before he left the country. She had a strong straight back, the smallest waist, probably seventeen or eighteen inches, he had ever seen and a wonderful low, round butt. Her measurements were probably 36-18-36 which seemed grossly out of proportion but worked perfectly on her. She had pretty bow legs; which on that day, ended at the huge black and white bunny rabbit bedroom shoes complete with ears and a pink nose, that adorned her feet. Only Lacy could look like that. He laughed at the contrast of those shoes on the feet of all that fine woman.

◊

Startled by his voice, she turned and saw him through equally ridiculous fifties cat glasses that had rhinestones on the corners. Immediately she realized who he was. Even though the years somehow made him look tired, he was still, in fact more beautiful than ever she thought a man could be as she gazed upon his face. She was almost tempted to say "You know Bernice Creech know she can make some fine black men,". Instead, she fought the urge remembering how uneasy flattery always made Clinton , and put down her files and hugged him.

"Clinton . . . how long have you been home?"

"Just got in last night to try and figure out what happened to Will."

"Your mother has been worried sick. I told her he said he might visit our London office while on this trip, but she kept complaining that he forgot her birthday. I guess he usually does make a big deal out of it after all."

"Lacy, how long has there been a London office and why would there be one at all for this type of business?"

"I guess about four years now. Will felt it was necessary because he did business there so often."

"And how often was that?"

"Oh I guess every other month or so. There was no definite schedule. I called the London office after your mother became so worried, but they just said they would give him the message."

Lacy looked through the giant roledex and found the number in London and gave it to Clinton. He dialed and a woman with a heavy British accent politely answered. He asked for Will Creech but was told that they no longer took calls for him at that answering service. They had not heard from him in a while and eventually dropped his service.

Clinton hung up, more bewildered and confused than ever. He wondered why Will would not tell his own secretary that he had a fake office in London? What would cause him to lie to Lacy, who had kept track of some of his most personal affairs like life insurance and burial plots for years? Will had always been prone to mysterious behavior since they were kids, but not usually when money was involved. Not much of what was happening made sense to Clinton.

"Lacy, have you actually ever reached Will at this number?"

"No, in fact I never even had it until one of the kids got sick and Barbara became hysterical because she couldn't reach Will. She cussed him out something awful when he got back in town, so he gave me the number right after that."

"What about a woman in his life? Is there one?"

"Not hardly. I don't even think he saw one member of that parade of women that came through here twice. Wait, I take that back. There was one that he even took to his cottage in Virginia for the weekend. Patrice or Patricka was her name, but I don't think I have a number for her though." Lacy began looking for the number before Clinton could stop her.

"Lacy, I'm more interested in the cottage in Virginia. You have a key for it?"

She stopped her number search and rifled through the top, middle desk drawer, found a set of keys for Clinton, then wrote down the address for him, which he took before giving her a quick hug and leaving the office. Bunny feet and all, she went back to her filing.

His head was in a fog as he drove down the peaceful country road in Virginia. Just the sight of animals grazing in their pastures and the long lines of electrical wire stretched across the horizon from their criss-crossed towers was enough to make him question everything he knew about his brother. Peaceful was not what he would have thought Will would seek out. An elegant townhouse on Dupont Circle maybe; a country cottage seemed too odd.

Following the map which lay on the seat of his mother's car, he finally found the address he was looking for on an impressive wrought iron gate at the beginning of a long driveway. Again, not quite what he expected. He used a key on Will's set to access the key pad on the left side of the granite and polished oak structure. The iron gate rolled open slowly, allowing him to drive on the granite and cobblestone driveway. The long ride up the tree lined road was shaded by massive oaks which led up to a perfectly manicured yard filled with rock gardens and low shrubs. The house itself was an enormous granite and polished oak nineteenth century English Tudor which matched the gate at the entrance of the driveway, which formed a circle around a flowerbed filled with shrubs, rose bushes, geraniums and day lilies.

Clinton stayed in the car for a moment looking at the "cottage" before him. Although he had been out of the country for a while, even he knew this place must have cost nearly a million dollars, if not more. Not in the budget of a kitchen appliance supplier he summed. Not even restaurant kitchens.

He turned off the car while sitting next to the three car garage. When Lacy gave him the keys, he wondered why there were six on the ring. Now he knew. The front door alone had three locks.

Nothing in his family history could have prepared him for what he saw. A foyer filled with tapestries and African Art. There was a sunken living room in the center of the house where the light wooden floors were covered by gorgeous Arab, Persian and Oriental rugs and a tasteful combination of antique and Art Deco modern furniture. The entire back wall of the room was glass, with sliding doors to a balcony spanning the length of the house overlooking a beautiful lake with a landing and a small speedboat anchored to it. This was nothing like the black lacquer and mauve apartment in the city.

Clinton moved from room to room, sixteen in all, finding more of the same. Catlett and Tolliver original paintings and sculpture, Benin and Yoruba figures adorned nearly every room in the house. There was a great recreation room which housed a pool table with a lap pool and sauna adjoined. The master bedroom was easily as big as the in-town apartment that Clinton had seen only a few hours before. The closets were filled with Armani suits and elegantly tailored silk and linen shirts that Clinton would have expected to find in Will's wardrobe. He just had not expected to find them in a closet the size of his mother's living room or stored with one hundred and ten pairs of shoes. He knew the number because he took the time to count them, hoping there would be further clues either inside the shoes, or a hidden meaning in the numbers of pairs.

Clinton settled in the office and surveyed the wall full of books and found a varied and broad selection which included subjects from learning Modern Japanese to Constitutional Law to Holistic healing. He sat at the wonderful mahogany and glass desk and fingered an antique Benin sculpture as he contemplated Will's situation. After a moment, he searched through the desk drawers until he found securities, bonds and a clear deed to this house in Will's son and daughter's name. All of the negotiable investments were in somebody else's name but never Will's. In fact, Clinton discovered that he, his mother, Clarissa, Will's kids, Justine and Jarrett, and even Lacy were all in much better financial shape than they thought due to Will's generosity or whatever the reason.

Clinton was unable to find any indication of how Will amassed such a fortune or where he might have disappeared. Calmly, he leaned back in the huge leather chair to contemplate the situation. He struggled to free his mind of the immediate and think of a way to access Will's behavior modes. He closed his eyes and slowly remembered a time then they were kids and none of the pain of their father's death or Will's divorce from Barbara or the incident invaded their lives.

◊

He could remember seeing his brother's long, lanky body as he followed him by a few feet on their way home from the traveling amusement park which set up in the community center parking lot off of Rhode Island

Avenue. It seemed to him that he spent half of his life following Will around, getting into trouble with him and being protected by his quick wit, fast fists and even faster mouth. As a kid, Will after all, was the best older brother he could have possibly imagined.

On this particular evening, fourteen year old Will was not particularly pleased with younger brother Clinton. They turned onto their street just as the brilliant orange sun completed its descent through the purple, gray and orange sky and behind the tree and building lined horizon of Washington, D.C.

After a half a block walk, they cut across the yard of the same house Bernice still lived in and went to the back porch. Clinton remembered being afraid of climbing up to the second story window; an activity he hated but nearly became accustomed to since he was often Will's excuse and unwilling accomplice for the numerous pranks and adventures Will steered them into during those years.

Will lifted Clinton up so that he could reach the top of the back porch overhanging. He patiently and quietly held the reluctant child up until he finally took hold of the ledge.

"Finally!" whispered Will. "Could we speed this up before they notice us out here?"

"I don't know why we just can't go through the front door like normal people."

"Because only one of us wants to be here. The other of us is not staying. And neither of us is normal. Now hurry up and climb up to the window."

"I'm normal," Clinton muttered as he pulled himself on top of the roof of the porch overhand and waited patiently for Will to hoist himself up to the same level, which he did with the ease of a circus acrobat. Clinton always loved to watch Will climb and often thought he should be a trapeze artist in the circus. He made tall climbing and swinging look so effortless and easy.

Once they were both in place, Will lifted Clinton up so that he could reach the top of the rose trellis which was anchored to the house. Clinton began to climb up to their third story attic bedroom with Will climbing up close behind. As they neared the window, the trellis stopped a few feet short of a comfortable spot for a nine year old to be able to open the portal. Clinton complained that his arms were not long enough to reach it and Will pushed his brother by the seat of his pants toward their destination. The extra boost threw Clinton off balance and he began falling out of control but oddly enough, he didn't panic and scream. With the ease of one who looked much stronger than the thin, long teenager that he was, Will caught Clinton around the waist and held onto him tightly. Clinton let out a sigh of relief.

"I'm surprised that you didn't scream and give us away."

"I knew you would catch me. I wasn't real, real worried. Only a little."

Clinton remembered the smile on Will's face as he carried him up to the window like a sack of potatoes, as sure footed as any person could be under the circumstances. Once they were inside, Will checked to see if his parents, who were downstairs playing cards, had heard any of the commotion they caused while entering the house.

The whooping and hollering of the four couples downstairs let them know that once again they had cheated death or punishment as would have been the case had Clinton Sr. gotten wind of their entry. However that could only have happened if he was able to tear himself away from running a "Boston" on Mr. and Ms. Echols from across the street, like he and Bernice did every other Saturday night.

They could hear their mother laughing and making the whooping crane noise she always did when she was happy, and the sound of Mr. Echols clearing his throat continuously as he always did when he became nervous about losing.

Will said, "They are a stoned trip aren't they?"

"Mama sounds like something is trying to choke the life out of her to me. Like a sick animal or something," Clinton said. The boys giggled at the adults and their strange behavior as Will carefully closed the bedroom door.

"Now you stay up here in our room until I get home. Don't go downstairs or make any noise."

"But what if I don't want to stay up here?"

Will reached into the top drawer of the nautical dresser and took out a screwdriver.

"Oh no, you wanted to come home remember? I was having a perfectly great time trying to find Elaine Jones. You know the only reason

Mom and Dad let me off of punishment was to take you to the carnival. If you're home, then I have to be too. It's your own fault for deciding you were too tired to stay."

Will pried the molding above the door off with the screwdriver, allowing a pack of condoms and a twenty dollar bill to fall to the floor from the space between the board and the wall. He smiled and put them in his pocket.

"Now I'm going back to find Elaine. I like that girl."

Will replaced the wood and quietly pushed the nail in with his shoe. Clinton undressed and put on his pajamas before getting up enough nerve to harass Will.

"I saw what you put in your pocket and I know what a rubber looks like. I oughta' tell Mama . . . making me stay up here in the room and . . . mumble, mumble, mumble."

Will turned and gave Clinton a playful smile, pleased at his nerve.

"If you wanna' go to the museum next week, you'll shut up and go to sleep."

Clinton turned away so that his brother could not see the look on his face, considering the fact called. He would not do anything to risk a trip to the museum and Will knew it. His older brother always did cut to the quick when it came to doing something that he wanted. No further words were necessary, so Clinton tried to get in the bed as quickly as possible without looking as if he had been bested, which he had. Will stopped by the bed on the way to the window and rubbed his brother's head playfully before continuing out for the evening. Young Clinton smiled and closed his eyes, knowing that all between them was as it should be.

◊

The memories of their young days together were still very pleasant to Clinton. Visions of his childhood often carried him through the utterly impossible emotional turmoil he had suffered that drove him from his home to foreign lands and customs. He tried to imagine what message Will might have left for him as he searched through the desk drawer for a screwdriver.

After a brief search which ended at the back of a lower drawer, he found a flathead screwdriver and went to the door. He removed the top molding, causing a small note with a key wrapped inside to fall to the floor. Carefully unfolding its contents, he slid down to the floor with his back to the door jamb and read the note from his brother.

◊

"Well Clinton, if you've found this, I suppose you're looking for me, which means I'm in deep shit. I can't tell you very much because I don't know much. All I know is that I've been called to Marrakech, Morocco to work, but I don't know who the employer is. Contact your partner Gerald to find out the kind of work I really do. Even now, in a letter, I find it difficult to tell you myself considering the path is quite divergent from yours and Big C's. Gerald has kept track of me for a couple of years now although he thinks I don't know it. I always leave you a note when I'm unsure of my jobs. You were real good and I know you still are, but please be careful, very careful. The crowd I run with can be pretty nasty. Take care of my kids if that's necessary, and of course Bernice. When you go through the papers, you'll see that I have provided for them, Jarrett and Lacy as well. It's all legal and clear . . .even Gerald can't touch it, or the IRS. There's a little something in black for you in the garage too. It's in your name already, and here's the key. The house is paid for and in the kid's name, but I guess you already found that out. I hope you're not still in pain. Please get on with your life little brother. It is too short to waste a minute. Tell Rissa and of course Bernice I love them, more than they could ever know, and well you know how I feel about you."

◊

Clinton sat quietly for a few moments after finishing the note. The moonlight through the blinds shone linear patterns across his face and upper torso, making disjointed lines which matched the confused pictures in his mind. The entire revelation of Will's secret lifestyle was incongruent with the rest of his picture of his brother. He could only imagine how a black man, not in entertainment, without several higher degrees, or inheritance -even one possessing considerable charm as Will did, would be able to amass such a fortune. In order to attract the attention of Gerald Bethany, Clinton's old associate, Will must have been doing something illegal and not only in Washington. What could he have gotten himself into that would cause him to be in Morocco, and purposefully leave a trail for Clinton to be able to follow? What had Will been doing with his life since he left? Clinton's mind raced in many directions as he passionately wished for some order in his thinking which would not come, but only matched the haphazard shadow picture that theblinds cast. At that moment there was only chaos in his mind.

Unable to think up a plan, he decided to continue down the winding path which might hopefully lead to his brother. He picked the key up off of the floor and moved through the house in search of the garage. There were so many nooks and crannies in the cavernous home, that he took two or three wrong turns before stumbling onto the correct door.

The damp cool air of the garage greeted him as he opened the entrance and searched for the light switch. An ever so slight smell of new paint drifted up the four or five stairs to ding his nose. He groped the walls until he found the light switch and turned it on. Cautiously, he moved into the garage where three black cars were parked. The one closest to him was a restored Bentley; next to it was a 1956 Chevrolet convertible with rolled and pleated black interior and the third and furthest from him was a 1961 Jaguar XKE convertible with gray interior. All three cars were a brilliant black with very expensive, slightly metallic finishes to them.

Will had not told him which car was his but after Clinton saw the choices he realized that there had been no need. When Clinton Sr. was alive, he always said that people, if equated with their transportation, always had a goal set for the end of their lives. Some people would still be walking, some would be in a raggedy old Pinto, some would be in a new Buick, some in a Mercedes and others in a jet plane. Will had always taken issue with portions of this analogy - secretly, behind his father's back. They never talked back to the huge cop if there was any possibility of his hearing.

Will's theory was that Clinton was actually a Jaguar type in disguise, suppressed by all the confines of duty and responsibility. He always felt that once Clinton stopped insisting on being straight, narrow and boring, he would be extremely comfortable in a Jag, preferably a vintage one. On the other hand, Will always considered himself worthy of a fleet of Concorde jets. Clinton had heretofore thought of himself as a BMW type and Will an Avanti. Apparently, from the discoveries made during Clinton's two days back in D.C., Will was actually in the runaway train category.

Clinton went to the Jaguar, put the key in the ignition and turned on the car. He opened the garage door with the automatic opener on the visor, returned to secure the house then drove the sleek black automobile away, closing the garage door behind him.

Driving down the streets of Washington in the Jag almost made him want to put the top down, despite the night chill. Better judgment took over though and he decided against that move. Maybe there was something to Will's lifestyle he thought. The months of aloneness without concern for material possessions had been what he needed, but there was something exhilarating about the sleekness of the machine beneath his feet. Driving the car in and out of the night traffic helped him to better understand Will's obvious propensity toward the life of a high roller. Will always did have a hint of gangster in him.

10 REUNION

Too many memories were brought to the forefront with this meeting and the dancing lights glistening down the shoreline of the Potomac River. It was like the dam he had held had cracks and tiny holes which threatened to let loose the entire reservoir of pain he had been able to contain for so long. Gerald was too much the same except for maybe two new gray hairs, and the restaurant had not changed one iota since he left. There were a few more lights along the waterfront, but they all shone as brightly as he remembered and served as a reminder of what once was and how happy he felt the last time he dined there at the Chopped Cherry Tree Restaurant. Happiness that went down in flames like a Kamikaze fighter.

Maybe they should have moved to the bar so that the new crowsfeet on Gerald's face would have reminded Clinton that these were different days and times. His old partner was in his mid-forties now, but still had the physique of a twenty-five year old and the ageless face of wisdom. His piercing, narrow blue eyes and sharp strong features fit well with the sharp, coolness of his personality. He spoke in the matter-of-fact manner and detachment necessary to be a successful FBI agent, with a highest arrest record.

As partners, they were an unbeatable duo. Gerald, shrewd and calculated and Clinton, instinctive and primal. They became one of the most respected teams in the agency. On this day, Gerald was telling Clinton that his only brother Will was a jewel thief and had been one for four or five years.

Gerald continued to explain how Will hooked up with Jack Wade, a careful, veteran second story man, who they could connect with several robberies along the east coast up until his death three years before. His apprentice, Will Creech took over the business and expanded to include a lucrative overseas market. The FBI became involved when the domestic robberies occurred.

"Will owned a seafood restaurant with a guy named Oscar Wade, about ten years before he started the equipment business. Any relation Gerald?"

"Yes. Oscar is Jack's nephew but he never went in for the robbery business as far as we can tell. He's always been clean. Jack and Will seemed to form a relationship right after Mack's Snacks went under."

Jack was a bored industrialist, turned international thief and his connections allowed Will to move into places he would never have been able to infiltrate without that affiliation. Jack's laundering and fencing contacts enabled Will to live very well and take few unnecessary or foolish chances. Even the house Will owned in Virginia had been left by Jack, via a will from him to Will's kids. Later Will renovated and improved the house, always careful to stay within the reasonable limits of his earnings in the equipment business.

"Once we thought we had him for selling emeralds from a London theft to a buyer in Los Angeles, but every connection we could find just dissipated into thin air. Will is usually very smart and careful when selling goods and only deals with a few fences, just like Jack."

"Gerald, why didn't you let me know what was going on?"

Gerald leaned back in his chair and watched Clinton carefully for a moment. They had been as close as two people who work together could possibly be. Over their five year partnership, they spent many weeks in hotels on stake outs for some of the country's best known racketeers. About sixteen months before Clinton left, they had transferred to the theft division. He studied the lines on Clinton's face in an attempt to read his level of commitment to the question he had just asked.

The question seemed sincere enough, albeit absurd. Gerald chuckled slightly at his friend's odd attempt at avoidance of the obvious by asking the obvious. Clearly, Clinton was still wrestling with his escape from the people who loved him and the pain that caused that flight. Gerald decided to lay things out on the table.

"Exactly how was I supposed to do that? Track you down in India or Australia or Switzerland? You left me no indication that you wanted to be bothered with anyone, including me. Clinton, you left without even saying good bye. I heard, from Will in fact, that you were in an emotional "no man's land." I wasn't certain you would ever recover. When I found out about Will, I assumed you did not need any of this added worry did you . . ?"

Clinton quietly sipped his drink as he stared out the window, wondering if Gerald truly intended to force him into a conversation about his leaving confirming his suspicion that home was a dangerous place to be. While pondering an escape route from this line of questioning, Gerald eased the burden and continued without waiting for a real response.

"At any rate, we know that Will took a flight to Marrakech a few weeks ago, about the time he seems to have disappeared. We have no record of telephone calls from that area to him, or correspondence of any kind. If he was contacted for a job as his note said, someone locally must have contacted him. The only person I can think of in Morocco who would have the money to hire Will, and a possible need, would be a very dangerous assassin in Marrakech named Saa'iqa Mastoora. Even though it is plausible that Will hired out his services I can't imagine what she might have hired him for. Her work is usually political in nature. She started out as a member of a Moroccan terrorist group akin to the Japanese Liberation Army. Since leaving the group, she has been available to the highest bidder. She's been linked to industrial and corporate murders as well as some political ones like John Westhelm of Westco Oil and Celestine in Belgium. She is independently wealthy and does not seem to be motivated by money, political loyalties or anything we can understand."

Although he was grateful for not having to deal with his own personal life and explaining to Gerald how he could have left without so much as a "see you later," this was clearly not what he expected or wanted to hear.

"Do you have any stronger leads than this? Something less fantastic maybe? You know like he was selling drugs, although I can't really imagine that either. This is all very strange Gerald."

"I know, but it's the best we can come up with at the moment. We are still looking for other scenarios, but this one fits the facts."

"Well, I guess that's where I need to go then. Do you think I can make myself an attractive enough prospect for her to add me to her organization?"

Gerald told Clinton about Naseer, Saa'iqa's right hand man, his skills as an assassin, and ability to speak at least four languages fluently - Arabic, French, German and English. They discussed the likelihood of her needing an explosives expert or another second story man like Will. Gerald reminded Clinton of Will's high skill level and presumed that he would not need help in most situations. He said several law agencies worldwide were patiently waiting for Will to slip up, but none had been able to catch him.

"I am going to assume that Will is in serious trouble and she may need a substitute for him, not an additional person. Either he never made it there or found trouble once he arrived. Missing a mother's birthday may not sound like a lot to most people, but for Will, it's a huge red flag."

"You might be right Clinton, but he has been so careful until now."

"What does this woman look like Gerald?"

"Part Moroccan, part French; long dark hair, strange blue-green eyes and drop dead gorgeous. That much we do know. I can probably get photos for you to see. If you're going, you will need to see her anyway. I'll work on it."

"Will wouldn't even be able to think with a woman like that around. He might be subject to anything. Why hasn't she been caught if you know who she is?"

"She's is simply too careful. It's almost as if she is laughing in our faces. It is nearly clear that it is her, but just when you think you have her in one city, she shows up on the other side of the world, with an alibi. She is well respected in the community, a real champion for the impoverished and children's health. Strange contrasts in her personality."

"Beautiful, smart, compassionate on some levels and careful. There you have your answer about Will's danger Gerald."

"All right, you may have a point but I'm just not sure about your going over there either."

"Why? I don't have Will's problem. I actually see more than bodies."

"That's not what I mean. You think you're ready for the rigors of the work?"

"I wouldn't jump out there without some training as a second story man. I had hoped you would help me with that."

Gerald reminded Clinton about Archie Dayton, the D.C. thief, who gave them nightmares. After Clinton left, Gerald finally caught him with an elaborate sting operation that took him months to pull together. Archie was in jail; joke that it was. Reports from the warden indicated that he let himself in and out of his cell at will, and was even found in the warden's office on occasion, waiting for morning coffee. Gerald was certain the only reason Archie bothered to stay in prison was so he wouldn't have to look over his shoulder the rest of his life. It would become a personal mission of Gerald's to hunt him down to the ends of the earth should he escape - an accurate assumption on Archie's part.

"Archie was as good as Will is, he just doesn't have the panaché. He never went international but he definitely made an impression on law enforcement here in the States. Maybe I can get an exchange . . . his training you for your helping us bring Will to justice. Can you handle that Clinton?"

Clinton seemed lost in thought as he stared out the restaurant window at a lone boat drifting slowly down the Potomac, draped deck lights twinkling faintly in the dark, casting their reflections on the calm water. "I'd rather see him in prison and alive than . . . Maybe some other agency wants this Moroccan woman more than Will. Sounds like they should anyway."

Gerald pushed his chair back from the table and rose. "Thanks for dinner buddy. It's great to have you back. I'll call you tomorrow as soon as I know something."

Clinton stood and the two men shook hands before Gerald left. Clinton sat down slowly, scarcely taking his eyes off of the glittering lights on the river until the yacht disappeared into the black horizon. The sudden sound of chair seats thumping against the restaurant tables intruded on his thoughtful solitude, forcing him outside into the Potomac chilled night air.

Will may have been right after all. He and the Jaguar seemed to be made for each other. The leather hugged his back and thighs like a comfortable, tailor made suit and carried Clinton easily through the streets of D.C. to 1795 Rosalyn Lane. He parked across the street and stared at the twelve year old contemporary home still laden and bursting with the happiest days of his life.

He gazed dewy eyed at the Yoshino cherry tree that he planted for Grace's thirtieth birthday as if he expected the beautiful white carnation like flowers to bloom before his eyes. He noticed every new shrub, flower and layer of pine needles around each tree, the gigantic television disk in the back yard, the tricycle parked on the side of the house next to the air conditioner, and the Fiberglas dog house by the driveway. He studied them hard, determined not to forget the changes when forced to look away. Life can alter drastically in the blink of an eye, so he wanted to take it all in.

He watched lights go on and off inside until the last glow in the upstairs front bedroom went out. He remembered Grace and Eddie's voices as the child called from his room and asked for one last drink of water while she answered him from behind their closed bedroom door. She struggled to keep the shudder out of her voice as Clinton played with the indentation around her navel with his tongue while she tried not to laugh or scream and prayed their son would not enter the door she forgot to lock.

Clinton laughed at the memory through tear filled eyes. He threw his head back and growled with frustration at seeing his home now occupied by others who he hoped were happy, but resented their presence. He stared almost blankly for another ten minutes before starting the car and slowly maneuvering down the winding lane for nearly half a block before turning on his lights.

◊

Gerald had been known to work wonders, but it appeared he was even faster at problem solving. It had only been three days and he could see Archie Dayton at the other end of the gym as he entered the doorway, which had two strong and fast looking guards on either side. Maybe those attributes would help them chase Archie if necessary, as long as they didn't give him time to out-think them. Gerald and Archie approached from the opposite end of the gymnasium as Clinton entered. Archie was about six foot one, a bit shorter than Clinton, and he wore a beard and shades, no matter how unnecessary they seemed. The men met in the middle of the floor and though one never would have imagined it, he and Archie actually did resemble each other despite the fact that Clinton had more upper body definition than his counterpart. Clinton never remembered any similarities while he was obsessed with catching Archie.

"Well Clinton, long time no see! Where have you been for the last few years. I suppose you know where I've been."

"Archie I figured you had given me enough heartburn for one lifetime. I was taking a much needed vacation away from you man."

Clinton listened to the sound of Archie's voice and wondered if he could duplicate the tiny midwestern nasal tone without sounding ridiculous. It fit Archie so perfectly but it might labor on Clinton's cooler, stoic personality. Archie smiled and laughed a lot more too. Clinton would have to take these matters into consideration.

"Well your partner done you proud here. Worked like a dog to get me. Ha, ha. Finally succeeded. Gave me some heartburn of my own. Pure stupidity on my end. Should've known better. Well let's get to the business of makin' you approach my extensive abilities. These nice folks here are takin' a good chunk off my time for this. Best earn my pay. Well, what kinda shape you in now?"

"Better than ever." Clinton wondered if Archie could possibly use the word "well" any more often, and hoped this was only a nervous habit that would go away and not have to be duplicated. After all, on numerous occasions, he and Gerald had promised him that he would never see the light of day again. He wouldn't want to mess up a shortened sentence. Gerald was a proper concern because he took everything personally. Too bad Archie didn't know that Clinton no longer gave a damn, but nervousness was a small price to pay for all the work he had caused.

"Being in good shape will help you. A lot of climbing, stretching and hoisting in this line of work."

"Work?!" Gerald couldn't help but laugh. He simply would not have Archie get away with calling theft "work" as if it were a legitimate nine to five job.

Archie ignored him with only a slight roll of his eyes. "Well, I am curious to know why you folks didn't get Will to do this training though. Surely you know what he does, but maybe nepotism keeps him out of my plush hotel accommodations. Word is, he has the strongest arms anybody's ever seen. Can climb anything."

Luckily, before Clinton could respond, Gerald reminded Archie that his continuous questions and chatter were very likely to land him back in jail. The less talk the better. Archie never was a slow man and it was greed that allowed Gerald to catch him, not stupidity. He quickly led Clinton toward the ropes hanging in the back of the gymnasium, ending the chatter abruptly.

They spent the next two weeks climbing ropes, scaling walls, opening safes, disarming alarms and using all the latest electronic devices and state of the art equipment available to burglars. Clinton ran, swam and lifted weights in order to get into better shape. He also took every opportunity to learn Archie's mannerisms and speech patterns.

At the end of the two week period, Clinton's beard was nearly as full as Archie's. He walked into the gym dressed in black sweats just as Archie had done each day during their training session. He wore shades and walked with that ever so slight bop that could identify Archie from two blocks away. He was a little more bow legged than Archie and had to be careful not to bounce too much on the down stroke of the walk so he wouldn't have too exaggerated an action and give himself away. He was nearly perfect. Unless the person actually knew Archie, they would be hard pressed to describe any discrepancies.

Archie, of course, was flabbergasted and flattered. "Man you could be my not quite so pretty brother or cousin or something. You almost got the walk, but the stride is too long. You got to be mo' cool brotha'. Take smaller steps like you got no particular place to go. Those long bow legs are trying to get you there too fast. Now don't be out there ruinin' my cool rep. I worked hard and long for that."

"Man . . .shut up and get to work. I need this last day to be sure about that window detection system. I feel comfortable with everything else. Come on."

Having said that, Clinton walked with smaller, slicker steps - Archie style, toward the window mock-up. Archie watched Clinton and smiled with admiration before joining him for their last lesson. He could feel that he was making the transition he was known for as an operative. As he adjusted his gait to match Archie's, he felt like he was in his element - back in the saddle again. Maybe, getting accustomed to being the shape changer he was before. Time would tell.

11 EMBERS

They were both silent for the last few minutes they shared over dinner. Clinton was uneasy with Bernice's apparent worry about his pending departure to search for his brother. She fingered the edge of her plate with her left hand and slid the fork between the sugar peas and the mashed potatoes, making little trails and separations that looked like railroad tracks. She never looked up from her plate, hoping that she could conceal the worry in her eyes if they didn't meet his. "Clinton . . . what time will you be leaving for London?"

"Ma, I still have two days left. Stop worrying please, you'll just work yourself into a frenzy."

Bernice began clearing away the dishes. He could tell by the slow, methodical way she scraped the plates that this would not be the end of it. He had seen the ritual many times before when Clinton Sr. had not come home from work on time, nor called to say why. Bernice nearly wiped off the glaze on a set of ceramic plates when he was a kid, waiting for his father during the 1967 and 1968 riots. Clinton hoped she wouldn't corner him into telling her something he wasn't ready to. He always had a hard time lying to her, but he certainly couldn't tell her the truth in this case. She'd lose her mind with worry.

"What do you really think happened to Will baby? Was that his house we went to that day to pick up my car and is that his black sports car you're driving? Where di . . . ?

"Mama, we aren't certain what Will is doing. That's why I'm going to get more information, but it does appear that he leads a life quite different from what we thought. Please don't ask me anymore questions 'til I get back. I'll have more information then."

"What if you don't get back? If you're tracking him, you might not make it back either! I'm sorry I ever asked you to come home now. I guess I thought he may have amnesia or been in an accident or something. But . . .I mean really! Secret houses and expensive cars and another life! This is like a bad Twilight Zone movie!"

She was far more upset than he imagined she would be. He left the table and hugged his mother tightly for a moment, then they both leaned back against the edge of the counter - his arm around her shoulder.

"Ma . . . whatever has happened, we need to know. I've never seen you shy away from reality. Even with all of the good traits, we all know that Will has a somewhat slick side. Huh?"

"I know you're right . . . but he is my child and whether he willfully got himself into something he couldn't handle or not, I hate to think of him needing me and my not being able to help him." Tears welled up in Bernice's eyes.

The pain and hopelessness was part of the reason he did not want to return. He could not understand why his family would not give up their vision of him as protector and problem solver, a position he was doubted he was qualified for. He had only seen his mother cry once, when Clinton Sr. died. He never wanted to see that again. She had been too worried about him to cry that other time . . . just before he left. She simply stared at him with an intensity matched only by his extreme grief. He simply did not want to be this close to the pain of everyday affairs. He did not want to feel this much empathy with a parent who longed for a child again. He pulled her close to him and held her for lack of a more intelligent action to execute, as his mind wandered back to Kenya and the peacefulness of the reserve. Then, fortunately, the doorbell rang.

"You expecting someone Ma?"

"Justine and Jarrett. I invited them over for dessert. You haven't seen them since you've been home and you won't believe how Jarrett has grown. Let them in for me honey, while I get the pie out of the oven."

His mother possessed incredible resilience. She could be in the throes of fear and despair, but transcend it when the circumstances called for her attention. He hugged her again before releasing her to pie duty, then went to answer the door.

Justine was a lot of fun, if she hadn't changed. She had a non-stop mouth that constantly talked trash. He had missed her while he was gone. He could hear his mother humming some spiritual he could no longer identify as he reached the door. She was resilient - not forgetful.

He opened the door to find eleven year old Jarrett, standing a couple of inches taller than his short, older, shapely, abrupt mother who began speaking to him with one hand on her hip.

"Well . . . did you forget your manners over the years? Don't you know how to ask folks to come in anymore?" Justine broke into his thoughts.

He had known Justine a long time he thought, and she was still a loud and brash hellion standing in front of him with her head cocked to one side as if it got stuck after that neck roll. He was about ready to enter into playful exchange with her, but was too distracted by Jarrett. He wondered who the child looked like.

"Hi Uncle Clinton . . . where's Nana Creech?"

Just as he completed his question, Jarrett noticed Bernice moving around in the kitchen humming and holding a pie. He ran past Clinton saying "That's O.K., I see her."

Clinton grabbed Justine by the collar and pulled her to him a little roughly, then hugged and kissed her on the forehead. Although she was fully grown, she was so small that she appeared nearly childlike as she clung to him.

"Well some things and people never change," he said as he pushed her away from him. He wanted to get a good look at her. She and Grace looked so much alike. Maybe he never really noticed before because their personalities were worlds apart. But tonight, not only did she look like Grace, but Jarrett looked like Clinton's son Eddie a little . . . or at least the way Eddie might have looked had he lived. After all, Justine and Grace were sisters. What did he expect?

The pain in his head pounded with each confused emotion. He moved away from Justine abruptly. He had spent five years running, jumping out of planes , and diving to the depths of three oceans in order to escape and replace pain with solitude and quiet. He had learned to live with the dulled emotions and certainly did not want the acute version he was feeling with increased family contact. He couldn't wait to get out of Washington and felt utter internal turmoil.

Bernice entered the room with a tray of sweet potato pie slices, coffees and a glass of milk. She and Justine exchanged looks, both aware of Clinton's retreat.

"Why don't you and Justine go out on the porch and have your dessert. This young man and I have a serious game of War waiting for us.

He beat me last week and that simply will not do!"

"You wish you had a chance Grandma! Heh, heh, heh!!!"

Bernice and Jarrett exchanged threatening glares as she gave Justine the tray with remaining desserts. "I see that he needs to be taught some respect for his elders. I feel I am that right person to do that."

"Of course Great Goddess of the gray hair and slow walk."

Bernice mocked him with a shocked look. "That's it!! Its on!!!"

Jarrett, delighted, got a deck of cards from the end table drawer, plopped down on the blue, green and purple plaid Early American sofa and the two of them prepared for battle. Justine and Clinton took their tray out to the porch and placed it on the wicker table between the two wing backed wicker rockers and sat down; Justine's feet dangling just above the floor. They sipped coffee and ate pie contentedly for a while before Justine asked what and where Clinton had been doing since he left home.

"Nothing special. Ranching, working on a wildlife preserve in Kenya. That's about it." he said.

"That's all! Clinton, you used to be my best friend. Talk to me. Not once in all this time have you written or called me directly, only through your mother have I heard anything."

He thought about their friendship. Nearly every bit of trouble he got into from elementary school to high school involved Justine. She had been his closest friend in life, but he'd never let her know that.

"Clinton! Can't you hear me talking to you! Is there some reason you don't respond?"

He stopped looking at the stars, jolted back into reality and the present by her abrasive and impatient tone. "Damn woman . . . you look like her, but all you have to do is open that mouth of yours in order to bring a body back ."

"So that's what's going on here. Grace. She was my only sibling Clinton. I miss her and Eddie terribly, but they are gone. Please Clinton, get it behind you. You insult her memory by sulking and moping or in your case, trying to self distrust."

Justine realized that she was annoyed with his emotional inertia, but felt she was more agitated than made sense. She tried to temper her conversation, paused for a second, lowered her voice and tried to clear her mind of all the thoughts racing through it. Visions of life gone by, a loved sister, her aspirations for her nephew and a mixture of emotions involving her son. She calmed the sea of feelings before speaking again.

"I've heard about these wild occupations you took up. Parachuting, cow rustling, snake charming, alligator wrestling and crazy stuff like that."

"Excuse me but I was flying the planes as a crop duster, and I wasn't wrestling alligators, it was a crocodile and that Clarissa can't get anything straight, she never could. It wasn't on purpose anyway. I don't know how that woman can keep a job that requires her to deliver straight facts. She never gets anything she tells right."

Clinton looked at Justine to see to read her agitation as he continued, but couldn't. "I worked on a ranch in Australia . . . and I have no idea what that snake crap is about. Rissa is exasperating."

Justine broke into a wonderful, easy laugh. He relaxed with her. She had the kind of personality that could make you forget your troubles, if that was what she chose to do. Or she could make you remember ancient problems and conjure up some new ones if she chose to do that as well. Tonight, she was helping him forget. Tonight, she was the best part of Grace and the best part of Justine.

From inside, Bernice heard laughter on the porch and looked through the screen door at Clinton's body movements. Of all her children, he was the most difficult to read. He had always been most protective of his feelings, even before the incident. When he was a very young child, he had been quiet and aloof, interested in introspective activities like building model cars and going to the Smithsonian. Will had been extremely outgoing and Clarissa a social animal, partying much too much in her high school years. But Clinton was more reclusive and exclusive. His social circle consisted of three males, Justine or Clarissa when she had the time, all through junior and high school. One of the guys, Stephen Letters even went to A & T State University in North Carolina with him, where both majored in mechanical engineering, became Kappas and contented to do well in school with seemingly very few new friends that Bernice could tell.

She watched and listened to Clinton with pleasure. Justine, if anybody, could always make him happy even when nobody else could.

Bernice thought it was a shame that he couldn't find solace in her company after Grace's death, but he didn't stay long enough to find out. She smiled, then returned to the card game and Jarrett's assault.

"Clinton, hasn't it gotten any better for you?" Justine asked. "I've been so worried about you. You just left!

"I know. I was living that horror. I couldn't get over the irony of it all Justine. On the very day I complete my career at the F.B.I.; a job I left, because my wife was afraid for my safety; I get home only to find that my wife and kid were killed by some drunk, coming home from the stupid grocery store!"

Clinton was shaking, and she could see every muscle in his body tense up instantly. He stood up abruptly and paced for a moment - fast at before he sat down on the steps of the porch. Justine watched him carefully, in revelation and with clarity. She always thought it was grief that consumed him when Grace and Eddie were killed. That they were partners in their sorrow for the loss of her precious life, soft, tender love and brilliant light which she shot directly into their souls. But at that moment, Justine understood that this was her take on the situation - not Clinton's. He was consumed with anger. Pure unmitigated rage, the likes of which she realized, she could not possibly imagine. What choice did he have but to leave? He must have considered himself a danger to anyone in sight. She knew of his work as an agent, but never considered what part of his being he called upon in order to execute a daily routine that puts your own life in danger and forces you to expect to kill at any given moment.

For all she thought she knew, she really didn't know him at all. What she thought was silence in sorrow after their deaths, was probably some internal struggle not to go off the deep end. She never even imagined that kind of anger or that sort of soul wrenching, boiling, deep seated contempt . She would never underestimate it again. Thank goodness, she thought, that it didn't seem directed at little black women who talked a lot of trash; however she wasn't sure who it was reserved for and while sitting there on the porch that night, she wondered if it was self directed. She focused on Grace's earring in Clinton's ear and watched him try to calm down.

◊

He sat on the steps and tried to get his emotions under control again. The part of himself he feared most had been brought to the forefront once again. There was the rise of the low boiling rage that arose from his utter despair. He had never been as happy in his life as he was with Grace. He rose each morning happy to have her arm across his face or all the cover pulled off him as she lay snug in a cocoon of sheets and blankets, unaware of his plight. He longed for the warmth of her body, and he seethed every day at the thought of her absence. His rage developed first in a lava, melting hot sort of way and now in small spurts which shot up with tiny geyser like motions rising only on rare occasions, with great unpre-dictability.

He could barely remember when he had goals and aspirations that didn't include Grace. He certainly had no long term goals since her death, only to get through the day - each one that came - often wishing for no more. Finding Will was the most result oriented task he had embarked upon since he left D.C.. When he first finished college, he worked for a firm in D.C. for a year before he went back to complete his masters degree in Criminal Justice because he had become bored with engineering. Working for the F.B.I. had been his only career goal since then.

All the jobs since he left D.C. were adventures exciting enough to make him forget, if only temporarily. Having to focus and keep his anger in check as opposed to working out his frustrations in physical work or tasks was taking its toll on him. He drew deep, deep breaths and tried to remember everything he knew about staying focused and centered. When he spoke again, it was with the slow deliberate tone of one who was attempting to keep himself together .

"Can you believe that? I couldn't. Some imbecile destroys my life in one fell swoop. What had I done to deserve that? It could not have been anything Grace had done . . . she was much too kind; and what the hell could a four year old do to warrant some shit like that? It just didn't make any damned sense!"

Justine left her chair and sat on the steps beside Clinton. She took his hand in hers, and kissed the back of it. He put his arm around her, brushed her long, thin dreadlocks away from her face and kissed her on the cheek, tilting her head over slightly so he could reach the place where her jawbone met her neck. She shuddered slightly, but he didn't notice.

He let go of her hair and stared straight ahead. She leaned her head against his chest and they sat quietly for a moment before she spoke again.

"Haven't you found any peace whatsoever since you've been gone? I thought that maybe time would help."

"I thought so too. I also thought that if I learned some of the mystical ways of the world, I could better understand the meaning of life and death. I went straight to Tibet when I left here, but that only put me slightly more at peace with myself. It didn't do much for the loss part. I kept moving around, examining the lifestyles of different groups of human beings, but I couldn't always relate other cultures to my situation either. You know what seems to have done the most good Justine?" She shook her head to say no. "Animals. Now they are real! Plain and simple in their actions. They tend to make things crystal clear. I thought I had internalized their essence enough to come home until I went by our old house a few nights ago. I'm not ready for this. I can't wait to get away from here."

They were silent for a moment as he stared into the night sky and she stared at him. She always considered him to be one of the most ruggedly, fine men she had ever seen.

"How is your dad Justine? Does he still drink like a fish and talk continuous shit?"

"Absolutely! Wouldn't know who he was if he didn't. Mama died though . . . the year after Grace. They were so much alike . . . soft and sweet. They always were, that's why I stayed with my dad after their divorce and Grace stayed with Mom in Memphis. Mother couldn't handle Grace's death either."

Tears welled up in her eyes as she leaned away from Clinton's embrace. He let her go placing both hands flat, behind him on the porch floor.

"Well, maybe we should have more uplifting conversations now, like discussions about hunters bludgeoning baby seals or children all over the world dying of starvation. Those topics should bring our spirits right on up to speed, you think?"

"Girl you are still crazy. So . . . do you still skate? We must have gone skating every weekend for two years straight."

"Yes, Jarrett and I go once a week. You remember the trips to New York we used to take when we were kids? I remember the first time you took me there. We saw some weird little play in which the guy pulled down his pants and showed his butt to the audience. I had never seen anything like it. Nor have I since, come to think of it."

"I remember that now, but I thought we were with a group of people. Somehow I remember a lot of foolishness on the ride back home as a result of that play. That crazy Greg Stamps with his ass hanging out of the window comes to mind."

"You're right. Just about everything we did was in a huge group it seems. We got in more trouble during high school before you and Grace rediscovered each other and became an "item.""

"Well not everything we did was a group project if I recall. Do you remember that week we spent sneaking in and out of your room at your father's house with the sex manuals?"

"Oh no Clinton, stop!"

"I don't know why you would be embarrassed. I was flattered to be your first. It made perfectly good sense to me that in such a delicate situation as giving up your virginity, you would want to be with someone you trust. Of course now I had no idea what I was unleashing onto the planet."

" We are supposed to remember other things about our youth that don't mortify us with utter embarrassment, please."

"Justine I thought it was a wonderful thing, and I think you should be glad to have had such a knowledgeable and attentive teacher."

Justine glared at him with a smirk on her face to match his smile. "Well if you hadn't been such a good teacher, I probably would not have been so hot to get involved with Jarrett's father, that fool. I'm going in the house and see how people who know how to act are doing."

She stood up and tossed her head back, causing her long dreadlocks to fly up and over her head and down her back as she started toward the door. Clinton grabbed her hand, bringing her stride to a halt.

"Do you ever hear from him? Does he see his son at all?"

"He has never thought of him as his son."

"Justine doesn't that bother you though?"

She smiled peacefully at him. "How could it when I have someone as wonderful as Jarrett in my life. There could only be good in that."

She picked up the dishes and he rose to open the door for her. Bernice and Jarrett were engaged in a heated card game. Justine took the dishes to the kitchen as Clinton watched the competition. He was happy that his mother had the extended family to support her since he, Clarissa and Will were away from home.

He was about to go help Justine with the dishes, when he noticed photos and trophies on the mantle and side shelves. On the top shelf were Will's football and Clinton's baseball trophies and medals. On the second shelf, a large portrait of the entire Creech family; Bernice, Clinton Sr. and all three kids, taking up the whole shelf. The third shelf down contained a framed photo of Justine and Jarrett at about age six or seven, looking very much like Eddie, who was born two years after Jarrett. To the right of them was an old straw hat with a huge bright, red feather. Clinton smiled and picked up the hat.

"Ma, who did this belong to?"

"Your great grandfather owned the hat, but the feather was handed down by your great, great, great grandfather. Don't quote me on this, but it was handed down from father to son several generations because it is a sign of great wisdom and humility, if I remember correctly."

"Was it tribal you think? I know we are part Indian."

"Its African. Yoruba I believe, but I know there's more to it than that . . . I can't remember anything else except that it has some religious meaning."

I'll find a book so that I'll know before talking to Malika about it."

He placed the hat on the shelf and looked at the photo of him, Grace and Eddie sitting next to it. His heart jumped at the sight. Since his abrupt departure, he had not seen their faces, at least not in concrete terms, since the visit to the morgue to identify them.

Although it was a struggle, he forced himself to look at the images. Clinton was holding her and she was holding Eddie, who was laughing as he tried to push his mother's arm away from his tiny waist. Clinton remembered what a major decision it was for them to choose the unorthodox pose as their family portrait. She was delighted that Eddie had not acted in a predictable manner.

Clinton leaned against the wall and tried to replace his misery with the happiness he felt on that day. Justine sat unobtrusively in the corner, trying to read his reactions.

◊

Two days later, Gerald and Clinton awaited the gate call for a New York flight that would connect to Royal Air Moroc to Casablanca, on to Marrakech. Clinton was dressed in typical Archie attire, black slacks and a Neru collar shirt, wore sunglasses and had a hard cover book about horses resting in his lap. Gerald gave him the number of Ann Taylor, Archie's romantic interest. Clinton was to check in every two days by leaving some general message for Ann at her number.

Gerald explained further that Archie and the real Ann Taylor were going to spend some time together while Clinton was using his identity. If a prison check was run, it would indicate that he had been released from prison one month before. Gerald also gave Clinton a list of pre-arranged robbery victims and major fences and laundering agents in Marrakech. Clinton spoke fluent French after living in Senegal, but his Arabic, especially Moroccan Arabic was weak.

They discussed Saa'iqa Mastoora's propensity toward the use of sharp knives and anesthetic drugs like Pavulon and Curare on her victims. She seldom used a gun and often concealed drugs in food and drinks. There had been reports of her utilizing new technology which allowed her to conceal weapons within artifacts which would only open in response to her specific body chemistry and touch. It would be difficult to tell whether or not she had a weapon hidden within an otherwise innocent looking personal item, clothing or piece of furniture. She didn't participate in loud and flagrant displays, if she could avoid it.

She was suspected of involvement in the murder of at least eighteen political figures and another twenty-four prominent business people around the world, although none could be proven. She was careful. Her identity was well known but she could not be linked to any incident. She was considered cunning, cold and vicious. She had no ties, no loyalties, no apparent politics, was well bred and shrewd. The Moroccan police seemed to consider her involvement too ridiculous to entertain, so all the agencies ceased involving them in any inquiries several years before.

Gerald completed his briefing just as the announcement for boarding came over the loud speaker.

"Gerald, my mother only knows that I am going to London. There seemed no need to tell her about an assassin in Morocco, o.k.?"

"I understand. I know what to do if I have to talk to her."

"Good. She's having a hard time with this."

"Clinton . . . there is one thing. I haven't said anything because . . . well, here goes. Archie doesn't wear an earring, you know and yours might . . . ."

Clinton cut him off. "He wears one now Gerald. The earring stays."

Gerald saw the blank expression on Clinton's face and dropped the subject. "O.K. then. Well you take care and I'm here if you need me."

The men parted with a hand shake before Clinton boarded the Boeing 727. Gerald left the gate area, leaving Clinton to walk down the jetway alone to board. For the first time he was genuinely fearful of Will's fate after hearing about Saa'iqa. He had to know but he wasn't sure he wanted to test his emotional fortitude with the disturbing possibilities that lay before him.

Once in the air, he was able to calm his thoughts somewhat, focus on the best strategy for the task at hand and consider the obstacles before him. He felt confident of his ability to imitate a thief. Archie had been a good teacher and demonstrated well his ability to allude the FBI for the time period in which he was successful. Clinton was also clear on the layout of the city of Marrakech and the customs, culture and rules which could not be ignored if one expected smooth sailing.

He was not sure how he felt about being close to a beautiful woman for any extended amount of time; especially one who would be distrustful and suspicious of him. He had sex with a woman about two years before, but it was as unfulfilling as he suspected it would be, so he had not pursued anyone since. The two non-sexual encounters he experienced with Justine while at home seemed awkward and strained, and she was as comfortable as any woman could be for him. He knew he would have to deal with his discomfort with women, and the lack of social savvy from years of isolation though. After all, he couldn't ruin Archie's "cool rep" could he?

Once he changed airplanes and settled into the first class seat of the L-1011, he began to relax a little. The billowy clouds afforded him a chance to think of his wife and son in less concrete, more ethereal and esoteric terms. He imagined them drifting peacefully through the soft, wispy matter like the angels depicted in Michaelangelo's work. No matter how absurd the literal interpretation of heaven seemed, he had come to understand why it was developed in the first place. It may well have been the creation of a grieving father and husband who longed for the distant, softer loves of his world to exist in peace . . . joy. . . bliss. . . warmth. . . happiness. . . tranquillity. . . love. . . harmony. . . serenity. . . . calm . . .

12 PERFECT LITTLE RICH GIRL

Naseer and Saa'iqa pulled up to the front of La Mamounia Hotel Casino and stopped. Naseer got out to open the car door for her but, as would be expected, was beaten to the task by a doorman dressed in an all white traditional shirt and pants, with a pale gray vest, yellow sash and burgundy fez. La Mamounia, built in 1923, was Marrakech's oldest luxury and most elegant hotel and was something to behold in itself. It was a pale shade of Persian red with a turquoise-green clay tile roof, and pale turquoise mosaic trim and marble. The grounds were filled with palm trees and perfectly manicured rosemary bushes and shrubs.

The surroundings complemented Naseer's tuxedo and Saa'iqa's elegant, black silk charmeuse Christian Dior evening gown and black velvet jacket. As was most socially acceptable, Saa'iqa's arms and back were covered. She was a pillar of Marrakech society, a highly respected princess of the aristocracy upon whom the duties of her father had devolved, and a benevolent benefactor to many causes. As she glided into the hotel, as always when visible, she looked and acted the part.

La Mamounia was just inside the old part of town about one half block from the ramparts wall near the entrance called Bab el-Jadid, opened in 1915. The wall itself, nearly 15 kilometers long, was constructed in 1126 by Ali ibn-Yusuf of the Almoravid dynasty as protection and fortification from attack, but barely made a difference to the Almohads who took over the city in 1147. The beautiful gardens surrounding La Mamounia were legendary, and though they would not rival Majorelle, Agdal or Yves St. Laurent's gardens, they were still peaceful and impressive. Originally a wedding present Prince el-Mamun, they included an abundance of orange, olive and palm trees, shrubs and assorted flowers with walkways between the rectangular areas of greenery. The casino in the hotel was perhaps the most ordinary feature it had.

On this particular night, the wealthy assembled to raise money for a children's home, a pet project of Saa'iqa's. Morocco, like many countries, held great disparity in its treatment of the rich versus the poor.

There was a substantial middle income group, but the most glaring difference, as usual, was between the wealthiest and the poorest. Several years before, Saa'iqa had visited some of the homes of farmers in the Atlas mountains and found people living with dirt floors, houses with no roof over the common areas - only the bedrooms. The houses had no refrigeration, no heat and air conditioning was provided by the lack of ceilings and sometimes walls. She could barely believe the conditions and found out that many children within the city were abandoned, or ran away from the country. Often their parents died and they had no other means of support, so they worked or stole their young, tender existence away simply trying to find food and shelter to survive another day. It had become her mission to assist their efforts.

As she and Naseer walked past the slot machines and into the main hall of the casino, there was a sea of people all dressed in their finest formal wear, mostly European, largely French, with a few people wearing traditional Berber formal wear. When they saw their hostess, a roaring applause rose to welcome who finally graced them with her.

She made a short speech in French, Arabic and then English, welcoming them to the "grand party" as she called it, while she smiled at the faces registering the politics behind most of their fortunes. The job of a government official was still highly respected and garnered a great amount of power in Marrakech. Many in the upper ranks in attendance to this event that she had convinced La Mamounia to sponsor as a fund-raiser for the Mohammed The Fifth Home for Children. The patrons would gamble and their losses and their earnings would be contributed to the home. In that manner, they could give away their money and have fun doing so.

Saa'iqa was quite pleased with the turnout, and Naseer was pleased that she was happy. They moved around the room and stopped to speak to Pierre' Bonet, a wealthy French real estate developer and his companion, a Nigerian woman, named Bisi Aminu who were playing blackjack. They seemed cordial, yet cool with each other before Naseer and Saa'iqa moved on to mingle with other guests. She nodded and smiled respectfully at Jalaal Abdullah, one of the older members of Marrakech society. He returned her acknowledgment, a slight and indistinguishable glimmer in his eyes. The chief of police Aatar Mohammed and his wife Toundam were seated at the bar. Saa'iqa smiled graciously and stopped. Naseer moved over to the bartender and ordered drinks.

"Aatar, how have you been. I'm quite pleased you could take the time out of your busy schedule to join this cause" Saa'iqa said.

"The more children serviced by your foundation, the less I will have to see coming through my jails from trying to pick the pockets of the tourists down at Place Djemaa el-Fna. Better for us all."

"So true, so spend lots of money so that can happen," she replied. Naseer brought her back an Amaretto on the rocks with a twist of lime. She thanked him and took a sip. "Toundam, how are your children?"

"All is well Saa'iqa. Our eldest will be attending the university next year. We are quite proud of her. Thank you for asking."

"Good, good. Well, we must move on and encourage others to spend, spend, spend."

They all smiled as Naseer and Saa'iqa left the Mohammeds and walked toward the blackjack tables. As soon as they were out of ears reach Naseer spoke. "Everytime we have contact with him I feel as if we are stealing the ball in a soccer game. Other times, like someone is walking on my mother's grave, as the Americans say."

"Relax. All he knows of us is what he sees right now. We have given him no reason to think otherwise."

"Until now," he replied.

Saa'iqa took a deep breath and looked up at him, stopped walking and linked her arm inside of his. "In all our years together we've not worked here in Marrakech. This job is a personal favor of sorts. I promise we will not work here again. Alright?"

Naseer looked down into Saa'iqa's face. He had seen her go through so many stages of growth, and yet still maintain her essence and wondered if she had taken this job because the others had grown too easy. They leaned toward worldwide tasks that righted some wrong in Saa'iqa's eyes. Even though they were being watched by Interpol, he knew in his heart that there was no support for what appeared to be absurd stories to the police department. Aatar was certainly instrumental in that because he held Saa'iqa in highest esteem and certainly tolerated no nonsense concerning the daughter of one of his Egyptian born childhood idols.

The Marrakech job somehow pleased her, maybe he thought, because it seemed to right past attitudes and arrogance. She strongly believed in reciprocity. Maybe it was the players involved and her ability to move among them undetected, that turned her on. It really didn't matter. As uneasy as working at home made him feel, he would not deny her the pleasure - whatever its origin. He smiled broadly at her and replied "Alright."

The evening went very well. Over ten million Dirhams were raised. Everyone ate, drank, gambled, laughed, talked, played politics, compared possessions and vacations, and basked in the social event of the year. She was in rare form, with the best, freest and most generous side of her personality loose and available. She floated throughout the room putting women at ease and making men wonder and worked the officials of La Mamounia so that they donated far more food, and far more time than they meant to. She laughed easily, at times in a light and airy manner and at other times in a deep and guttural, animalistic way that made Naseer's heart jump. It was a perfect evening of fun before the massive amount of work she was about to undertake.

The silence between them on the drive home was laden with a sense of satisfaction. They passed an old van about three blocks away from the house. They both looked at it and laughed, but neither said a word about it. When they arrived at home, Naseer opened the garden door and went in first, searched the bottom floor and turned on the lights before Saa'iqa entered. It was a ritual they had done for years, and despite her ability to protect herself, she appreciated his concern and meticulous protection.

Once he was certain the coast was clear, she entered, he secured the house and they went up to their respective rooms on the second floor, parting with "goodnights" as he watched her go into her room first, and close the door behind her. He waited momentarily until she opened the door and said "All is fine." He knew it was true because if not, she would have said "the room is clear". It was their private code to alert the other of an intruder. He walked to his room, and closed the door behind him.

He had put the word out to all the fences in town that they needed someone very good, who was not local. He thought for a few moments about the task of finding a replacement for the thief Will Creech and though he had suggested to Saa'iqa that they find a Marrakechii candidate, he agreed to some degree that someone from outside their country might be a more reasonable choice. He only hoped it would not be an American from the United States. They tended, it seemed to him to be quick tempered and irrational. Just before he fell off to sleep, he wondered which way the wind would blow in the days to come.

Her thoughts were a pleasant jumble of assorted visions and sounds. She lay in her soft white bed surrounded by both printed and live, yellow and white flowers on all surfaces in the room. Dreamily, she watched the sheer curtains blow back and forth from the breeze of her open balcony door as she looked out at the remnants of a barely glowing moon in its last stage, and thought about the tasks at hand, and the programs provided by the money raised. She had accomplished one of her more pleasant goals in life. Her last mental vision before sleep took over was of her mother's beautiful, peaceful face reading a story to her when she was a small child.

13 GETTING ACQUAINTED

When Clinton stepped out of the rented Fiat carrying two black leather bags, with black slacks and a black silk shirt on, bearded and wearing black rimmed shades, very few people including those who knew Archie, would have questioned his identity. If a person was not acquainted with either one, there was no reason whatsoever to be suspicious.

Le Mansour Eddahbi Hotel was a fairly new establishment and one of the finest in Marrakech with palatial courtyards and stunning sitting rooms with twenty-five foot ceilings. It was in the New City, Hivernage off of Avenue De France almost too close to Saa'iqa's home, but the logical choice for Archie Dayton to stay in because it was slightly flashy and ostentatious. It had tennis courts, a large pool, was close to the Medina and the Airport, and next to the Marrakech Congress Center, the conference center. There were numerous bars and restaurants within the hotel complex, a jazz club and a disco.

He walked into the lobby in a perfected Archie bop as if he hadn't a care in the world, which of course he seemed to own. There were a few Europeans and Africans from other countries going about their various tasks in the lobby. No one paid particular attention to him. He checked in and followed the bell captain to his room. He wondered for a moment why the captain had chosen to take him up, but noticed that there wasn't a bellmen around at that moment. Clinton would watch him though. He was amazed at how suspicious he had become after years of paying no particular attention to his surroundings, and liked the feel of his edge coming back.

Once he was settled, he sat on the balcony and watched the radiant Moroccan sun setting over the plains just outside the city, splashed with tones of rust, magenta, gold and lavender. He could see the workday business travelers on the streets below as they made the journey home for the evening. Clinton was amazed at the mix of vehicles on the streets and the strange carts that farmers drove which seemed to be a combination wagon and tractor, yet pulled by a donkey. The sound of horse hooves against the pavement, the constant engines of the small French and Japanese cars and the diesel Mercedes contributed to the serenity encompassing the landscape and helped lull him into the proper state of mind for his first professional theft and the bait he was to become. He remained calm and quiet as he watched the final rays of melted color ease below the horizon.

As the pitch black of night replaced the sky's splash of brilliance, he also shifted to a deep, sullen state which always came over him when he worked undercover. It had been a strong force which he could call upon easily before he left the United States, and would often send him into a near trance. Grace disliked his behavior with a passion when he went undercover. She always considered his transformation similar to a multiple personality syndrome or such. He considered it more like an acting assignment or maybe temporary amnesia which targeted only those things in his real life.

It was sometimes difficult for Clinton to return home to Grace and Eddie during such assignments, opting to either stay away from them if the mission was short, or keep emotional distance if the job was lengthy. His love for them caused him to become unfocused and made his work less effective though he could never have said such a thing to Grace. He suspected she knew. It seemed to him that she was quite concerned about his safety, but for him, the greater danger was in his ability to so thoroughly become his assignment cover.

Sometimes he even frightened himself and felt he had to struggle not to plummet into some removed and deranged existence. At times like those, it was thinking about the life and love they shared that kept him on solid footing and steady ground. He wondered what could pull him back without them. He contemplated how to make the best of this new-found freedom from his wire's worry.

An hour later when he rose from the chair on the balcony with the dark, he was as close to Archie as anyone could possibly become.

His only thoughts were of horses and the pretty, tall, honey colored woman named Ann Taylor, Archie's woman for nine years. He felt her love for Archie as if it were truly his own. He had been briefed on her birthmarks, and the scar on her back beneath her right shoulder blade from when her brother accidentally rammed an open ended pipe into her back while helping their father with the plumbing. Clinton could imagine the crescent shaped keloid mark, as if he had touched it the day before.

He put on a black hat, picked up his small black leather bag and left the hotel in the rented car. There was no need for him to read the map because he had studied his route very carefully on the flight over, but he took it with him anyway.

He parked the car two blocks away from his target, the home of a wealthy European businessman who lived in the Amelkis, a wealthy golfing community with a grand golf course and beautiful new homes, built in the "Oasis of Marrakech." Gerald had already contacted the man, a British man named Joseph Wainwright and a friend for eight years, and arranged to reimburse him for any losses he might incur should they be unable to retrieve his artifacts. Wainwright, somewhat excited by the thought of being part of an underground operation, agreed. Wainwright and his wife were on holiday in Germany and would not be home during the theft, however the actual break-in had to be performed as if it were real in order to avoid discovery. It would be reported two days later when they returned and it would be treated in the appropriate manner, therefore giving Saa'iqa nothing to be suspicious of.

Clinton walked down the deserted street and around a corner to the elegant, three story rose colored stucco mansion on the outskirts of town and the six foot stone wall surrounding it. It sat on a fairly large lot, and was a farther distance from the houses next to and around it than those in the city. The street was quite still and dark since there was no moon. Only the sound of a dog barking several streets over could be heard and the whir of sprinklers on the greens across the street as they dispersed water onto the golf course.

Once certain he was free of watchful eyes, Clinton removed a rope and hook from his bag and tossed the four pronged, metal instrument to the top of the wall. He noiselessly climbed the wall with ease and disappeared on the other side with only a small thud.

◊

Late the next morning, the sun glistened on the backs of the sea of black, white, green, rust, blue and yellow djellabahs that moved ahead of him down the busy street of the merchant's district in the Medina, just beyond the souks - the intertwined shopping area filled with artisans of all sort. He struggled with the signs on the front of the shops, his minuscule Arabic failing him miserably. Finally, he saw the store he was looking for - the one which belonged to one of the biggest fences in the city.

Clinton put the shades on once again and went inside. The store was narrow and well lit with four large square, glass jewelry cases in the front room and bright, internally lit glass cases built into the walls, all around the room. All displays were locked. There were antiquities from the Berber culture in three of the cases, and one case of more European looking jewelry in the last floor case. The walls had an assortment of necklaces, earrings and bracelets in them, hanging on the walls. He was greeted by the owner, a short man in a well-worn blue knit shirt and burgundy lightweight wool pants, black socks and brown Hushpuppies. He had gray hair and beard, appeared to be in his late sixties, wore glasses and , his teeth showed much need of dental care. He walked out from a second display room to greet Clinton, cleaning a silver chalice.

"SbaH lxair, salam alekum." Salem said.

"Hello, and how are you also?" Clinton replied.

"Ah, you are American?"

"Yes . . . straight from the states." Said Clinton.

"You speak Arabic or French, my English is not too good."

"No, I'm sorry I don't, and your English is fine with me, and certainly better than my Arabic."

Both men smiled, the old man pleased that Clinton recognized his ability to speak the language, and happy that he was atypically humble, for an American.

"And so, what see here this room is more jewelry for woman, but have more for man in back room and silverware, china, statues, chalices like this one here and figures from Ancient Berber tribes passed down for many family and some ceramic and clay works and glowe rugs the special rugs that be knotted, embroidered and woven pattern. They quite nice - some cheap, some not so cheap but I can make you good price."

After a quick look toward the back of the shop, Clinton asked his name. Salem replied " Noir Salem".

Comfortable with his identity he said "Thanks man, but I think I may have something for you instead." Clinton looked around the room to see if anyone else was listening or had entered unnoticed. Salem watched him carefully, followed his lead and also looked for an intruder into their conversation. Clinton, seeing no one, continued.

"I have a hooked Berber knife, a solid silver musket, five silver powder boxes and some Berber jewelry which date back to the early 1800s to sell."

Salem went to the front door, closed and locked it, still holding the chalice in his hand and putting silver polish all over the doorknob, before he wiped it off. He pulled down the shade which covered the glass door right after pulling down the "At Mosque" sign which was written in French, Arabic and English so it would be visible to patrons. Then he beckoned Clinton to follow him into the back room, which he did. The older man put down his work and wiped the silver cleaner from his hands as he curiously watched the tall black man meander around the back room of the shop looking in the cases.

Noir Salem cast his eagle eyes upon the delicate antique gun, powder cases, knife and exquisite jewelry for defects and damage, with wrinkled, weather beaten hands. Clinton watched carefully. Salem tried to read Clinton's actions. He knew full well whose possessions they were having made some of the purchases for Wainwright himself. Clinton stood back and watched as the old man muttered to himself in a combination of Arabic and French. Clinton spoke only when asked questions, never letting on that he understood bits and pieces of the sentence in which Salem called Wainwright a fool for paying so much for a particular powder case in the first place.

The older man finished his query about other fences Clinton had worked for and an examination of all the artifacts. Confident he would be unable to secure more information from the American, he told Clinton he would check out his references and see him the next day at the same time. Clinton collected his loot, placed it in the bag and left.

As soon as Clinton was gone, Salem picked up the telephone and told the listener that the tall American just might possess the skills they needed. He also informed the listener that he would return the following day to check on the possible sale of the items. He listened for a moment before hanging up the telephone.

Clinton took the car and the artifacts back to the hotel and dropped them off. He decided to walk through the streets to take in the atmosphere. It was Africa, but different . The Moslem influence and Arab flavor saturated every sound, smell and sight. It was marked with the customs of passionate wars, unshakable religious beliefs, sensual dances and hidden desires. There was a timelessness that made Clinton feel like a child. The place seemed all knowing in contrast to his blind naiveté.

On the way back to the Medina, he awed at the fields of sheep, alongside the course of cars and foot traffic right in the heart of the city. It was amazing to see and difficult to comprehend why they would be kept so close to the road. A tourist ride camel decided that it did not want its picture taken with a tourist seated on its back. Generally camels were very gentle and cooperative, however this one was running across the field with a frightened Swedish woman screaming on its back and the frantic trainer trying to regain control. It clearly was not happy. After watching a moment, Clinton headed for the inner city square.

Place Djemaa El-Fna was filled with life. It was called the "Place of the Dead" because it was the Sultan's location for the execution of criminals. The purpose seemed in great contrast to all of the hustling, bustling, color and movement of present times. He stopped to watch the dentist seated at the edge of the square with a table full of bloody rooted teeth in front of him, and wondered about the purpose of the display. He moved on to watch the beautiful, male, black as coal Gnawa dancers from Sudan in their brightly colored blue, and white costumes with tassels swinging around in circles on their heads as they moved to the music. They were splendidly tall, straight with even, brilliant white teeth and performed a dance that put him in mind of a Russian dance. When they moved, swinging the tassels around and around, Clinton was reminded of the brothers and sisters back in the United States dancing in nightclubs, at festivals and in church. Everywhere he went in Marrakech, he saw familiar mannerisms. He wandered around watching the people and the many variations of shows, tipping every once in a while, but discretely so that he would not be accosted by a horde of quiet but relentless children, as he had seen many tourists suffer. He looked at clothes, people and smelled and tasted the wondrous food well into the evening before returning to the hotel.

The entire day helped to relax his mind and put him more at ease. When he arrived back at the hotel late that night, he stopped in the bar and got a bottle of wine, a rarity for him, before going to his room to retire. There was no need for dinner as he had spent the better part of the day eating fruit, dates, and pastry while at the Place Djemaa El Fna. He considered the beauty of the people in Morocco and his spirit became temporarily lighter. He sipped a glass of wine, looked down at the busy streets below, and listened to the sounds of the night.

He sat on the balcony watching the stars until he fell asleep, his dreams a mixture of Ann Taylor and Grace, his fantasies of Ann being more prominent as the night went on. He dreamt of her at home, preparing dinner for him - Archie, and he could even imagine her soft spoken, calm and even voice talking to him through the evening meal, and he could even feel the touch of her skin against his and the light rose smell of her hair as he dreamt of sleeping in bed with her. His fantasy limited itself to things he could handle in real life, therefore he never drifted into visions of sex with her. He was working up to speed, and moving his psyche into the deep cover of which he was once master.

◊

The next morning, at eleven o'clock, Clinton walked into Noir Salem's shop with the same black bag. From across the street, Saa'iqa's two men, Yakub and Aamil quietly watched him enter the store . Clinton and Salem concluded their business. Clinton was paid liberally for the artifacts, and left the store. Salem walked to the edge of the street and signaled to the two men, indicating that Clinton was the person they sought.

They waited until he drove off, then followed him back to the hotel. He parked and went up to his room. Yakub asked the desk clerk who he was. Without much hesitation, she gave him the name, Archie Dayton. The two men left.

That night, Clinton drove down a secluded, palm tree lined, side street of the Palmeries subdivision, one of the wealthiest in Marrakech, extinguished the headlights and coasted to a stop. He turned off the ignition, waited for a few minutes to be certain he had not been noticed then got out of the car. He walked about three blocks down a sparsely populated street before turning a corner and walking the remaining block to the single, gigantic mansion on the street. Unlike Joseph Wainwright's urban mansion, this magnificent villa had a large gate at the end of a stone driveway. Clinton used an electronic decoding device to break the lock on the massive gate. When it opened, he quietly entered the isolated grounds unnoticed, or so he thought.

The dark blue Mercedes rolled slowly, silently and without illumination, down the street until it reached the corner next to the house. From inside, Saa'iqa and Naseer watched the gate close behind Clinton. They waited for a while in silent anticipation of Clinton's return but saw no sign of him for at least thirty minutes - far too long for a professional. In that amount of time he should have either been long finished or thoroughly caught.

Concerned about his actions or lack thereof, the assassin and her protector left the Mercedes and moved stealthily around the outer perimeter of the house in search of Clinton. Saa'iqa maneuvered around the rear of the house in the dark and Naseer circled the front until they met in the shadows near the gate. Neither of them was able to find Clinton and therefore returned to the car confused.

As soon as they were seated they began to analyze the situation.

"Was there no sign of him anywhere?"

"No."

"Naseer, I cannot imagine that he is still inside that house. Drive around to . . ."

Her words were cut short by a long sharp knife extended from the back seat of the car. Clinton placed the blade of the knife against Naseer's jugular vein while grabbing a handful of his hair in one swift movement. Saa'iqa turned to look at the assailant but was quickly stopped by Clinton's cold and chilling voice. She recognized the voice of danger, and perhaps a killer as well as she knew her own. It was calm and low as he spoke to her.

"Do not turn around woman."

She turned to face the front once again, but maintained an angle which allowed her to see Naseer, the man's hand and the knife. She considered her options but waited patiently to better ascertain the situation.

Clinton watched her intensely before speaking. She was more visually memorable and smaller than he would have thought a woman in her line of work would dare be, but then again obscurity, and physical strength were probably not her strong points. He pulled the knife closer into the big man's throat before speaking.

"Obviously you people are not the authorities or you would have taken other action. I saw this car following me earlier today . . . and badly so, I must say. The two men in it checked the desk to see who I was. Not your brightest recruits I hope. Now I want to know who you are and what you want."

Saa'iqa had considered the fact that Yakub and Aamil often exercised the common sense of a door mat, but she really thought she could trust them with such a small job, a tiny, little task. On the other hand, maybe they did her a favor by flushing him out in a more casual manner than the formal introduction she had planned. In their present situation, she could see more of his personality and character. The sheer size of Naseer, even seated, would make most men fainthearted. This one had nerve if nothing else.

"You want to speak a little faster?" Clinton said. He tightened his grip on Naseer's head in slow deliberate movements and raised the knife from his jugular to the fleshy portion beneath his chin. Very slightly he cut into the skin with only enough force to draw blood. Naseer neither moved nor made a sound.

Saa'iqa on the other hand, turned her head to look forward out of the window. She struggled hard to conceal the smile which was taking over her face. There was something quite invigorating about a man who successfully executed intimidation in a foreign land, upon people with unfamiliar customs.

She knew that Naseer could probably disarm this Archie Dayton before he was seriously hurt, but then again, maybe not. She noticed that he allowed the lower edge of the knife to remain close to the vein while using the tip to incise the chin. Quite a knowledgeable act . Usually thieves were not killers but the hard streets of the U.S. may have produced a combination of both. Her sources informed her that Archie Dayton was a Philadelphia street kid. No telling what his origins really were. No telling how he happened upon a life of crime.

"I am Saa'iqa Mastoora, and this is Naseer Aajiz. We have been hired to do a very complex job for which we need a good second story man. We were informed that your work is of the highest caliber. After some checking into your past, I found that you were released from prison recently and are obviously branching out into international waters. I would like to discuss your employment with us Mr. Dayton. That is your name, correct?'

Clinton withdrew the point of the knife slightly, but only enough to stop the active draw of blood.

"My employment is of no concern to you. I have no interest in your venture and much prefer working alone, thank you. Now give me your left hand."

Saa'iqa held her left hand out over the middle console of the car. Clinton threw a double set of handcuffs into her lap without losing his vantage point over Naseer. Saa'iqa slowly picked up the cuffs.

"Pick up the handcuffs with your left hand only and secure one end to the hand hold on your door." Saa'iqa complied, and listened closely to Clinton's breathing. He was calm, controlled and steady.

"Now take the other end that's connected to the second pair and put one cuff on his left wrist and the other on your left, slowly."

Clinton could feel that she was examining every choice he made. He moved the knife only enough for Naseer to participate in their confinement, but he tightened the grip on his hair.

Once the cuffs were on both of them he told Saa'iqa to pull against the connecting chains so that he could be certain of their security. She did as she was told. Keeping the knife in place, Clinton used his left hand to open the rear car door.

"Now I'm going to leave. The keys to the cuffs will be on top of the car . . . I know you'll figure out how to get them. Good luck with your work, and stay very far out of my life please."

In one fluid motion, Clinton exited the automobile and closed the door with a small click . The muffled sound of keys being placed on the roof of the car was heard in the next few seconds, and then there was silence. No foot steps, no car starting, nothing. Saa'iqa looked in the side mirror for him, to no avail. Naseer looked in his side mirror but saw nothing. They listened for a moment before either one spoke. There was a tiny smile on her face.

"Saa'iqa, I truly dislike this man with great vehemence. Please reconsider. A skilled Marrakechii would be so much easier to handle. This one appears to be far too independent for our needs."

She reached into her purse with great difficulty considering their position, and pulled out a handkerchief for Naseer's bloody chin. She gave it to him and he wiped away the blood with his free hand. The same hand he thought would have knocked Archie Dayton out had Saa'iqa not been so intent on examining him.

"Naseer, we need a foreigner. Someone who would have no loyalty to Muntasir Zaid. We cannot take a chance that a Marrakechii might turn on us and inform. Zaid has many eyes in Morocco, and more ears in this city than you or I."

"All right, I understand your reasoning and of course this is true, but there are others. Although I feel that I could find a Moroccan, maybe from Casablanca, I still think that the person we use should have some understanding of our customs and besides, there is one other very important factor. This man seems to have no interest whatsoever."

"I have ways to persuade him, and besides, I like this one."

Naseer cleared his throat and tried not to look at Saa'iqa, especially with the twinge of annoyance he knew must be evident in his eyes. She was in another world, and therefore did not notice his reaction . . . a range of comfort she seldom experienced, and that was reserved only for him. She was rarely relaxed enough not to read the people around her, on a constant basis. Only with Naseer because he always watched her back.

"Tomorrow, Naseer, I want to check into Mr. Dayton a bit closer before pursuing him further. Now, please find a way to free us."

14 A SLOW BOIL

Saa'iqa looked out over the flower and fountain filled yard of her beautiful home, the same home she grew up in. She tried to concentrate on the paperwork on her desk - the same desk that Will Creech had looked through only weeks before in his search for jewels and valuables. He had no way of knowing that the most precious items in the room were the clear and distinct memories of a loving father and devoted mother. She often spent time as a child drawing pictures as she was perched on the floor, her father cutting real estate deals on the telephone only a few feet away. At times, her mother would bring lunch or NAA-NAA and pastries.

Saa'iqa watched his face carefully during those times as he looked at her mother. It seemed as if her every word sustained his very existence. The love they had for each other amazed and enthralled Saa'iqa, and made her feel even more loved not only by each of them individually , but also by the parent unit they seemed to be. She forced her mind to drift back to the work at hand lest it drift to some of the uglier days that followed.

Naseer, who was seated across the desk, continued to hold, while waiting for a telephone connection to the United States.

"Naseer, what did your contact at Interpol say about Archie Dayton's capture? If he was not intelligent enough to stay free, maybe he is not the right one for this job."

"He said the only way they caught Dayton was with an elaborate sting operation that required a great deal of manpower and many months of preparation."

"If he was only a local criminal, why did Interpol have any information on him at all?"

"Seems he burglarized the home of one of their undercover agents, and broke into a safe which held some semi-sensitive documents. He either didn't know what they were, or did not care, because he left them. They watched him carefully for several months, but did not make an issue of the theft since it was not to their advantage to do . . ."

"Is this Jessica Lash?" Naseer asked, then gave the telephone to Saa'iqa.

Jessica Lash was a beautiful, dark chocolate brown woman with a short natural haircut, a diamond stud in her nose and three in each ear, and gigantic doe-like dark brown eyes. She was medium height, about five feet six inches tall, thin with a small frame, a large, round behind, a low waist and long, big legs. She was the daughter of a wealthy New York commercial real estate attorney and a father who was an importer and exporter of specialty goods.

Her office was in the back of a large gallery with glass across the front of the building and across the length of her office. The office furniture - desk, sidebar and end tables were glass with massive ivory tusks for legs, gold trimmed bands around the base of the feet of the desk and on the ivory knobs of the drawers of an accompanying white wooden file cabinet on the opposite side of the room. The couch was white raw silk with gold piping around the edge of the pillows, and fine gold threads woven into the fabric. There was a white and bronze simulated leopard rug underneath her desk and a bronze leather, high backed chair in which she sat, and two low backed, matching chairs across her desk for guests. A sleek gold shaded floor lamp atop a long ivory tusk sat in one corner, and three matching ivory tusked based lamps with gold shades sat on her desk and the two tables at either end of the couch.

"Hello Jessica . . . this is Saa' iqa. Do you have a minute? I need some information please."

Saa'iqa picked up the photograph that the FBI and Interpol had been circulating as Archie Dayton, which in fact was Clinton's picture. She played with the edges of the picture as she listened to her old school chum on the telephone.

"In your line of work, have you come across a professional by the name of Archie Dayton?"

Jessica answered from her New York gallery, "Yes Saa, I know Archie."

" Good, describe him for me. Recently, I've been asked to do some business with him, and want to know more about him."

As Jessica sat in her Fifth Avenue Gallery, surrounded by the work of some of the greatest visual artists, quilt makers and sculptors of modern times like Valerie Maynard, Elizabeth Catlett, Jacob Lawrence, Charles White, Charles Bibbs and William Tolliver as well as Donald Locke, Chevelle Makeba Moore, Wadsworth Jarrell, Carolyn Mazloomi and Michael Cummings, Jessica thought back to the time when she and Saa'iqa attended Le' Chateau Campagne together, a private French high school for girls.

Saa'iqa had been one of the most striking girls she or anyone else at the school had ever seen. She had also been a loner and deadly quiet. Once a foolish classmate, Jacqline Duviér, became angry because the boy she was interested in, Jean LeBeau', who attended a nearby school, fell madly in love with Saa'iqa, though she had little interest in him. He was tall and scrawny with a long, goose neck with a pronounced Adam's apple, black hair, hazel eyes and knocked knees, but Jacqline loved him immensely. For two consecutive years during spring, he would sneak away from his schoolwork and watch Saa'iqa through the southern side of the classroom building that overlooked the rolling countryside, behind foliage that hid him from the view of the mathematics teachers who generally taught in that room. Saa'iqa minded her own business, intent on a good education.

Jacqline determined that Saa'iqa was responsible for the boy's advances, and that she had to find a way to eliminate her from the equation. In her childish, lack of wisdom, she devised a plot to get Saa'iqa and the boy in trouble, assuming that this would dissuade him from his fantasies, and that Saa'iqa would take an active role in discouraging him, as opposed to her continued indifference of the prior two years. Jacqline decided to write two torrid, steamy letters - one from the boy and one from Saa'iqa, which she allowed to fall into the hands of the schoolmaster. According to her twisted thought patterns, once they got into trouble, Saa'iqa would beg for mercy in an attempt not to be expelled, would do everything to keep the boy away, and would be humiliated sufficiently enough for Jacqline to feel avenged for her wounded heart.

Part of the equation was correct. The boy was discouraged and afraid of further trouble, however Saa'iqa never responded to the schoolmaster's false allegations except to say that she did not write the letter and had never seen his letter to her before. Saa'iqa was suspended, and remanded in her room for two whole days. On the sixth day, early one morning a package arrived for Jacqline.

The entire dormitory awoke to Jacqline's hysterical screams as her shrill pleas for help filled the building, and perhaps the entire hillside of the normally quiet village. The dormitory mother raced into Jacqline's room to find the teenager dancing in fear on top of her bed, as a dozen multicolored snakes and vipers slithered around the room with some moving toward the open door and the girls in the dormitory who went to check out the commotion. Nearly every girl on the floor was standing at that doorway, at least until they saw the snakes headed their way.

As she sat on the phone, Jessica remembered that as she passed Saa'iqa's room that day, she could see her inside seated at her desk reading- while all hell was breaking loose around. The memory was especially strong since Jacqline died from the bites of three of the snakes.

After Jacqline's death, Naseer, who was in his early twenties at the time, drove to the school and moved into a nearby apartment. Each day, he would sit outside the school in the family estate owned black Mercedes, and watch the building. He was concerned for both her physical and spiritual safety. Saa'iqa would go out during her breaks and talk to him. When asked by the schoolmaster why he was there, he told them that since the school had experienced such a dangerous incident with the young girl and the snakes, as Saa'iqa's protector, it was his duty to remain close to her to prevent her from harm. The school was uneasy about it, but did not interfere considering her family situation. They never found out how the poisonous snakes appeared in Jacqline's room, and after the incident, they appreciated any extra security they could get.

From that time on, Jessica always locked her room door and windows , even when she was in class. About four months later, Saa'iqa was seated beside Jessica during lunch. They were talking about their French class for which Saa'iqa was tutoring Jessica. From nowhere, completely out of context with the conversation, Saa'iqa spoke to Jessica in a very matter of fact tone.

"Jessica you have nothing to fear and no reason to lock your door unless you are intent on causing problems" Saa'iqa smiled pleasantly.

Jessica noted that she appeared to be pleased that only this lone American seemed to suspect what actually happened, and Saa'iqa's responsibility in Jacqline's death. Before the stunned girl could figure out the correct response to the statement, Saa'iqa moved the discussion on to the next French lesson as if nothing important had been said. That night and subsequent nights, Jessica left her doors unlocked because she was more afraid of appearing afraid of and offending Saa'iqa further, than she was before the conversation. At least up until that point she felt she was hidden in a cloak of false security. With the veil off, she knew that all she could do was take her chances that Saa'iqa would not take an interest in destroying her as long as she appeared calm. The remainder of the year before their graduation was uneventful, but it was with these memories that Jessica considered the phone call she was engaged in with Saa'iqa.

"Jessica? Are you still there?"

"Oh yes Saa, I'm sorry, my secretary brought in an invoice that was incorrect. Forgive me for being distracted. Archie Dayton, right? You want a description?"

"Jessica, you are still easily distracted. I know you're busy, but it won't take long."

"It's just me, not you. O.K.. Archie. Well, he is a black man, about six one or two, a medium brown color sort of like Ethiopians, but more red than yellow. Not nearly as much brown as me, nor as dark. He wears a beard and sunglasses most of the time. In fact, I'm not sure I have ever seen him without either. Good looking, nice body, in good shape. There is something kind of dangerous about him, and distant."

"Dangerous? How?"

"I don't know how to describe him, but aside from his obvious line of work, you kind of feel like you ought to cross your legs, or hide your underwear and run or something."

"Uh huhm."

"I think his most recognizable feature is the disarming quality he has with women. I'm not sure how to describe it . . . you know what I mean?"

"Yes . . . I think I do. Well thanks Jessica, you have helped a lot."

"Well I hope so, he seems like a nice enough guy . . . stoned sexy . . worth consideration, O.K.?"

"It's business, just business. Thanks Jess. I'll keep in touch."

"O.K., take care of yourself and keep those lingerie drawers closed."

Saa'iqa smiled and hung up the phone.

◊

Jessica sat at her desk for a moment, the receiver dangling from her hand as she contemplated the enormity of her actions. Just as the telephone began making that obnoxious repeated, half-freight whistle and half siren noise that indicates that the phone is off the hook, a man reached across the desk and took the receiver from her. He replaced it on the base of the telephone. As she looked up from the desk, with tears filling her eyes, she could not shake the terror she felt even while looking into the serene, calm face of Gerald Bethany, a face that usually calmed fears.

"Jessica, you did good. It will be alright."

"Gerald, you have no real idea what you are talking about."

Another agent came from a back room, carrying a set of flowered suitcases. He stopped beside the desk where Jessica and Gerald were talking.

"O.K. boss, the secretary and the packing guy have been released and paid for the next month, the rent and utilities have been paid, and the security system paid. We are ready to take Ms. Lash."

"Take Ms. Lash where exactly? Where do you think Ms. Lash can go, huh? Just tell me, huh?" Jessica answered, although unsolicited.

The agent seemed somewhat confused, and looked to Gerald for assistance.

Gerald said " Take her things to the car and wait." The agent complied, grateful not be have to continue dialog with the distraught woman.

"Jessica, exactly what did they feed you little girls at that nice French school to make you turn out so crooked?"

With a half smile on her face, Jessica looked deep into Gerald's eyes in a way that made him know that she depended on him.

"First I have to put my life in jeopardy by deceiving my friend, then I have to suffer your insults too?! You and that damned Creech have made my life miserable for years. How in the hell did you find out that I knew her anyway? I thought he left town or found a new occupation. Why in the hell is he back . . . and for that matter, why are you back annoying me?"

"Jessica, please calm down, cease the bitching and come on so that we can get you to a safe house until this is over." Gerald rose to help her leave.

"Over? Safe house?!? What a joke? Saa'iqa hates two things. Betrayal and weakness, both of which I have just exhibited. You think this will be over for me?"

She paced around the room slightly, olive colored pants suit molded to her body and her long legs ending in four inch heels. "Gerald, I had forgotten how her voice sounded, but that call reminded me of the cool edge that she has. I should have taken my chances in prison for possession of stolen goods. How in the hell did I let you talk me into this when I know better. How?! When will this ever be over for me if it doesn't go like you think it will?"

"Jessica . . .everything will be just fine."

Gerald was at a loss for further words which might comfort Jessica. He knew her hysteria could only come from one who knew well the basis for her fears. He contemplated the incidents in her past that had so thoroughly convinced Jessica of what his research had told him of Saa'iqa Mastoora. He knew Jessica was playing both sides against the middle as much as possible, and would not reveal everything she knew about Saa'iqa to him. He wondered if there was more reason for her fear than what he had uncovered, as if what he knew was not enough to strike terror into the heart of even the most lionhearted. All he could really do was help her lock up and take her to the most secure place he could think of, a remote beach house on a secluded island off the coast of North Carolina where he had successfully stored witnesses for federal cases before.

It had been his call not to leave an employee at the Gallery, for fear Saa'iqa might need information from them should something go wrong. Jessica had agreed with this, despite the loss of business for the month and had settled for the FBI reimbursement, although everyone knew it was insufficient for her ritzy clientele and the above the table and under the table sales she would probably lose.

Just as they were leaving the gallery, she turned and looked up at him with a mixture of contempt, fear and longing on her face. She moved closer to him, put her arms around his waist, rested her head on his chest and took a deep breath. She was really afraid and he knew it. He had not suspected that his ultimatum for her to help or feel the heat of the bureau would cause her quite so much pain, and did not like the position he was in at that moment. He pulled her closer to him and gently rubbed the back of her neck, across her shoulder and upper back, and took in the softness of her hair against his neck and chin and the light scent of perfume that wafted up into his nostrils as he held her silently.

Before Clinton became his partner at the bureau, Gerald, like many whites, had never spent much time around black people. He had gone to predominantly white elementary and high schools in his home in Des Moines, Iowa, and although he went to the University of Wisconsin where he had somewhat more contact with blacks, he was never really close to anyone. He did not play any sports and the only black person he had regular contact with was an arrogant young teammate on this debate team who chose to argue about everything and deem political conspiracy as the basis for nearly all events in America, a view that Gerald had been reconsidering in recent years. During college, Gerald did not like him well enough to develop or even want to pursue a relationship with Boice.

After his failed marriage to his wife of two years, Roberta, a midwesterner as well, he went through a phase where he only wanted to date women who were not like him in any way. Roberta had bored him to tears with her thoroughly conventional thoughts and pastel, flowered shirts with little bow ties, khaki dockers and penny loafers. It seemed to him that she droned on about nothing all the time. Investments, planning for kids - a thought which frightened him tremendously when he considered such a permanent attachment to her - and paying off bills were exciting conversations for her. She was too familiar, stable and regular - qualities he thought he needed and wanted at the beginning of their relationship, but the same traits that ultimately made him get up in the middle of the night after yet another session of boring sex and move into a hotel. He never returned really except to pick up his clothes when she was not at home. He gave her everything, willingly, just to be free. She didn't even seem to hate him appropriately but he supposed that would require more passion and fire than she could muster.

The women he dated over the next three years seemed to be cut from a template that said "anybody who is not remotely like Roberta." He dated Asians, Hispanics from the entire Spanish Diaspora, Africans, southerners, African American, German and Malaysian women and had more fun than he had in his entire life before. It was during that time period that he and Clinton began watching Jessica's activities. Clinton seemed unaffected by Jessica, probably because he was so in love with Grace, but although Gerald never even told Clinton, he was taken by her the moment he saw her. It was then that he also realized that Clinton really did not know him as well as he thought because he should have known the conflict that being around Jessica caused for Gerald.

There was something about the gentleness in her huge, childlike eyes that made his heart skip a beat then and still on the day he was transporting her away from all that was familiar and comfortable to her. He sometimes had trouble concentrating around her, but was very careful not to show it. He fought hard when he first met her not to arrange unnecessary meetings or pop harassment surprise encounters just to see her, that probably would have tainted his investigation. When he was around her, he felt wild and crazed inside. Had she not been a suspected criminal, he certainly would have pursued her but her high maintenance needs and apparent lack of concern as to how those needs would be cared for always kept him at bay. Being so close to her, when he could feel the softness of her skin and the muscle tightness in her shoulders caused by fear was stressful, and he struggled to keep his heart rate steady. Her head lay against his chest and he hoped she would not notice his attempts to control his breathing, and the pounding in his heart. He prayed that her fear of Saa'iqa would distract her.

He couldn't really pinpoint the emotions he had for her. Certainly there was lust, but there seemed to be more genuine concern than physical need. He was prone to fixing things for and about people, but with her, he only wanted to safeguard and protect her just as she was - minus the criminal activity that would force him to stay away from her. He was amazed that his feelings had remained as strong over the years he had known her without the nurturing that emotions generally required for sustenance and growth. Even though he was in a stable relationship with a German woman who had moved to Washington to work at the embassy, he still had a twinge of reaction for Jessica. Not one he would ever act on, and probably not one she was aware of, but nonetheless it was there.

They remained in that position for a few seconds before Jessica pulled away, stood straight and picked up one of her bags to leave. She turned and looked into the steady face with the steel blue eyes. He returned her gaze with as much confidence and assurance as he could output, fueled by the years of being an agent and experience of executing the task of building trust with his informants, despite whatever contradictory gut feelings he might have. It worked and she seemed reassured.

"Gerald, I hope you're right."

"I'm right. Come on."

◊

With the identity of Archie Dayton no longer at issue, Naseer went about the business of making their work go smoothly. As he sat in the blue Mercedes, parked on a busy street near Bahia Palace, he considered the changes in the mission since their original plan. He thought about the American Will Creech, and the necessity of his disposal. For some reason this job did not feel like most to him.

He considered his dislike for Americans and tried to find its origin. He could not remember any particular incident that had occurred, it was simply a general annoyance he had with most Europeans . . . although Americans from the United States or from Montreal for that matter, seemed to be collectively more arrogant.

He did remember a visiting businessman from Texas who came to do business with Master Mastoora about thirty years before. He was a big man with a loud, obnoxious voice, the table manners of an orphaned goat and the social graces of a wild boar. Naseer disliked him in a general fashion, not particularly for any direct actions.

Dashing, dressed in a black djellabah, Naseer stood at the edge of a crowd enthralled with one of the snake charmers in the square. He watched Thamar Ali through the window of Restaurant Relais Al Baraka, next to the offices of the Commissariat de Police in the far northwest corner of Djemaa El-Fna and tried to rid himself of the general annoyance he felt for anything European. Even the expensive European suit that Thamar wore as he quietly ate his lunch seemed to grate on Naseer's nerves at that moment because Moroccans who had become as Europeanized as Thamar were cause for aggravation to him.

After a few moments, Thamar pushed his chair back from the table and disappeared from Naseer's view for a moment before reappearing at the entrance of the restaurant. He walked out into the square, looked both ways - but not in Naseer's direction, before walking down the street to his car and driving off.

Naseer strolled casually past a crowd of young boys who were talking to some tourists as they determined if they could get money out of them and went into the same restaurant. Since no disguise could really conceal the huge man's identity, the work he completed in public was seldom of a very sensitive nature. They were usually lightweight tasks, that were better executed with the distraction created by his size. People seldom remembered Naseer's activities. They always had a vivid memory of his appearance however.

He went directly to the same table where Thamar had been seated, waited for the waiter to clear the table and ordered lunch. Discretely, right after the waiter left to place the order, Naseer reached under the table and retrieved the key that Thamar had left tape to its underside for him, and slipped it into his pocket.

◊

Later that day, after his exquisite lunch, Naseer drove to the airport, and parked and went inside to the few public lockers found in the building. Using the key that Thamar had left for him, he opened number 364, and removed the large bound folder before closing the locker and going home. An easy day's work for the big man. He knew he should enjoy it, for it was likely to be the last one for a while. With that in mind, he went to the garden, sat in the lounge chair, and read a book on the life of the poet Aimee' Cesaire, until he was awakened by the Saa'iqa's soft hand against the side of his face. He smiled as he looked up into her face, held her hand in his and kissed it.

"How did everything go? Did Thamar Ali deliver?

"Yes, just as he promised. Everything was in order."

"Good. Very good. Are you hungry?"

"Not hardly. I ate a glorious meal at the restaurant. I hadn't been there in a while so it was quite pleasant."

"Well I'm a little hungry. I think I will swim a few laps, then see what cook has put together for dinner."

"Sounds good."

"You don't need me for anything do you?"

He smiled at the thought. Everything in his life had depended on her for so long, his emotional, physical, financial and mental well-being were all wrapped up in her existence. He held her hand in his and pressed it to his lips again, absorbing all her essence through the pores, osmotically into his bloodstream and straight to his heart - the immobile collection of Saa'iqa that lay heavily in his soul and yet floated throughout his being with the weight of a feather.

"No, I'm fine. I'll just finish reading my book."

"O.K.."

She bent over and kissed him gently on the forehead and rubbed the moisture from his hairline before parting. He let go of her hand and watched her walk away, the feather in his soul floating around and tickling his throat inside.

◊

The next day, Saa'iqa and Naseer sat in the Mercedes, in front of the Marrakech Train Station. Naseer was in traditional dress, but Saa'iqa wore a short, low cut red dress, clearly not made for tradition, at least not an Arabic one.

"Did you put the rest of the papers Thamar Ali forged for us in the safe?"

"Correct, along with the journal. What if you cannot convince this Archie Dayton person to work with us?"

"I feel certain I can, but if not, Jean Lelong will be available for the last two jobs, and you and I will have to perform the first two. I'm sure we can handle them if we must. They are the least difficult of the set."

"Shall I pick you up?"

"No. I will use public transportation. If it goes badly, I will need the cover."

Saa'iqa got out of the car, carrying a purse and a large flowered bag, and entered the train station. Once inside, she went to the lady's rest room and fiddled with the hem of her skirt while she waited for the area to clear of people. She then took a deep purple djellabah and head scarf out of the bag and quickly put them on. Then she attached a purple veil over the lower part of her face, inserted two brown contact lenses in her eyes, and turned the flowered bag inside out to the black side, just as another woman was entering the area. Without ever making eye contact, Saa'iqa quickly left the rest room in her new disguise, walked through the terminal, out of the front door and caught a taxi.

◊

As she rode in the back of the taxi, she contemplated the events at hand and wondered if there were signs that she was missing in this unusual scenario. She had never pursued an employee in this manner before because her method of securing talent was fairly standard. She sent for them, watched them and then brought them into the fold. It was somewhat exhilarating to operate with less surety as was the case with Archie Dayton. Quite exciting indeed, and she needed some excitement these days. She kept her face down, careful not to allow the cab driver to see her in full. After a few moments, he stopped trying, afraid that he might be offending the shy woman in his back seat. Saa'iqa appreciated the way Morocco's customs aided her work so completely.

15 FLAMES

Clinton walked down the hallway of the beautiful hotel, soaking up the grandeur of one of Morocco's finest abodes. The people who passed him on the way to his room were from many different countries and customs, but the one thing they had in common was money. Clinton wondered whether or not Archie would have chosen this hotel had he actually been the one to come. Probably not, but then again, Ann Taylor most certainly would have, he thought as he reached his room door.

Just as he was about to place the key in the door, Clinton saw a faint light, glimmering through the crack underneath. He stopped cold and listened carefully. Although he could not hear anything, he smelled the slight odor of candle wax and a light, expensive perfume as it drifted ever so lightly up to his nostrils. He knew it was expensive because it was not overpowering and had no chemical smell to it. He suspected it was Saa'iqa inside, and contemplated his options first before he inserted the key and unlocked the door.

Once inside, barely visible in the candlelight, he saw her seated on the couch in a short, red, low cut dress with small pearl buttons down the front. The nine candles around the room put out far less light than Clinton would have imagined, but seemed to have a special scent that did not compete with her perfume and was both exotic and intoxicating at once. Saa'iqa sat with her long legs on the couch, completely comfortable with her surroundings, despite the fact that she was uninvited. On a white linen covered room service table on the opposite side of the room was an array of food including caviar, olives, oranges, assorted French hors deurves and canapés, champagne, mineral water, bread, fruit and cheese. The champagne had beads of water on it, assuring Clinton that she and it had been there a while. He wondered if she had bribed the waiter to let her in, or the maid, or if she just killed one of them for the key.

Cautious and clearly wary of the situation, Clinton looked behind the door before fully entering and closing it. Saa'iqa was silent as she watched. Clinton turned on the overhead light and walked toward the bathroom door, never taking his eyes off of one of the most beautiful women he had ever seen in life. She squinted slightly, her blue green eyes reducing to slits as she tried to adjust to the light, while she sipped her champagne.

As he entered the bathroom, he turned to look at her as well as the rest of the bedroom, just in case they were not alone. She watched him watching her, neither one speaking. He looked behind the door and inside the shower but found no person lurking in the shadows. As he re-entered the main room, he spoke.

"Where is that gigantic man who accompanied you on our last encounter? Didn't he want to come to this party?"

Saa'iqa just smiled and sipped her champagne while Clinton looked underneath the bed, careful not to turn his back on her.

"If he had come, I seriously doubt that he could fit under that small bed, don't you?"

Satisfied that the bed harbored no secret attacker, Clinton stood up. "Well you do have a point, however one of those other two guys who can't trail somebody worth shit might be able to fit under there." Clinton looked inside the closet.

"Archie, I am alone. I thought I would try a little different approach toward securing your services."

Comfortable that the suite was free of intruders, Clinton took off his black leather jacket and hung it in the closet. Saa'iqa poured a glass of champagne for him. "Good, relax a while." She carried the drink over to where he stood by the closet door. The closer she got to him, the more lightheaded he became but he dismissed the feeling as ridiculous in the beginning.

He stared at her for a moment, and then at the glass, but did not move to take it from her. She smiled, understanding his hesitation, then sipped from the glass intended for him. He watched her for a moment, so she took another sip.

"If you make me taste much more of it, I'll just get drunk and you won't have enough left to enjoy."

He took the glass from her, but eyed her suspiciously. She smiled slightly, returned to the table and placed caviar on a few crackers. He followed her to the table, partly to be more hospitable, partly to watch her

145

actions and partly because it seemed like the thing to do. Once she finished, she held one of the crackers close to his lips. He did not move to eat it, so she took a bite herself then held it to his lips once again. He watched her for a moment, until she swallowed, then allowed her to feed him in the erotic manner she was doing so with her body too close to his for the action to be considered just cordial, but far enough away for any man, including him, to want her to move in even closer.

There was something about her that reminded him of Grace. No other woman he had ever met other than her blood relative Justine, had ever really reminded him of Grace. He could not put his finger on the root of the familiarity. Something in her mannerisms that he was able to catch only in glimpses, that sent him to a place in his heart that felt like home. Not just familiar like someone he had seen before and was seeing again, but like the place where his soul lived and his weaknesses were accepted. He had only felt that way in Grace's presence and to a lesser extent with Justine. It was as if Saa'iqa was shooting massive doses of the feeling, straight inside his body. He felt as if he was standing next to and absorbing the electrical charge of the woman who had endured twenty-two hours of labor pain in order to bring his child into the world, and had allowed him the room to feel as if he had been a major part of the experience. He understood Saa'iqa's talent better. She was a chameleon, like him, internally able to become whatever you needed, but unlike him, able to do so without background information.

He was barely touching her, her breasts gently brushed against his stomach every once in a while as she raised a cracker to his mouth, but he could feel the heat generated between them that was caused by his being in her energy field. It was mesmerizing, immediate and lethal. He could not imagine the origin of her effect, but he could not deny its presence. He was clearheaded enough to know that it was completely her own like an outbreak of dengue in the Everglades, and that she was not some reincarnation of Grace, but he felt drawn to her spiritually and yet wanton, simultaneously.

He tried to step back and away from her, but couldn't move for some reason. Luckily, she turned away from him to walk back across toward the couch. He could feel her energy field snap away from him like a rubber band recoiling to itself after having been stretched. He steadied himself so that he wouldn't bend into the recoil. He thought about her and wondered if she was into some ancient, ritualistic witchcraft. He struggled to stay calm, but he was afraid of her and he generally was afraid of nothing, and worse, he had no real idea why.

"Mr. Dayton, why are you so suspicious of me?" she said as she sauntered across the room.

"Let's say I'm a bit leery of people who follow me in the night."

He was still reeling from her contact, but dug deep within in order to fortify his own energy force so that she would not be able to consume him again. He decided that as in any good fight, staying on the offense was always better than being on the defense.

Saa'iqa sat on the couch, and so Clinton sat extremely close to her, with his arm behind her head and his face close to her ear. She was still a small woman, and he a fairly big man so he used the size difference to gain leverage over her energy pull. He needed to intimidate her physically somehow, though he felt no real issues of safety were presently in question. She felt his warm breath rustle the hair around her temples and crossed her legs in response, an unusual reaction for her.

"Mr. Dayton, you have no reason to fear me. My motives are just as I have told you."

"Uh, huh", he replied.

He reached across her, placing his champagne glass on the end table next to her, rubbing his arm across her breasts as he retracted it, causing her nipples to immediately stand erect. She took a deep breath. He smiled as he unified with her energy instead of being indiscriminately snatched in by it or opposing it.

"I didn't say I feared you. I am suspect of your actions. You may still be armed." He nuzzled and sniffed her ear, then breathed out a slow guttural breath as he moved to her jawbone, his lips close to her face. She was calm and did not flinch.

"Feel free to search me if that is your concern Mr. Dayton."

"Is that an invitation?" he asked.

"We have business to discuss Mr. Dayton, whatever facilitates that must be done."

"I see", he said.

Clinton moved away from her but only enough to have free movement and stared deeply into Saa'iqa's eyes, the glasslike aquamarine crystals cutting into his soul. Without breaking eye contact, he slid his hand from the nape of her neck, down her back as he moved it thoroughly from one side to the other, through her clothing. She tried to sit up slightly but he gently pressed her back with the palm of his hand on her chest, just below her neck, indicating that she should not help him. She took another swig of her champagne.

With both hands, he removed the huge silver embossed comb from her hair, causing the colossal bun of thick, not completely straight hair to cascade down her chest, over her shoulders and down her sides. Clinton found a small release button hidden in the decoration of the comb. He pressed it and the blunt comb sheathing came off to reveal six razor sharp blades hiding beneath the harmless looking hair ornament. Saa'iqa sipped her champagne calmly. Clinton sat back a little and looked at her with little expression on his face.

"Well yes . . . I believe this looks like the hair comb of someone I should trust completely, wouldn't you say so?"

Without breaking her composure, Saa'iqa put a bite of cracker in her mouth and chewed before replying. "It is a very dangerous world out there for a woman in my line of work, you know. I have to protect myself."

He looked at her calm demeanor and had genuine respect for her, covered and placed the comb on the table and resumed his search. He ran his hands thoroughly through her hair, fascinated by the texture and feel of it - sort of like course yarn, in thin strands - a blending of African and French cultures. The bed of waves and curls could have easily hidden and concealed an arsenal.

Finished, he brought the hand closest to the table around the front and down her chest slowly, until he reached the top button of her dress. Her breath wavered for a beat, but neither of them broke eye contact. Slowly, he unbuttoned the first, and then the second button then skillfully slid his hand inside and underneath her left breast, allowing the tip of his small finger to lay in the crevice under her breast while the rest of his hand cupped the smooth bottom half and his thumb gently brushed across her nipple as he moved toward her underarm and the soft down of hair there.

Only her breathing changed to a deeper, slower intake of air.

He moved back to the center of her chest and examined her other side in the same manner. Saa'iqa sipped her champagne slowly, their eyes always meeting and their faces about six inches apart. He spoke to her in a deep, raspy voice that made her insides shiver, although she would not show it.

"Hum . . . Women have far more interesting places to hide things than men do. I don't know when I have found a search so pleasant."

She sipped her champagne as he removed his hand from inside her dress and in one fluid movement, kneeled in front of her, with both knees on the floor. His action made her eyebrow raise, only. He smiled in a slick sort of way as he gently uncrossed her legs and spread them wide enough for him to move his body between her knees. Then he leaned into her, forcing her legs wider apart and gently raised her arms to rest on each side of her on the back of the couch, careful not to make her spill her drink. In a slow deliberate movement, he placed both hands under each of her armpits and began rubbing gently, back and forth as he worked his way down both of her sides, past her narrow waist and hips and thighs to her knees, and the end of her dress.

"And so Saa'iqa Mastoora, how much does this job pay?"

He rose and sat back on the couch beside her in his original spot, sipped some champagne, propped his elbow up on the back of the couch, and rested his head in his hand. She crossed her legs and sipped. He lay his free hand on her hard, flat stomach and began moving in a crosswise motion from under her breasts to her knees.

"Seven hundred and fifty thousand for four separate jobs."

Clinton unfastened the two lowest buttons on her dress and gently pressed his open palm between her thighs until she uncrossed her legs again. "You may as well keep your legs open for me baby" he said with barely a smile and began to move his hand back and forth from one side of her thigh to the other, beginning at her knees, slowly working his way up toward her hips and deeper beneath the red fabric, her right thigh first. Satisfied that there were no thigh weapons, he moved gently toward her crotch, brushing his hand lightly across and watching her facial expression change as he did. He lingered there a little longer than was necessary but could not resist once he saw her eyes close, the champagne glass tipping toward the floor, and this magnificent woman let go . . . albeit ever so slightly. He spoke to her in a soft, low voice.

"Saa'iqa, put the glass on the table baby."

Without ever removing his other hand from his head or his elbow from the propped position, he gradually withdrew the roaming hand from under her dress, pressing into the skin on her thigh with thus far, uncharacteristic pressure. She opened her eyes and placed the glass on the table.

"Your search was extremely thorough."

"In a strange country with a woman who wears knives for adornment and has a sidekick who looks like a giant genie, I don't think I can be too careful, do you?

"Well did you enjoy the quest for weapons?"

"I don't recall saying that it was over yet."

He sat straight on the couch again, lifted both of her legs and placed them in his lap.

"I didn't know I had anything else left to search."

"There's always more on a woman . . . you just have to know where to look."

"And does this take a lot of practice Mr. Dayton?"

He smiled as he removed one of her shoes. "I suppose it's like everything else. Skill does not always come from repetition. Some of it is inherent. I spent quite a bit of time in jail. Your fantasies of women get more efficient as the days go by. You might be surprised at the places I can find."

He flashed that slick smile that she found somewhat disconcerting, then pulled the foot pad from inside the shoe and searched underneath it. "And exactly what do I have to do for this money?"

Finding nothing inside, he careful attempted to pull up the sole and turn or pull off the heel.

"You need only do what you do best."

"I do a couple of things fairly well."

Having found nothing in the first shoe, Clinton threw it into the bathroom. Saa'iqa watched her expensive Parisian imports fly through the air and hoped the heel would not break so that if she had to kill this man, she would not look like a fool as she walked down the street, drawing attention to the strange manner of walking that comes with a broken heel, or her bare feet if that became too absurd. It never occurred to her to bring another pair of shoes. She would have to remember to do so in the future, especially if she dealt with U.S. Americans. She continued watching curiously.

"You only need to do the thing that involves tall buildings and hanging from ropes."

Clinton searched the second shoe in the same manner.

"My two most proficient skills involve hanging from rafters."

The shoe search complete, he threw it into the bathroom causing Saa'iqa to cringe when she heard the awkward thud as it hit the wall. Clinton reached across her and picked up a glass of champagne, sipped from it, then held it to her lips for her to sip. As she did, he ran the tip of his tongue along the length of her eyebrow and stopped, keeping his face close to hers. He took the glass away from her lips.

"Archie Dayton . . . I think that I am the one who should be cautious here."

They could see the evening sun set through the window as the call for Adan, evening prayer, could be heard in some distant square near the heart of town. The warm colors of the orange and purple sky enhanced the mood that was building between them and the cat and mouse game that the lion and mongoose were playing within the hotel walls. Clinton thought of the contrasts between the predominantly Muslim city and others he had been in throughout Africa since he left D.C. years before. Somehow, the people were less straightforward and held more hidden information than more southern countries on the continent, or at least it seemed that way to him. It may have been because of the dueling colonialism of the French and Spanish for Moroccan land that the original people had endured and the amount of subterfuge under which they operated in order to survive that made them seem less direct. Possibly it was just the culture.

He watched the twinkling on the champagne glass as he placed it next to Saa'iqa's lips again, and considered the history she carried in the fullness of her lips. As she sipped once again, he considered that many years of anger, hatred, love and dependence had occurred between the people of her father and the people of her mother. Many battles, and dependence, hatred, need and joy darted through the lessons learned by school children from both cultures, both in Morocco and in France. As he looked at her long, wavy, course hair, her thin nose, full lips, startling blue-green eyes, straight black eyebrows and honey colored skin, he understood somehow, the confusion she must have experienced as a child when faced with the mixed messages that bombarded her and others like her when they were young. As he lowered the glass, the light cast a reflection of the rim that bounced across her velvet smooth skin casting a vision that made him shudder inside ever so slightly.

He placed the glass back on the delicate lace of the end table. He took both of her hands in his and carefully examined the manicured nails, painted in clear polish and the thin, soft fingers that lay lightly in his hands. He removed all of her rings, two on each hand. For the first time he noticed a slight shift in her seating position and wondered if she was nervous about something. He tried not to look up, not wanting to make eye contact with her, as it would become a certain distraction.

◊

She tried not to show the alarm inside as he removed her rings and held them in his hands. Two of them were harmless, but the other two were not nearly as benign. One had been constructed by a friend of hers whose hobby was duplicating ancient Japanese weaponry, and had four tiny, razor sharp, slashing daggers that could be exposed, but only through her touch on the appropriate button, which was triggered by the chemical elements of her skin, activated by her body composition. It was designed for close combat and especially useful for putting out an eye or raking quickly across a jugular vein. The other ring, a Khatem adorned with stones, was activated in the same manner, but contained a needle that she kept full of Curare, the same anesthetic she used to kill Will. She had three different styles of this ancient Berber ring as she had grown fond of this method of execution over the years.

A comb with daggers in it was one thing. She could pass it off for self protection, albeit unusual, but a ring with daggers was a bit different and an emerald one filled with poison was altogether something else. She hoped that his probing and touching her body had not left enough of her essence for his fingers to simulate her touch. She did not want this minor issue to stop negotiations. Time for the completion of the project was running out and although she had no feelings one way or the other about killing him, she certainly did not need another delay. He was disarming for her somehow, and she hoped a confrontation was not about to occur.

◊

He looked at all of the rings, but the one with the sapphires circling a giant emerald drew his attention for some reason. He pressed all of the small sapphires systematically and then turned his sites toward the giant emerald and pressed and probed the top, bottom and sides of the ring, but to no avail. Ultimately he was unable to obtain a reaction from it, so he gathered all the rings together in one hand, and was about to place them on the table when she spoke.

"You're not going to fling them across the room also are you?"

He smiled as he leaned across her, brushing his face against hers as he placed the jewelry on the table. "I never harm beauty."

He returned to his normal sitting position and gently lifted her right foot up to his lap and began rubbing it with the skill of an expert reflexologist. She relaxed after a few moments and he placed that foot on the floor and massaged her left foot before placing it gently on the floor also, leaving her in slight expectation. He then rose, walked to the opposite side of the room and removed his pullover sweater, folded it neatly and placed it on the dresser.

"Tell me what I am supposed to steal, and how many other people are involved."

With his back turned to her, she quickly grabbed the poison Khatem and put it back on her finger, turning the decorative weapon side inside her palm. "This is not information you need to know. For the protection of all the professionals on this job, your interaction with each other will be minimal. Your only contact will be with Naseer and me, and one other man later. As is, you know much too much for a man who is not certain he will take the job."

"Alright . . . that's fair. Are there any other second story professionals? Is that the position of the other man I will be working with later?"

"No . . .you are the only one."

She rose from the couch and walked over to Clinton. Standing very close to him, she unbuttoned the top button of his shirt with one hand, while keeping the other hand with the ring on it behind his neck.

"How long will the work take?"

"Only a few weeks . . . yours is the last position to fill."

"So your entire operation is waiting for me? Why haven't you hired someone before now?"

"We did, but he fell ill. You ask too may questions. What is your decision Archie?"

She began unbuttoning the second button on his shirt. He steeled himself, struggling against her electricity.

"Any other requirements or benefits I should know about?" he asked in a slightly lowered voice.

"A couple. You must cease all of your private career activities, which would never have been allowed had we hired you before your arrival in Marrakech. We watched you and hope that you are always as careful as you were the night we followed you. Were there any other jobs here in the city that we don't know about?"

"No, that was my first."

"Good. I want no unnecessary attention brought upon our cause."

"Cause? Now look, I have no interest in any political crap. I'm just a crook, trying to make a living. That's all."

"No, it is not political and the dangers are no more than your normal risks, considering your occupation. However . . . the benefits may be far greater than you can imagine."

She unbuttoned the third button on his shirt and caressed the hair on his chest as she pulled his face down toward hers and they kissed long, slow and passionately, the ring positioned squarely at the base of his neck. The kiss broke slowly and she asked if he had made a decision about working for her.

He experienced an array of emotions that ranged from confusion about Will and whether or not he was the person who "fell ill" as she called it, to weak knees from the intimate contact with her. He knew he would get better as he continued to have contact with her, and he hoped his reactions occurred because he had not been very close to women a lot in recent years. He struggled to stay in control but knew he couldn't take much more of the fondling, even though he was fully aware that there might be malice lurking in her heart. He felt as if he was in a pre-copulation dance with a black widow, and was foolish enough to think he would be the one male spider to live after sex. He contented himself with the fact that as long as she needed him, he might be safe.

Clinton laced his fingers through her hair so that he had a secure handful of the mane held gently at the back of her head, but strong enough to be certain of her inability to get away. She noticed the gesture but remained calm. He pulled her very close to his body. Close enough to feel the hardness of her thighs as they pressed into his legs, and close enough for her to feel the growing hardness of his penis. He kissed her while calmly removing her hand from behind his neck, bringing it down between them, holding her hand in his - the ring between his forefinger and thumb. He slowly removed his lips from hers, licking the indentation of her full lips that rested directly below her nose ever so slightly and quickly with the tip of his tongue.

"And what do you have for me if I refuse?"

◊

He slid the ring from her finger and closed it in his palm. She looked into Clinton's strong face and watched his jaw muscles tense and release beneath the beard. She was amazed and ecstatic. She was generally quite bored with the men she had to work with, and was pleased that this man would not be dull.

As she watched his cool expression and his narrowed but unafraid eyes, she wondered what it would all mean by the end of their relationship. She wondered if it was possible for her to have a real relationship with such a man, one that could continue past the job. She wondered if he could accept her for who she really was, and if she could ever let him know that much about her.

She suddenly felt afraid because it was apparent that he wanted her sexually, she could feel him pressing against her hip, but he was still very much in control and very careful not to allow her to hurt him. She had immediate respect for him and even more contempt for the fools she had killed over the years who were governed by their sex drive. She suddenly felt that whoever he was in his past and in the present was absolutely perfect with her. She had never felt so accepting of another person other than Naseer, and the thought nearly brought her to tears of joy and anger at the same time because acceptance of a man she had just met was certainly not in her program. She wondered if she should kill him simply for having the audacity to invade her psychological space, lest he reach her heart. She tensed slightly, then smiled and stared into his eyes for a moment before answering.

"And will you refuse?"

He felt her tense up, but could not read the reason behind it. She seemed to be struggling with something, but he didn't know her well enough to hazard a guess. Without releasing Saa'iqa, he reached behind him, opened the top dresser drawer and dropped the ring into it. With both of his hands, one on each of her arms, he placed her arms around his neck, then slowly slid his hands up the back of her dress, one on each thigh and up to her buttocks then lifted her up so that her legs straddled his waist. She moved into the position easily and he could feel the strength of her muscular thighs as her small body clung to his waist, with ease.

"The pay and benefits sound attractive. I'm in."

She chuckled softly as he kissed her neck and chest, then ran his tongue across the indentation of her collarbone and up the underside of her neck until he reached her mouth. They kissed passionately, deliberately and slowly as he carried her into the bedroom.

16 BUSINESS

The morning seemed slightly more crisp, and clear, and wonderful, she thought as she walked briskly down the street. It was pleasant to wear regular clothes - a long dress and flat, sensible shoes. She tired of the disguises sometimes, including the vamp outfits although they were the most fun, and the endless array of contact lenses in nearly every color of the rainbow. Good sex always made the next day brighter.

She wondered if men felt the same way. She remembered reading an article in an American medical journal that said that men had a physiological need for sex every seventy-two hours. The reason had something to do with their need to release sperm and the inherent, uncontrollable desire to make more - pro-creation and all . It seemed to make sense to her and fit well into the pattern that Naseer seemed to have of going out and staying late about every fourth night. In a way she pitied men for being such slaves to nature and a physical system that appeared to run their thought processes, although it probably made her work a lot easier. She had never had an intimate relationship long enough to judge the accuracy of this theory for herself. The men in her life only came in snatches, and seldom lasted for more than a month, at least not in a way that was close enough for her to watch any habitual behavior. She liked it that way.

Although her sexual needs were far less often, there was nothing worse than a bad lover and nothing better than a good one. She always had a couple of lovers in her life that she could go to if she wanted, that she might only see once every six or eight weeks or so, but they usually started talking marriage after six months and she would drop them. They only knew her as a real estate investor and her father's daughter. The two flavors for the current six month period had been fairly adequate lovers - one Moroccan and one French, but they were nothing to write home about - so unimpressive in fact, that she had not bothered to see either one of them for the past two months.

However Archie Dayton had been extraordinary, although a bit anxious - the first time. He most certainly made up for it the rest of the night though, had slowed down, moved deliberately and was most adept at a lot of different things - far more interesting than her usual fare. Black men seemed to have a rhythm to their lovemaking that reached into her soul and held on. Moroccan men had it somewhat, but black Americans from the United States and South America seemed to be most noticeable. She loved to work in Brazil, almost as much as in Paris or Canada where so many Black American men fled in order to avoid serving in the Viet Nam War. There was music to their fluid movements, and if they knew what they were doing, she could feel the music throughout every muscle and every bone until she felt the shivering deep down to her toes and fingers and sounds of ancient rhythms pounding inside her uncontrollably. Archie knew what he was doing, and it felt like he had not made love for years, and missed it terribly. She guessed it was the jail sentence that made him that way.

The shops were busy and full of morning business people and shoppers. The sounds of cars, horns, animals in the square and an approaching train busied her mind as she made her way toward the train station. Although her clothing was usual fare, wearing the auburn colored wig was much more than a notion considering how much hair she had to conceal beneath it. The contacts for the day were dark gray. Her disguises were sometimes cumbersome, but seldom boring.

She checked her watch as she crossed the street and headed toward the train station. A large train could be heard as it pulled away from the station. The 9:15 had been running since she was a young child and her father used to take her to the station to watch during the happy times of their life. She sat on a bench out front and listened as the train left earshot as she remembered the stares they would get when he, her mother and she would come to the station together. People were not as open at the time, and a French wife drew some attention. Although most people were polite, she could feel the contempt of a woman standing on the side, sheltering her children as if Saa'iqa's interracial genes would rub off on them or a man who sucked his teeth and stared her father down when he realized that he was married to her mother. She could feel the disdain of thirty years before as if it had happened the day before. The thoughts once brought her a mixture of pain and joy, but in the brightness of the morning and in the afterglow of great sex, the pleasant memories were most prominent in her mind. Immediately after the sound of the wheels began to die down, the pay telephone closest to her seat rang. She answered.

"Hello . . . Yes, how are you? . . . Yes, he has agreed to the jobs . . . I checked him with FBI and Interpol records, as well as a personal friend who knows him through their mutual work . . . Yes . . . Archibald Dayton . . . Of course if you would feel better if you did so. When will you be in town? . . . Yes that will be one week prior to the most important task he will do for us . . . I can meet you wherever you wish . . . Alright.

She hung up the telephone and walked down the street, admiring the beautiful sun, the hustle and bustle all around her, the people and their varied, interchanged languages spoken from conversation to conversation as she passed them by, and the glow of life of her homeland as seen through the eyes of the camouflaged person she had grown to become. She was at peace, at least as much as any killer could be. She had the eternal devotion of Naseer, there was the possibility of great sex for the next few weeks, her politics were in order, she was rich and beautiful, and men were in their place with her. They neither ran her nor did she need them uncontrollably as so many women she had known. All was right in her world.

◊

Later that day, on the other side of town, Clinton, in his best Archie Dayton black attire and disguise, cautiously picked the lock and entered the home of Saleem Asad through the back door - his first assignment from Saa'iqa. He carried a small bag with him, and wore surgical gloves. The house was modestly, but elegantly decorated with sparse traditional Moroccan furnishings, Arab rugs, tortoise shell artifacts, brass vases and trays and highly polished wooden figurines.

As he moved down the hallway, the most noticeable thing to him was the smell of the house. Spices, exotic and foreign. He could make out cumin and coriander, maybe curry but there were other scents which were indistinguishable to him. Sort of sweet smelling but earthy at the same time like raisins, prunes or currants. He wondered what the residents had for dinner the night before as he turned into the bedroom where Saleem and his wife had slept together every night for the prior twenty-four years.

Clinton contemplated the dangers of his situation and how thoroughly such an action went against his basic nature. He went across the room to the chest next to the window and began searching through the drawers, grateful that he had not been asked to execute the task while they were at home. He had secured documents while in the FBI, but there were no real people involved, they were usually obtained from a felon's office possessions and they were mostly available through some other source. However, stealing from regular, everyday people was a very different matter. He wondered how anyone could do it for a living. The heightened tension from executing a task which was morally wrong to him was almost too much to bear. He had felt a little of it while doing the initial thefts to attract Saa'iqa, but those were controlled, safe situations which allowed him to think only of the mechanics of stealing. He never considered the exhilaration and fear that came with the emotional difference inherent in the task of random theft in an open environment that might include discovery, danger, alarm, retaliation, surprise and reaction on the part of the victim. The array of possibilities must have fed Will's need for adventure.

His search of the first chest was futile so he turned to a smaller chest on the opposite side of the window. As soon as he opened the red velvet lined top drawer, he found a brown leather journal, removed it from the drawer and glanced at the pages filled with Arabic writing. He exchanged it with an identical one he took from his bag, carefully closed the drawer and left the house.

◊

The next morning Naseer rubbed Saa'iqa's shoulders as they discussed Clinton's performance in a mixture of Arabic and French, as many Moroccans tended to speak. As usual for morning, she wore backless, workout tights, in preparation for their early exercise. Their current job seemed to cause more anxiety in her than most, and she often woke with pulls in her upper torso. She sat at her desk as the hulking man stood over her and massaged the tension from her neck and back with the expertise of the well trained, personal assistant and valet that he was - as was his father, and his father's father before him - although they had both served men. As he spoke to her, it was difficult to tell whether or not his look of adoration was based in loyalty or lust. Whichever it was, he never stepped out of line, but clearly present was the question of which line Saa'iqa may have drawn for him over the years. At that moment, she was lost in the pleasure of his touch and he was enveloped in the joy of touching her.

"Is the journal in place Naseer?"

"Yes. Mr. Dayton performed with complete professionalism, and I blindfolded him and drove two extra hours both ways. It is lucky for us that Saleem Asad only records in his journal once a week."

"True. Are Yakub and Aamil certain of their duties? I question Yakub's thought processes at times."

"My cousin will perform well. Do not concern yourself. Saa'iqa . . . is it entirely necessary for Dayton to stay here at the house?"

She took satisfaction in his concern and had always marveled at what she suspected was his deepest affection for her. She would never hurt him intentionally, but her life was clearly her own. She not only wanted to watch Archie Dayton, but she wanted him close by for all the obvious reasons his presence sparked in her and that seemed to cause Naseer's jaws to tighten a bit when he said his name. He was exciting, different, sexy and she had no intention of not enjoying his company. Naseer would have to adjust.

"What better way to keep track of him?"

The vein on the left side of Naseer's neck seemed to stand out, despite the fact that his voice remained calm and smooth when he answered, "Of course you are right."

From the hallway, near the door on the other side of the office wall, Clinton listened quietly to their conversation. He stayed until their thoughts turned to personal matters about a foundation her father started and the disbursement of funds for sick children. He had listened past the point of safety and could only understand a little more than half of what was being said anyway, as his Moroccan Arabic was very weak. He did understand that he had done well in Naseer's eyes, that Saa'iqa wanted to watch him and something about two cars an hour. That part was real shaky. He also heard two names, Aamil and Yakub, but had no idea what they described or meant in the scheme of things.

Clinton went quietly up the winding staircase and into the guest room in which he stayed, since leaving the hotel three days before. It was very large, probably seven or eight hundred square feet, about the size of Will's bogus apartment back in D.C.. The huge cherry, four poster bed had a flowing navy blue canopy, navy blue and white Swiss dotted comforter and sheets with opposing background and dot colors, and gigantic floor pillows covered in traditional Moroccan fabric of gold, white, navy and burgundy . Huge, thick white throw rugs lay all around the room and the balcony door was covered by white sheers that danced and swayed to the music in the square as the call for Fajr, the morning prayer - and the faithful, could be heard over a loudspeaker.

He walked out on the balcony and marveled at the many houses around the city and the view of Hivernage which was filled with trees and foliage. He fully understood the seduction of the kind of power and money which enabled a person to live so lavishly, and wondered if those elements drove Saa'iqa. He breathed the fresh air of morning and hoped that all would be well.

◊

From a block away, Yakub and Aamil watched Saleem Asad's house carefully as the early morning sun brought more than a glorious day to the Asads. The two men were seated in a gray Peugeot, sipping mint tea when they saw Saleem and his fully covered and veiled wife come to the front door of their home. He spoke to her briefly before bidding her good day. Aamil talked into the walkie talkie he held in his hand.

"Saleem is leaving. Move quickly!"

Suddenly, a small, older Renault carrying two white Frenchmen , turned the corner at the opposite end of the street and sped toward Saleem, who was stepping from his beautifully flowered, small courtyard onto the street. The man on the passenger side of the Renault raised a machine gun just as Mrs. Asad closed the door after her entrance back into their home. Saleem stopped to adjust the strained latch on his over-stuffed briefcase when the assailant sprayed him with machine gun fire, striking him down to the ground. The car turned right past Yakub and

Aamil, in fast escape.

Mrs. Asad ran from the house screaming, crying and calling out to her dead husband who lay motionless on the ground, his body riddled with bullets as he gasped his last few breaths. He stared up into the crying eyes of his wife, and whispered for her to take off the veil , so that he could see her face. She removed the veil which covered all but her eyes, barely considering the social implications of such, but only the importance of her husband's last wish. She placed his hand on her face, her tears streaming down her cheek and his arm. He smiled faintly as she kissed the back of his hand, then gasped two long breaths and died, staring at the face he had awaken to every morning for nearly a quarter of a century.

She sat beside him, cradling his head in her lap and mumbled and cried out his name in grief, until her neighbors, most of whom were headed her way, ran from their homes to assist her. The papers from the briefcase lay scattered in the street, their importance of no significance at that moment in time. As a shocked community yelled, screamed, comforted a widow and called for the authorities, Yakub backed the Peugeot around the corner, into a perpendicular street and drove away, slowly and calmly in the direction opposite of the two assassins, toward the glorious morning sun, which brought disaster to the Asads.

◊

An hour later and less than eight blocks away, Muntasir Zaid, Saleem's partner of fourteen years approached the building which housed their office, one of the largest industrial farming businesses in the country. He noticed a lot of people, and what appeared to be news reporters hovering around the front door of the building. As he attempted to enter through a quieter doorway, a particularly zealous reporter from Liberation newspaper approached him, and suddenly all the others followed. Muntasir could not make out what they were all shouting at him, but in the midst of the madness, he heard the word "murder."

" What was that about a murder?"

"Your partner Saleem Asad was killed in an execution style murder early this morning."

"What? What are you talking about? What murder? There must be some mistake. I talked to him just last night around eleven!"

The reporter tried to read Muntasir's face, always suspect of powerful people and their possible complicity. He continued speaking, but also listened intently to the tone and heart of Zaid.

"I was certain you knew of this. It happened early this morning."

Muntasir's head was reeling. He simply could not believe what he was hearing about his dearest and oldest friend.

"I stopped early to see an elderly relative and did not listen to the radio. Where did it happen and was his family . . .?"

"In front of his home. No one else was hurt. It appears to have been a machine gun that killed him. Has he been receiving threats of any sort lately? Anything to explain this act?"

Muntasir stumbled backward slightly, searching for the wall of the building to lean against. the reporter grabbed him by his jacket sleeve and helped to steady the shocked man.

"Thank you. I am alright now. I just have to . . . get to my office I think."

"Of course, but before you go, could you tell me about any threats or enemies of late? Any reason for this tragedy?"

"We both have received telephone calls at the office telling us to cease the activities of the Pure Moroccan Business Cartel and our efforts to rid Marrakech of so many French and Spanish owned businesses. Saleem and I have worked very hard . . ." his voice trailed off as he shook his head and bowed it. After a couple of seconds, he looked up at the reporter, tears welling up in his eyes. "I must leave now and see to his family."

"I understand," said the reporter.

Muntasir turned to walk up the remaining steps and into the building. He could barely compose himself, and did not want to break down in front of all the watchful and wondering eyes outside of the office. The reporter bowed in respect for his loss, and ended his questions. The rest of the mob either wandered away or set up camp around the steps in hopes that Muntasir would want to talk again.

Muntasir opened the door and began walking toward the elevator. His heart was pounding and he felt as if the lump in his throat threatened to close his air passageway. He could not imagine what could have caused such apparent senseless violence, and worse, he wondered if it was truly a planned event. He thought of his friend, and though they did not always agree, he suffered greatly at the prospect of life without him. He boarded the lift, dreading the coming conversation with their staff and the duty bound act of seeing to Saleem's wife. He could only imagine the devastation she was experiencing at that moment. She was a strongly traditional Moslem wife and Saleem and their children were without a doubt, her entire life.

◊

At Saa'iqa's mansion, she and Naseer practiced judo and akido movements in the spacious exercise room in their basement with a lap pool originating from an indoor fountain positioned at the far end of the massive room which was mirrored on two sides, with ladders, weights, ropes and equipment against the third. They were dressed in black ghia, loose fitting pants, with no shirt for Naseer and backless tights on Saa'iqa. Although she was possibly a foot and a half shorter than Naseer, she held her own during the exercises, and skillfully avoided his aggressions, staying clear of his strength - moving in quickly and delivering quick, distinct, devastating blows before moving back from harm's way. As they worked, they discussed ways in which she could compensate for her lack of size in similar situations, and continued to work with the ease that comes with years of repetition.

Clinton entered the gym dressed in sweats, and watched the duo as they concluded their practice. He could not decide if they cut practice short for his benefit or not. If so, they did it without discussing it, and without any apparent signals to each other. He considered how many methods of communication that they shared, and that he needed to be aware of. He would try not to take this factor for granted, as he felt it would be dangerous for him to do so.

Naseer walked toward Clinton as Saa'iqa attempted to coax him into working out with Naseer. Clinton watched the walking set of rippling muscles, bulging biceps and protruding veins that approached him in the form of Naseer, and politely declined Saa'iqa's suggestion.

"Ah . . .no . . .I don't think so. I get the feeling that my man Naseer here still has a grudge about that little, bitty incident in the car on that first night. I think I'll just go on over here and work on the rope for a while since I will supposedly get the opportunity to do more than be a petty house thief eventually."

Saa'iqa laughed and continued walking toward the door, not a drop of sweat visible on her body. Only the slightest minute amount of moisture collected above her top lip. Clinton watched her lick it off with the tip of her tongue just as she reached him. He had an immediate sexual, emotional internal jolt of electricity rush through his body as if it remembered all to clearly the way she tasted when he attempted to lick nearly every part of her that he could find during their first night of sex. He struggled to stay non-expressive.

Naseer glared at Clinton as he rubbed sweat from underneath his neck. Clinton moved his attention to Naseer, sensing that it was probably not a good idea to become distracted in his presence. There was an undercurrent of dislike emanating from him toward Clinton and the feeling was that given an inkling of a chance, Naseer would just as soon be rid of Clinton, and possibly any man who took even the slightest bit of attention away from Saa'iqa that could be focused on him and their life together, however distorted it might be.

"I see your wisdom is increasing Dayton. You may do alright at any rate." Naseer said as he passed Clinton.

"Be patient Archie. I have another task for you tomorrow which is slightly more difficult." Saa'iqa added.

"Good. I mean I don't mind taking your money and all, but almost any kid on the streets of any major American city could have done what I've done so far."

"Patience Archie." Saa'iqa said as she stopped and sipped on a glass of water near the doorway of the gym, then pulled a lightweight sweatshirt over her head. Both Clinton and Naseer were aware of the smooth, even colored skin of her back being hidden from their eyes, as the tail of the shirt drifted down around her thighs.

"Do you speak a second language Archie?"

"No . . . do I need to?"

"It would help, but no it is not necessary."

She picked up her glass and walked out of the door, the words "be patient" flowing out of her as she turned the corner and disappeared from sight. Naseer and Clinton stared at the door momentarily before Naseer followed her and Clinton walked toward the rope. Neither man looked at the other, as if their eyes would betray their thoughts.

17 DRIFTING

The mist was so thick that it looked like cotton, swirling and sailing through the space surrounding his head and shoulders. The density made his figure hard to make out, but he looked so much like his father that she could hardly miss those straight, broad shoulders and his doelike eyes before the white cloud of condensation covered him, obstructing her view. She listened carefully, hoping she could distinguish his voice amidst the sounds of frogs calling and crickets chirping. She could hear the water parting softly as some small slithering creature moved its way into the cool, wet lagoon. She could not hear him call her name.

She waited patiently, just to get a glimpse of him, as she had every other night for weeks now. She hoped tonight would be different, and that she would be able to hear the words that she could see him saying when the fog allowed her a true look at his face - the same face she had washed dirt from for so many years, and winced about when his nose was broken while playing football in high school. She stared into the last spot where she had seen him, with determination not to miss him should he appear and with concentration so great that it gave her a headache. There was only fog and deafening silence.

All was extremely quiet for a few moments, so much so that it made her nervous. On this night she stood in her tennis shoes, a nightgown and bathrobe and hoped for a glimmer of him. She hated the feel of mud as her toes sank into the bank of the lagoon, so she remembered not to wear her bedroom shoes, however, for the life of her, she could not figure out why she had not put on some slacks and a shirt. She had been here enough times by now to know better. Just as she was about to look down to check her footing, she saw the back end of the boat drifting in and out of the fog, about thirty feet from her. Will was standing on the back, saying something to her, but she couldn't hear what it was.

She called out his name and reached her arms toward the boat, as far as possible, but her voice cracked and wheezed like static on a radio with a loose connection, playing during a rainstorm. Her mouth was asking him to come back, but the words only came out in assorted syllables, and letters. She yelled as loudly as possible, but the static was only more pronounced. She watched him drift further away from her. He had stopped trying to talk to her, understanding that he could not be heard at all. She watched him as he disappeared into the mist again, crickets singing, frogs calling and water lapping sounds all clear and audible as the boat left her sight.

From her warm bed in Washington, D.C., Bernice opened her eyes from the night's dream and tried to remember what was different about it. As she reached up to pull the fan cord on, she remembered that she could hear herself, although in broken, static type tones, but she could not hear Will at all. She wondered why she had a headache as she hoped the static meant progress and wished she could better understand the dreams.

18 DOUBT

The night was cool, aided by the soft showers that filled the late afternoon. Morocco could be unforgivingly hot or pleasantly cool all in the same day, and at times, freezing cold in the morning if the wind traveled off the Atlas range in just the right way. Many of the houses in the New City had their doors open on this particular evening, their residents hoping to enjoy the welcome breezes and the break from the week's heat.

Trying to be inconspicuous in the plush, well groomed neighborhood, the two agents watching Saa'iqa's house were quiet and careful not to draw attention to themselves or the parked van they were sitting inside. State of the art surveillance equipment filled the inner space of the somewhat beat up, older, blue, Fiat van. The agents, both men, appeared to be Moroccan, one with a full turban and no beard and the other with a full beard and no hat. Both men wore headsets over their ears, and listened intensely to the happenings inside of Saa'iqa's house.

Suddenly, the one with the beard snatched the headphones off and threw them down on the floor. "She found it again! I was just cut off. I don't know why I give a damn anyway. When we do hear her, all she does is order fucking groceries!!

The turbaned agent quietly removed the headphones from his ears, laid them on the console and folded his arms as he watched and listened to his frustrated partner's complaints.

"What in the absolute hell did I learn Arabic for anyway?! A damned Cuban speaking Arabic . . . what . . . so they could dress me up like a genie and put me in east hell to listen to some killer buy groceries for a year?!? I hope this Creech is still the hot shit they say he was so I can go home. I am more than sick of this!

There was silence for a couple of seconds before the turbaned agent yawned and stretched his arms and back. The Cuban agent cracked his knuckles, put his elbows on the console and rested his head in his hands in disgust before the other agent spoke again.

"Well . . . . look at it this way. You could be wearing body makeup every damned day."

He snatched the turban off of his head in an exaggerated and flamboyant manner, revealing a full head of bright red hair. "And you could have your head in a sauna."

The Cuban agent stared at the brilliant, carrot topped head of his partner, then laughed at his partner's contrasting painted, olive skin and red hair. "Good point," he said, "I could have freckles."

◊

Saa'iqa sat on the edge of her desk, holding a brown folder containing forged papers in her gloved hands. She removed a smaller, thinner folder from within and gave it to Clinton. Leaning against the door from across the room, Naseer watched the exchange carefully if not somewhat suspiciously. It was difficult to tell whether or not he suspected Clinton's intentions, or Saa'iqa's. Although aware of his pointed attention to the transaction, Saa'iqa did not acknowledge Naseer's concern.

"Archie, these papers are to be placed inside the safe. It is just a small office safe . . . easy work for you. Entry must be from the roof. Any questions?" she asked.

"Any time limit?"

"The guard makes his rounds every thirty-five minutes. I'd like for you to be in and out between that time. It should be simple for you considering your performance during our practice sessions. The office is on the second floor. Naseer will answer any other questions you might have during your ride over. I have an errand to run, and will see you both later."

Naseer considered what the errand might be, but knew better than to ask. He was not fond of being an escort to Archie and unaware of Saa'iqa's whereabouts all in the same day. It was a bit much to handle for one so accustomed to being in control. He watched her as she left the room and thought about how rare it was for her to omit telling him of her whereabouts and considered the implications. Clinton watched Naseer watching her and contemplated the extent of their relationship. Naseer sensed he was being scrutinized.

"Dayton, why don't we get started. I'll get dressed. Generally, a jacket and a tie are appropriate or a high buttoned collar with no tie."

"That would be easier to work in. Ties and ropes often don't mix."

"Suit yourself," Naseer replied.

He put on loose fitting black pants, a white silk shirt and an elegant black and white hounds tooth raw silk blazer, then went downstairs to wait for Naseer.

He poured himself a vodka and tonic and waited. First Saa'iqa came in dressed in the most benign, Moroccan housewife attire he had ever seen. Her contacts were dark brown, and her head and the lower part of her face was covered. She wore a long drab, olive colored dress with long sleeves. She barely spoke, only a couple of grunts and a nod and then went out of the back door of the house carrying only her purse.

A couple of minutes and two sips of his drink later, Naseer came down the steps wearing as European a look as hers was Moroccan. He wore all black linen - suit and shirt, as made sense with the enormity of his size and black shoes with no socks. His head was uncovered. He was actually quite dashing, and probably a ladies' man in his own right.

"Well Mr. Dayton . . . are you ready for a night out?"

"Whatever is cool with you man."

They left the house unwatched, as the two U.S. agents had followed Saa'iqa earlier - that is until they lost her at the museum. At any rate, they were not outside the house when Clinton and Naseer left the house in a light rain that was drizzling just enough to haze the windows but not enough to dampen their clothing. By the time they reached the entrance to the Old City, the rain had increased to a steady but light fall. Clinton was pleased because he knew that patrons would not be seated on the roof for dinner in the warm, wet Moroccan rain.

The two men drove to the Riad Diaffa in one of the oldest buildings in the Marrakech Medina and allowed the valet to park the car as they entered through the front door. The fully restored structure was one of the most breath-taking restaurants in the city with its sculpted, highly polished cedar ceilings, delicate zelliges covering the walls, embellished woodwork and navy flowered upholstered couches and chairs. There were silver water pitchers atop silver bowls on silver filigree stands for the ritual of hand washing, and six foot tall silver candelabras around the room. Soft artificial lighting blended with the flickering candlelight on each table and the flame of the giant, lit, mosaic, rust, gold and blue fireplace at the opposite end of the large side room in the restaurant. Crisp white tablecloths with blue and rust embroidered diamond shaped designs adorned each table and plush Berber rugs lay peacefully on the tile floor. White lace curtains held in place by golden, braided ropes hung unobtrusively beside archways leading to additional dining space on either side of the large main room.

As they walked toward a private table, there was a female Moroccan singer on a small stage area, along with a piano player. She was elegant, slightly heavier and taller than most of the women he had seen in Morocco, and although more heavily clothed than he might have expected of her counterparts in the states - in a black pants suit with a high collar shell, she seemed to be comfortable in the atmosphere. Her sound was exquisite as she sang a lilting Berber tune that made her voice soar high and light as air before falling deep and lower than seemed possible for such an angelic tone. The song and her delivery were amazingly beautiful and though Clinton could not understand about half of the lyrics, he was drawn to her and halted as he moved toward the table. The Maitre'd and Naseer waited patiently until he began moving again.

Once they reached their table, Naseer thanked the Maitre'd and spoke in Arabic to the two women who were waiting for them. Clinton, still a bit distracted by the singer, barely noticed that they had arrived at their destination.

"I really like that song."

"Saa'iqa said you would like this place. It has many Moroccan specialties, with a few universal dishes. She was pleased with its convenience."

Clinton turned and looked Naseer squarely in the eyes before replying. He though for a moment about the few opportunities he had to separate Naseer and Saa'iqa, their thoughts and actions. To try to pit one against the other in order to obtain information about Will would be useless he surmised, and rightly so. But to isolate Naseer's feelings and bait him by dwelling on any possible insecurities he might have about his place with Saa'iqa might work he hoped, if he could do it subtly on one hand and obviously on the other.

"It bothers you that she might know so much about me doesn't it?"

Naseer met his gaze with stone cold eyes as a small, sinister smile came over his face. "Another time and place Mr. Dayton. Let me introduce you to Ameera and Gauhar."

He turned and indicated that he was speaking of the two women seated in the isolated booth. Clinton was stunned by their beauty. Naseer introduced them in Arabic and then informed Clinton that Gauhar spoke a little bit of English. He then seated himself next to Ameera, as if staking claim.

"It is very nice to meet you ladies. Pronounce your name for me again please. Gu - hair?" he said.

"Gau-har," she answered, "It is Gau-har. The jewel."

"Oh yes Mam" he said in his best Archie Dayton imitation. "I'll bet you are precious."

They talked for a few moments before Clinton excused himself and asked Naseer to order for them. Naseer confirmed that he would and Clinton left the table, headed for the staircase and the upstairs rest room, pausing momentarily to listen to the singer. After a few lines, he proceeded up the stairs, entered the rest room and locked the door. He reached behind the door to find a tall, thin compartment concealed in the wall, then turned the small twist handle on the metal door of the hiding place and found a bag filled with supplies necessary for his job.

He removed the black sweater from the bag and put it on over his white shirt, hanging the jacket on a hanger inside the compartment. He then took a rope, with four pronged umbrella hooks attached out of the bag and draped it over one shoulder. He closed the door to the hiding place, then threw the bag over the other shoulder.

He unlocked the bathroom door and peeked out into the corridor to see if anyone was approaching. Pleased that he was alone, he closed the door quietly and left it unlocked, as a locked rest room door for ten or fifteen minutes might tend to draw attention. Quickly, he went to the window, climbed out of it and onto the back side of the roof, away from the empty terrace dining area.

Once hidden by the dark of night, he threw the hook up and anchored it to the roof of the three story building beside the restaurant. Convinced of its security, he climbed up and pulled himself on top of the roof, then wrapped the rope again and put it over his shoulder. He ran across two connected buildings until he reached a twelve foot gap of open space and ground below. Undaunted by the challenge, he reached into the bag and removed what appeared to be a Billy club, about eighteen inches long. He pressed a release button on the side of the club, and pulled out slightly rubbery extensions until the club transformed into a flexible pole of about ten feet.

With a running leap, he vaulted across the twelve foot expanse onto the next building, holding the pole high as he landed to assure it wouldn't drop and give away his position. Once steady, he pressed the release button and the pole snapped back into its original eighteen inch club. He returned it to the bag and proceeded to the rooftop door on the front, street side of the roof, and entered cautiously.

Wearing surgical gloves, Clinton opened the door from the stairwell and looked into the corridor in time to see the back of the night watchman turn the corner at the opposite end of the hall, and disappear. Carefully, he tipped down the hallway to the third office on the left and used the tool in his hand to unlock the door. Once inside, he took a stethoscope from the black bag and opened the safe. Quickly, he placed the folder with the papers Saa'iqa had given him into the safe, closed the door and returned to the restaurant without incident.

Dressed in his jacket again, Clinton returned to the table as another woman, a Moroccan belly dancer, danced in a white chiffon, sequined and silver beaded outfit. Her midriff swayed and gyrated to the sound of drums and a lute that two musicians were playing who accompanied her. The dance was sensual, but not crass like the exotic dancers and lap dances in the states. It appeared to have a spiritual connection of which Clinton did not know the history, but was becoming increasingly curious about.

He sat at the round table beside Guhar, and a feast of Variété Salades, a giant seven salad dish of lentils, lamb's brain, candied carrots, avocado, tomatoes, beans and vegetables. The head waiter brought over the water bowl and towel for Clinton to wash his hands as Naseer searched his face for an indication of the success of his work. Clinton was calm and confident as he nodded knowingly toward Naseer, assuring him of the success of his task, and asked what he ordered for dinner. Naseer smiled comfortably and replied that he ordered several local dishes that he felt he would like - Tajine d'agneau aus pruneaux - lamb with prunes, and Harira Marakechia, Pastilla aux Amandes et Pigeonnaux, - pastry with almonds and pigeons, Tajin de poulet au citron - chicken with lemons, and seven legume couscous. Clinton was beginning to acquire a real taste for Moroccan food and was quite pleased with the selection, confident that Naseer had not missed many meals and certainly knew how to order exceptional ones, as evidenced by his size.

◊

The next morning Clinton awoke just before sunrise feeling refreshed and rejuvenated. It had been good to hear music and get out, even if it was with Naseer. He rather wished that they had been out with Saa'iqa so that he could watch her and learn more about her. He doubted seriously that the two of them would ever spend much time in public together unless she was in disguise, although he barely understood why she had allowed Naseer to be seen with him either. It seemed illogical. As he considered their whole situation, he marveled at the audacity she displayed and reconsidered the amount of caution he originally thought she would use.

The police chief came by the house one evening to drop off collections from the policemen for a children's fund that Saa'iqa ran. Saa'iqa had introduced Clinton as the son of an old business acquaintance of her father who was visiting Africa for a few months. The police chief never questioned the tale, Saa'iqa or Clinton. It all seemed so bold to Clinton, as if she and Naseer were laughing at all of them, yet it didn't seem to be their state of mind. They were simply carrying out an agenda and they had covered themselves so well in the eyes of the community that there was no apprehension at all. Then it dawned on him that what better alibi could the big man have than to have been out with the visiting American in a public restaurant - and she, after all, had been heavily disguised when she left the house the night before. He shuddered to think what she might have been doing while they were out having dinner. She was a frightening and yet exhilarating woman he thought as he heard the call for Fajr from the loud speaker in the square.

Clinton opened the French entrance doors and stood on his balcony and looked out at the hazed sky and made a mental note of how mellow and easy the morning felt and smelled as scents of nuts and fruit baking in some pastry dish wafted through his window, to his nose. He never wanted to forget this experience. He doubted that he would ever have another like it in life. After listening to the call for prayer for a few moments, he dressed and prepared to make his prearranged contact.

When he left the house, all was quiet and calm. There were birds chirping in the garden, many of whom were not indigenous to the area, but had been flown in from South America, Austrailia, South Asia, India and other parts of Africa. It was an amazing feat that all the different birds in her collection were able to reside in harmony together considering their vastly different origins. She had two brilliant green long tailed Quetzals from Central America, a Toucan, two Great Birds of Paradise with their widely feathered tails and bright green chins, and Indian Red Hornbill, two Cocks of the Rock, a Macaw, an Emerald Cuckoo and a Golden-Fronted Leaf Bird from South Asia. They were Saa'iqa's passion, although she never seemed to want close contact with them, only to listen to their morning songs. Each morning, the maid uncovered their huge cages at 5:30, fifteen minutes before Saa'iqa awakened, so that the birds would wake and in turn wake their benefactor. She said that they gave her solace. He could not imagine how the woman he was beginning to know could have been guilty of all the dastardly deeds he had been informed of - and then at other times, when those strange bluegreen eyes fixed on his eyes and seemed to carry a deep seated hatred for all humankind, it became quite clear to him. On this particular morning, the birds had just begun singing as he closed the door to leave.

He walked briskly through the street until he reached the news stand, stopped and bought the New York Times. Then he walked three more blocks down a less busy side street to a lone telephone, picked up the receiver and dialed. Just as he did, he became aware that the blue Mercedes pulled into an inconspicuous parking space and stayed about two blocks away . Although it was difficult to see that far, Naseer's unmistakable size gave them away as he loomed large in the driver's seat of the car. Neither Naseer or Saa'iqa got out. Clinton pretended not to notice and proceeded to dial information in New York, and asked for Bergdorff's, not his original intention, but who knew what kind of devices

Saa'iqa carried at that moment.

From inside the car, they watched him carefully.

"Saa'iqa, he makes a call about every second day. I've not been able to get a handle on who he talks to, the length of time varies. I just don't like it. You think I should bring the electronic equipment and check him out?"

"Naseer, he is a very long way from home. He probably calls his woman and wants privacy. I will question him if you will feel better, but I wouldn't be that concerned if the length is varied. I would be if they were short . . . like a check-in."

"Maybe, but it doesn't feel right."

Saa'iqa rubbed the back of his hand gently, as only she could and said, "Do whatever you feel most comfortable with, but I think you are worrying too much."

The muscles in Naseer's neck relaxed considerably as Saa'iqa picked up his hand and massaged it momentarily before placing it back on the seat. They had watched Clinton for about fifteen minutes after all, so Naseer smiled at her, started the car, drove about fifty feet to the closest cross street and turned, driving out of Clinton's view.

Clinton finished his nonsensical conversation with some poor sales clerk about a fictitious suit that he claimed to have seen there and wanted shipped to him. The woman was near total exasperation in her attempts to help him identify the suit properly so that she could find one to fit him. No longer needing the cover, he set her free and hung up. Immediately, and cognizant of his tardiness, he called the appointed phone number and checked in, then walked to the park and read the newspaper.

As he sat down to read the paper, he wished he had a way to connect the dots on Saa'iqa's activities. She kept all her contacts so isolated and the activities of each operative separated so that it was difficult to get a picture of the whole operation. But after all, that probably was the point.

19 THE ICE WOMAN COMETH

As they drove toward the airport in the early morning light, at least one of them seemed fairly satisfied that Clinton's phone calls were reasonable and appropriate for his distance from home - and it wasn't Naseer. He drove in silence and thought about how different her behavior seemed with this job. She was too calm. The edge was not as sharp as usual and he could not figure out what was going on. He had never encountered this with her before. As he pulled up to the front door of the modest, older, small airport, he couldn't shake the wish to be rid of the job, the situation and most of all, Archie Dayton. He stopped the car for her to get out.

"Wouldn't it be easier to just kill Muntasir Zaid? I could do it, you wouldn't even have to bother. I don't relish a drive to Essaouira."

Saa'iqa laughed at his suggestion. He had to smile back at her, clear that he had been nearly whining - a first for him. This job was raising many new emotions. She took a small detonator from her flowered bag and held it in the palm of her hand before answering.

"Naseer, our client does not want him dead . . . that is much too simple, and non gratifying. I rather prefer this to his death myself, and only wish I had his father's throat to slit once again. Had I been as experienced as I am now, I'm sure I could have thought of more painful ways for him to die."

Naseer hung his head slightly, aware of the pain that any thought of Muntasir's father conjured for Saa'iqa. He wished he had not gone down any path that would have brought up such memories. Saa'iqa gave him the detonator. As he took it from her small hand, he could see that she was fighting back tears. Any mention of her father could reduce her to incredible emotion and it was the only thing that could. He certainly had not meant to take her to that kind of emotional state before such an important task. He tried to touch her hand, but could feel the tension in her muscles build just as she gently pulled away from him. He looked into her eyes again and the watery, dewy look was replaced with the familiar, cold stare of determination . . . and death. Somehow, this transformation was at least comfortable and therefore eased his worried mind a bit. Without another word, she got out of the car dressed in European clothing, a black pants suit and carrying the large flowered bag.

Even as a tiny woman, her stride demanded respect as she walked through the airport doors. The two agents in the blue van that they were fully aware had followed them, left their curbside spot and followed her to the building, careful not to get too close. Naseer pulled off, checking the rear view mirror closely. Once she was clear and just as they reached the door, he pressed a button on the detonator and a huge explosion occurred in a trash can a few feet inside. The two agents, along with three or four other people, were thrown back by flying debris and nearly stampeded by screaming people trying to exit the airport.

Inside the terminal, Saa'iqa coolly walked down the main terminal until she reached an unmarked door on the left side of the corridor. No agents in sight, and after checking to be certain she had not been followed, she went through the door and into the janitor's closet. There she put on a man's pair of pants and a black djellabah. Quickly she placed the brown contact lenses in her eyes and a pair of black, elevated men's shoes. As a final touch, she expertly secured a fake beard and mustache to her face and donned a black turban. She turned the flowered bag inside out, exposing only the black side and put all of her belongings into it before cautiously leaving the closet in the appearance of a man. She walked back down the corridor, toward an exit and out toward the parking lot.

Only a few feet away, Tasneem Faz, dressed in black, traditional clothing with every part of her body covered except for her eyes, which were covered in blue green contacts, walked up to the ticket counter and picked up a ticket for Saa'iqa Mastoora for her upcoming business trip to England - should anyone wonder what she was doing at the airport.

Meanwhile, Naseer parked the Mercedes in the parking lot, got out and locked the doors. He walked over to the next row of cars and opened the door of an older, white Peugeot and got in. From the front seat, he retrieved a white djellabah and a white turban and put them on. He started the car and headed toward the exit of the parking lot.

Back inside the airport, Saa'iqa walked past the commotion unnoticed as the two agents searched the area for any sign of the small woman with the long hair - not the taller man with the turban, and certainly not the woman in traditional clothing who was picking up Saa'iqa's ticket. She exited the airport and got into the white Peugeot with Naseer, who was waiting at the last entrance to the building from the parking lot. They paid their parking fee for the past three days rental, and left.

Just as they were leaving, Yakub drove the same gray Peugeot used during Saleem Asad's murder, into the airport parking lot and stopped behind the blue Mercedes. Aamil, who was in the passenger seat, got out of the Peugeot and into the Mercedes. He turned on the ignition, and both men, driving their respective cars, left the parking lot.

◊

The drive to Essaouria on such a beautiful morning, could only be extraordinary despite the fact that it was uneventful. They passed scores of school children on their way to a day's education and farmers working with their sheep and goats in the fields. Acres of olive trees lined each side of the two lane road and fields of Argan trees filled with goats, both young and adults, that had climbed to the top to eat the choicest of fruit amazed and baffled them as if they were tourists, despite the fact that they had seen this strange occurrence their entire lives. Mounds of hay lay in the fields and adobe looking huts often made of the homes of the farmers, with large casbahs spotted throughout the countryside. Occasionally, there was a potters store on the side of the rode with scores of pottery waiting for those with an eye for the subdued hues of turquoise, greens, reds and terra cotta.

As they drove the one hundred and seventy six kilometers on route number ten, Saa'iqa and Naseer talked pleasantly of mundane and simple things of life, like the plumbing needing fixing in the main level guest bathroom, and new tile for the garden walkway. They were practiced, efficient and thorough, so she was more relaxed than she had been for weeks, and he was grateful for the peace she seemed to have at that moment although he could seldom tell whether or not her moods were related to the task at hand or the sun shining hotly down from the Moroccan sky.

When conversation fell off, she read The Complete Kama Sutra by Alain Danielou. She had compared it to The Kama Sutra of Vatsyayana as translated by Sir Richard Burton and found it less Victorian and provincial. She considered the Kama Sutra to be one of the most fascinating and telling books in history. It was an absolutely informative guide into the way men viewed sex, women and in some ways, their place in the world. Despite the fact that it was Hindu in origin, the teachings seemed to echo the habits and thoughts of many cultures, at least from a male point of view. One of the most interesting aspects to her was the fact that even though it seldom described the process by which women arrive at the conclusions they reach accurately, the end result in behavior was usually on target.

It was also fascinating to her that the book described a less selfish male need for immediate satisfaction and gratification, greatly liberal sexual practices and men who displayed a deeper understanding of women in general even though some of the expectations were archaic - as well they would be for a book written in the fourth century B.C.. The specific instructions on oral sex, multiple sex partners and hermaphrodites and the very detailed conditions under which certain acts were considered appropriate with one person but a sin with another caused Saa'iqa to study ancient India and its practices in her spare time. Any group of people who could develop a sexual position called the Queen of Heaven, needed closer attention and evaluation she felt.

She studied the Kama Sutra on a continuing basis since most of her clients, victims and workers were men, and sex often became a means of controlling a situation. She thought about the reasonableness of the sexual position identification method in the Kama Sutra and how often she had relied on its accuracy during the years. She almost laughed out loud as she looked out in a field at a horse and a few cows and thought of the descriptions, but did not dare alert Naseer to her private thoughts. She suppressed the laugh.

They could see the beautiful city from the hillside as they ascended from their overlook position. Just at Marrakech had all Persian red buildings, the seaside town was filled with houses that were white with blue trim. Only a few structures were terra cotta in color, and most of them were very old.

Essaouira, formerly called Mogador and famous for their woodworkers, pottery and fishing. The water was crystal clear blue-green and the shoreline filled with birds hoping to catch the leftovers from the fishermen's catch of the day. The walls of a long gone fort herald the glory of civilizations past, ancestors gone by and descendants who battle through commerce and cabinet making. The souks were filled with herb shops, fabric stores, pastry makers, art galleries, museums and Mosques. The beautiful, clean city by the sea transmitted the best of Morocco to locals and visitors alike. Although the city paled in size in comparison to Marrakech, it excelled in a peacefulness and lack of concern for tourists and visitors. There was no constant tourist hustle as in Marrakech so the people were far less focused on visitors. It was easy for two Marrakechiiis to get lost in the scheme of things, their actions unnoticed. They took no chances though, and did not ride through the heart of the city.

When they reached her vacation home on an isolated beach outside of town, they did not go inside for fear of leaving clues. Instead, they parked the car in the garage and went to the small speedboat parked in a covered, locked boathouse behind the garage. They filled it with fuel brought from Marrakech in portable cans. Stopping to fill the tank at a local stop for boats was too risky. Using the contents of the pump designed for their personal use on the dock was out of the question because it was too easy for a good detective to match the ordered quantity, the reported usage, and actual amount used. They parked the Peugeot in the garage and left in the speedboat with the concealing Biminy top, a present Saa'iqa's father gave her Mother on her thirty fifth birthday.

Naseer and Saa'iqa raced through the water with great determination and direction. She was dressed in a bathing suit, covered by a long red and black kimono, and he in white shorts and a tee shirt, the picture of a vacationing couple. The shore was quite deserted and barely visible from the boat as they sped toward a lone motor yacht, anchored some distance from the shore.

As they approached the beautiful, antique, mahogany Chris Craft motor yacht, Naseer slowed their speed in preparation for boarding. When he reached the side, he stopped and helped Saa'iqa disembark and board the cabin cruiser to join an older man who appeared to be in his late sixties, who stood on deck. Once she was safely on board, Naseer left the immediate vicinity, returning in the direction from which they came. The man, Jalaal Abdullah, greeted Saa'iqa with open arms and a warm lover's kiss.

Saa'iqa responded by letting him know how nice it was to be missed, a warm, affectionate tender and gentle touch and embrace that nearly melted him onto the wooden flooring. He was obviously smitten with her.

"I am becoming accustomed to these weekly meetings with you. Sometimes however, it is difficult to believe that I am seeing Hanna Mastoora's daughter romantically though. I remember when you were a child. You were almost as beautiful then as you are now."

Saa'iqa preened and tossed her hair, taunting the older man sexually, as if she enjoyed the fact that he was so infatuated with her. She allowed her kimono to fall to the deck, revealing a matching red and black one piece bathing suit. Jalaal removed the large silver comb from her hair allowing the long, dark curls and swirls to fall their full length past her waist. She took it from his hand, held it between her fingers as though contemplating some hidden thought inside it, then lay it on the console beside her.

She leaned against the console and fingered the controls carefully, as if they were delicate and fragile. She rubbed the wood with her palm and then with the back of her hand, akin to savoring the feel of velvet or rose petals or the soft down of a duckling.

"This is such a wonderful boat Jalaal. I have never seen another like it."

"I had to wait for three years to find one, it is a 1948. Very few left in the world."

"Huhm. I remember you also when I was a child. I remember well those times when you were all friends . . . you, my father, Karraar Zaid, Ihsaan Asad and a couple of others. Your daughter Jameela and I were in school together when independence came . . . and everything changed. We were very young in 1956, but I remember it."

She rubbed the console again and in one continuous movement caressed not only the boat, but moved up Jalaal's arm to the side of his face, just before turning to go downstairs. The older man's breath became labored, heavy with anticipation, but was only allowed to continue as long as her tease was in play. He thought of how wonderful she was to touch. She stopped and returned to his side when she heard him speak, ever attentive to his every word.

"I have always regretted the events which occurred shortly after that . . . but . . . it was imperative that we Moroccans banned together and freed ourselves of as much of the foreign financial and cultural influences as possible. Your father never understood that. We are Moorish people . . . not European."

Saa'iqa stroked his cheek gently, a calm, serene look on her face, covering the thoughts that brewed in her heart.

"My father was blinded by his love for his French wife and half French child. I am alone and have no such attachments. I fully understand my social responsibilities . . . that is why I arranged for the sale of that property you and Muntasir own to the broker from Rabat. This way it is retained by Moroccan blood."

She walked down to the bar to prepare some drinks, but their conversation continued as he assumed control of the boat and began moving them forward very slowly. Once downstairs, she opened the cabinets and took out two glasses. She had worked on the old man for more than three months. The planning and set up for the job had been quite extensive and she was pleased that everything had fallen into place. She could still hear Jalaal's voice as she poured two glasses of wine.

"I can still see Naseer about a half a kilometer behind us. It isn't necessary that he wait. You care about being discreet far more than I do. I am a widower now."

"Jalaal, he does not mind the wait. Besides, there are those who might not understand a member of the purity cartel being with a half French woman."

She opened a small ring on her finger, removed a tiny capsule from it and placed it on the counter. Then she wiped the fingerprints from the bottle. The boat began picking up speed.

"I'm going to take us over to a cove I know of. It is very beautiful there. As for being seen with you, I am an old man now . . . people don't really care what I do anymore. I leave most of the battles to the sons now, like Muntasir and Saleem, before he died."

Saa'iqa wiped fingerprints from the small refrigerator. Jalaal continued speaking to her from the deck of the loping boat with an engine that purred like a big cat.

"I am not even sure our efforts were fruitful anyway. So much is owned by foreigners now that it is quite unbelievable. Who would have ever considered the Asian and Oriental countries as a threat to our financial control all those years ago."

Saa'iqa picked up the small pill and prepared to drop it into one of the glasses of wine.

"You know Saa'iqa, all of the loss and the fights. I'm not certain it was worth it. Karrar, Ihsaan, and of course your father. I regret his death most."

Saa'iqa halted placing the pill in the drink and stared out of the window at the beautiful sea as it bobbed and rocked gently along, the boat moving smoothly through the water. The sounds of the engine matched the nonsense she heard coming from Jalaal's mouth as she thought of the idiotic words he uttered from his mouth. She could see her Father's strong and patient face as he tucked her into bed and sang an Egyptian lullaby his Great Grandmother had taught him. She could still hear the sound of his baritone voice as he tried to sing the part of the ant in a high, squeaky voice that made her laugh until she cried and fought not to wet herself - the only worry of a four year old. Her eyes flashed green fire as her mind returned to Jalaal and she put the pill back into the compartment on the ring.

She picked up the drinks and walked up the stairs to the deck above and Jalaal, who was seated at the controls. She gave him one of the glasses, then sat the other one on the console. She then walked further back on the deck, picked up her kimono and put it on.

"It is a little cool with the boat moving" she said.

Jalaal looked around to see if Naseer was still following. He was, but maintained his distance at about a half mile. Jalaal shook his head slightly, as if awed that the man was so alert and aware of their movements.

"Will he follow us all the way there?"

"Yes, but he will not intrude."

"He is as loyal to you as his father was to Hannaan. He was a good man . . . Naseer's father. At least he has lived a long life. I hear he has moved to Agadir in his retirement."

Saa'iqa put her hair in a bun on top of her head and secured it with the silver comb, then picked up the wine and sipped.

"Oh, young one, did you remember to bring the papers for the sale of that property? Muntasir was nervous about sending signed papers . . . even with me. I told him the buyer had been checked thoroughly, and that I met him during the transaction. He seemed reassured. He has been jumpy lately, since Saleem's death. I guess that makes sense though."

"You did not tell him I had anything to do with the sale did you? He still holds some hatred of the French, and would surely react badly to your involvement with me."

She moved in close behind Jalaal and gently rubbed his shoulders as he drove. He moaned a little, as if he had been longing for her touch for years instead of the week since he last saw her. She nibbled his earlobe and kissed the side of his neck softly.

"No . . . you worry too much about me. I did not tell him though."

Saa'iqa reached in the pocket of the kimono with her right hand and removed a long, sharp scalpel. She held it at her side as she continued to rub the back of his neck. All the years of agony that her father had suffered for being outside the desires of the cartel and their narrow minded thinking rose to the top of her brain and threatened to burst through to the open air, but she remained calm. She always did. She was a professional.

"Well that's good. Yes . . . the papers are well cared for. They are safe."

She rubbed his neck with the back of her hand. He was still looking straight ahead, piloting the boat toward the cove with expectations of love and bliss with the beautiful young woman who had taken a love interest in a lonely old man. He had been amazed when she seemed open to the proposition and in fact, he considered that she was actually more interested in him than he in her at first. His feelings were mostly of lust and loneliness at first, but he had grown quite fond of her over the past few weeks. He kept his eyes on the cove ahead.

Saa'iqa kissed him on the side of his forehead and then on his cheek just before she quickly and skillfully pulled the sharp knife across the front of his throat, making a deep, clean cut from one side to the other. Blood gushed out of his jugular vein with incredible force, spraying the console and windshield. His eyes remained opened, but his death was swift. He never had time to respond or talk. He never even saw the flaming eyes that stared at the back of his head as he slumped forward on the wheel, his right hand falling off of the throttle. The boat drifted to a stop as his life came to an end and the involuntary jerking reactions ceased. She wiped the blade of the knife clean on his shirt and put it deep inside the brassier of her swimsuit so that it would not move.

"My father and mother both died as a result of your actions you old fool. The least you could do is be sure you were right! You and that damned self righteous Karrar Zaid."

She took surgical gloves from her kimono pocket and put them on her hands, which had remarkably little blood on them due to the speed with which she used the knife. Then she pushed Jalaal from the seat onto the floor and took command of the controls. She turned the steering wheel hard to the right and accelerated, causing the boat to make one large circle in the water, then throttled back and brought the boat to a stop, pointed toward the shore. Naseer saw her make the signal with the boat and hurried toward her.

Still clad in surgical gloves, Saa'iqa went downstairs and finished erasing her prints from the kitchenette. She carried the wine bottle and ice bucket back up on deck, wiped off the bottle and glasses and dropped them into the ocean. With Naseer approaching fast, she got a can of reserve fuel from the deck and poured the contents into the open ice bucket, then placed it on the aft most portion of the engine door on the deck. Using the Jerry can of extra fuel, she poured some over Jalaal's dead body then steered the boat toward a sea wall on shore and secured the position with the lashings on the spoke wheel.

Once the collision course was stabilized, Saa'iqa throttled forward, causing the cruiser to slowly accelerate. She walked to the transom, or rear of the Chris Craft and dove into the ocean, kimono and all, just as Naseer arrived, cautiously clearing the engine and careful not to be in ocean water to long, with blood on her - lest she attract sharks. She had been treading for only a minute or so when he pulled up along side, reached down into the water, pulled her onto the boat and wrapped a towel around her. He then resumed his navigational position, turned the boat back in the direction they originally came from and they sped away.

Saa'iqa removed the kimono, and dried her hair with the towel. In the distance, the beautiful wooden yacht carrying the older widow - the last of his bloodline, smashed into the seawall on the beach and caused a huge explosion. The speeding boat with the biminy top was long gone, leaving no witnesses to his murder let alone his final burning on the deserted beach in Essaouria.

They replaced the boat without being seen, retrieved the car from the garage and drove directly back to Marrakech, just in time for a late lunch.

◊

Dressed in a stunning, high collared, long, black dress with a slit that went up the side from the floor to her knee, Saa'iqa left the table where she and Naseer were having a fabulous lunch at one of Marrakech's finest restaurants, Restaurant Yacout. She wore no contacts and no wig. Along with being opportune, it seemed appropriate and respectful of the events of the day and the cartel member who fought as a young man for Moroccan purity, that she should look as Moroccan and French as she possibly could and show the brilliant blue green eyes made possible by the genes of her French mother, her impurities flaunted completely in rejection of all he had lived for and all he abandoned in doubt in his older years. Somehow, she felt as if his death offered justice to her employer and his mission and granted her the extra pleasure of a job well done. She neither despised nor loathed Jalaal. She actually had very little feeling about him one way of the other. She felt it was a leveling of the universe's score to settle hypocrisy. Reciprocity from the ether. Equilibrium from the forces of nature and justice. She felt exceptionally good.

She excused herself from the table and walked to the phone booth around the corner, pleased that they could find no agents following them. It was pleasant not to be followed for just one night and yet to be able to fulfill alibi requirements while having a wonderful meal out on the town, at one of her favorite restaurants, seen and recognized by people who knew her well and respected her completely. She inserted enough coins in the phone to call her employer in Paris, and let him know that Jalaal had been taken care of and that the papers were placed in his safe beforehand.

From a public telephone in Paris, their prearranged contact spot, Claude DuParc talked to his employee, Saa'iqa. He was dashing to say the least. Actually, he and Saa'iqa looked as if they were related, but he was quite tall, with golden skin, straight black hair and a mustache. He had on a dark Armani suit, and thousand dollar shoes.

"Yes, good. Now when you had the land transferred to Pierre´ Bonet´, you were careful not to be implicated, were you not?"

"Most certainly" she answered.

"Yes . . . good. You sent him to Brazil and he knows when to return? (pause) No, the money can't be traced . . . I made sure of that. I will be there this week, and I want to see Dayton in person. I am certain you were most thorough but I would prefer to see him for myself. There can be no mistake on the last job. Place the money. We have been on long enough. Call in two days, at time number eight, and location number twelve, for a rendezvous location. Au revoir."

He hung up the telephone and smiled to himself as he went back to the museum tour of the Lourve.

20 THROW IN THE CORN STARCH TOO!

A couple of days later, as a dazed Muntasir arrived at his office one morning, two policemen approached him and informed him that they had questions that they wanted him to answer in their office. Willing to cooperate, he went to the police station with them and found himself there for the next six hours, under grueling interrogation. The two policemen looked almost cartoonish in their determination to get the truth. One was short and thin the other was tall and thin. It appeared to Muntasir that thinness was a prerequisite for working for the police.

As the hours drudged by filled with questions he could not answer, he wished he had never agreed, but alas he really had no choice. Most of the time they had him seated in a small room with no ventilation, and filled with the horrible stench of too many prisoners, treated too harshly for too many years. He was not in danger of physical abuse, partly because of his standing in the community, and partially because they obviously had no absolute evidence. But he certainly could not figure out why everyone he knew was dying. Partially, he was there because he hoped they knew more than he did.

Luckily for him, he too knew the chief of police, Aatar, but unlike Saa'iqa, he was not held in quite as high esteem. Although they were benevolent to their causes and good businessmen, many more liberal Moroccans felt his father was too harsh and extreme for their subtler, more forgiving and tolerant natures. His father was considered a bully my many, including Aatar - though Moroccan sensibilities would never allow one to say such. The diplomatic if not open minded police chief would work hard to be certain Muntasir was treated fairly. His detectives knew better than to affront their boss' sensibilities.

"Mr. Zaid, don't you think we should be suspicious considering the entry in Saleem Asad's journal which states his doubts in your loyalty to the cartel, and your recent desires to do business with several French businessmen. Then there is the small matter of his death!"

"There were no conflicts whatsoever I tell you. He had no such sus-

191

picions. He was like my own brother . . . I would no more hurt him than hurt myself. I tell you we had been receiving threats!"

"The second officer joined in at that point. "The journal states that he received no such threats, and thought you claimed to have received some in order to conceal your involvement with foreign investors."

Muntasir was getting more and more frustrated with the accusations he felt had no basis whatsoever. He could not figure out why Saleed would make up such things.

"There is no involvement with foreign investors!! These things are just not true!

"We are being patient with you because your family has always been highly respected in this community, but you push our patience with your constant lack of knowledge. You deny involvement when there were papers found in Jalaal Abdullah's safe with your verified signature on them, selling land to a Frenchman, Pierre Bonet'. Then when we attempt to reach Bonet', he is conveniently out of the country. This is just too much Zaid."

An exasperated Muntasir attempted to explain, for the fortieth or fifti-eth time. "I told you that it was my signature and that we were selling that property to a Moroccan businessman in Rabat. Jalaal was handling that. I never saw the buyer."

"But this supports the writings in Saleem's journal which imply that you and Jalaal were both interested in expanding to international inter-ests. Maybe you decided to work alone, and that is why you had Jalaal killed."

"I was at a luncheon today when that happened. I could not possibly have done that . . . there were two hundred people at the event!"

"That is the only reason you have not been arrested, though I doubt you would have done this work yourself. We will be watching you very carefully from now on. Do you understand?"

"I hope you will better spend your time searching for the murderer who did this."

It was early that evening when Muntasir left the police station reeling from the interrogation and all the events of the past couple of weeks. He walked to his car through the dark, barely lit street, stumbling from the overload of the day. He wondered why these things were happening to him? Why had Jalaal and Saleem been killed? Was he in danger of being killed himself? It appeared so to him.

Just as he reached the car he felt he was being watched. He looked all around but saw no one. He quickly, nervously unlocked his new Mercedes jumped inside and locked the car doors, heart racing as he fumbled with the keys in an effort to get them into the ignition. Sweat poured from his forehead, his head was pounding and his hands were shaking violently but no one came to the car to assault him. No one ran from the shadows with a gun or a knife, but he couldn't calm down.

He fumbled to get the key in the ignition and just before he started the car, the thought flashed through his mind that the ignition might be rigged to trigger a bomb which would explode the whole car. He hesitated turning the key, but the fear of someone coming to get him was too great for him to waiver for long. He took a deep breath and turned on the ignition. There was no explosion, Praise Allah! He drove out of the parking lot like a bat out of hell, terrified of being followed and looking desperately into the rear view mirror until her turned a corner and could no longer see the street, the square or the station.

Out of the shadows stepped Naseer and Saa'iqa.

"Saa'iqa, I would say the man is having great difficulty coping with the situation, wouldn't you?"

"Appears that way."

"If he doesn't calm down, he may have a heart attack."

"Even better, makes our job easier."

"Feels like we ought to light a cigarette or something like one of those forties, American movies. I think I need a Fedora."

Saa'iqa looked up at him and his attempt at humor. It was rare for him. She laughed, as did he.

"Aren't we witty and fun tonight ."

"I have my moments. You go first."

She smiled at him and walked to the exit of the parking lot and down the street. Other than when they were obviously doing public tasks, while they were working, it was rare that they were ever in the same place at the same time and when they were, they almost never left together. He got into the blue Mercedes and drove home. She liked walking in the dark and of course he never worried about her.

Occasionally, a foolish mugger or rapist might attack her, fooled by her size, thinking she was easy prey. Although rape did not happen often in Morocco, and public rape was nearly nonexistent, it had been an issue in major American and a few European cities. But this only kept her in practice. She was appalled by the audacity of those attackers so they seldom survived.

As she turned a corner onto a more secluded street, she became aware of a male presence moving closer to her but remaining hidden. She turned around and looked in the direction she felt it coming from and saw a medium sized figure in the shadows. She smiled to herself, turned around and continued walking. After a few seconds, she could tell that he was no longer focused on her. She looked again and saw him cross the street and walk in another direction.

It happened sometimes to the lucky ones. She suspected they were men with heightened powers of awareness. Somehow they were able to sense that she was not exactly what she appeared to be and shied away. Wise of them. She would have to learn to mask the confidence level a little better. She would practice that element more often. The rest of her walk home was quite pleasant and undisturbed. She appreciated the peace and needed calm for a moment. Calm from the tasks at hand.

◊

When she arrived at home, food was nearly prepared by the cook for the evening meal. After a shower and change into casual clothing, a light silk golden djellabah, Saa'iqa went downstairs to the to eat with Naseer and Clinton. There were several ornate, low tables with large, low chairs around each one. Many candles adorned the walls and hand carved sideboards that bordered the room. The chairs and tablecloth were blues, golds and orange and the windows were open, allowing the cool night air to bounce the sheers lazily from side to side.

She sat at the table with Naseer and Clinton. They washed their hands and got comfortable as the cook, Hani brought in the food. Clinton waited until she left the room before speaking.

"Other than our activities, and the clients you have, what legitimate business activities do you participate in?"

"My father was a wealthy man with vast real estate holdings. I manage them and several businesses he left me."

"I see. Was he born into money or did he build this fortune?"

"He was born poor. Everything he had and I now have, he earned."

Clinton poured more wine into all three glasses. Naseer stared at him with great intensity.

"You said was. Are both of your parents deceased?"

"Yes."

The cook brought in another platter of couscous, and lamb with prunes and placed it on the table. They all ate in silence for a moment, until they were alone again. It almost seemed a natural reaction for three people with so much to hide to stop talking when another person entered the room.

"What happened, if I may ask?"

Naseer could barely contain himself at that moment, but as a dutiful compatriot, he waited for Saa'iqa's response, hoping he would be allowed to smash in Dayton's face for being so bold as to ask personal questions. To his surprise, she answered, affirming that he should be very concerned about this thief's control over her. It was all too unfamiliar for the big man. He straightened his back stiffly.

Saa'iqa noticed Naseer's reaction but did not respond. She simply would not allow him to dictate how she should act with another man, and she saw no reason to be overly cautious with Dayton. She was not in the habit of giving away information that was secret, and she was not about to begin over the dinner table. In her mind, Naseer was overreacting and acting out of his own agenda.

"It is fairly common knowledge in Marrakech. My father only had one wife in a country where having more than one was common during his time. My mother was a French woman; very soft spoken, kind and gentle. They loved each other very much. In 1956 when Morocco became independent, the mood was clearly anti-French. An organization was formed by some of the prominent business leaders in the city to eliminate as many French owned businesses and encourage Marrakechii ownership. It was not widespread, but there were some very powerful members in it, some close friends of my father's. One man in particular was so obsessed with the cause that he sent his second wife, a French woman he had been married to for thirteen years, and their eleven year old son back to France. He never saw them again. They pressured my father to send us away but he refused. They harass . . ."

Unable to contain himself any longer, Naseer abruptly broke into their conversation.

"Excuse me, but I think I will leave now."

He stood and left the room. He was disgusted with this new phenomenon - Saa'iqa trusting a total stranger enough to tell about her life - that he was beside himself and unable to listen to the diatribe any longer.

"Naseer, Yakub will be here at four to get Archie, correct?"

Without bothering to return or even look back, Naseer answered from the hallway.

"Correct . . . I will meet him."

Clinton stared at the hallway as if he thought Naseer would return, but he did not. "Naseer seemed a bit abrupt, didn't he?"

" Naseer grew up with in this house with me and had great affection for my father."

Clinton acknowledged "It must be very difficult to lose a loved one. Go on. Tell me about your parents" he said as he moved his chair a little closer to her. They ate a few more bites of food and drank in silence as he waited patiently for her to continue.

"They badgered my father constantly, making his life very difficult., always trying to discredit him in the community. He was a powerful man and they felt they needed his participation to the cause in order to gain more public support. The most adamant one, Karrar Zaid, the one who sent his son away, constantly tormented my father in many different ways. It finally took its toll on his health. He suffered a stroke at an early age. Even while he tried to recuperate, they tried to gain control of his land."

She stopped talking for a moment and took a few sips of wine. Clinton leaned back in the chair and placed his hands behind his head. He watched her expression and could feel the pain building as she recounted the story. He could feel it because he knew it too well, and although there were few outward signs of her pain, he recognized it completely on a gut level that transmitted ions of grief from her body to his. It was much too familiar. He understood the covering up and the suppression of emotion and could recognize it in the tiny twitch that occurred on the left side of her face as she calmly told her story. It made him nearly physically ill and he rushed to stop her from reliving the account.

"Saa'iqa, you don't have to go on. I understand what it means. I know the depths. It's alright."

He quickly placed his hand on top of hers and held it. He was trembling. She jumped ever so slightly and stared at his brown hand and studied the protruding venation, perfectly manicured and even nails and distinctive look of power. For a moment they looked quite familiar but she couldn't figure out why. She felt the slight trembling and it almost made her feel comfortable and understood, then she thought better of it. Other than during games of seduction and with the exception of Naseer, men generally did not touch her if they knew her as well as Archie Dayton did. Not if they knew what she was capable of. Not if they suspected any of what she had done and might do. Discovery of the true purpose of the hair comb alone would be enough to make most men run for their lives. Even if they knew no more they kept their distance, as well they should.

His action confused her for a moment. She took a sip of wine and gently eased her hand from under his with a smile and the unspoken pretense of needing it to get her napkin to dry the corner of her mouth.

There were no tears to wipe from her eyes because there were no real tears left for her parents. She watched him calmly. She no longer had to practice hiding the pain generally because other than Naseer, there were no real human souls to her - only walking vessels of disappointment, greed and hidden agendas. She had told their story so many times as if it was a play with rehearsed lines to be executed. She straightened her sitting position and before speaking.

"It was horrible for my mother. After thirteen highly stress filled weeks, he died. The cartel started plans to have my mother deported and focused on doing so but they didn't get the chance. My mother was so grief stricken that she committed suicide a month and a half later. She slit her wrists and bled to death in the bathtub. I found her that way one morning."

"You found her? I'm so sorry. Do you have brothers and sisters? What happened to you?"

"I am an only child. My aunt, my father's sister, sent me to boarding school in France. She was a good woman. The extra responsibilities forced upon her by my father's death. Karrar Zaid made relentless attempts to control my father's property by Karrar Zaid, and wore her health down. She died of a heart attack within a year. Although some land was lost in those early weeks as my aunt took over my father's affairs, the bulk of my father's estate remained in trust, safe from Zaid until I came of age. Naseer and his parents continued to live here and care for the house for many years until I returned. When they retired, Naseer stayed with me."

"What did you do all those years?"

"Well, I finished my doctorate in Japanese history. Spent a few years in Japan . . . you see . . . traveled a lot."

"How do they accept you here now? Is the mood still the same?"

"Times change. They were a small but hateful group even before independence. Enough about me. What about you? I know you are a street child from New York. Any brothers and sisters?"

Clinton answered her questions with the prepared Archie Dayton life history. He said that his father was a drunk, but always kept him with him and did the best he supposed he could. His mother had run off with another man when Archie was six years old and was never heard from again. They finished eating, leaned back in the soft, pillowy chairs, sipped wine and talked easily.

"Why do you call your father a drunk?"

"Cause he was! Worked in a linen plant every day and got drunk every night and weekend. I suppose they would call him a functional alcoholic or something today. But I'm sure you knew that. I'll bet Naseer had every part of my life checked out before you ever approached me."

"Well yes, but that doesn't tell me how you feel, or who you really are."

"Yeah . . . well . . . he was alright. He was there. He didn't go anywhere even if he was comatose half the time. He's still the same, except he did quit drinking as much because the doctor told him he was going to die if he didn't. He is a survivor. What about you? How do you feel about all that happened to you?"

"I learned that values are relative and have little to do with the outcome of your life. I live my life however I choose and make my own justice. Being right or wrong won't make much difference one way or the other as to the final results."

He considered what she said momentarily and realized that it made perfect sense for her set of circumstances. It didn't matter if you were a good man who refused to desert your family for some ridiculous financial power mechanisms, or a woman who only did volunteer work and helped the needy and loved her husband and son, or a five year old who only rode to the store with his mother, or a kid who had committed no crime other than being interracial. There was no real justice in this world. The cards were indiscriminately unkind, and if you wanted retribution or fair play, it was very likely that you had to exact it yourself. He could see how easily a child could make the leap that she had. It had been hard for him as an adult not to take that same road, even processing his pain through a myriad of adult experiences. What if all you had was extreme joy and extreme pain and anguish, with no middle of the road occurrences to balance out your thinking? He contemplated the vast emotional differences in her world as a child as he watched her sipping her wine.

At that moment he felt a sweeping range of feelings for her. He stood and pulled her up from the chair and close to him so that her head rested against his chest. She moved willingly and rested peacefully against him as they half danced, and half rocked while they sipped wine contentedly, the slow Moroccan music playing in the background.

"Saa'iqa. Who named you and what does it mean?

"My father. It means thunderbolt or lightning. Together with my last name, which means concealed or hidden, my name means hidden thunderbolt. Why?"

All Clinton could say was "Malika."

"You say something?"

"Nothing important."

He pulled her close to him and kissed her like the kindred spirit he knew her to be, as did she. Although she did not know as many details about the man she was kissing, she could feel the commonalty of their pain and sorrow. They held each other tightly, the depths of their souls converging, even through their deception. When he released her, they both felt the passion of years of loneliness and despair release, if not fully, then more than had been in a long time.

"If you're not too tired, we have a few hours before Yakub will come to pick you up for tonight's job. If you have an interest, give me a few minutes, then I would certainly wish your company in my boudoir. Only if you are interested though" she smiled.

"I can't imagine I could get too tired for, or not be interested in such an invitation."

She kissed him lightly before going out of the door. "I will get the dishes later while you and Yakub are on your job. Hani has left for tonight."

At the top of the stairs there was Naseer. He spoke to her in low, forced calm, hushed tones. "You think it wise to tell this outsider so much?"

She replied, "I only gave Archie information that was common knowledge. Nothing I said would help him connect all the events around him to me. Even if he was dangerous, which I don't believe he is, it wouldn't matter."

Naseer contemplated her words and realized that she was right. Any Marrakechii could have told the stranger of the Mastoora history and its trials and tribulations. He was furious that he had no real right to be furious. There was something wrong, but he had no proof.

"Naseer, if he betrays us, I will not hesitate to kill him. It is that simple. Do not worry so."

He took her hand in his and kissed the back of it. "Of course. Of course. Goodnight."

He left her alone without another word. She watched him leave, and wondered if she should heed his warnings and give them more credence. She simply could not muster up much more suspicion at that moment. Her thoughts turned to another bath in some of the scented oils her aunt left her from years before.

She went into her bath area which was on the opposite side of her bedroom and began running water into the Jacuzzi tub, then added Egyptian Musk Oil and bubbling beads to the water in generous doses. She undressed and put on a flowing yellow and white kimono that matched the vases filled with giant yellow flowers and pale pastel green wallpaper, with small pale yellow flowers. She disrobed and climbed into the tub, immersing herself in the bubbles.

There was a faint knock at the door. It was Clinton. He came into the lavish yellow and white room with a huge round bed, overstuffed comforters, thick throw rugs and a smell which nearly made him melt to into a pile on the floor. She beckoned him to join her in the tub. Without hesitation, he peeled off his clothes and lowered himself into the pool of water filled with bubbles and oil.

He faced her, slid in close, straddled her body with his and kissed her, as she held onto the side of the tub with both arms spread wide, struggling quietly not to sink under his weight. He wrapped one leg around the back of her thigh, forcing her to wrap the other thigh around his waist in order to hang on. His weight forced her hands free from the sides and she held onto him tightly, both determined not to break the kiss, laughing as they sank into the water. After a couple of seconds, he lifted her back above water level and she grabbed hold of the side of the tub and anchored herself again. They continued kissing for a few moments before he broke away and looked as her. He had not felt as free with a woman in years. He tried to read in her face the part of her that released him from some of the sorrow he had felt for so long. Her expression was non-committal. He wanted to say something, but he didn't know what. As if she read his mind, she pulled him toward her and kissed and nuzzled his Adam's apple, forcing any words that might have been spoken into silence. She pulled him close to her then turned him over so that his back was against the side of the tub and she was straddling him. She took the giant sponge from the soap dish and began lathering his body slowly. He lay his head back allowing her room to wash under her chin and down his neck to his collarbone. She took shampoo from a shelf beside the tub and lathered his beard then brushed it, just before she pushed his head under the water.

He was calm, and although the thought did occur to him that it might be a cleaver method of drowning him, he didn't overreact and allowed her to complete the rinsing and bring him above water level at her own pace. She did so and smiled at him as she wiped the water from his eyes with the corner of a towel and kissed him slowly and passionately. He was neither stupid nor unnecessarily afraid of her. After replacing the towel, she used the sponge to lather his chest and arms first, playing with the dense curls of hair on his deep chest with the tips of her fingernails, tugging and pulling them sharply every once in a while and causing him to wince slightly just before she rinsed the soap from his skin. Then she would kiss the spots gently and rub her chin across the hairs and into the tight flesh across his muscular chest. He relaxed and closed his eyes as she caressed the sore spots with her hands first and then her tongue until she was kneading, licking and sucking his nipples gently. He sighed audibly. She smiled as she felt his penis growing hard against her stomach.

It was difficult for him to lay still, remain loose and receptive and stay halfway afloat. He had to concentrate in order not to become the aggressor because at that moment he wanted to be wrapped all around her, joined tightly to her and be deep inside of her. He fought hard to keep his breath steady and not give in to the total abandon he felt with every pore of his body. He could feel her hair in the water encircling his chest and waist like the fir of some small animal moving around him, brushing gently against his body. He could scarcely understand his reaction to her, and was only mildly concerned about its boundaries and limits at that moment.

◊

Naseer lay in the bed counting every crack and crevice in the ceiling. He could endure most things and was accustomed to other men in Saa'iqa's life, but Archie Dayton felt like too much as he thought of his hands all over her. Sleep was most difficult for him. He was grateful that the walls were thick and carried no sound. Audio to accompany his own manufactured visuals would be more than he could bear.

◊

After a lot of lathering and washing, one thing led to another, and another, and another that continued for several hours until both Clinton and Saa'iqa were exhausted and fell asleep. Clinton set his internal clock to wake him an hour later. He awoke more rested and calm than he had been in years and quietly left Saa'iqa sleeping soundly in the soft moonlight seeping in through cracks in the windows and doors. He checked his pants pocket for a penlight and metal tool, then put them on and carefully opened the door and left the room.

Guided by the glow from the skylight, Clinton tipped downstairs to the office, entered and went to the desk. He unlocked the bottom drawer where Saa'iqa kept the brown folder containing his work assignments with the metal tool. Once he found the folder and opened it, he viewed the contents with the penlight. Inside were the brown journal from Saleem Asad's house, and envelope containing the equivalent of two hundred thousand dollars in francs and a folder containing French securities and bills, made payable to Muntasir Zaid. The securities equaled another six million American, but in French Currency. In a manila folder were papers, written in French, transferring possession of two office buildings to Pierre´ Bonet´. Luckily for Clinton, he could read the transfer papers

◊

Drifting in and out of sleep, Naseer listened carefully, thinking he heard a sound downstairs. He lay quietly on his back and attempted to hone in on the noise, unclear whether or not is was real or just a feeling induced by some vague and unrewarding dream state. He decided that something really was wrong. He knew the house too well, having spent his entire life living there. He strained to listen and although he did not hear anything, he rose to check.

◊

Downstairs Clinton heard slight movement and a creaking of the stairs as Naseer slowly descended and entered the courtyard. Quickly, Clinton closed the folder and replaced it in the drawer as he extinguished the flashlight and silently hid behind the door. A few seconds later Naseer appeared in the doorway, turned on the light and looked around the room. Considering the coast clear, he turned off the light and moved back into the courtyard. After a couple of seconds Clinton left his safe spot and moved to the doorway to look into the moonlit courtyard.

Naseer moved toward the next room off of the courtyard as Clinton peeked from the office in an effort to locate him. The big man turned to look behind, but Clinton quickly pulled his head back into the doorway. Satisfied he was alone, Naseer entered the room in which they had eaten dinner and turned on the light. Clinton raced into the courtyard toward the staircase, but stopped short in the shadows at the base of the stairs to avoid detection. Naseer went into the large room to search its numerous nooks and crannies. Remaining on the shadowed side of the staircase, hidden from the light pouring in from the skylight over the fountain, Clinton safely tipped upstairs.

Naseer continued his systematic search of the lower floor. Satisfied that there was no intruder, he made an equally tedious search of the upstairs area and after searching his own room, he determined that the only place left was Saa'iqa's room, and that the only intruder was a creeping Archie Dayton. He went to her room and threw open the door, prepared to alert her to Clinton's absence from his room. Instead, he turned on the light, and found her naked, and cuddled in Clinton's arms. Startled, she struggled to focus her eyes and sit up as she questioned his actions.

"What? Is something wrong? Has something happened?

Naseer glared at Clinton who released Saa'iqa so that she could cover herself with the sheet. Clinton sat up straight in the bed and leaned against the headboard, apparently waiting for the same news as Saa'iqa. Naseer looked at them both, a sneer of disgust on his face.

"I thought there was an intruder and wanted to check on your safety. Excuse me please."

He slowly backed out of the room and closed the door. Clinton fought back a smirk - which he certainly could not afford to allow to be seen. Although he felt some admiration for Naseer, he was pleased to best him at any time.

21 AGE OLD

Bernice finished washing pots from the evening meal and was drying her hands as she thought about her sons, and the fact that she had not heard from Clinton since he left weeks before. She got caught up in the ritual of wiping the kitchen counter, as she was doing at that moment, and noticed that the yellow and gray countertop was beginning to show wear in the spot beside the sink - her worry spot as Justine had deemed it. Anytime she was worried or lost in thought, she did seem to wipe the exact same spot on the counter over and over again. She looked down and could see the flecks of gray taking over in spots where yellow was predominant before. She stopped and listened to Jarrett's cheers for the Power Rangers in the movie he watching in the living room . She smiled at the sound of childish delight over childish concerns.

Bernice hung the dishtowel on the rack and left the kitchen. Justine came from upstairs and grabbed her jacket from the chair by the door on her way out , and called back to Bernice as she stepped onto the porch.

"Mama Creech, its cool out tonight. Bring a sweater."

"O.K., I'll get one from upstairs."

Justine was in a rocking chair rocking gently and humming some nonsensical tune from one of Jarrett's Saturday morning kid's shows when Bernice joined her on the porch. The older woman sat in the chair next to her and patted her hand gently, then covered her lower body with an afghan.

Justine watched her as she began rocking gently, in rhythm with her own movements.

"Have you heard from Clinton yet?"

"No, but I suppose he was still in London. Gerald calls me every couple of days and lets me know that he is alright. He "feels" good - not like he's in trouble or anything."

Justine was amazed at the connection and the "feelings" that Bernice seemed to have between her children and herself. Bernice said that he must be getting closer to the real issues and the truth because of the change in her dreams and the new development of hearing her own voice in broken static though she admitted being unable to hear Will's voice at all.

The conversation broke off and the women sat in silence, looking at the bright moon as the clouds drifted across the face of it, obscuring the craters and coloration from time to time. They rocked sometimes in unison and at other times out of synch, with Bernice's chair making an occasional creaking noise as it pushed against the wooden planks of the old porch that Clinton Sr. had built during their first year in the house so that she could rock Clarissa to sleep. She was their most colicky baby and anything that would help her find peace was prominent in the agenda of the exasperated parents of young twins. Bernice tried to remember what Clinton looked like as a child, and then Will and then she tried to stop her mind from mutating into some lost state of mother worry. She fought hard to calm her emotions and just require her heard to be quiet. She thought of the moon and the stars and breathed as deeply and slowly as she could. After a few moments of silence Bernice continued their conversation.

"But that is not why I wanted to talk to you. I want you to do something for me honey."

"Of course Mama Creech. Anything you want. You've been very sweet to me and Jarrett over the years. What can I do?"

Bernice took Justine's hand in her own and stroked it gently. Then she rubbed Justine's hair a couple of strokes, allowing her fingers to feel the cylindrical roughness of the slender dreadlocks that framed her small face, showing a hint of gray intertwined within the mass of hair on Justine's head.

"No baby don't volunteer so fast. You've put a lot of effort over the years into not doing what I'm about to ask you to do. It might not be so simple."

"You're worrying me. What is it? You sound so serious."

"Well, I suppose I'm getting old and lonely. This thing with Will has made me think about how alone I have been since Clinton Sr. died. It has been eight years now. I miss him terribly and with Clarissa with a French husband and two children . . . it isn't likely she will ever move back to Washington or the United States even, for that matter. And Will . . . you know Will and I were alone for nearly five years before I met Clinton Sr. and fell in love. I guess that's why we have always been so close. It was hard before. Those were not times when an unmarried woman had a child alone. Especially not a teacher!"

"I can imagine Mama Creech."

"I know you can honey. I know it hasn't been a bed of roses for you either. I was lucky though . . . Clinton Sr. treated Will just as if he had been his own child. Never once did he do any less, and I think that his being a policeman probably kept Will straight while he was young. Will loved him dearly. His real father wasn't much good. Well the twins came and life was wonderful . . . and then Will divorced Barbara and I hardly ever see his kids. Then the tragedy with Grace and Eddie . . . . now Clinton's so hurt . . ."

"Please don't put yourself through this. I've never seen you like this. What's wrong?"

"I want you to consider moving in with me. You and Jarrett. You're in that small apartment and since your dad moved to Florida you've got no family here except me."

"Well, Mama Creech . . . that is a real sweet offer but do you really think it's a good idea? You're just feeling real low right now. We will always be close by."

Bernice considered the conversation and how far she could go with this young woman who had become so important in her life. She thought about the wonderful times they spent together as a family, she, Justine and Jarrett. One of their favorite things to do was to go to the Smithsonian to see the Dinosaur exhibit. Even as a very young child, Jarrett was more fascinated than frightened by the gigantic creatures. He had the spirit of her own children when they were young. She rubbed Justine's hand, and then held it in her own.

"Mama Creech, what's wrong?"

"There is one more thing Justine. I want you . . . I want you to tell Clinton that Jarrett is his son. I want my son home and he needs a reason to exist . . . and a reason to come home."

Justine slowly pulled her had away and sat on the edge of the rocking chair, trying not to look at Bernice. She weighed her options carefully and Bernice waited patiently.

"What are you talking about? Jarrett is not Clinton's son? Where did you ever get such a notion?"

"Honey, Jarrett is the mirror image of my father at that age. If Clinton weren't so grief struck, he might remember those old pictures up in the attic like this one."

She reached into her pocket and removed an old photograph of her father at age twelve. He looked exactly like Jarrett in turn of the century clothing. Justine gasped, shocked at how much they looked alike. She stared at the sky and contemplated the concept of heaven for a moment. She wondered whether or not Grace was looking down at that moment, listening, absorbing the conversation she was having with Bernice . . . her sister's mother-in-law. She thought about Clinton Sr. and whether or not he was watching them and angry that he might have missed out on a relationship with a child that meant more to him than he might have known. Or might he have known?

"Baby," Bernice said, "even if Clinton had not paid attention to the resemblance, any fool can see how you look at Clinton . . . and always have when I really think about it. It used to worry me because I thought you and Clinton were having an affair at first. Somehow I don't remember you being anything except one of the gang of folks he hung out with in high school but after they got married, I saw the look in your eyes. I noticed how you and Grace felt about each other and knew you would never do anything to hurt her. Then I was confused . . . thought it was strange until Jarrett got to be about five. I guess they didn't notice because he doesn't look as much like Clinton as he does my father. I think if Clinton had stayed here he would have figured it out. Tell him honey . . . I want my son home."

Justine turned away from Bernice, tears streaming down her face. She had endured years of silence. Of never being able to tell her child that he spent at least three evenings a week with the only grandmother he had, his real grandmother. Many times they discussed the fact that he never got to know her mother, or his aunt Grace very well and therefore missed the connection to other women in his biological family. There were times when she wanted to scream from the deception and what she felt she was taking away from his memories as a child. Although she could not tell him, she made sure he saw his grandmother often.

"Justine . . . talk to me."

"You know . . .while we were part of that loud and crazy gang, I was hopelessly in love. Clinton never seemed to notice, and I figured we had time. He didn't see Grace for three summers straight before the year they turned twenty."

Justine stopped for a moment, overcome by the emotion of all the events surrounding her decision to discuss this subject with her surrogate mother and friend. Bernice began rocking slowly, and patting the back of Justine's hand. Justine eased back into her rocker and allowed herself to rock in rhythm with Bernice. They just stared at the sky for a few moments before Justine continued.

"I saw the look on his face the moment he saw her. It scared me, there was so much adoration in his eyes. I tried to figure out what was so different about her that he would respond to her the way he did . . . the way I had wished for years he would respond to me."

She choked up again, the tears rolling down her face. She stopped rocking and had the urge to take off running down the street like the mad woman she felt she was at that moment, with her hair aflame and her clothes flying off and up to the sky as she did - or at least that was her best vision of an insane woman and she certainly felt that she fit the bill at that moment. It was all just too much. She had suppressed the whole issue for so long, hidden it so well that even her own father had no idea of the truth - or at least she thought not. Suddenly she became fearful that he too had known all along and that she was not fooling a soul, but that they were all just waiting for her to gain some sense, or maybe even laughing at her adolescent attempt at deception. She was nearly dumb struck at the thought that she was only kidding herself and that the whole world knew her secret. Her mind raced with insanity, doubts, questions, guilt, love, anger, hate, lust, relief and every other thought and emotion she could conjure. She thought her head would explode. As she was trying to decide if she would run or not and if hair combustion was spontaneous when insanity took over, Bernice reached over and patted her hand , soothing her back into the rocking rhythm that the two women shared again and calming her down from her state of multiple madness to at least a narrower condition.

"It's alright baby. It's alright. Try to get it all out."

Justine took a deep breath and continued, her voice shaky.

"I panicked. I was determined to make him forget about her and think about me. I cooked up this stupid, childish scheme to get him in bed because I thought that was all guys his age thought about. I was sure he would be so preoccupied with our new relationship that he wouldn't have time to think about Grace, and I knew she wasn't prone to give up any parts of sex. I wouldn't have either . . . except to him. That was my plan. We spent one week together, and then he lost interest and gradually started spending more time with Grace. To save face, I immediately made up a relationship. Well when the summer was over, and Grace went back to Fisk University, Clinton started burning up the road every other weekend to see her. They were in love and I was pregnant."

"Why didn't you tell Clinton? I'm certain he would not have let you go through that alone if he realized . . ."

"Tell him what? Nothing he could have done would have been right. He loved Grace . . . she loved him. It just would have been a huge mess. This way was much better. An abortion was out of the question for me, and entrapment was plain disgusting."

"What about now? Don't you think he should know now? And what about Jarrett?"

"You know . . . I thought I had it under control. That after all that has happened, I would feel differently when I saw him again. When he opened the front door for Jarrett and me right after he came home, I felt just like I did when I was fourteen and first saw him. My knees got weak, my heart started racing, I got chills and was shaky inside. I am a grown woman now and I have no idea why that man affects me like he does. It is just ridiculous." Justine wiped the tears from her face with her hand. Bernice handed her a tissue from her pocket.

Justine smiled and said "Oh, you were ready for this huh."

"I wasn't certain what to be ready for. Frankly, I thought you might try to keep up the lie, but I'm glad you didn't.

"I'm too exhausted. Actually, it has been very difficult since Clinton came home but I will say this, as far as Jarrett is concerned, he has done alright without a father so far."

"Yes, and a most wonderful child he is but I want you to think about this. There's a lot of secrecy here, and there is just no need for it to continue baby. No need. I loved Grace, but she could not be hurt by this any longer."

Justine wiped the tears from her face with her free hand, the other one still under Bernice's loving touch. She stopped staring at the stars and finally turned to look at Bernice, who was looking at her. They smiled at each other and squeezed one another's hand.

"Mama Creech . . . if you knew all these years, why didn't you say something?"

"It just wasn't my place. It was clear . . . the emotional turmoil you were in. I was not going to add to it by having you worry about your secret too. With all that has happened with Will though, I just think there have been too many secrets in this family. But know now that if you decide not to tell him, I won't . . . but I think we will all benefit if you do. Besides, you always stayed close to me so I got to see my grandchild grow up."

"I thought it was important for him to know you."

"Then maybe now you'll think that it is important for him to know who I really am to him. You just think about what I've said baby. You won't know what Clinton thinks until you talk to him."

"But I am so afraid of what that might be. I understand how angry he has been. What guarantee do I have that he won't direct that rage at me? I don't know if I could take it and I can't tell which way he might go."

"And you can't know that. Only he can."

22 MALACHITE AND FOOLS

Clinton felt like a Humphrey Bogart character as he stood on the corner of the small neighborhood market, contemplating the eerie, pre-dawn, night sky. A strange mist, uncommon to a dry, inland area hovered over the city. There was an odd chill running up his back and on the underside of his wrists that made him shudder.

He had taken a walk to clear his head before he and Yakub were to execute their job. He was grateful to be able to walk the streets freely, without concern of being recognized. Even if someone he knew saw him, it was not likely that they would be clear that it was him and not someone else, and he knew Arabic just well enough to fool a foreigner who knew none if he had to. He watched some men unpacking wares for the day's trading and realized that it was time to go back to Saa'iqa's. With plenty of time remaining, he casually walked through the streets toward the house past expensive houses that were deceiving behind tall walls of over-grown greenery and unkempt grounds and medium houses with perfectly manicured gardens and courtyards.

He had no idea where all of the jobs were leading really, and that made him extremely nervous. It was impossible to gauge what ill effects he was causing, and he could only hope that Gerald and the agents stationed in Marrakech had a handle on what was going on. Naseer and Saa'iqa kept such a close watch on him that he had not been able to connect in any way to any one since he arrived other than the phone check in's, and those were becoming increasingly hazardous. Heretofore, there was no real reason for Naseer to use electronic surveillance equipment during his monitoring of the calls, but after he and Saa'iqa spent the night together with no real regard for his presence, Clinton suspected that he would start. At that time, neither hearing a real check-in or the jumbled conversation caused by Clinton's electronic scrambler would be a safe prospect. He knew his life would be worthless.

Without justification for such a thought, Clinton genuinely hoped that there had been no agent intervention because their suspicions about

Saa'iqa's involvement with Will had been unfounded. At times he alternated between that thought and whether or not Saa'iqa could see any part of Will in him, if she had known him. He and Will looked unlike enough for resemblance not to be too much of a threat. About the time he decided that she might be innocent of any involvement with Will, he also realized that the thought might be folly and in his confused state, arrived at the mansion.

When he reached the office, she was sitting at the desk talking to her cousin. Their conversation was in French, so he understood it well. It was warm and loving, and there was some concern for the relative's health. He could not figure out why the cousin was up at three thirty in the morning, having casual conversation. When she saw him arrive, she cut the conversation short, ending it with love and peace for her cousin and his family. She hung up the telephone and greeted Clinton warmly.

"How was your walk?'

"Pleasant enough. The night is a little strange and the fog is heavy in scattered areas. Does fog happen often here?"

"Not really. It seems to depend on the rainfall and the conditions caused by the Atlas."

He walked toward her mostly out of a desire to be close to her. She smiled and after a pleasant peck on the mouth, she put on surgical gloves and opened the drawer where she kept his assignments.

"Yakub will accompany you to a bank where you will need to place the contents of this envelope into safety deposit box number 467. You should use gloves at all times."

She gave him the envelope containing the money. He didn't have a clue of what they were setting up.

"If it is just a safety deposit box . . . why don't I just go in during the day instead of all this cloak and dagger stuff?"

"There can be no visual connection whatsoever. I don't want anyone remembering you or even you in disguise. It's not like breaking into a vault and our connection will take care of the surveillance cameras and make it very easy for you. All you have to do is get in the box. Yakub will drive you."

Although there was no impatience in her voice, it was certainly all and only about business. Any softness from the hours of lovemaking they

213

shared most of the night was over and done with. He listened to her tone and tried to hear her clearly - intent and all. At that moment, Naseer and Yakub entered the room.

"SbaH lxair Yakub." said Saa'iqa. "This is Archie Dayton. He is ready to go Do you have any questions?"

"No Saa'iqa, I understand clearly."

Saa'iqa turned her back as she walked behind the desk to put away the large folder. She was not looking at any of them as she inquired the time. Yakub checked the time on his new gold and malachite watch, the same watch that Will had worn for the last twenty five years and took off only while sleeping. The one his father gave him. The one that left no doubt in Clinton's mind that the house he was standing in, or the people he was standing with constituted in some way, his beloved brother's last stop. The notion that Will might be dead was no longer apodictic.

"Fifteen minutes before four o'clock," Yakub answered.

Clinton felt physically ill. He struggled harder than ever before for composure, anchoring himself to the desk with one hand. Although quite calm and unaffected on the outside, his insides were aflame.

"That is a beautiful watch. Is it Jade?" Clinton asked.

Saa'iqa had not seen Yakub or the watch since Will's murder, but she knew exactly which one Clinton must have meant, even with her back turned, and she knew that Yakub was a fool. She stopped in her tracks and turned slowly to see for herself how the idiot standing in her office, her dear Naseer's blood relative had jeopardized the operation and her. Her demeanor was calm but her eyes flashed fire!

"Malachite and thank you." said Yakub, foolishly pleased with the attention.

The blundering, small minded Yakub caught the look on Saa'iqa's face and realized he was in serious trouble. He became nervous and looked toward his cousin for back up and aid. Naseer, who had been standing quietly nearby hung his head slightly in shame once Saa'iqa took the time to shift her glare from Yakub to him. He could not look her in the eyes and he feared the fire inside them, not so much physical fear for himself, but his cousin had caused him to lose some of her confidence. This notion was far beyond unacceptable. If she did not rid the world of the idiocy that made up Yakub, he would have to in order to save an inkling of face, and it was not a pleasant notion for a cousin he played with as a child.

"Where did you get it . . . I really like it." Clinton said in his most casual and unconcerned voice.

Clinton noticed Saa'iqa's flashing eyes. The same eyes that only three hours before had taken him to places he had not known for years. He looked at her small perfect body, glasslike skin and the gorgeous hair. At that moment, he wished to pluck every hair from her head, one by one, and choke the beautiful neck he could not get enough of just one hour before.

He looked at Naseer's lowered head and understood clearly that Yakub was one track they could not cover. He was too stupid to control completely and therefore dangerous, but he could not figure out why he had been allowed to remain in their midst. He did know that it had something to do with Naseer though. His own anger was almost unbearable and his knuckles were losing their color from the tight grip he held on the desk. It was the only way not to react violently so he held on, hoping they would not notice. That would be difficult as they were so focused on Yakub at the moment, and he was sweating bullets.

Yakub cleared his throat and answered. "In London, on a trip a few years ago."

Saa'iqa calmly walked toward Yakub until she was very close to him. Enough talk, time was running out. Looking straight into Yakub's eyes, Saa'iqa informed Clinton that he would have forty five minutes to complete his task. Then she spoke in a low, deadly soft voice to Yakub in French.

"You constantly amaze me with your stupidity. You will come here immediately after you have finished at the bank. You and I have much to discuss."

Sweating profusely, Yakub said "yes". He and Clinton left the room as she went to the window and stared into the dense, bizarre fog that hung over the garage. Naseer quietly closed the door behind them as they left.

◊

Inside the bank, Clinton was on the verge of throwing up. The ride over was excruciating. He did not know how much longer he could stay in control. As he opened the small locked door to the safety deposit box with a pointed instrument, his gloved hand began to shake so violently that he had to stop. He removed the black ski mask up to his nose, in an attempt to get more air, and turned away from the surveillance camera. Alone in the small room, his composure seemed to be vanishing. He leaned against the wall and took a few deep breaths.

He remembered the watch and how important it was to Will. His mind went back to the graduation of the senior class of 1971 on the campus of Howard University. Banners were all around the open field, commemorating the occasion. Many graduating students and their proud parents were milling around after the ceremony. An anxious younger Bernice Creech and her husband Clinton, Sr. searched the area for their newly graduated son Will.

Sixteen year old twins Clinton and Clarissa, helped search with the assistance of fourteen year old Justine.

Clinton Jr. could remember it all as if it were yesterday. Clinton Sr. took a watch case from his pocket and gave it to Will. Will opened the case and found a beautiful gold watch with a malachite and gold wrist band. Clinton remembered the tears that welled up in his father's eyes as he shook his eldest son's hand with pride. Bernice and Clarissa were well into full blown tears while he and Justine smiled quietly. Will hugged his father, making him blush. Will ignored his father's embarrassment and hugged him again, causing everyone, even Clinton Sr. to laugh. Clinton remembered that all was right between them on that day, and how much Will cherished the token of his stepfather's affection and would never have parted with it willingly.

Coming back to the reality of the moment, Clinton pulled the ski mask over his face again and resumed work. He quickly opened the door, reached into the envelope, got the money and placed it in the box. Then he adjusted his surgical gloves, packed up and left the area.

Outside the bank, Clinton got into the white Peugeot where Yakub was waiting patiently. Yakub turned on the ignition and moved easily down the street.

"Any problems Mr. Dayton?"

"No, not really. Is that it for the night?"

"Yes. We are finished. A short night, huh?

"And will we be working together again?"

"No. Saa'iqa is very careful not to overuse her assistants because it keeps mistakes and recognition low. I was not expected to do anything else on this articular job."

Clinton bent over and held his stomach. He warned Yakub, telling him that he must have been more nervous about the job than he realized. Yakub quickly pulled over for Clinton to get out and deal with his malady.

Yakub slowly pulled the car onto the shoulder of the dark deserted road. As soon as the car came to a stop and Yakub put on the brake, Clinton opened his car door and in one fluid motion, he kicked the door open wide and grabbed Yakub, who was about his same size, from the driver's side and across the passenger seat and out of the car as he himself got out. Once he had the shocked Yakub out and onto the ground, he grabbed him by the collar and threw him up against the side of the car, slamming him a couple of times for emphasis and release of some of his anger before attempting to communicate with words.

"Where is the man you got that watch from? Tell me now!"

"Who are you and what are you talking about," said a horrified Yakub.

"Even an idiot like you can understand what I am saying. The man . . . tall . . . black . . . my brother! Where is he?"

Yakub stared into Clinton's face, assessing the possibility of a blood relationship between he and Will. He could not think of any prayer which would help him at the moment considering all the bad dealings he had done in his past. He had more respect and fear of blood relation than any other circumstances in life, including that of a spouse. He knew this could be very bad for him.

"Your brother! Oh no I . . . I do not know what you are . . ."

Clinton banged his head against the side of the car a couple of times again, then he threw him down on the ground, which caused Yakub to lose balance and roll a few feet away. As Clinton started toward him, Yakub reached in his pocket, took out a knife and opened the blade. Clinton stopped short of grabbing him when he saw the knife.

"I suggest you make this easy on yourself because right now that thing isn't going to do you any good. I intend to beat the shit out of you until you tell me what happened to Will."

Yakub lunged at Clinton, barely missing him as he jumped out of reach. He was a desperate man, but he had no idea the years of anger, bubbling to the surface for all the injustices done against his family that he had standing in front of him. He simply had no idea.

"Mr. Dayton, there is nothing you can do to me at this point that will be any worse than what Saa'iqa will do. How did you find me?"

"You stupid son of a bitch, Saa'iqa's not your problem right now. I am."

Yakub actually laughed at the absurdity of Clinton's statement, his perspective developed from years of tales of the small, heartless woman and her exploits and horrors.

"And you call me stupid. She is always a problem. She will be for you too when she finds out how you have deceived her."

Yakub lunged toward Clinton again. Clinton moved away from him and caught him across the head with the back of his hand. Yakub recovered and turned to face him, but was still off-balance. With the momentary advantage, Clinton was able to subdue the hand with the knife and get behind Yakub, his other arm about his throat, cutting off the air supply.

"Again, when is the last time you saw him and where is he now?"

Yakub struggled to breathe, grasping at Clinton's arm with his free hand. He mustered up strength and simultaneously jabbed his elbow into Clinton's ribs and stomped on the top of his foot, causing him to break his grip. Yakub turned quickly, ready to attack.

"Your brother has long since been food for some ocean fish because he was as arrogant and foolish as you!"

He rushed Clinton head on and they struggled, the knife between them. Clinton grabbed the knife as Yakub pushed Clinton away from him with his arm across his chest. In contrast, Clinton pulled Yakub toward him forcing Yakub's hand that was holding the knife, back toward his own solarplexis region. Realizing the trouble he was in, Yakub struggled to push the enraged Clinton away but succumbed to Clinton's superior strength as the knife jabbed deeply into the man's upper abdomen. He gurgled, his eyes rolled and he fell to the ground.

Exhausted, struggling to escape from the rage which had consumed him, Clinton fell to the ground and leaned his back against the car. He had shot six men during his career on the force, and purposely, shot them in extremities like arms and legs, except for one. John Lexington had been a particularly bad customer who was tenacious and viscous and had knocked Gerald to the ground during a joint DEA/FBI investigation, and picked up a led pipe and was about to beat Gerald in his head with it. Clinton had not choice except to shoot to kill, or lose his partner. Even then, John was so mean that he tried to beat Gerald with his last and dying breath and would have succeeded had Gerald not rolled out of his way. After his last flailing attempt, Lexington fell to his knees and then dropped over on his side, still holding the iron pipe to his death. Somehow killing Lexington seemed necessary in order to save Gerald. Killing Yakub, although necessary to save his own life, seemed to come from a place that Clinton did not want to go again. There was anger so deep inside of him that it made him shake and shudder at his own lack of humanity. He tried to get himself under control as he fought not to succumb to the meanness he felt inside.

After staring at the dead man for a few seconds, Clinton got up and put Yakub's body in the back seat of the car and closed the door. Then he wiped blood from his hands and got behind the wheel and drove to Djemaa el Fna, the large market place in the city.

23 REALITIES

He parked on a side street opposite the police department and got out of the car, went to a telephone inside the lobby of a small hotel, dialed a number and waited for an answer. He looked around cautiously to see if he could be overheard, while watching the car to be certain no one was paying too much attention to what he hoped appeared to be a sleeping Yakub in the back seat of the car. When the phone was picked up, but no voice came over the line, Clinton spoke.

"Yeah . . . well a horse named Passion is in deep shit at Place Djemaa el Fna right now and needs your immediate help. Things got out of hand, and I'm expected back about now."

He waited, listening patiently for instructions, then agreed and hung up the telephone. He checked inside the car to be certain that Yakub had no surprises left in him, then went over to a wall, leaned against it and waited. He looked around at the market, and the few vendors who were beginning to set up for the day. He tried to envision the shrunken heads hanging around in ancient times that the market was so famous for and the gaze of those dead in the square of the dead. He wondered if the shrunken heads he read about were of the people hung by the Sultan as punishment for their deeds in medieval times or if any malicious predator in the country side could bring in his day's work of killing people for the purpose of selling their heads like the farmers who slaughtered sheep and hung them in the food courts in the souks.

Suddenly, Morocco seemed dark and evil to him. Dangerous and full of malice. Only days before he considered it one of the loveliest places he had ever been in with its honest and warm people. Now, he doubted their honesty and questioned their sincerity. He watched the vendors constructing their carts and tables and wondered how many people they had killed before their breakfast on the way to work . It all seemed an appropriate historical setting for the wild and bizarre and widening state of mind that Clinton was in. The sky was beginning darken less, and yet was not quite light, but the fog was still all around. It was early enough for him to feel comfortable that Saa'iqa and Naseer would not to be too suspicious about his return yet. He hoped he would be away from the square before the call to prayer.

After about ten minutes, the turbaned agent, Jim McKinney and the bearded agent Jorgé Ruiz pulled up in the van they used for surveillance on Saa'iqa's home. They got out and talked to Clinton very briefly, then Jim got into Yakub's car, and Jorgé and Clinton got in the van. Jim proceeded straight ahead while Jorgé and Clinton turned left and went down a side street.

The soft glow of daylight was slowly, but steadily approaching as Clinton and Jorgé drove through the mostly deserted streets, while Clinton thoroughly cleaned the blood from his hands with towels and an odorless solution Jorgé gave him. He felt certain he would be under greater scrutiny by Saa'iqa than the hotel clerk, and couldn't afford to have one drop of blood on his clothing or person.

"Jorge, I'm certain that Saa'iqa killed Will now, but I can't imagine why."

"I'm sorry about your brother, but remember this woman is an assassin. She doesn't reason like the rest of us. She is so hard to catch because she is thorough. That hulk started sweeping an eight block area at random intervals with electronic detectors early this afternoon. They do that fairly often. Today he banged on the van and spoke! The arrogant son of a bitch. We knew she would not move freely if she thought she'd been watched, otherwise we would have followed you. What was your assignment tonight?"

"To place money in safety deposit box number 467 at Banque' du Maroc. There were some papers written in Arabic that I couldn't decipher well enough to tell you what they said, and one French land contract. Have you been able to figure out whose house I put the journal in?"

"Not really, you and Naseer could have driven halfway to Casablanca in that amount of time. The safe next to the club was a smaller office of a local businessman named Jalaal Abdullah. He kept his first office for sentimental reasons. We know there is some connection between his death and another businessman's death, Saleem Asad. We think the link is Asad's partner Muntasir Zaid."

As they drove, Jorgé explained their speculations and how they wondered if the journal was Saleem's, but that both his wife and the local police expert Thamar Ali confirmed that the one found in his house was in his handwriting. That made sense of course, considering how well Naseer had paid Thamar for the forgery.

Jorgé went on to say that after intense police interrogations, Muntasir Zaid had continued to deny any involvement in both deaths most emphatically, but it was clear that he would profit financially from Jalaal's death in particular. It appeared that the two men joined together to sell land to a French developer, Pierre´ Bonet´, but he was out of the country and could not be reached until his return at the end of the week.

"I know that name Zaid. Saa'iqa mentioned a man named Zaid but the first name started with a K, like Kara or something. She said he was so adamant about maintaining a pure Moroccan society that he sent his French son and wife away after independence from French rule."

"Karrar Zaid was Muntasir's cold-hearted father, and that part is true. The woman and their son moved to a small town in southern France where she worked as a domestic because her wealthy Parisian family had disowned her for marrying a Moroccan. She and her son were in a freak bus accident which killed about fifteen people. A bridge collapsed and the bus fell into a river. Her body was found but Jameel's, along with four others, was never recovered. I reviewed Muntasir's life once he became a suspect."

"What about revenge? She said that the senior Zaid contributed to her father's death. Maybe she is out to get him."

"We suspect that she already did. He was murdered a few years back, in about her style, but that does not explain this new development with his son. If she considered him responsible, she'd have killed him off long ago. We think she's working for Pierre´ Bonet´. He stands to benefit most. The land contracts in Jallal's safe sell him lucrative property rights that have successfully stayed in the hands of the cartel for many years. Also, Åsad's journal refers to more deals in the works between Jallal, Muntasir and Pierre. We suspect that the three of them were trying to make a lot of money from a tract of land foreign investors have been trying to get hold of for years. Pierre' must have gotten greedy when he realized that Muntasir was the chief owner of much of the land. Jallal was an old man and no longer cared who knew he had sold out, so Muntasir signed over small pieces of the property to Jallal who in turn sold to Pierre, thus remaining a true Marrakechii nationalist. We think that then he double-crossed Bonet' and held onto a small parcel without which the rest of the land would be worthless for development. In some twisted way it appears he thought he could get away with the money and still not sell out to a Frenchman. What could Pierre' do? He could not prove direct involvement because everything went through Jallal. That's when he hired Saa'iqa to frame Muntasir for the murder of Saleem Asad in order to force him to sell the last parcel. That's our theory anyway."

"But why would he kill Jalaal, and if Muntasir already owned the land, why sell at all?"

"A Moroccan could not modernize that area without public outrage, but Jalaal's death is unclear. There's no real smoking gun yet."

"You said Pierre' would be back this week? Saa'iqa said I would have an anonymous and unannounced encounter with our employer because he wants to see me in person. There is something incomplete about this theory though. You have a picture of Bonet'?"

Jorgé pulled the van over to the side of the street, around the corner from Saa'iqa's house and stopped. Then he reached into a folder behind the passenger's seat and pulled out a picture and gave it to Clinton. Clinton looked hard at the picture of Bonet', trying to remember if he had seen him at Saa'iqa's house or in the neighborhood. He had no memory of Bonet's face whatsoever, but said that he would look out for him. He informed Jorgé that he was scheduled to complete one more job for Saa'iqa, but had no idea what it might be, and that she must have at least ten or twelve different people working on this project, none knowing what the other was doing or meeting by chance, ever. Only she and Naseer seemed to know what was really going on. He bade Jorgé farewell, and left the van.

He did not relish entering the house and trying to convince Saa'iqa that he had no idea where Yakub was - but he had no choice. As he turned the corner he noticed that he could not remember if any metropolitan area he had been in before had as many varied sidewalks as this city of Marrakech. Even in the semi-dark of the rising sunlight, he could see the small blocks in these wide walkways, but there were no slabs with peri-odic cracks two feet apart in the cement to send his mind back to child's play and the concerns of his luck, should he step on the line. Somehow the mind wanderings actually helped him focus on the task at hand. There weren't many people out yet, and as he reached his destination, he noticed that only Saa'iqa's office light was on.

He took a deep breath and looked up through the scattered fog above him now, and could see the beginnings of daylight in the sky, although it was at times obstructed by the drifts of dense fog. Just as he reached for the doorknob, he could hear the male voice singing in Arabic over the loudspeaker in the morning call for prayer. After steeling himself for the task at hand, he entered the house and joined Saa'iqa and Naseer in the office.

"Any problems with the deposit?" she asked just as he came inside the office door.

"Not a one until we were leaving. Yakub's car stopped on us about halfway here, but he was finally able to fix the problem. It took a while though."

"Where is Yakub now?"

"He said he was afraid the car would not start again if he stopped, so he kept going. He asked me to tell you that he would see you later."

Saa'iqa cut her eyes at Naseer. "Yes I suppose he did have his reasons for not returning."

"Well unless you need me further, I think I'll go to bed now."

Saa'iqa moved closer to Clinton, stroked his face gently and said, "You think you might want company?"

It was all he could do not to react to the same touch that hours before made him warm and peaceful inside but now set his soul ablaze with anger. He removed her hand from his face and placed it gently by her side. Naseer noticed the action but was too busy dwelling on the fact that it met his personal needs to try to consider the cause.

"I'm really tired now. I'll see you tomorrow, O.K.?"

Bewildered, Saa'iqa answered, "Alright," but she watched him carefully as he left the room, curious about the new behavior.

24   TWINS AND SOULMATES

He survived being in the same house with Saa'iqa and avoided intimate contact with her for two full days. He was tense and angry, but no longer felt numb and dead inside. He had to be cautious, because he realized, he wanted to live - and to live fully, if only to see Will's murders come to justice.

A couple of days later, as Naseer drove the three of them through the noon traffic, the silence seemed unusual in the car. She was reading a book, her constant pastime, about poisonous plants. Clinton engaged neither of them in conversation while Naseer casually watched his less than normal behavior in the rear view mirror. They arrived and parked the car.

Naseer, Saa'iqa and Clinton entered the Sofitel Hotel Restaurant and were escorted to a table by the maitre' d. As they passed a table near a window where a black woman and three men were seated, the woman, who was least visible from their point of view called out to Clinton, using his real name. The tone of her voice cut into his heart and made him physically ill inside, the pit of his stomach aching and burning in a slow sensation like lava seeping through his body. It was Clarissa! He knew for certain that she was pregnant at that moment, because he could not imagine how else she could have been that close to him and he not sense her. He dismissed the communication breakdown in Kenya. That was a mistake.

His mind raced but he ignored her, knowing it was their only hope. She assumed he had not heard her, excused herself from the table and rushed to catch up with him. He continued walking, thinking that he could somehow relate the message to her telepathically to go back and sit down. It didn't work this time, although sometimes such non-verbal communication had worked in the past. She touched him on the shoulder.

"Excuse me sir . . . sir . . ."

Her three companions watched her carefully as did Saa'iqa and Naseer, as Clinton turned to greet her.

"Clinton . . . what are you doing here?"

Clinton flashed a beautiful, white toothed, brilliant cordial Archie Dayton smile from behind the beard and removed his sunglasses so that she could see his eyes as he spoke to her. He was Archie in rare form.

"Although at the moment I regret being unfamiliar with such radiant beauty, I'm afraid you have me confused with someone else dear lady."

The intensity of his eye contact cued Clarissa into the proper behavior for the moment. She responded easily knowing that if your twin says he doesn't know you, you know the seriousness of the situation and you don't know him either.

"I'm very sorry. I guess I have . . . for a moment you looked like a man I used to work with."

"That's quite alright."

She returned to the table allowing Clinton time to observe the glare on the face of one of her lunch companions, a well dressed, fair skinned Moroccan named Claude DuParc, whose eyes were riveted on Saa'iqa. Aware of the intensity focused on her, Clinton turned to see Saa'iqa's reaction. She returned his stare but the look on her face was one of utter confusion. Clinton turned to follow Naseer and the patient Maitre d' to their table. Saa'iqa followed.

Once seated both Clinton and Saa'iqa ordered alcoholic drinks, an unusual occurrence for either of them. Naseer watched them both in curiosity as they waited for their meal. Clinton attempted small talk but it was very hard to sustain for some reason. After a few sips of his drink, Clinton excused himself stating that he had promised to call his sick father about mid-day, Moroccan time.

He walked across the room and into an alcove to the telephones and dialed. As soon as he heard Gerald's voice on the other end, he began talking.

"Gerald I only have a moment . . . Clarissa is here, and I think she is in danger. Call her law firm in Paris and find out who's with her in Morocco today. Then get me a background brief on each of them. (He paused to listen.) There are three men but I am most interested in the Moroccan. He appears to be the tallest of the three, and is definitely the youngest. (pause) In particular, I need to know about his parents, childhood, and where he was born. (pause) I've got to go. I'll call you back in ten minutes . . .oh . . . and if you have time, contact Jim and Jorgé and ask them to hang outside the Sofitel Hotel. If they see Clarissa and the men leave, they should stay with her. I don't want her hurt! (pause) I'll call back.

Clinton hung up the telephone and walked past Claude Duparc enroute to the phones, as he returned to Naseer and Saa'iqa. Offering no acknowledgment, Clinton disappeared as Claude reached his destination. Clinton could not believe what was happening. His gut was telling him that Saa'iqa and the Moroccan knew each other, and considering that he was to be seen by his employer on that particular day, Clinton was only left with the possibility that this man was Saa'iqa's boss. Worse, he certainly was not Pierre Bonet', but some new element in this convoluted game of subterfuge and duplicitous behavior. He could not think of a worse nightmare in his entire life than to have Clarissa involved somehow. He should have told her that he would not really be in London so that she would not have been thrown off like that. Had she expected him to be in Morocco, she would have been more cautious he thought as he sat at the table.

Claude arrived at the telephones, unable to use his cellular telephone at the table. He picked up the receiver of a wall phone and dialed, made his connection and spoke in French.

"Chantal, I need you to pull up Clarissa Pillonel's file please. I'll wait."

As he waited, he was such a nervous wreck that he nearly paced a hole in the two foot square patch of carpet that the telephone cord would allow him to walk. After all, the only reason he was able to recommend Will as a possibility for Saa'iqa's work was because when he had his attorney checked out thoroughly, he also found out what he suspected she did not know. That one of her brothers was a jewel thief.

"Yes, yes, I'm here. I recall her telling me that her sister-in-law and nephew were killed a few years ago. What is her brother's name? Is it Clinton? (pause) What? I'll call later."

Claude unbuttoned his jacket and wiped his forehead before picking up the telephone receiver again.

Clinton arrived at the table, struggling not to look overly concerned. Saa'iqa was a little nervous and casually kept an eye on the telephone bays as they ate their lunch. The waiter brought over a telephone and asked if she was Saa'iqa Mastoora. She took the phone and greeted her caller in Arabic. Claude was on the other end, calling her from the phone bays. He asked her to listen without reacting. She agreed and he continued.

"I suspect that the man you think is Archie Dayton is actually my attorney's brother, Clinton Creech, Clarissa and Will Creech's brother. I never made the connection because we were looking at Archie Dayton's photos, I thought. This brother was out of the U.S. for a long time, and I was unable to track him closely when I checked him out. I knew he was a traumatized former FBI agent who lost his family. Will, I found out, was a thief, and a really good one at that. That is why I was able to connect you to him. I know Clarissa well enough to know when she is shaken, and she is badly shaken right now. That man rattled her so I checked her files. We have been set up Saa'iqa! He must be here to look for Will. Have you understood what I've said?"

Without altering her expression, and continuing to talk pleasantly as if discussing a fashion show, Saa'iqa replied that she understood everything perfectly well. Claude continued, his palms sweating so badly that he had to use his handkerchief to dry them so that the receiver would not slip out of his hand. He had been so careful not to have complications. He hired Saa'iqa because she had always been such a perfectionist. What could possibly be happening to his plans?

"Saa'iqa, I'm waiting for my secretary to fax a photograph of Clinton Creech to me for verification. This is very bad. The last papers must be properly placed, and I suspect he knows who I am and that we are on to him. Clarissa is staying in this hotel . . . so I want you to have Naseer abduct her from room 284 this afternoon, and take her somewhere to be held as insurance toward his cooperation. Once we have finished with my brother's destruction, get rid of them both."

Smiling and laughing cheerfully, Saa'iqa agreed that it sounded like a marvelous plan and said she would await his call. Nervous from all the cheer and happiness, Clinton rose from the table and was about to leave when Saa'iqa asked where he was going.

"I did not reach my father earlier and need to try to call him again. Why, is there something wrong?"

"Oh no, all is fine. I was only wondering."

As Clinton made his way toward the telephones, Saa'iqa warned Claude that he was coming his way. Claude responded by saying that he would return to the table but for her to continue talking as if someone was still on the other line in order to avoid suspicion. She did.

As Clinton dialed Gerald, a clear and sudden panic wracked every bone in his body. Although he still appeared calm, his stomach was turning flips and the muscles of one of his calves were tightening, working their way toward a severe charley horse. He fought hard to remain still inside but the battle was tremendous. There was no way he could tell his mother that two of her children were dead, or that Clarissa had been hurt, or worst of all, for her to hear that all of her children had died at the hands of a Moroccan assassin. Bernice would lose her mind if she lost all three children within three months, and heaven forbid, an unborn grandchild as well. He watched the physical reactions that losing Will had caused her to have. She tried to hide it, but he suspected she had experienced some nausea, and she certainly lost weight during his stay in D.C..

He steeled himself as he heard the easy, even voice of his long time friend on the other line.

"Well Gerald . . .what's the deal? Who is this man?"

"Clinton, you are probably right about your hunch. He appeared at a convent at age fourteen with no memory except for his name . . .Claude DuParc. He went to the finest schools and became successful in the clothing industry. I checked on Karrar Zaid's French wife's maiden name. Her family name was DuParc. He may well be . . ."

Clinton had been watching Clarissa's table while on the telephone and saw the other two men leave Claude and Clarissa alone.

"Oh shit Gerald! Something's up! I don't like this at all. Get Jorgé and Jim here now!"

Clinton hung us the telephone abruptly as Gerald was informing him that the two agents had already been contacted. As he walked back to the table, Claude and Clarissa got up from their table and left. He took an alternate route to his table in an effort to follow his sister, but was cut off by Saa'iqa as she approached him from the side.

"Archie, there you are. I was on my way to the washroom, then we can leave if you are ready."

Clinton read the ever so slight narrowing of Saa'iqa's eyes, and tried to understand their meaning while remaining calm and staying in character.

"Alright. That's fine by me."

He looked at Claude and Clarissa as they left the building, and saw Claude take Clarissa's arm, with a little more purpose than Clinton supposed would be normal for the occasion. Clarissa though not over reacting, turned to look for Clinton, a somewhat desperate and confused look on her face. Clinton saw her and struggled not to knock Saa'iqa down and run to his sister. Saa'iqa studied Clinton's face as his sister's panic registered throughout his being. Her suspicions confirmed, Saa'iqa blazed chilling ice eyes at Clinton, forcing him back into character.

"Go ahead Saa, take your time, I'll be at the table when you return." he said in a cool and casual manner.

"Saa" she thought as she left him and moved toward the lavatories. This was evidence to her that he was nervous. He had not tried shortening her name before, not that she could remember. It was one of the things that she liked about him. Unlike most Americans from the U.S., he never tried to make Moroccan names convenient and fit into a narrow American speech pattern, too lazy to call a person by their correct name.

As she opened the door of the rest room, Clinton looked at the table where Naseer was watching his every move. He could almost see the steam coming out of the big man's ears. Certain at that moment when his eyes connected with Naseer's, and the smirk which had been hidden underneath the dutiful facade came upon the big man's face, as it slowly surfaced and told a tale of gleeful revenge in his eyes, Clinton knew with all certainty that the charade was over. With speed and agility he headed for the door, where his sister was just clearing the large foyer of the hotel. Naseer left the table and followed him, but there was considerable distance between them, thwarting the big man's efforts.

Clinton ran out of the main entrance and onto the sidewalk, looking both ways for any sign of Clarissa, but to no avail. Panic struck his soul. He was annoyed that he could not feel her presence and that he could not determine which way she had gone? When they were kids, hide and seek was a useless game for the two of them, but they played so that they could interact with the other children. Suddenly he resented the fact that she had chosen this time period in her life to have another child.

Aware that he was being followed by Naseer, he quickly ducked behind a support column at the far end of the entranceway. Seconds after he was well hidden, Naseer ran from the door, looked around quickly then returned inside when he could not find Clinton. As Naseer hurriedly disappeared through the doorway, Jim and Jorgé pulled up in the blue van alongside Clinton. Immediately Clinton jumped into the van.

"Drive down the street and turn right down that alley. Maybe he has Clarissa there! They haven't had much time to escape."

Jim moved quickly down the street and whipped a right turn into the alley. They moved slowly, checking the area for signs of Clarissa. The three men searched the area from the van at first, then Clinton jumped out and ran quietly through the clearing, looking for his sister, Claude or any sign of an open doorway. After a couple of minutes, he jumped back in the van and asked Jim to take him to Saa'iqa's house as fast as possible so that he could get some bargaining power. The van sped onto the main thoroughfare and down the relatively quiet streets for a workday in the perpetually busy Marrakech.

When they arrived at Saa'iqa's they appeared to be alone, much to Clinton's relief. He unlocked the door and ran upstairs to his room, grabbed the suitcase packed with clothes that he always kept under the bed and his bag of tools and ran downstairs toward the office. As he moved through the courtyard he heard the housekeeper, Hani, in the kitchen singing an old folk song, but was careful not to let her hear him.

He understood enough Arabic now to get the gist of her words. It was a song about a mother who lost her child in the market, and sent the men of the village to find her. She was concerned about whether or not the child had eaten all of her food during the last meal that she had. The mother prayed to Allah to take care of her child, and not let her be hungry until she found her way back to her family. Clinton considered the irony of mothers and their lost children and how appropriate the song was for the moment. It was as if she could read the situation in the air. He reached the office and hurried to complete his tasks.

He threw the bag on top of the desk, unzipped it, removed a set of lock opening devices and opened the bottom drawer of the desk with ease. He grabbed the brown folder full of the papers he was to place for the last job, put it in his black work bag, picked up both bags and ran from the office into the courtyard. To his dismay, he heard Saa'iqa and Naseer coming in the front door. Quickly, he turned and escaped through the patio door without a sound, the same patio door that Will broke into when he stole Saa'iqa's jewels.

Saa'iqa and Naseer entered the office, still discussing the events of the past couple of hours. Naseer was mostly quiet as Saa'iqa, in a much too calm voice acknowledged that she should have listened to her best friend and loyal companion. He responded that they were only hunches and that he too had begun to trust Clinton, alias Archie as well. She sat on the edge of the desk and noticed the open drawer and missing folder . She went into the seething but calm rage that was betrayed only by the flash of fire in her eyes.

"That bastard took the contracts intended for Pierre' Bonet." How could he have been here and gone so quickly? Search the house Naseer and I'll check with Hani."

Naseer left the office just as Saa'iqa slammed the desk drawer shut, an action rare enough to make Naseer stop momentarily to examine her expression. He was unaccustomed to emotionalism from her. She was always cool, despite the situation. She saw him turn and look at her from the courtyard. She lowered her head for a moment.

"I'm fine. Just a temporary reaction to my own stupidity. Sorry."

"Not a problem, only curious." He replied.

He went upstairs. She started toward the kitchen, but stopped abruptly when the office telephone rang.

"Hello."

It was Clinton calling from the mobile phone in the van.

"Saa'iqa, we need to talk."

"Yes I suppose we do. You have something I want and we have your sister Clinton Creech. I'd like to know how you were able to get Jessica Lash to participate in your deception. I know she knows better."

"That's not important right now. I doubt you have time for more forgeries to be made or to replace me before tomorrow. We should be able to work something out. All I want is Clarissa and to get the hell out of Morocco."

"And I am supposed to believe what you say, huh? Aside from that, I do not have the authority to make any decisions about yours or your sister's future. Call me back in two hours and I will have an answer for you."

She hung up the telephone receiver and disconnected, before picking it up and dialing. As the phone rang, Naseer walked back into the room and leaned against the door while he listened to Saa'iqa's conversation. He looked at her on that day as he had every day of her life, with undying and unaltered love. He remembered the first time he saw her as a baby. He had never seen a newborn with so much hair on its head, and eyes that were nearly Kelly green, with hints of yellow in them. They were so bright. Her eyes generally frightened people because they were so odd, but as a baby, they looked like a cat or moreso, like a snake. She had many an old conjure woman visit her in those early years, trying to drive out the spirits that must have been inside. Finally, her eyes became a little darker and more blue-green. The old bats finally stopped making daily visits. Naseer remembered being happy that the visits were less frequent, thereby leaving him more time to be with her.

It was how he became a logical choice as her protector. He always considered it his job from the day she was born and he knew he was hopelessly smitten with her. As she grew up, she was a happy, smart little girl who learned at the speed of lightning. She was open and generous, and only gave love and sweetness. Her days were filled with thinking up ways to make her mother and father happy, doing good deeds for the needy, and teaching less fortunate children her own age how to read. She was devout to the teachings of Islam, and was one of the few children he knew who prayed at least five times a day and never protested any of the rituals. Her heart was open and warm with an enormous amount of love left over for all with whom she came in contact. Her world was wonderful and bright, her future filled with joy and happiness, and the conjure women were pleased with their early work. All was great, calm and praise to Allah, most highest in its existence . . until her parents died.

When her father first had the stroke she was hopeful, supportive and cried only when he could not see. She thrived on the hope of his full recovery.

Naseer would never forget the despair she felt when her father died and the affect it had on him as well. It was one of the most traumatic events of his life, even moreso than his own uncle's death. Aside from his personal loss of the man he admired so greatly as a businessman, a father, a husband and the epitome of a good Moslem man, the effect it had on

Saa'iqa was devastating to Naseer.

She cried every day for weeks. Her face was swollen and her beautiful blazon eyes were only slits of puffed skin, with red rims around the edges. He was severely pained, every tear she shed. He sometimes felt it was unbearable to feel so much pain and incredible to feel it through someone else's sorrow. At least at that time, she would talk to him and keep some dialog about what she was feeling. He had never known anyone who felt so deeply and so much. He was in awe of the depth of her love for her father, in awe of her depth of love for any other human, in awe of the warm and wonderful places in her soul that allowed her to so thoroughly give her being and essence to another person. He became even more enamored with her and longed for the kind of love he knew she was capable of giving.

He understood then how connected he was to her and how intertwined their lives were. He prayed to Allah more than five times a day to bring her peace and tranquillity, for her and for his own sanity. There were times when her pain was so great that he felt physical reactions of many varieties. During those early days, he would often have shooting stomach aches or chest pains and would lose weight, as did she. He could stand the loss, but she nearly wasted away, being too small to handle the drop in poundage.

Just as her tears were beginning to lessen - to only eight or ten times a week - and he thought they might make it through the emotional storm, her mother killed herself. It was as if the bottom fell out of the sky. It rained torrents for three days causing floods and stopping commerce that so many of the farmers and craftspersons depended upon on a daily basis in Morocco. Naseer would never forget those days. It was as if Allah himself was reacting out of umbrageous yet righteous indignation.

Saa'iqa sat in a room for three weeks in a catatonic state, a constant stream of tears running down her face, but not filled with the sobbing emotionalism after he Father's death. Only water, constant water. She lost about thirty pounds and looked like a skeleton or an anorexic. She did not care if she bathed or ate and would not look at a book, her favorite activity generally. Naseer and his family cared for her as if she were the emotional invalid that she was. It was the only thing they could do. She would not talk, not even to him. She could not, he came to understand.

He had the worst weeks of his life after the suicide. He wasn't suffering the physical pain from her pain, but he was in mortal fear and spiritual despair. He could find no way to get through to her, and she was unreadable.

He waited. And waited, and waited.

He waited everyday, in the corner of her room, during the light of day and the dark of night. He waited in the middle of storms when the violent sounds of thunder and torrential rain forced farm animals into hiding and people indoors. He waited through the hordes of well-wishers who visited and tried to offer advice to the family of servants caring for the orphaned child. He waited and sang songs to her from shadows across the room as he stood and lifted his baritone voice in the folk songs of both Morocco and France, the homes of the parents she missed so deeply. He stayed in her room all day and all night for weeks, and prayed to Allah for hours on end. Prayed for her sanity. Prayed for her return. Prayed that she would not leave him.

She sat in a corner staring out of the window at the sky, and he sat in the opposite corner staring at her. She would not eat, and he could not eat. She would not sleep and he was afraid to lest she hurt herself or come back to him and he miss that first moment when she recognized his face or touched his hand. A week went by, then two, then three and he waited. He was becoming more and more afraid that she would never return to him. On the fourth week of her despair, she turned and looked at him, wiped the last tears from her eyes and spoke.

"I will never cry again. I will not love this much again. And I will destroy those who have brought me so much sorrow and any others who have such great greed as those who have caused my family such destruction. I hold only you close to my heart, but even you cannot come inside. There's no space there anymore. Allah has deserted me."

She looked out of the window again and he watched as the last tear rolled down her face. The last one he would ever see. He could not begin to understand how to respond to her statements. She was still a child, but her words were certainly not that of a child. He was flabbergasted. He sat quietly and waited. She stared out of the window. They stayed that way for another two days, without a word or a tear. At the end of the second day, she stood up walked over to him and sat down in his lap, looked deep into his eyes, put her arm around his neck and kissed him on the mouth. He remembered that the action was so inappropriate for a young girl that he started to react, but fear of her emotional state and her reaction to any rejection at that moment made him stay calm. She pulled away from him and stared deeply into his eyes. He felt he had to respond and attempted to do so.

"Saa'iqa, it is not proper for you to kiss a man like that. You are a well brought up young lady, and in the eyes of Allah this is improper behavior, let alone the fact that you are much too young to think like that. Now I . . ."

"Naseer, my dearest Naseer. Protector of mine. I no longer live by anyone's rules. If I am to survive, I will do it in any manner I see fit. If you do not want me to act in this way with you I will not, but do not try to tell me how I am to act. It is useless. I have done what was appropriate. I have been a dutiful daughter of Islam. It has done me no good. I will do what I want now and if you care for me, you will leave me alone. Now let's go see what Mother cook has fixed for dinner. I am hungry."

With that, she left the room for the kitchen. He followed, fearful yet exhilarated by her new behavior. Grateful there was any behavior to be fearful or exhilarated by. She ate like a ravenous animal after a hunt and kill in the wild. She ate lamb, and couscous, vegetables, oranges, pastries -both Moroccan and French, pasta and Pastilla, grapes, melon and dates. She drank mineral water, mint tea, and fruit juice.

He watched her for an hour and realized that she was just that - an animal after a kill. She had killed off the person that she was and was feeding the new creature she was becoming. He was witnessing the birth of an entirely new being. He shuddered with fear for what was to come. No one else seemed to notice the difference in her, they were simply grateful that she had returned to them. She appeared the same.

The only visible difference in her demeanor was that she never raised her voice again. Not in play, or in anger. She was always soft spoken, and the more hostile she became, the lower the tone and volume of her voice would descend. She was still very kind to those who deserved it, she showed family love and devotion in the same way, but she never prayed again, at least not in the early years. She had gone through the act of the ritual in recent years only because it was a good disguise for a

Moslem woman, but the words were hollow and had no meaning to her whatsoever . She could have been reciting from a cookbook, or saying the national anthem of a foreign country for all it meant to her.

Once she made the transformation, the conjure women seemed to be the only people who were clear that a change had occurred. They came around a couple of times and tried to talk to her. She was smart and did not say anything to them that would let them know how her heart had changed . . . but they knew, and they stayed away. They were quiet, but they never returned.

Because of the age difference between them, it was easy to keep his feelings in check when they were young. But as she grew up, as she became a woman, he had increasing difficulty staying in line because even though a part of her had changed drastically, he and possibly he alone could see the bright shining light still burning inside of her. He could feel the place where her heart once was and hoped with all his being that the child with the warm soul would return to him once again. Until then, he would do whatever she wanted in order to stay close to her, even kill.

Over the years he had seen her guard almost come down, never with anyone else but once or twice with him. She had been in complete control of their relationship over the years. Others thought it was because of his station in life and although that was part of it, he was too modern a man for those restrictions to completely support his caution and submission to her.

He could have left years ago, and nearly considered it when offered an opportunity to play professional football in the U.S. after he finished college. He was afraid to miss any time out of her life however , and therefore did not leave. He also did not know what effect his leaving would have on her. He feared she might have no restraint; no control; no compassion. Despite the ice, he knew she loved him in the only way she could. Her words that day were true. He was as close as anyone could get to her, and that sustained him through many years, many men, and many, many murders and deaths.

Had he left, he would have missed the first time that they made love. She had been wild over her late teenage years and early twenties, or maybe a better way to describe it would have been calculatedly promiscuous when it met her needs. She was twenty two and home from college before attending graduate school when she set her sights on him. He felt it was a moment of weakness, when she was trying to decide if she should remain heartless and whether or not the coldness in her veins would still feel good to her. He hoped that if she felt warm and secure, the light would come back on and she would release some of the ice coursing through her body. She made him promise that the one sexual encounter would not have any emotional effect on their relationship. Fool that he was, he promised. It had proven to be one he held fast with his honor, but certainly not with his heart.

He drove her to the resort house in Al Hoceima that belonged to her estate. They began their mini vacation walking on the beach between the cliffs and along the rocky inlets, gazing dreamily at the blue water and white sand. They scuba dove the coral reefs, absorbing the beauty of the breathtaking, expansive colors, plants and fish beneath the surface of the clear waters. They rented a boat and went deep sea fishing, took long rides out on the ocean in the moonlight and gave each other sensuous massages in warm oils and made long, slow love under the bright starlit sky.

Every time he looked at her, he could remember the soft touch of her hair as it brushed across his chest and thighs when it fell in all directions while she sat naked on top of him. It was love making for him, and for her he believed - not just sex. It was a natural succession for the relationship they shared, and an act that he hoped would make her comfortable enough to let him into her heart.

It was a two day fest of love that he would never forget. He did everything he could think of to make it a wonderful experience for her. She was as willing and participatory as he was gentle and attentive. When it was over, they basked in the warmth of each other and he was hopelessly in love. He waited to see if there was any effect on her emotional state. Any possibility of her softening. He saw a glimpse of something happen, but before he could get a handle on her emotions and plan an assault on the hardness she recuperated and returned to her usual position, forcing him into his usual position and station in life. The Ice Goddess returned within a week.

The second time they were together sexually was when she decided that her biological clock was ticking and she needed to have a baby. She was distracted and preoccupied with odd emotions relating to her biology and was strangely scary to him at that time. She made the decision that if she was going to have a baby, that he and only he could be the father because she was clear that no other man could be close enough to her to be a participating father and her child had to have a full time father. Religious protocol went straight out of the window for him and he had been elated at the thought, though he struggled not to show too much joy because he was certain it would scare her off.

However, once they embarked upon their mission, her own insecurities got in the way of any meaningful lovemaking that might actually produce a child. Even he knew that. She was tense, sporadic and nervous. They couldn't get positions right as the missionary position proved useless because of their difference in size. Every sexual attempt was awkward and strange. Once, a bat flew into the open window of her bedroom and flapped around the room wildly in an attempt to find freedom. The fight to get it out deflated all interest in sex and frustrated him tremendously. Saa'iqa took it as a sign of negative energy surrounding the conception of a baby, and became unusually emotional.

He could do nothing to calm her mood and he tried everything he could think of. He lured her into the tub for a long relaxing soak, but the water kept getting cold; the bubbles kept dying down as if the soap and oils had gone flat. He tried giving her a massage, but her tight muscles simply would not relax. They would give way momentarily and then lock up as soon as he moved to another part of her body, so that by the time he moved back to her shoulders they felt hard and constricted as if he had done no work at all.

He had picked her up and carried her to the balcony and lay her on the chaise lounge there and kissed every part of her body from her ears to her toes, and licked everything in between with his tongue, lingering at her neck, breasts and clitoris in hopes that the light touch would help her lose the tension plaguing every sinew she had. After a while she leapt from the lounge and went back inside, sat down and began braiding her hair into one long braid, while he was in mid nuzzle behind her knees.

"I simply cannot concentrate Naseer."

"You don't need to concentrate Saa'iqa. That is the purpose of this act. To be free and not concentrate. Just relax." he said to her retreating back as she left and sat at the vanity.

Finally, baffled by her behavior, he went to her and rubbed her back gently while she looked into the mirror and braided. He stood behind her, astounded by the emotion she rose in him. She leaned against his thigh, rested her head against his stomach and kissed his navel gently.

"I'm sorry. I don't know why but this just isn't working. I can't be calm inside for some reason. You know its not you."

Her touch against his bare skin and the half braided hair brushing against his thigh and down his leg to his knee was nearly more than he could endure. He turned her body around to face his, opened her legs wide and knelt down on both knees between her thighs. Even kneeling, he was still slightly taller than she was in her sitting position. He kissed her forehead, pulled her head back with his hand and kissed her gently on the neck before speaking to her.

"You may have all the time you want. You do whatever it takes to feel comfortable."

She hugged him around the neck and buried her face in his chest. He held her tightly for a few minutes then stood, put on his robe and sat out on the balcony. She joined him, he opened the robe and encompassed her naked body with it and she curled her small body under his arm and into his side. They sat in silence until she fell asleep then he carried her to bed, tucked her in and left her. To sleep with her all night and smell her hair and skin, and feel her touch, or have her roll up under him would have created more disappointment the next morning for him, and although he was far more patient than many men, he was not a glutton for punishment.

It had been a painful experience for him to have something that he waited seventeen years for to have gone so wrong. He deduced that the thought of loving some small creature which might leave her, or get sick or die was much too much for her to bear. The next morning, she woke up and turned off the damned biological clock . . . for good she said. Needless to say, that one time was the only effort toward baby making that ever happened for them.

He was patient. He would wait for that light forever if necessary. But that was when he started finding sexual partners a little more often . . .

every three or four days now. He seemed to have needs that he had not noticed were so often before. It allowed him the calm to wait. Watching her with other men though was difficult for him , especially Clinton Creech. All he wanted was to break his neck into tiny little pieces to get his hands off of Saa'iqa.

As he watched her talking on the telephone, he was clear about why he loved her so much. He could see the little girl as she pushed her toes around the tip of the four inch heels she had taken off, and played with the edge of the desk with her heel while sitting on the desk. He smiled at the thought of spending the rest of his life with her, and hoped one day they could have enough peace between them to enjoy the last days of their lives together as the lovers he knew they should be and the soulmates they already were.

She had Claude on the line.

25 TORMENT

She reached him at a sleazy hotel in a the Old City, in poor section of town. He was sitting on a bed watching Clarissa, who was sitting in a chair near a desk, gagged, with her hands tied behind her back. Aamil stood near the door in a relaxed guard like stance. Claude looked very worried as he talked to Saa'iqa on the telephone.

"Yes. When? . . . no, I have a better idea. Maybe we can take care of everything at once. Have him meet us at Pierre Bonet's house tomorrow night at eight o'clock, but tell him to call back at seven thirty tomorrow night to tell him of the location . . . Don't argue with me! You've made a big enough mess of things haven't you? We can still accomplish everything and take care of these new matters . . . No! I have planned this too long for it to fall apart now. Do what I say!

Claude hung up the telephone and walked over to Clarissa. He stood over her for a moment without speaking, only the heavy sighs of a man with immense worries could be heard. The weight of the moment sent chills through Clarissa's body. She began to shake slightly though she put up a brave front. The call for evening prayer came up from the square. The strong Arabic voice sang with the clarity of a bird in beautiful phrasing and lilting tones that coasted across the city to Claude's ears. Claude began singing in Arabic, joining the voice of the call. Clarissa looked up into his face and realized he was possessed by the spirit of the religion. She wished at that moment that he was as clear about the intent of the message of the prayer which although she couldn't be certain of its words, she felt certain did not include telling him to kill her or Clinton.

As she watched him, she knew all too well that she was in deep trouble and that he was on a mission which would not be dissuaded by Clinton, the Moroccan woman with the long hair or his relationship with her and the knowledge of her having children to love and raise and care for. Nothing in her world mattered to him as much as, as far as she could figure, his revenge.

When the call stopped, Claude began stroking Clarissa's face very gently as he talked to her. He paced slowly around her in circles, rubbing her face first with the back and then the front of his hand.

"Clarissa, I deeply regret your stumbling into this mess. Your brothers have made my life a bit more complicated though and now I'm afraid your mother will lose all three of her children in such a short time span. I am sorry for her. I know you have been concerned about her. . . I understand loss of a loved one, in fact that is one of the reasons my brother must die now. Before Clinton interfered he would have been framed for the murder of Bonet' but now, I suppose Pierre can shoot both Muntasir and his accomplice Archie Dayton when they come to steal back the incriminating contracts and to eliminate Pierre'."

He was getting more and more animated, stopped circling, stood in front of her and began rubbing Clarissa's face with both hands, as if working out his new plan gave him energy and power. Clarissa became more and more nervous, and Aamil watched Claude cautiously out of one eye.

"Yes . . . that will work Clarissa. Not as well as Muntasir rotting in prison, but I guess he has been sufficiently discredited. I'm certain Pierre' will prefer this method since in the prior plan, his dying was one of the requirements that he was unaware of."

He chuckled to himself, walked behind her and began rubbing her neck and back with both hands, pushing her hair up and her head forward every few strokes of contact with her. Her eyes widened as she wondered if he had other, more sexual plans for her. The thought made her even more nervous. He continued rubbing her shoulders.

"You are so tense Clarissa. Relax."

Under any other circumstances in the world, his shoulder rub would have felt great. Possibly inappropriate for their work relationship but a pleasant sensation anyway. As was in this case, she could not think of when last she wanted a beautiful, rich man to get as far away from her as she wanted Claude DuParc to at that moment.

"You didn't know I had a brother did you. Well nobody does . . . not even him. He either thinks I'm dead or could care less. You see, I was born Jameel Zaid, son of Karrar Zaid."

He went on to tell the tale of his and his mother's banishment and how he watched Karrar and fourteen year old Muntasir as they stood pompously in the center of the great foyer of the Zaid's house. He remembered that day too well and how Jallal Abdullah was standing next to the door with a suitcase in his hand, and six more sitting by the door. A man servant picked up the luggage and carried it out of the door, while his mother Yvette Zaid and he, Jameel, stood talking to the stocky, strongly built Karrar. He talked of how he remembered Karrar's Moroccan wife Khalilah standing quietly in the background, with tears streaming down her face.

He always liked Khalilah. In fact he had waited so many years to exact his revenge because he did not want to cause her any pain by his actions against Muntasir. She died six months before he hired Saa'iqa. Khalilah was kind and gentle, and she treated him like her own son. She and his mother, a second, foreign wife, never had any problems that he could see and they lived together in harmony and with happiness between them. The look on her face was as pained as his own mother, but she stood quietly on the sidelines.

Claude told Clarissa that he had not faulted her because as a woman, there was little she could do. He had seen Karrar have her locked in a room, and not allowed her to come out for weeks for as little as expressing an opinion albeit mildly and with the greatest respect. Her words meant nothing if he did not want to hear what she had to say, and it was hard to predict what his reaction would be. She had been pleading and promising him all she could offer for days before the official banishment, in hopes that he would reconsider and allow them to stay. Claude had heard her promise to have more sons for him; to allow him more wives if that was what he wanted; she offered herself sexually as often as he wanted and she offered to work harder in the community to escalate his standing if he would simply allow Yvette and Jameel to stay. None of her words meant anything to Karrar. One thing for certain was that he would not take kindly to her speaking while he was in the middle of ridding himself of his French wife and child. Even through his quiet rage while recounting his story, Claude bore no anger toward her.

"Clarissa, my Mother dropped to her knees and begged for him to allow us to stay and not yield to the wishes of the cartel and the pressures of the independence movement."

Claude dropped to his knees abruptly, and tears ran down his face as he told of the indignities his mother suffered that tearful day, as he continued.

"Karrar's only retort was 'We are Moroccan now . . . only!'" Claude said in Arabic then translated for Clarissa, so that she could understand fully the weight of the situation.

Clarissa listened carefully.

Claude told of how after his father of eleven years issued his command, he turned and left the foyer. Tearfully Khalilah had moved to comfort Yvette but thought better of it, hung her head and followed her husband from the room. Claude stood up and sat on the edge of the bed while he continued.

"My mother was inconsolable. Jalaal helped her up from the floor and toward the door. He often cleaned up my father's messes. I tried to talk to Muntasir." I said, "Muntasir, please you talk to him. He will listen to you. He will not send us away if you explain that we are not like the French he talks about. Do you know what my fourteen year old brother said Clarissa?"

Clarissa shook her head, letting him know that she was still listening, still with him - afraid not to be.

"He said, why would I do that? He is correct. All French are alike." Claude said. "I asked him how he could say such a thing and reminded him that we had been brothers all our lives. We had played together . . . and besides . . . why did he marry my mother at all. She was always French, I said."

Claude was becoming more and more agitated. He stood up and walked around the room, then began flailing his arms around and nearly shouting as he asked Clarissa his next question.

"Do you know what he said Clarissa? Do you know what he said?"

Claude hit the dresser with his fist causing a loud banging sound that made Clarissa jump and made Aamil put his hand a little closer to the knife on his side, and take a couple of steps closer to the window to look out to see if they were attracting attention. Claude realized from their reactions that he had been a little loud.

"I apologize for being emotional. I can seldom stay in full control when I think about that day."

He sat on the side of the bed again but he was shaken and he was scaring the daylights out of Clarissa. He wasn't making Aamil too comfortable either. He gained his composure again and spoke very calmly to Clarissa, albeit through slightly clinched teeth.

"Muntasir said it was true that my mother was always French, and that on that day, Karrar had rectified his mistake. We were a mistake to him Clarissa. One that could be gotten rid of after nearly fifteen years of marriage to my mother. I could not believe what he was saying to me. I said how can you say these things to me? She has cared for you when you were sick and I am your brother!"

Claude sat straight as an arrow, adjusting the several thousand dollars worth of clothing on his body. He stared into Clarissa's eyes with great intent and resolve.

"Clarissa, he said to me that I was French, and that he had no brother. Then he turned his pompous ass around and walked out of the room. My mother began wailing again as that snake Jalaal guided her out of the house. I stood there for a few minutes because I wanted to remember the hatred I felt for Karrar and Muntasir at that moment. I cannot tell you how hurt and humiliated I was that my mother would be reduced to begging a man with no heart as she was that day."

Claude began mindlessly fingering the intricate workmanship on the top of the night table as a couple of tears fell from his eyes. Clarissa was duly terrified as she gained new understanding of the extent of his anger, devastation and resentment for his brother and father.

"My mother died . . . drowned . . . when our bus fell as the bridge collapsed that we were on. I tried to save her but the current in the river was too strong. I was a good swimmer, but she was so beat down into the ground by life that I believe she had no will to live, so when I caught her hand, I held onto a tree limb and though I was small, I think I could have held onto her if she had tried. She smiled at me when I started slipping from the limb. Her weight was a bit much, but I'm certain I could have held her. I'm certain we both could have survived. She called out to me that she was too heavy and was going to cause me to go under. Then she told me I was a wonderful son and let go of my hand and drifted with the current until she went under. I yelled and screamed, but she went under"

He paused and began rubbing Clarissa's hair, allowing his fingers to run through it and forming small curls with his fingers in the ends of her hair. He played with it as if he were a child.

"I lived, but told no one who I was. I needed to disappear in order to come back as an unknown and destroy Muntasir and Karrar. Karrar was killed by other means, but Muntasir has been a pleasure to annihilate."

Clarissa realized that he would go through anything to exact his revenge and she understood fully that she probably would not live through this, nor would Clinton. She shuddered to think that maybe Will had not either, although she could not figure out what his involvement might have been. One thing was clear though, Clinton was checking on Will and he was in Morocco and Claude had mentioned Will also. Things did not look good for Bernice Creech's children that day.

Her eyes welled up with water as she thought of her two children and the unborn child she was carrying inside of her; the one she only learned of the week before. She thought of her husband, the most loving man she had ever known, with the exception of pre-trauma Clinton. But most of all, she thought of her mother. Of the pain that she wasn't certain she could endure from the loss of three children. She knew her mother was very strong, but this was a bit much. The grief of it all sent Clarissa into sobs, tears rolling down her face and over the gauze and tape that made up the gag in her mouth.

Claude looked at her then knelt on both knees, on the floor in front of Clarissa. He spread her legs gently, wide enough for him to move between them, placing his stomach against the edge of the seat of her chair. She was looking more and more panicked, uneasy about anything he might do in his crazed state and appalled at the thought of it being sexual, as was Aamil, who was still quite Muslim and most uneasy with the thought of rape.

Aamil placed his hand on his knife and contemplated Saa'iqa's reaction to him stabbing their boss if he tried to rape a woman. Murder was one thing, loose sex with agreement was another, but rape was inexcusable. He decided that she would back him on the rape issue because he knew of the midnight hunts for rapist that she had a propensity toward. Part of her training. He prepared for the worst.

Claude took off his jacket and threw it on the bed. Clarissa's eyes grew as she whimpered. Aamil breathed deeply, hoping for the best. Claude spoke to her.

"Clarissa. I am so sorry you are involved in this ugliness. I have always had the greatest respect for you and your abilities as an attorney."

He laid his head gently on her breasts and cried, hugging her around the waist as she sat tied to the chair, sobbing. She cried for her mother, for Will, for Clinton, her husband and for the pitiful child who lost his mother and was exiled by a hateful father that lay across her chest, crying for the losses he had suffered and the pain he was about to cause his faithful and brilliant attorney. The same child and boss that she had been happy to work for up until just one hour before.

Aamil eased his grip on his knife, pleased that he would not have to act, but touched by the pain and loss of family all around him. He wished he was somewhere else.

Clarissa and Claude stayed in that position as he held her tightly and she began shaking nearly uncontrollably from the exhaustion, the effects of pregnancy, fear, and the utter disparity of it all.

◊

At that very moment, back in the United States, it was early in the morning and Bernice was making coffee. Justine was beginning to make breakfast and Jarrett came downstairs to ask where his socks were.

"In the third drawer from the top . . ." she was answering when she heard the glass coffee pot hit the floor. She ran over to Bernice, whose left hand was shaking violently. Bernice held the shaking wrist with her right hand in an effort to stop the movement, but to no avail.

Justine became frightened. "Mama Creech! What's wrong? What's wrong?"

Bernice leaned against the counter in an effort to stop the shaking from throwing her body around. Justine grabbed and held her as Jarrett looked on in horror. The shaking was so violent that it made appliances on the counter rattle loudly as the two women held on tightly, Bernice to the sink and Justine to Bernice. Finally, the shaking subsided enough for Bernice to speak.

"I don't know what's wrong baby but something is. . . something is terribly wrong!"

26 A PROFESSIONAL'S NIGHTMARE

That night, Saa'iqa and Naseer sat in an old red Mercedes on a deserted street about a block away from Pierre´ Bonet´s large modern home. Both of them were dressed in black, loose fitting clothing, clearly ready for their type of work.

"Be extremely careful Naseer. I don't like any of this. I think Claude has lost his mind, having all of these people in the same place for some insane finale. I tried my best to talk him out of this meeting but he is obsessed and irrational."

"Yes . . . but he is still our employer."

"I should have known better than to take this job. He was always prone to highly emotional states when we were children. You remember?"

"Yes . . . I remember."

"We had a common bond when we were young, being the outsiders, the half-breeds - but now I just don't understand his actions."

"Well, it will all be over tonight then maybe you can take a vacation."

"I've been considering a permanent one from this work. This has been messy Naseer. I've made mistakes I never would have made a few years ago. You and I both know this man should not have been able to fool me this way. My instincts are muddled."

Naseer could scarcely believe his ears. He was hearing the conversation that he wished for, for nearly twenty years. All the killing could stop, the looking over his shoulder as well as looking over hers could stop. Maybe she could calm her inner spirit and just live without all the fire and anger she had held onto so tightly for so long. Maybe she felt she had aided enough justice in the world, evened enough scores for the portion of abused and tattered lives that needed reparation and resolution, that she felt a duty to aid in their needs. Even though he was happy about the news he was concerned about her spirit. He did not want her broken and doubtful of herself, he wanted her free.

"Nonsense Saa'iqa. Just this one man. He caught you off guard. He does have a quality about him."

"But you warned me Naseer! I should have listened because you have never failed me. You've been the one constant in my life."

Naseer placed his hand over hers as it rested on the front seat of the car. He was pleased with the thoughts going on in her head, but afraid of her self doubt. He had seen her as a broken child, and it had caused him more pain than he ever wanted to endure again. He wanted the light to shine, not to be snuffed out. He hoped she was in a temporary state, and that she didn't only have two sides - retribution and anger, and submission and emotional retreat. He was nervous about the days to come, but eager to get their present situation over and done with.

"And know that I will always be your constant for as long as you want me there. We'll go someplace you enjoy when this is finished, like Austria. For now, how about a checklist? Have you got the detonator?"

"Yes. As soon as we have the papers, have taken care of Clinton, and Claude is satisfied with Muntasir's death, we blow this car . . . with Clarissa in it. Naseer, I don't ever remember killing off all the siblings in one family before. This will be a first. Very messy. Will was stupid and Clinton will be a pleasure for his deception, but this woman is just plain unlucky."

She was quiet for a moment, contemplating the ludicrous situation she found herself in before speaking again.

"We might have to prove she is alive, the way Claude has this insanity planned."

Saa'iqa stared out at the clear Moroccan sky and the stars twinkling for as far as she could see, an infinite mass of light and sparkles. She wondered if her mother and father could see her from wherever they were. She wondered for the first time in many, many years if there was an afterlife - a thought she had dismissed after one week of calling her father after his death with no answer. It was an easily dropped concept at that time, because she knew if there were such a thing, he would have been in touch with her and not let her suffer so alone. As she looked at the sky, she felt small and insignificant, in a way she had never felt before. She felt for the first time, some remorse for the woman in the trunk of the car and the fate she was about to suffer. She was experiencing a new emotion, one that as a professional who was top in her field, she could not afford to have.

"Naseer, Claude tells me she has a husband and two children in Paris."

Naseer was nearly awestruck as he began to recognize what was happening to her but he was deeply frightened as well, because this was certainly not the time to question herself and the necessity of her actions.

"Saa'iqa, don't think about those things now. It will on . . . . ."

"I brought a second gun for you."

"What?! A gun?! Why a gun? You will need one for the plan, but I don't need one, I never do."

Saa'iqa's eyes set ablaze, and she was nervous. She frightened Naseer. Her voice nearly cracked when she spoke. He had never seen anything like these events happen to her before. What did it all mean he wondered. He wished he fully understood before they had to work.

"This entire situation is highly irregular and flamboyant? I do not like any of it. We don't know if Clinton is working alone or with those two men who watch us constantly or for that matter, how many there might be. For the first time I am unsure of a job and I want you to act accordingly! Do you understand me? Now Please take this gun!"

She reached into one of the folds of her loose fitting black overskirt and retrieved a handgun, a 44, which she offered to Naseer. He stared at her and wondered what the best reaction would be. He had spent years learning Tae Kwon Do, Tung Soo Do, Akido, Capoiera, Kimbuktu, and Judo. He knew knives and blade weapons but he knew nothing about guns, and had only shot one once. They were loud and drew attention, and to use a silencer seemed unethical and sneaky to him. In fact guns seemed less than honorable. If a person was going to kill someone, they should have the decency to allow them to die with honor he always thought. Guns and explosives were too easy and detached. He shared this basic concept with Saa'iqa. He would not take the gun, and hoped the annoyance she would have with him for not doing as she asked would keep her high enough for her not to slip into a dysfunctional state about killing Clarissa.

"I think you are overly concerned, but I will be careful and alert. I will not take the gun though. They're much too foreign to me. I'll go check the woman's gag. The drug was very mild and she might wake up."

Naseer got out of the car and walked around to the back and opened the trunk. Saa'iqa sat quietly for a moment, somewhat annoyed by his refusal yet renewed by his confidence that the job they were on was much like any other, and caused no particular alarm. She stared at the gun for a moment and could not remember the last time she had used one. She didn't like them either. They were the mark of a coward she felt. She breathed in heavily, then let the breath out in a long, drawn out release of anxiety, preparing herself for the night's work, then she put the extra gun in the glove compartment.

She heard Naseer close the trunk so she got out of the car. He met her as she was closing the door. She reached out and took his hand in hers, then rubbed the back of his hand against her face. He smiled at her, though secretly inside he felt the heart stopping chills that her touch always gave him. For the first time in a long time, he was hopeful that the light was trying to shine through.

"Naseer, please be careful. I can't lose you."

"And you never will."

She released his hand and they started toward the house, quietly and cautiously, checking for abnormalities. It appeared clear, so she took one side of the house and he took the other agreeing to meet in the back where they expected Claude and Pierre' to be inside waiting.

Naseer walked to the left of the large single house whose back sat on a beautiful lake with exotic plants which had been imported by the wealthy homeowners in the area. He widened his approach so that he could take in a complete view of the area and saw Jim hidden behind a clump of olive trees. Skillfully, he positioned himself out of Jim's peripheral vision and silently approached from behind.

Jim was watching the house, oblivious to the danger he was in. Naseer grabbed him from behind with one hand over his mouth and the other arm across Jim's chest. In one quick, powerful motion he broke Jim's neck and eased his dead body to the ground. With the quiet of a cat, he resumed his trek toward the back door of the house.

Clinton and Jorgé drove up in the blue van and parked a few car lengths behind the red Mercedes. They got out and approached the Mercedes cautiously to avoid detection. Clinton opened the door of the car and began searching, his body only half in the car.

"See if you can find any clue to Clarissa's whereabouts." He said to Jorgé.

Jorgé walked to the opposite door and opened it with intentions of assisting when a banging and bumping sound came from the trunk. Clinton opened the trunk with the release button located in the glove compartment. He took the gun, and put it into his pocket, then met Jorgé at the back of the car where he helped a groggy Clarissa out of the trunk and removed her gag.

"Clinton," she said, "I've never been so happy to hear your voice in my life!"

Clinton untied her hands, as Jorgé closed the trunk.

"Let's get away from the car. I heard the woman say she had a detonator and would blow it up with me in it once they have papers and take care of you. What is going on Clinton? How did you get mixed up in that crazy man Claude's madness. Lord I never imagined that man could be that loony . . . and I've known him for years!"

Clinton picked her up and carried her back to the van, away from the rigged car. Jorgé followed quickly and opened the door for Clinton to put Clarissa in the back with the surveillance equipment. Jorgé closed the door, while Clinton removed the ropes from Clarissa's feet.

"Clarissa I will fill you in on everything later, but right now, Jorgé and I have to go. Don't get out of the van, no matter what goes on. If the local police don't show in twenty minutes, drive to the police station and tell them what you know. We are a little concerned about Jim, Jorgés partner since he did not meet us out front as planned. Under no circumstances whatsoever, are you to come into the house. None."

"But Clinton. . ."

"No buts Rissa. Under no circumstances. Agreed?"

"Yes Clinton. None, but why do you have to go into the house since I am safe." She was trying not to panic, but she had gone too long without food for a pregnant woman and she was getting more and more shaky. Clinton noticed how ill she was.

"Rissa, are you pregnant?"

"Yeah . . . I messed up the communication system, didn't I? I'm sorry, I didn't know it would be so vital on this routine trip to Morocco. Gees Clinton. So many things are out of synch here. I just found out last week. For some reason I just couldn't tell, and I'm three months pregnant."

"Well it does explain a few things." Clinton said. " I have to go in Rissa, that woman killed Will, and Claude was her employer at the time. If I can catch them and turn them over, then at least Will's death would be partially vindicated. Besides, I promised I would work toward her capture. Now stay here please."

Clinton kissed his sister on the forehead and he and Jorgé got out of the van. Enroute, they saw Muntasir Zaid walking the narrow walkway to Pierre's house. He was too far away to warn without creating a commotion and had reached the front door, just as a door opened. Clinton was not happy about the surprise of seeing Muntasir.

"What the hell is going on here? Why is he here? Damn where are the police?"

"The bigger question is, will they come. We didn't tell them that we thought Saa'iqa was involved, only Pierre and Muntasir. That should peak their interest. A chance to catch Muntasir, their prime suspect, should be enough reason."

"You did ask them to make a silent approach didn't you?"

"Sure I did" answered Jorgé, "but this whole situation with Muntasir here, and no notice looks bad, real bad."

Clinton stopped at the red Mercedes and searched under the wheel wells for the explosive device. Jorgé was thrown, and watched carefully before asking what Clinton was doing.

"It isn't likely that I'll be able to get inside carrying a gun. If she uses the detonator, it will serve as a diversion. I don't know but anything will help, especially with Zaid in there now."

He found the explosives under the left rear wheel well. He gave the gun to Jorgé in exchange for the forged papers, then hurried quietly to the front door of Pierre's home, where the light was still on for his arrival. Clinton looked around for observers, then placed the explosive pack behind a large clay vase on the front porch. He knocked on the door and awaited an answer. After a moment, Pierre' opened the door, greeted Clinton and invited him inside.

Clinton followed Pierre' into a large open living room with a wide patio door overlooking the lake. To his surprise, only Muntasir was in the room. He looked around for Claude, Saa'iqa or Naseer but didn't see them. Pierre offered him a seat and a drink, then asked for the papers. "I don't think so Mr. Bonet', not until I have my sister back." Muntasir cut into their conversation. "As I asked you before Bonet', what is going on here and who is this man?" "I see." said Bonet, "Not only are you incompassionate but you are impatient also."

"I came here because you said on the telephone that you knew who was behind the murders of Jalaal Abdullah and Saleem Asad, and the effort to make it appear as if their deaths are my doing. That is why I am here and I would like that information."

"Well say hello to him," Bonet continued, "This is Clinton Creech . . . who has contributed very heavily to the deception."

Muntasir turned abruptly and stared at Clinton, searching for any signs of familiarity. He searched all his memory banks and simply could not find any indication that he knew Clinton. Clinton sat quietly, absorbing information.

"But why? I don't know you sir, nor have I caused you any harm. Why would you do this and what is his connection to you Pierre'?"

Clinton decided it was time to speak.

"Mr. Zaid . . . I was hired to do a series of tasks which at the time, I had no idea who would be affected by their completion. I now know that this conspiracy has been directed toward your political and character destruction, and possibly your death. I suspect that both you and I are in extreme danger and suggest we get out of here now."

Alone, Claude entered from a side corridor, pointing a gun at Muntasir and Clinton. He had a smirk of satisfaction on his face that indicated that he felt he was sitting in the catbird's seat.

"A very wise suggestion Mr. Creech, but I'm afraid it comes far too late. There is no escape for my brother at this point."

Muntasir gasped in amazement. He rose quickly to his feet, as startled look on his face.

"Jameel! It cannot be you!"

Clinton looked around for an escape, Saa'iqa and Naseer. At that moment, all were illusive.

"Muntasir, I'm surprised you recognize me. It has been many years since you turned your back on me."

"I have spent as many years being ashamed of the way I behaved. I tried to find you after father died and was told about the bus accident. I regret my moment of weakness but I could never dispute our father all of my life, even when I knew he was wrong. Many nights I thin . . ."

Claude cut him off. "Save your disgusting sorrow and penitence! I have neither the desire nor the stomach for it. Now is a time for dying brother. I must admit however that I have not the make up for murder; not even when the object is something I loathe as much as you, so I have called in professional help. You may remember our childhood friend Saa'iqa."

Saa'iqa came in from the same corridor carrying a gun with a silencer attached. All she could think about was the grandiose manner in which Claude had staged the "finale," as she had grown to think of it. It was overstated, melodramatic and inefficient, and she was embarrassed with the tackiness and gaudiness of it all. Clean and efficient was her style. Quick and quiet. She stood by Claude for a second or two, then moved closer to the patio door for a look into the secluded backyard, careful not to be in clear view.

Claude continued with his speech. "She will rid me of you permanently as she did that snake you called father. You would have been allowed to live in prison had Mr. Creech not interfered with my plans. You have him to thank for your death."

Saa'iqa cut her eyes at Clinton only briefly, but then returned her gaze to the back of the house.

"Saa'iqa Mastoora? What do you have to do with this madness? What is he talking about?"

"Quiet Muntasir. I'm not quite who you think I am. However, before now, I had enough sense not to work at home. I am regaining that thinking power back even as we speak. This will not be happening again. Not ever."

Outside, Jorgé was sneaking around the side of the house toward the back when he discovered Jim's body, contorted from the waist up in a bizarre position, his neck broken. He bent over to close his partner's opens eyes, said a small prayer for him and made the sign of the cross before standing again. He looked over the area carefully in search of

Naseer or Saa'iqa. Feeling he was safe, he continued his journey to the back.

Back in Pierre's living room Clinton and Muntasir held their hands high in the air. Using gloved hands, Saa'iqa checked Clinton for weapons. Her eyes met his, but she was over being angry. She only stared at him as if looking at any other dead bug on the sidewalk, since that was the way she envisioned him. Yet still, something about him made her regret all the negative that had happened between them, but only casually. Betrayal was high on her list of don'ts. Very high. Claude held the gun on Clinton while she checked.

Outside, Jorgé positioned himself so that he could see some of the action inside through the sheer curtains covering the patio entrance. Carefully, he moved closer toward the door, unaware that Naseer was moving up behind him. The big man tipped quietly up behind Jorgé until he was about fifteen feet away. Jorgé, in a ready stance with gun drawn, moved closer toward the door. Naseer moved closer toward him.

Inside, Saa'iqa checked Muntasir for weapons. Finding none, she reached into the folds of her big shirt and withdrew yet another gun. She put the gun with the silencer against Muntasir's head and placed the new one in his right hand. With her gun at the back of his head, he readily took the newly appeared firearm. She raised his right hand with the gun in it and aimed at Pierre', who immediately protested.

"Claude?! What is this? I have done everything you asked of me. I have worked for you for years!"

"Shut up Pierre," Saa'iqa said, "or you really will be dead! Now stand still."

Compensating for her lack of height by standing on her toes, she took careful aim from behind Muntasir. Clinton spoke up, mostly because he could not quite figure out what else to do at that moment. He needed time, Jim and Jorgé.

"Oh . . . I see. We're supposed to be in cahoots here and the deal has gone bad. So Muntasir and I come in here to do you in Pierre', but you get us first. But don't you understand that you know too much of this whole show? As soon as all suspicion is off of Claude, they will get rid of you too man. Don't you see?"

"Mr. Creech," interrupted Claude, "I said I wouldn't like to kill, but make no mistake . . . I will. Be quiet now and let her work, besides they think I'm dead. That is a ridiculous hypothesis."

Saa'iqa was very careful with her aim, and Pierre was very shaken and nervous as one might expect. Clinton pushed the chatter in hopes of distracting everyone.

"Oh no . . . they know exactly who you are and all about the Catholic schools and the nuns and your mother . . . Yvette DuParc. The connection is already made Mr. DuParc.

Unfazed by the entire situation, Saa'iqa aimed Muntasir's hand skillfully, even though he was sweating bullets, and fired. The bullet hit Pierre squarely in the lower shoulder, causing him to cry out in pain, fall to the couch and pass out.

Clinton had to admit as he watched that it was truly a pleasure watching an expert of her caliber. She was calm, she controlled every inkling of resistance, and she was not easily unnerved by noise or nonsense. Even with the physical difficulty of holding one gun at a man's head who was at least ten inches taller than she was, and forcing him to shoot with the other hand, that she was actually controlling, she was quite accurate and incredible. She hit Pierre' in a place which would not cause him permanent damage, yet would be believable as the target achieved by an amateur in the heat of passion type shooting. He was duly impressed.

Jorgé jumped at the sound of the bullet, and looked around for more trouble in just enough time to see Naseer nearly upon him. He reacted quickly and shot the big man in the shoulder. Naseer steeled himself and made no sound but only continued to charge. He shot again and caught the giant in the stomach just as Naseer reached him. Naseer attempted to strangle him but could not sustain his hold because of the injuries. He settled for knocking the agent out cold with the back of his hand, and then stumbled around the side of the house toward the front door.

In the house, with the momentary advantage of the gunshots, Clinton used the hand closest to Saa'iqa to backhand her hard enough to knock her a few feet across the room. The force caused her to release the gun with the silencer on it and sent it sliding toward the front of the house.

Muntasir, who still had the gun in his hand from the staging of Pierre's shooting, turned the gun on Claude, and they shot one another nearly simultaneously, with Claude firing only seconds before. Muntasir was hit in the chest and fell, and Claude was hit in the head, between the eyes. He fell a few feet away from Pierre'.

Saa'iqa leapt quickly to her feet and Clinton went for Muntasir's gun, which was closest to him. She reached inside her big shirt and pulled out a lethal five pointed Chinese star weapon and threw it directly into Clinton's arm making it impossible for him to pick up the gun. She charged him attacking with a flying Tae Kwon Do sidekick, aimed for his chest. He ducked, rolled his shoulder underneath her highest leg, then rose quickly, throwing his elbow into her side as her body reached him, which threw her off to her right and onto the floor. She rolled into the fall and quickly rose to her feet again. She reached into her shirt and got the detonator and pulled out a long sharp knife with the other hand.

"I've had enough of this nonsense. I'm certain you are expecting help and the only thing that would keep Naseer out of this house at this point is that he is dead. I want to be done with this and you!"

At the front of the house, Naseer was about to open the front door, but was moving very, very slowly due to his extensive injuries. Most men would have died from the wounds he had endured, long before that point. He was about seven or eight feet from the door when three police cars pulled up without alarms and sirens blaring. The policemen inside got out and readied themselves for combat. They saw Naseer bent over, attempting to reach the door, that was only three feet away from him. One of the policemen raised a megaphone to speak to him.

"You on the porch . . . stop and . . ."

Before the policeman could finish his sentence there was a huge explosion on the front porch which knocked a large chunk out of the front of the house and made it impossible to see what was left of the giant man. The policemen all ran for cover.

With the explosion, Clinton, who lay prone as soon as Saa'iqa pushed the detonation button, had a few pieces of debris thrown on him. The room was not destroyed, but several flying objects from the front of the house landed in various places around the room. Clinton got up and searched the room for Saa'iqa, but could not find her. What he did see was the patio door open, and the sheer curtains blowing freely in the wind. He ran out of the door in time to see Saa'iqa's back as she ran toward the lake. He grabbed the gun from beside the unconscious Jorgé and ran after her.

He was only able to get off one shot before she reached the edge and dove into the lake. He ran to the shore and looked into the dark water for any sign of her. Seeing none, and furious with the situation, he fired twice into the water in the direction he supposed she would have gone, but without clear success. He stared at the water and growled in disgust as the policemen, alerted by the shots, cautiously approached him as they demanded that he drop the gun. He did and they immediately began questioning him.

He heard little of what was being asked of him and said to him. All he could think about in the dark of the night with bodies strewn all over the living room and outside the house, was the laser eyed woman who had probably survived and who he felt he was destined to cross paths with again. He turned and went back inside with the policemen, hoping to explain his presence in their beautiful city of Marrakech. He listened carefully and though he heard the sound of something moving in the water. He turned to see if his suspicions would be confirmed, but the angry and confused police roughly escorted him into the house - the only standing survivor of a fiasco.

27 YOU BETTER GET A MOJO TOO!

A week later, Clinton and Clarissa sat in an airplane, approaching the terminal of Washington National Airport.

"Clinton, how much should we really tell Mama about Will?"

"Rissa, we have been over and over this. I say nothing, except he was there on business and was killed in a boating accident."

"You know that is not going to work. We can't think of enough manufactured details to answer all the questions that will come up over the next few months. Even if we could, coordination between us would be too difficult."

"I know you are right, but the alternative of telling her Will was a crook and Saa'iqa threw her baby's body into the ocean just doesn't work for me."

"Yeah. I'm chicken too. But, we never get away with lying to her so what is the point?"

"Um. You're right. Well you do the usual and start, and when you finish messing up the details and getting everything all backwards, I'll have an easier time of filling in the real information. But the initial shock will be over."

"You can kiss my rear end!" she laughed.

He kissed her forehead and they held hands in silence till they reached the gate. As they walked from the jetway and into the gatehouse, they could see Gerald, Bernice, Justine, Jarrett, and Clarissa's husband, a native of Martinique' and her two children anxiously awaiting their arrival. There were also five agents standing in the general area. Clinton noticed the FBI and cut Gerald an inquisitive look, but Gerald only smiled. As soon as she could reach them, Bernice hugged her two children as tears streamed down her's and Clarissa's faces. After a moment Clinton excused himself to speak to Gerald, who had been waiting patiently on the sidelines, out of the family beeline to them.

"Clinton, it sure is good to see you again. I can't tell you the horror I felt for those four hours that I did not hear from you. I think you should keep Clarissa and her family here until we can find Saa'iqa."

"Gerald do you think . . ."

"Clinton we found Jessica Lash and the two agents assigned to protect her, all dead in the safe house we had her in. That woman has connections all over, including our organization. I've assigned twelve agents to your entire family, and by the end of the week, I should have a safe house large enough for all of you to live in. Your best bet is to stay together right now. Alright?"

Clinton looked at the furrowed brow on Gerald's face and decided protest was useless as well as foolish. Gerald only carried the deeps rows when he was worried and serious.

"Alright Gerald. My mother will like that."

"Yeah . . . she does. She was delighted in fact. I'll call you tomorrow. Your escorts are here and I've got to go."

"Thank you man for everything. I'm sorry I couldn't deliver her. It was very . . ."

"Don't even think about apologizing. You accomplished more than they've been able to do in years. She's in the light now. She can't just hide behind her facade like business is usual. You did real good."

Gerald left, dispatching the new and constant entourage of bodyguards on his way. Justine approached Clinton. "Clinton, how did you hurt you arm?"

"Oh that, I can hardly feel it anymore."

"Clinton, are you going back to Kenya? Are you still so ready to get away from here again . . . tell me how you are doing?"

He laughed at the rapid-fire questioning, her trademark.

"I don't really know Justine. Anyway, it's out of the question for the moment. It appears we will all be living together for a while. I understand you moved in with my mother, so I guess you will be coming with us. What brought that on may I ask?"

"Well it is sort of what I've been wanting to talk to you about. There's a reason I'm there and well . . . I've been talking to your mother, and I think . . . I think it is about time I told you something I probably should have said years ago. Maybe now is definitely the right time."

Clinton watched her fidget and shift her weight, and wondered what could be been so serious. She smiled at him with tears welling up in her eyes. He lifted her face so that he could see her better, a little frightened by her behavior.

"So serious Justine?"

She linked her arm inside of Clinton's and they strolled toward a set of seats, leaving the reunion gang on the other side of the gate. Quietly, one of the guards followed them as they sat down, keeping a safe but unobtrusive distance. Justine waited until they were seated to answer, full blown tears trickling down her face by then.

"Well yeah, it is pretty heavy duty. I'm a little afraid of how you'll react."

"Baby, nothing you could do could be very bad. I've spent the last few weeks with real bad, I now know the difference if I didn't before."

She smiled. He kissed her on the cheek and put his arms around her and held her for a moment.

28 ONLY A JOY

The mist was heavy, and the fog filled the lagoon where Will Creech stood on the back of an old fishing boat. His arms were outstretched toward his mother Bernice, who was standing on the end of a pier reaching toward him . . . complete with street clothes and shoes. The peaceful sound of water lapping gently against the side of the boat could be heard as the boat calmly drifted away from the shore, drifting deeper into the mist, deeper into the fog - but she could still see his beautiful face. She could see the lines of his father and the character of his stepfather in him. She could see the future of his children and the connection to Jarrett, Clinton and Clarissa and her children, even the unborn grand baby she couldn't wait to see . . . all in the lines of the peaceful, all too handsome face of her first child. He was a wild thing, and she knew that Clinton and Clarissa were trying not to tell her everything that happened to him. But she knew who he was, she had always known and had always loved him. Period. There would never be another person like him, and she would never have another first child. He spoke to her through the cracks in the fog.

"Mama . . . I never meant to cause you so much grief."

"Baby, you have only been a joy."

She couldn't see him as well now, only a glimpse here and there, but she could still hear his rich deep voice that had player running all through it, that held a family tightly in its reach, the voice that carried her through so many trials and tribulations, that she listened to from the tiny baby sounds through the cracking of puberty and into manhood.

"Bernice, I will always love you."

"And I you Will."

Will's face was barely visible. The tips of his outstretched fingers only occasionally coming into view, his voice progressively fainter. She thought of how he must be going to Clinton Sr., the only rightful father he ever had. She was pleased with the thought that they could be together. She heard him one last time.

"Good-bye mama."

She slowly lowered her arms to her sides, a calm, peaceful serenity overtaking her entire body and soul.

"Good-bye son."

THE END - maybe . . .